"Obviously you were right and I was wrong," said Westley. "He is clearly not just another nut. He is a nut with style, good instincts, and enormous appeal. He puts on a rubber mask and proceeds, in the full glare of the media, to act out every man's fantasy. My wife, my entire family, adore him. So do all my friends. They can't wait to hear about his latest exploit. He's Robin Hood, Zorro, and Spiderman rolled into one. He cuts through all the nonsense and does whatever has to be done. I swear, sometimes I'm jealous." The commissioner smiled rather wistfully. "Naturally, he's a menace to the established order and must be stopped. And of course he will be. But the day he is, I think it might be best for us both to disappear for a while."

GAYNOR'S PASSION

Fawcett Crest Books
by Norman Garbo:

SPY

TURNER'S WIFE

GAYNOR'S PASSION

Norman Garbo

FAWCETT CREST • NEW YORK

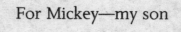

For Mickey—my son

A sudden madness came down upon the unwary lover—forgivable, surely, if Death knew how to forgive.

—Virgil

The ruling passion, be it what it will,
The ruling passion conquers reason still.

—Pope, *Moral Essays*

ACKNOWLEDGMENTS

The author would like to thank Gerard Van der Leun, editor, and Arthur and Richard Pine, agents, for their respective roles in the shaping of this book.

The no smoking sign went on for their final approach to Kennedy Airport and Richard Gaynor thought, These past few days have probably been the finest and most satisfying of my life.

The twins were sitting just across the aisle, and Gaynor glanced over for perhaps the fourth time in as many minutes to assure himself that their seat belts were properly fastened. Asleep, their faces looked soft, guileless, and even younger than their ten years.

His sons were not identical twins. Tommy had the Gaynor face: dark, deeply set eyes, a slightly long nose, and a wide mouth. His features even held that vague hint of melancholy, as much a part of him as his shy half smile. Joshua, on the other hand, was entirely his mother, with the kind of fair, classic good looks that everyone said was wasted on a boy but that he was already learning to use to advantage. He had Jane's hard core of stubbornness, too, as Gaynor knew only too well.

Enclosed in the night, buoyed up by the jet, Gaynor went soft with tenderness for them. They were his sons.

The flight attendants were busy with their final cleaning up. It was one of the more popular late evening flights from Chicago and the cabin crew had been working steadily since takeoff. A petite stewardess with the kind of sharp, knowing eyes that could pick out a divorced, reasonably eligible father at fifty feet paused to smile at the sleeping twins, then at Gaynor. Her name was Emily, and she had made a point of letting Gaynor know she was based in New York and was uncommitted. Gaynor was not interested. He did not feel divorced when he was with his children. Even away from them he found it hard to feel that way. It was still too new. He still found himself waking in the night and reaching for his wife. And who was Jane reaching for these nights?

The question gripped his heart. He saw his face reflected in one of the plane's windows: dark, wavering, wet with fog. Yet it appeared undisturbed, tranquil, the face of a man wholly at peace with himself and the way that life had chosen to treat him. His face was a lie. It lied outright. If he should ever be so foolish as to add up the really joyous hours Richard Gaynor had lived, the hours free of frustration, anger, anxiety, or pain, he knew that the final figure would depress him for a month.

Yet, in considering his life to date, he knew he had only himself to blame. To begin with, no one had forced him to become a classical painter at a time when the absurdities of abstract expressionism were infecting the art world. Then, too, it was no one's fault but his own that he had allowed himself the luxury of falling in love. Surely he should have known he was too hopelessly committed to his painting to offer any woman the time, thought, and attention necessary to love. And finally, as if these two errors in judgment were not enough, he had foolishly married, sired two children (although only one had been intended), and expected to live happily ever after as husband, father, and family provider.

Not surprisingly, he had done poorly in all his assumed roles. The critics had consistently dismissed his art as out of step or derivative. The public, having little taste of its own, had believed the critics and bought little. The only woman he had ever loved, his wife, had considered him an abstract lover, a neglectful husband, a preoccupied father, and so unsuccessful a provider that she had gone to work herself to improve a family standard of living that government statistics described as barely above poverty level. For the past several years Jane had, in fact, earned considerably more than Richard. And in a society that tended to equate human worth with annual income, this was the final blow to his crippled marriage as well as to his self-esteem.

*   *   *

With his wife and children gone, Gaynor had considered his life laid waste. He was unable to paint. He brooded. He searched his soul and found little of lasting value. After a time, however, he decided that inasmuch as his life had never been especially outstanding, there was really not that much to regret. He went back to work. And a bit more than a month ago, the Art Institute of Chicago had actually bought one of his paintings.

Emily appeared beside him, took away his empty brandy glass, and left a warm glance and the electric touch of her fingers in its place. An airborne predator. But why him? God knows, he was no Robert Redford. Did the museum sale somehow reflect from his eyes and send out sexual signals? The sale had certainly given him a greater load of confidence than he had carried in years. Another few sales like that and legions of women would be camping on his doorstep. Perhaps even Jane would find him freshly exciting. She had, once. Ah, but would he choose to take her back? Letting his mind drift, he indulged the fantasy. Marvelous. A single museum sale, his first, and he was already envisioning the world flat on its back, opening its arms to him. Yet it was typical. He made instant quantum leaps from despair to euphoria. He shrugged. In a few weeks he would be moaning and beating his breast again.

Or perhaps not.

Every life had its turning point and this might be his. Anything was possible after the joy and exultation of the past few days. The reception in his honor, his sons sitting so proudly in that great marble hall. He was their father, for God's sake! Speeches were made by celebrated men and women. The canvas the museum had bought, *his work,* was extravagantly praised. Words like "powerful," "moving," "remarkably sensitive" were used. What else could they say? They had already bought it. Ironically, it was a painting that Gaynor had never especially cared for, a large oil of three old men sitting together on a park bench, bodies touching but eyes solitary and lost in a distant landscape. The composition had always depressed him. It was so pathetically without hope that once, alone with it on a rainy March afternoon, he was tempted to destroy either the painting or himself. Yet this was the canvas they had chosen to buy for an unbelievable

3

forty thousand dollars—more money than he had ever earned in any two years running.

The plane lurched through some heavy turbulence and Tommy woke with a start. His dark eyes were frightened, disoriented. "What's happened, Dad?"

"Nothing." Gaynor smiled and pressed his son's arm for reassurance. "Just some rough spots. We'll be landing in a few minutes."

"Can I have a Coke?"

Gaynor shook his head. The American opiate. "You'll have to wait till we're on the ground. They're not serving anymore."

"I'll ask Emily. She has a real thing for you."

"Don't ask anybody. And what does a pipsqueak like you know about having things for people?"

Tommy smirked. "Ha."

Joshua, now also awake, joined in. "We've decided, Dad. We think you should call Emily for a date when we get back. We like her."

"Fine. Then one of you can call her."

"We're too young."

"So am I," said Gaynor.

"Come on," said Tommy. "You'll be thirty-five next month. It's unhealthy for a person your age not to have sex."

"Where did you hear that?"

"It's common knowledge."

"Jesus Christ."

Joshua leaned over as far as his seat belt would allow. "We got her all primed, Dad. We gave her the famous artist routine. We told her this big Chicago museum just bought a painting for forty thou."

"Fantastic." Gaynor shook his head. No wonder Emily was in heat. "Did you also tell her that's before taxes and my gallery's forty percent?"

"We didn't think that was necessary."

Tommy dug a scrap of paper out of his pocket and handed it to his father. "Here's her phone number. She's off shift Thursday and Friday this week. She said the best time to call is in the evenings."

"Do you guys take care of your mother's needs this well?"

The twins exchanged awkward glances. "Mom's doing okay," said Joshua.

At least they had the grace to be embarrassed, thought Gaynor. The human soul had more parts than he would ever touch or understand. His own blood. But two separate individuals, each with thoughts and emotions wholly unrelated to him. He shoved the piece of paper into his pocket without glancing at it.

There was a sudden opening in the fog and the lights of New York broke through. The twins leaned toward the window and looked down. Gaynor worked his jaw until his ears popped. He felt a surge of unreasoning anger toward his former wife. How dare she take his sons? What right had she to deprive him of their closeness? But the questions were as unreasoning as his anger. He knew the answers as well as he knew his own failings. The two were inescapably linked. Jane had left him and taken the twins because she considered him a bad husband and a worse father. And who was he to argue? His wife had read endless books and articles on such subjects. She was an acknowledged expert. The only thing he was a expert on was painting pictures. And often, at least according to the critics, not even that.

The fog closed in once more and the lights disappeared.

Tommy turned from the window and grinned. "Maybe Mom will marry you again now that you're rich and famous."

"I'm not rich and famous."

"Well, you're at least more rich and famous than you were last month."

About to explain piously that it was not his lack of money and fame that had broken apart their family, Gaynor changed his mind. There was little chance of fooling these two. They had lived too closely for too many years.

There was another break in the clouds and lights were again visible below. The lights were much closer this time, making the plane's speed seem greater. Gaynor peered out along with his sons. This great, hurtling machine. Flying was still something he could never take for granted. He still found it fascinating, a continuing source of wonder. And the closer they drew to earth, the more wondrous it seemed. In the heavens, above the clouds, it lacked reality. It was when they approached the ground that the enormity of what they were daring struck him.

He glanced curiously at his fellow passengers. Some dozed, others read, still others stared off into space, already absorbed with whatever problems awaited them on the ground. Only a few youngsters and some of the elderly seemed to share Gaynor's sense of wonder. Those close to either the beginning or the end of the spectrum. The rest appeared to take the whole miraculous adventure for granted. How sad. Gaynor had more than once tried to capture on canvas the way he felt about flying, but each time he had failed. Art, paint and canvas, had definite limitations. Unless the limitations were his own. Still, he had yet to see any other artist do better.

They were only about a thousand feet from the ground, but occasional patches of fog still broke Gaynor's view of the lights. He had grown up in Rockaway Beach, one of the areas adjoining Kennedy, and he was looking for landmarks. It was hard to orient himself in the darkness, but he felt he should be able to pick out at least a few familiar places. With the threads of his early years stretched out below, he searched for them the way a stubborn detective might search for clues to an unsolved crime. He spotted the huge gas tanks, strung with ribbons of lights, that he used to ride his bike past on the way to the beach. Then he recognized the steeple of a church that stood just a few blocks from one of half a dozen houses his family had lived in in a period of less than ten years. At that particular stage of his father's sagging fortunes, it had apparently been simpler to move than to pay rent.

"Hey!" Gaynor pointed in sudden excitement. "There's the school I went to."

Joshua looked. "Where?"

"Come on, Dad," said Tommy. "You know you never went to school."

Gaynor unbuckled his seat belt and leaned across the aisle. "See those two gas tanks with all the lights? Well, a little to the right there's a long, dark building shaped like a stretched-out *H*. Do you see the one I mean? It's the one that has the—"

There was a loud, crackling explosion and the interior of the jet seemed to flower bright red. Gaynor felt himself lifted, soaring. A radiance traveled like a streak of light across his eyes and into his brain. It set fire to a forest of nerves and he thought, My God, my sons. He saw cities of sparkling, jeweled lights. Then the lights went out and he wheeled in absolute darkness.

He was floating upward. Halting. Then ascending, heavily,

slowly, senses flickering at each level. Pain enclosed him like a shroud. It had neither beginning nor end, only a terrible weight. He opened his eyes. But he could not see. Nor could he hear. Or if he could hear, there was nothing to hear. Then he heard a faint wailing in the distance and the darkness took him again. When he came back, the wailing began to reach him, dimly, as the sound of sirens.

The roar of flames washed over him. He felt great heat. His brain stopped. Then began again. He sensed he was being lifted and carried. "My sons," he gasped in a broken whisper. Then he fell back into a long oblivion. Being luckier this time, he stayed out.

Not more than twenty minutes earlier, Jay Newman, an off-duty lieutenant of detectives with the New York Police Department, had wandered out of the Shannon Bar and Grill on Cross Bay Boulevard in Queens. He located his car and started to get in, then changed his mind and went for a walk instead. He walked with the careful precision of a man who had drunk a great deal, was accustomed to drinking a great deal, and knew exactly how to handle its varying effects. At the moment, one of these effects was a vague stirring of sexual excitement, and he considered that perhaps it might not be too bad an idea to drop by and see Mary. He was fifty-six years old and sexual arousal was no longer the instant reflex it had once been. On general principle, it seemed foolish to waste anything that promised to be in increasingly short supply. Then, recalling Shakespeare's warning that although alcohol might stimulate desire, it invariably diminished performance, Lieutenant Newman thought, Hell, why take it out on Mary.

So he walked.

Ambling along the dark road edging the wetlands of Jamaica Bay, he soon found himself refreshed by the cool, foggy night. It was certainly better than going back to an empty apartment before he was ready for sleep, and he knew he was still several hours away from that. He breathed deeply and felt the sharp tang of the salt air blend agreeably with the accumulation of bourbon inside him. Interesting. It seemed to heighten his sexual awareness further, which, even without any immediate prospects of satisfaction, was really quite pleasurable.

Dirty old man, he thought, and he smiled. The ugly, denigrating expression happened to be one of his pet peeves. Invented by the young, it gave voice to an arrogance that not only stamped physical love as exclusively theirs but rendered it obscene for anyone over forty. The unmitigated chutzpah. And this from a generation that had required drugs to make life's most exciting physical experience a bit less boring.

Landing lights blazing, a steady stream of jets roared close overhead as they approached Kennedy Airport. Newman glanced up after them, a compact, solidly built man whose wide shoulders and deep chest made him appear heavier than he really was and not nearly as tall. When he had first tried to join the department, the medical charts revealed him to be quite a bit overweight for his six-foot-two height. But the examiners, taking into account his Doctor of Law degree and superior scoring in all other areas, had chosen to overlook the problem. Now, thirty-some years later, twenty-five pounds lighter, and nearing the end of what he coldly considered a less than spectacular career, Newman tended to wish that the examiners might have been a bit less lenient. Whatever their intentions, they had done neither him nor the New York Police Department any favors.

Yet, walking, the lieutenant did not look like the aging, daunted, functioning alcoholic he knew himself to be. It was as if his brain and body had never been granted any true awareness of the condition or stage of life through which he was currently passing. He carried himself with the style and manner of a good, even superior, heavyweight fighter who, though perhaps a bit past his prime, was still not to be fooled with. Even now, his steps were naturally light and quick, the thick, graying hair at his temples stirring in a westerly breeze, big-knuckled hands swinging loose at his sides. One of his more loving black detectives had once said without malice, "For a sweet, li'l ole Jewish gentleman, Lieutenant, you sure do walk big and mean."

But the truth was, Newman did not feel big and mean these days. He felt tired and depressed. What he seemed to want, mostly, was simply to be left alone. A condition that he sometimes laughingly dismissed as male menopause. Yet he was not deceived. During the worst of it, he knew that although much of his plight could be blamed on his age and the bitter underview of the world to which those in his line of work were normally heir, he also knew that an almost equal part had to do with his missing Jenny, his wife, whom he had lost almost fifteen years before. Although, of course, he had not really *lost* her. A stupid euphemism. He had in no way misplaced her. She had simply been killed: shot twice, once through the head and once through the chest. And there was nothing euphemistic about that.

The lieutenant walked lightly and carefully between acres of marshgrass on the one side and the nearly deserted road on the other. The tall grass overgrew the sidewalk and brushed against his legs. Behind him, the bar he had just left was no longer visible, lost in the fog. Killing, he thought, a never-ending conspiracy against the sanctity of life. Jenny was just another in a long line of victims. With a couple of major differences, of course. One, he had loved her. And two, he was the one who was supposed to have been killed. Her death had been a mistake, a simple case of poor marksmanship. Both bullets had been intended for him. Typical. Even the killers were incompetent. It was hardly worth the effort to pick them up. And if you did catch them, they were soon set free. The courts were overcrowded and there was no room in the jails. The statistics were a nightmare. And the rich were being ripped off, right along with the poor. Urban barbarism had become the great leveler. It had succeeded where generations of pious efforts and good intentions had failed. It had finally achieved its own social equality.

Newman smiled dimly. Some theory. Properly developed, it might even make the op-ed page of the *Times*. He could imagine department brass reading it and having a collective hemorrhage. Except that most ranks below deputy commissioner were more likely to read the *Daily News* than the *Times*. They would not even see it. In itself a fair indication of department mentality. Or was he just being superior? The final refuge of the failed, defeated, and damned.

A jet roared by, sounding so close that Newman almost ducked. They were coming in pretty low tonight. If the weather got much worse, they would probably have to shut down for landings. Living so near the airport, Newman often felt himself part of its operations. Others in the area complained about the noise, but it never bothered him. Sometimes he even welcomed it. It made him feel less alone.

He paused to light a cigarette, then stood at the edge of the marshgrass, staring across the dark waters of Jamaica Bay. In the distance, Kennedy's lights shimmered, ghostlike, through shifting layers of fog. It was April, the beginning of spring, but winter's chill still clung to the salt air. The lieutenant suddenly shivered. He took a half pint of Old Grand-dad from his pocket, drank deeply, and put the bottle away. The bourbon felt warm and reassuring going down. Moments before, Newman had noticed a car slow and stop at the curb about fifty yards back. It was parked there now, a dark sedan with its lights on and what sounded like a souped-up motor going. The lieutenant stood staring off into the darkness. Then he started to walk away from the car, moving slowly and erratically, even stumbling from time to time. He did it well. Why not? He had had enough experience with the real thing.

The motor grew louder and the car pulled up alongside him. "Hey, man, wanna lift?"

Newman looked but kept walking. The car was a highly polished Trans Am with four young men in it. Incredibly, two were black and two were white. Heart-warming. At least they were starting to go interracial.

He shook his head. "Jus' out gettin' a li'l air." The words were slurred, a drunk's. He continued walking.

The car stopped a few yards ahead and all four of them came out. They were grinning. Along with rolling him, they obviously expected to have some fun. Perhaps pour on some gasoline and light a match to him. There had been a rash of such attacks on drunks and vagrants in the area lately, and this bunch had the look. The new barbarians. And the eldest could not have been more than twenty. Somehow, the very young seemed to be the worst. Any hint of human compassion seemed to have been bred out of them. The two whites brandished open switchblades. The blacks carried short lengths of iron pipe. And what had happened to that particular stereotype?

They formed a tight line across the walk and Newman stopped, facing them. The only visible traffic was in the air. Cross Bay Boulevard was deserted, abandoned to the fog, as if all the decent, law-abiding inhabitants of Queens had been ordered to remain safely behind their locked doors.

"What do you want?" Newman's voice and manner were no longer those of a drunk, but these four were too deep inside themselves to notice or care.

One of the blacks laughed, a tall, graceful African prince in royal purple. "What you got, man?"

"Nothing for you."

A white youth lifted his knife, weaving it back and forth like a snake. "You lookin' to get cut, mister?"

"No."

"Then hand over your bread right now."

"Sheet, Angie," drawled the other black, "stick that fat ol' Jew jus' for laughs."

Newman found himself smiling. That was all that had been missing . . . the single word, Jew. Now it was complete, the traditional circle closed. "What's the matter? Don't you guys like Jews?"

"Sure. Like dog shit on new shoes." It was the second white knife-wielder. "Come on, Angie. Let's take another inch off his li'l kosher pecker."

The lieutenant knew they were capable of it. Genital mutilation was getting to be almost as popular as burning. Like changing fashions, old perversions were rediscovered by new generations. It was a two-thousand-year continuum. He still smiled. There was a soft purring in his chest.

"What you grinnin' for, ole man?" said one of the blacks. "You think we kiddin'?"

"No. I don't think you're kidding."

"Then wipe that dumb grin off your face."

"Why don't you animals try wiping it off?"

The answer was so flat, cold, and unexpected that for a moment they just stood staring at him. Newman, moving into the breach, stepped back, drew his service revolver, and leveled it at them. "Okay. Who's first?"

No one stirred. Angie said something, but a plane was passing directly overhead at that moment and his words were lost in the roar.

"Drop the knives and the irons," said Newman.

"You some fucking cop?" asked the other white.

"I'm a fat old Jew with a loaded thirty-eight." He cocked the hammer and they dropped their weapons. "Now turn around."

"Hey, man, we was only foolin'."

Newman nodded. "Sure. But I'm not. Turn!"

They considered his face. They were young, but all four

had been around long enough to recognize what they saw. They turned.

"Now start walking."

"Where?" said Angie.

"Off to your right."

Newman marched them through the marshgrass for about thirty yards. When they were out of sight of the road, he said, "Okay, stop here. And don't turn around."

They did as they were told.

"Now I'm going to give you a choice," said Newman, "which is more than you sweet mothers were about to give me. You can either take a bullet in the back where you stand, or you can start running when I tell you to and take your chances on the fly."

They all began babbling at once.

"Shut up!" snapped the lieutenant. "The next one who opens his mouth gets it right now. You disgust me. You make me ashamed to be human. You're good for nothing but causing pain. I don't know how you got this way and I don't care. I only know that filth like you don't deserve to live."

They stood silent and unmoving in the cold fog, a contemporary tableau. Newman could see their bodies trembling. The message had gotten through. One way or another, they expected to die. One of the white youths, Angie, made soft, whimpering sounds.

It was at least a human indication. When Newman heard another plane thundering in behind him, its engines loud enough to cover the sound of any shots, he said, "All right. Take off or take it here."

He fired a single shot over their heads to get them moving. Then he watched as they fled, a covey of frightened quail flushed out of the tall grass, running wildly, arms flailing as though truly feathered for flight. He fired twice more over their heads and saw them jostling one another in panic. Insanely, they seemed to be deliberately holding together in a tight cluster, as if to break up into four targets would make each of them more vulnerable. Group courage. And what about group fear? Watching the knot of fleeing runners grow smaller in the darkness, Newman fired his three remaining bullets harmlessly at the sky. But suddenly, as though the shots themselves had somehow set off a larger explosion, there was a crackling, thunderous roar, and Newman saw what appeared to be a great ball of lightning break open the dark directly ahead. The four runners were held, frozen in its glare, and Newman could feel heat shifting inside him. The ground trembled beneath his feet and there was a sound like a thousand freight cars crashing. Then great clusters of fire and other, darker things began falling from the sky.

"Dear, sweet God," Newman whispered and dropped to his knees in the grass.

There were actually two planes involved, but because they had collided in midair, they came down, struck the ground, and exploded as one. Fountains of sparks and waves of flame cascaded over the place where Newman had last seen the four youths running. They were swallowed up, gone. The night was orange, red, green, yellow, blue: a kaleidoscope. Newman knelt in the grass, rocking gently, the empty revolver forgotten in his hand. The scene held the dim, misty glow of a nightmare, a deadly landscape where something terrible was calling. And the lieutenant had a moment, then, when something in the deep of that dreadful carnage, perhaps a silent cry out of the newly dead and near dead, took a leap through the night and into him. Cold with shock, he rose and trembled toward the maelstrom.

There were great gouges in the earth where hell shone brightly. Newman breathed the stink of brimstone. Exploding jet fuel splashed crazily, igniting into sheets of flames. There were acres of large and small fires. Steam rose from tidal pools. The marshgrass smoldered and burned deep purple. Bodies were everywhere. Some were aflame, sitting, still strapped to their seats. Others were in bloody sections. Newman stumbled over something and a head rolled away. Dark thunder blossomed from the soil. Fetid smoke rolled over the marshes. The tall grass shimmied back and forth, trying to rip itself up. Newman wandered helplessly, looking for a sign of life. Faintly, in the distance, he heard the sound of sirens. His lips moved, but without sound.

Once, in Korea, badly wounded and left for dead as the battle moved away, Newman had crawled among a silent host of bodies. He was the last living creature on earth. Death oozed out of the ground. He felt the same way now, felt whatever small good was left in him going away. It was more than pain, more than sickness. It was the obliteration of everything human. The glow of fire was everywhere. It placed separate pink aureoles over everything. Then Newman heard a groan off to his right and caught a glimpse of movement.

The man lay on his back, all but his head covered by a shallow pool of water. The grass was afire beside his hair. He was alive. But if he moved, he would drown. If he did not move, he would burn. Newman carried him away from the fire. His face was bloody and a red froth bubbled from his lips. He was trying to speak. Newman leaned closer.

"My sons," breathed the man as he lost consciousness.

Newman left him in a safe area away from the fires and went to search for other survivors. He found five more. Two were women and one was a young boy. They were terribly maimed. Newman did not think any of them would live. He placed them beside the first man. What remained of the two planes was an inferno of twisted, melting aluminum. Newman could get no closer than fifty yards. He choked off his brain to keep out what he saw. The horror was everywhere; the smell of death turned solid as stone in his throat. The flames penetrated his mind, clogging his ears. It was hard to breathe. Still, he wandered through the smoldering marshgrass, picking his way between burning pools, looking for further signs of life. There were none. It was the final circle of hell.

When the first rescue team arrived from Kennedy, they found him sitting in the high grass beside his six survivors, an empty bottle in his hand, silently weeping.

The Reverend Clayton Taylor was working late at the Atlanta headquarters of the American Fundamental Church when a public relations aide came in with the first news of the crash. The minister's eyes were pale and flat.

"How bad was it, Martin?"

"They say the worst since Tenerife, worse than Chicago. Around three hundred dead."

Taylor seemed to stare off somewhere. It was as though he hadn't heard. But of course he had. His thoughts were already well past the event itself. "Any survivors?"

"Less than a half dozen. But they're not expected to live."

"Aah . . ." It came out softly, almost a sigh.

"How do you want it handled, Reverend?"

"The usual senseless tragedy approach. Why does God permit such things to happen? Isn't God fair? Is there a God?

That sort of thing. Use the argument that God could never stop manmade calamities from happening without forcing men to behave according to *his* will, thereby taking from them a free will of their own. Something, of course, he would never do." Taylor looked at him. "Do you understand the tone?"

"Yes, sir. What about distribution?"

"All major city newspapers. And I'll also do a thirty-second radio and TV spot on it."

"Any preferences about who I should give it to?"

"Try Arthur for the press piece and Thomas for the broadcast material. They've both been doing excellent work on this sort of mood sermon. And I want it fast, while the crash is still making headlines."

"Yes, Reverend." The PR man started to leave.

"Oh, and Martin"—Taylor caught him at the door—"please keep me informed on the survivors. If and when they die, we'll need an appropriate follow-up."

2

Newman, having his own key, silently let himself into Mary Logan's apartment. It was a few hours before dawn. He showered without waking her, downed a fair-sized tumbler of bourbon, and slipped naked into the big double bed. Lying very still, he kept himself separate from her flesh.

But moments later she turned, felt his presence, and reached for him. At which point it all broke loose, and he grasped her across a landscape gutted with horror, grasped her with such force and intensity that she cried out with shock. And because she knew him well, she felt sensations playing apart from her own nerve endings, felt him moved by something outside and beyond her body, something of which she was only an incidental part. Then darkness flew in like an unwelcome bird, and there was more concern than pleasure in even the coming.

His head lay, unmoving, on her breast.

"What is it?" she said. "What's happened?" They were not new questions for her. He was in a line of work in which the dark underside of things was always tearing loose. Even so, tonight's rupture seemed especially bad.

"Aah . . ." He breathed softly against her breast, all sweet balm to his flesh.

"Jay . . ."

He rolled apart from her and lit a cigarette. "There was a crash in the wetlands near Kennedy. It was terrible. Almost three hundred dead. I happened to be first on the scene. First? Christ, it came down all around me as I stood there. I thought I'd seen everything, but this was like nothing else. Men . . . women . . . children . . ." He looked away from her toward the window. "You can't imagine what it was like."

"Sweet Mary, Mother of God," she whispered and crossed herself. The words and act were instinctive, out of her childhood. She had not been to church in more than twenty years. Though close to forty, she had a round child's face, innocent blue eyes, and a softly voluptuous body that seemed to have stopped aging on her seventeenth birthday. Newman, sometimes teasing, called it a terminal case of arrested development. Still, he was pleased to accept its rewards. "Those poor souls. Were there any survivors?"

"Only six. And they're not going to make it. The human body was never intended to fly through the air at the speed of sound. So we make regular payments. Which are growing with the size and speed of our planes. The blessings of science."

"Do you want to go back to the horse and buggy?"

"At least they'd have gotten you home."

"Yes," she said. "And probably have died there of TB, polio, diphtheria, pneumonia, or plague. We can't have it all ways, darling."

It was a characteristic exchange for them. Among other

things, they shared a curious reversal of job stereotypes. She was Irish in a welfare department dominated by Jews, and he was a greatly outnumbered Jew among mostly Catholic cops. They also shared a poor but long-standing joke that described their attraction for one another as basically ethnic. Consider. Where else could a middle-aged Irish spinster find an alcoholic Jewish detective so worth saving? Conversely, where else could an over-the-hill yid find himself another blue-eyed shiksa with a seventeen-year-old body housing a warm Jewish heart?

He ground out his cigarette and reached for all of that sweet warmth that had finally come to be his single acknowledged refuge. He spoke into a scented cave at the side of her throat. "I may have been near to hell before, but tonight I was right in it. Fire everywhere . . . the torn, broken bodies . . . what was left of those poor children. God, the little ones. Your senses cloud. You can't take it straight out. Your heart bleeds, Mary, it bleeds."

She held him. The fog had cleared, and the curtains at the window were silver. Overhead the moon was a cold stone, a dead thing.

"It's not worth it," he said. "Nothing is worth that. Dear God, I swear we should have stayed with the horse."

Mary held him until he slept.

Lieutenant Newman was summoned to the office of the New York police commissioner at nine o'clock that morning.

He passed through an infinity of doors and offices until he entered a large, ornate, high-ceilinged room with paneled walls, a marble fireplace, baroque chandeliers, and red velvet drapes. Incredible. His reaction was the same each time he walked in. The man was at the head of an armed force of more than twenty-five thousand police officers, and he still ran it all from the front parlor of a Victorian whorehouse.

"Sit down, Jay," said the commissioner. "I'll be with you in a minute."

Newman watched a continuing parade of secretaries march in and out, most of them detectives in shirtsleeves with holstered revolvers on their hips. The commissioner himself, Michael Westley, sat behind an oversized desk, a slender, almost excessively handsome man, whose graying temples and crinkling laugh lines seemed to add more distinction than age to his appearance. The guy looks better than he did thirty years ago at law school, thought Newman. He thought it matter-of-factly, in much the same way he might have reacted to an exceptionally handsome show horse. There was no resentment or jealousy. He and Westley were barely members of the same species.

Speaking to his secretaries, the commissioner's voice was so low that even sitting in the same room, Newman was unable to hear what he was saying. It was a manner of speech that Westley had already begun to cultivate at Harvard. "Speak softly and people will always pay more attention to what you're saying," he had told Newman during their first year as roommates. No mention of carrying a big stick, but the thought had to be implicit. To which end, a portrait of the former police commissioner, Theodore Roosevelt himself, still hung over the fireplace, a continuing reminder to all who entered the office that it was quite possible to reach as high as the White House from here.

The last of the detectives left, closing the big double doors behind him. The commissioner leaned back in his chair and looked at Newman. His eyes were pale gold, like an expensive animal's.

"I hear you had quite a night," he said.

The lieutenant lit a cigarette without asking permission. "I could have done without it."

"Where were you coming from when it happened?"

"A bar. Where else?" He smiled faintly. "It's okay, Mr. Commissioner. I was off duty."

"A police officer is never off duty."

"Absolutely correct, sir."

"How much did you have to drink?"

"Nowhere near enough."

Westley studied several papers on his desk. "And you were alone when the crash occurred?"

"Yes."

"There was an abandoned car, a Pontiac Trans Am, picked up on Cross Bay Boulevard. There were also four extra bodies in the wreckage that were neither passengers nor crew. Do you know anything about either of these items?"

"Yes," said Newman, and briefly told the commissioner about the four would-be muggers.

Westley's pale eyes flickered. It might have been with

amusement, but it was hard to tell. "Talk about poetic justice. Or would you call it divine intervention?"

"I'd just say it was lousy luck."

"I assume you haven't told anyone else about this."

"I may drink too much, Mr. Commissioner, but I'm not stupid."

"I know that, Jay. But I must say, it would be hard to judge from some of your less well considered performances."

Newman carefully left that one alone.

"In any case," said Westley, "I want to congratulate you. You saved six lives last night."

"They're not going to last."

"That's beside the point."

"Not to them. As I see it, they'll be dead in less than seventy-two hours. All I did was extend their pain."

"In the meantime they're alive, and it was you who saved them. Jay, you're a hero."

"I'm no hero. I just happened to be walking along Cross Bay Boulevard, half tanked as usual. It was all an accident."

"That's how heroes are made, Jay. By accident."

"Bullshit." Newman's voice was flat. "Sir."

"Now listen," said the commissioner, speaking even more softly than usual. "I have a press conference scheduled to take place in this office in a few minutes. It's being held for the express purpose of making the most of your participation in last night's disaster. And I'm telling you right now that I expect your full cooperation. A little humility, a little self-deprecation, may be all right, even appealing. But for God's sake, don't overdo it. And I especially don't want any of your wry, misplaced humor and sarcasm. I want this handled straight, Jay."

"Jesus Christ. I don't believe it."

Westley chose a cigar from a humidor on his desk, lit it, and said nothing.

"Wrong," said Newman. "I do believe it. In fact I'd say it was a fairly characteristic response. Almost three hundred dead and you call a goddamned press conference to make the most of it."

"Don't twist my words. I'm exploiting your heroics, not the dead. Nothing can touch them anymore."

"I beg your pardon. Sir, you're marvelous, a humanitarian of the highest order."

Norman Garbo

"Cut the sarcasm, Jay. We can't all afford your noble indifference to life's more sordid practicalities. Whether you approve or not, there are certain responsibilities that come with my job and I take them seriously." Westley contemplated the tip of his cigar. "On general principle, nobody likes a cop. Even some cops don't like cops. So an important part of my time goes to trying to improve our image. And giving the public an occasional police hero to cheer is one of the best ways I know of doing it. Unless you can come up with a better suggestion."

"How about cutting back on some of our garden-variety corruption and brutality for a week or two?"

Westley was not amused. Sitting in his high-backed chair, he looked cold, aristocratic, and dangerous. "I hope you haven't had too much of the sauce this morning, Jay. I'd really hate for you to mess this up."

Newman saw that he had finally touched Westley's anger. Over the years, he had developed a finely tuned awareness of just how far he could safely push something like this; at the moment he knew he was very near the limit. Often tempted to go over the edge, he somehow never did. Which, when he considered it, merely added to an already high level of self-disgust. What was he afraid of? There was depressingly little about his life and work that appealed to him anymore. Still, the alternative of waking up one morning to nothing at all was even less appealing. Today, at least, he was not about to push it.

"Don't worry. I'm sober."

"Excellent." The commissioner gestured approvingly with his cigar, all knives sheathed. "Providence placed you smack in the middle of a terrible calamity last night. It had to be a deeply humbling, humanizing, searing experience. Regardless of what you may say, you had to be affected by it. From what I've seen of these reports on my desk, you single-handedly managed to keep six people alive who would otherwise be dead this morning. No one could have done more. And because you're a police officer, this reflects on the entire department. So let's make the most of it. I know what you're capable of at your best, Jay, and I'd appreciate your giving it to the media. Will you do that for me?"

Newman nodded. He was tempted to stand up and cheer. No wonder Michael was commissioner. It was what he had

20

set out to be and it was what he had become. And unlike most commissioners of police, it was not simply a political appointment offered as patronage to an outsider. He had started as a patrolman right along with Newman himself and come up through the ranks. No mean thing. There was something so neat, so perfectly rounded, so wholly satisfying about the man's entire life and career that Newman was tempted to believe in predestination. Still, it had been Westley and his youthful ideals that had convinced Newman to be a cop in the first place, that had persuaded him that their law degrees could contribute more to the public good out on the streets, enforcing the law, than in a courtroom, arguing about it.

"Were you hurt, were you injured in any way last night?" asked Westley.

"No."

The commissioner studied him closely. "What are those red marks on your forehead and cheek? And there seems to be another on the back of your hand."

"There were flying sparks. I guess I caught a few. They're nothing."

"Nothing is nothing." Westley picked up a phone. "Send Dr. Burke in," he told someone.

"You can't be serious," said Newman.

The police surgeon must have been waiting just outside the door because he appeared almost immediately, a plump, white-coated man carrying a black leather bag.

"Lieutenant Newman suffered several burns during last night's rescue operation," said Westley. "I'd appreciate your checking them out, Doctor."

The police surgeon, having been briefed, knew exactly what was expected of him. When he was finished with his examination and ministrations, Newman's forehead and left hand were swathed in surgical gauze and there was a large strip of tape high across his cheek.

"Better give him a sling for added support," ordered the commissioner.

When that, too, was taken care of, the doctor left.

"I'm relieving you of all regular line duties," said Westley. "I'm putting you on temporary assignment to the commissioner's office. Call it special sick leave, if you will."

"For how long?"

"We'll see how things work out."

21

Norman Garbo

Newman struggled to light a cigarette with his bandaged hand. "When do I get my Actors Equity card?"

Westley was silent.

"What are you trying to tell me, Mr. Commissioner?"

"It just seems that if—"

"Come on, Michael. It's *me*. Remember?"

Westley studied the ash at the tip of his cigar. "All right. Here it is straight. Though it should hardly come as a surprise. We both know you've been pretty much of a joke as a lieutenant of detectives for years. The wonder of it is that you're still alive and on the job. In fact, if it wasn't for—" The commissioner cut himself off.

"I know," said Newman. "If it wasn't for you I'd have been flopped or shoved out long ago. I guess I've neglected to say thanks lately. Forgive me."

Westley rose and came out from behind his desk. A very tall, lean man, he literally towered over Newman's wide, compact bulk. Once, working as partners, they had been nicknamed the Reed and the Rock, and some of the old-timers still referred to them that way. "I'm not looking for thanks. You know me better than that. It's just that you represent such an unholy waste of human resources that sometimes I want to strangle you. You've got more real heart, talent, and brains for this work than anyone on the force and you've pissed it all into a bottle."

"So what else is new?"

"What's new is that both the DA's office and the Internal Affairs Division haven't been off my back about you in months. And your record this past year has finally become too much for even me to cover. The fact is, they want you out, retired, before you do even more harm to yourself and others. And in all good conscience, I can't say they're wrong."

Newman had been standing, but now he sat down. "I can't believe it's really been that bad."

"Can't you?" Westley sighed as he might have sighed to a child. He turned back to his desk, took a folder out of the top drawer, and leafed through it. "Okay. Here's a brief list of your year's more sparkling highlights. On two separate occasions you had your service revolver taken from you by suspects, who then proceeded to fire at and wound either you or one of your men before being disarmed. You were personally involved in four traffic accidents that resulted in either bodily

22

injury, property damage, or both. You had three reported off-duty fistfights in bars and God knows how many others that weren't reported. You were determined to be the direct cause of several major street disturbances that might easily have turned into riots and from which you were barely rescued by a Signal Thirteen. You actually beat a hit-and-run suspect unconscious before dragging him into the station house and dumping him onto the floor in front of the booking desk."

"The sonofabitch was doing sixty in a fifteen-mile zone and hit a kid."

"Sure," said Westley, then continued without glancing up. "Also, you let several suspects go without booking them because they were allegedly friends who had done you favors. At two different times, you allowed yourself to be entrapped in ridiculously compromising sexual situations by female suspects, when even the greenest recruit would have had enough common sense to know better." He paused. "Shall I continue?"

"If you're having fun."

Westley returned the folder to his desk drawer. "Your drinking, of course, is at the heart of everything. But quite apart from that, you're abstracted both on and off the job, you're careless, you're contentious, and you're given to extreme and precipitous action. My honest opinion is that the IAD and the DA are right. You should be retired before something really calamitous happens." He paused and looked at the lieutenant. "But you don't want that, do you?"

Newman shook his head. At that moment he was unwilling to trust his voice. Nor did he trust his eyes to meet Westley's. He was afraid there was too much of what he was feeling visible in them. He had to keep something in reserve. He didn't want to strip himself naked in front of his friend.

"I'm sorry," said the commissioner softly. "There's no joy in this for me. I remember too well what you were. It sticks in my throat like an old piece of meat. I can't seem to get it down. One day I suppose it will finally choke me." He made an impatient gesture. "Oh, to hell with it. That's all history, anyway. In the meantime, I'm still the police commissioner in this city, and what you did last night was no small thing. It has to help. So with a little judicious effort, maybe we can hold them off."

The commissioner studied Newman carefully. Then, like a

film director going through a final costume check before the cameras start to roll, he made a small adjustment in one of the lieutenant's newly applied bandages. When he was satisfied, he went back to his desk and picked up the phone. "All right," he said in his controlled, barely audible voice. "Lieutenant Newman is ready to be interviewed."

3

At certain moments Richard Gaynor thought he might simply be asleep and dreaming. Bad dreams were often like that. You floated on a cloud of foul intent, unable to move and not really caring. At times in the past he had sat up in bed, feeling invisible claws ripping his chest, an oppression clogging his throat, and a stranger's eyes staring through the dark. So perhaps this, too, was a dream, and he would soon waken and get on with his life. But, increasingly, he began to sense that this was not a dream and that all the tubes connected to his arms and body were real, and that the nurses sticking needles into him were real, along with the blinking lights of the monitoring equipment, and the doctors in white coats peering at him, and God only knew what else. All were real. But perhaps most real of all was the fear of regaining clear awareness and knowing exactly why he was there.

As it was, he just drifted in and out of things. Once, it was dimly in his thoughts that his wife was looking at him. But then he remembered that he no longer had a wife, so he assumed he was imagining it. Also, this woman was weeping and Jane never wept. Or hardly ever. And certainly not for him.

Then for whom?

"My sons!"

He must have said it aloud because a nurse was suddenly bending over him and there were other people in the room. Then he had a misty vision of waving arms and sending his tubes flying. He had once tried LSD, and the sensations then were not too different from those he was experiencing now. At that time everything had quivered with a brilliant light, rainbows curved across the ceiling, and a heavy red rain was falling. Now the rain was his blood. It spurted outward, spraying the room. The nurse was very excited and did something to his arms. The woman who looked like his wife was gone. Then men were holding him and injecting needles and the red rain turned black. His mind had been reasonably lucid for almost a full day and night, but he had been careful to keep it hidden. He wanted to watch and listen for a while. There were things he had to find out. Much of his face and head were bandaged, and there was a cast on his right leg. When anyone was in the room, he kept his eyes closed and his breathing regular. He felt very sly and superior. Doctors and nurses came and went in groups. They leaned over him, talked in whispers, and checked his tubes and monitoring devices. At one point, three men in business suits came in with the doctors and stood there, gravely studying him. He learned they were from the Civil Aeronautics Board and wanted to question him. One particular nurse seemed to be with him more than any of the others. She was young, with very dark hair, and she wore a ridiculous little starched lace cap on the top of her head. When she was not busy checking his tubes and equipment, she sat in a corner of the room, watching him. Through slitted eyes, he watched her in return. Her eyes were as black as her hair and shockingly candid. Gaynor lay silently considering the nurse's eyes. Then he opened his own.

For several moments they just looked at one another. Then the nurse rose and approached the bed.

"My sons," he said. They seemed to be the only words left to him.

"Welcome back, Mr. Gaynor."

"My sons."

25

"We've all been waiting for you."

"My sons."

This time he gripped her wrist, holding on with whatever strength he could muster. She did not try to pull away. Nor did she say anything. There was no need. All she had to do was let him see her eyes.

"Aah . . ." He closed her out along with everything else.

Jane, his former wife, was there the following day. The moment she walked into the room she started to cry. She was utterly unable to look at him. Even when she touched his hand and spoke, she was looking somewhere else.

"I killed them," he said.

She shook her head, a pretty, fair-haired woman with pallid cheeks and new, dark circles under her eyes. Uncharacteristically, she had not even tried to cover them with makeup.

"I never should have taken them on that trip. It was pure ego. I had to let my sons see what a great artist their father was."

She said nothing.

His bandaged head bolstered by two pillows, he seemed to see her in parts: the straight, delicate nose, the full, curved lips, the firm jaw. She was all Joshua. A necessary reversal since Joshua was no longer there to be all her.

"God, how you must despise me," he said.

Weeping quietly, she failed to deny it.

But so modest a punishment was not enough for him. He needed more. "Why did you come here?"

"Richard . . ."

"You don't care about me. You never did. What I was never mattered to you. I didn't fit your holy image of what a husband and father should be, so you threw me out."

She stared directly at him for the first time. "What are you trying to do?"

"I'm trying to make an honest woman of you. I'm trying to get you to say what you really feel."

She shook her head.

"Come on, Jane." Half muffled by bandages, his voice was harsh. This mother of dead children. He looked fully into her face, then at the long, graceful neck, the lights shining from her hair. She must have washed her hair that morning. Bereft of her two sons, she shampooed her head. Still, her mouth trembled. Her grief was real. Could she suffer more with unwashed hair? "Come on and say it. It will make you feel better. Come on and say what you're thinking."

"Please, Richard."

"Say it!"

"Don't—"

"Say it! You've torn my guts out for a thousand lesser reasons. Now you've got real cause. Say it, damn you."

Eyes shut, she leaned against the bed, rocking gently. The bed, Gaynor, his tubes, all swayed to her rhythm. "No."

"Don't you want payment from me? Wouldn't you love to see me bleed?"

"No . . . no . . . no."

"Sure you would," he said, and without warning he jerked a tube out of his arm. Blood shot over his ex-wife in a crimson spray, a soaring fountain.

She recoiled in horror. "You're insane. Your brain has been damaged."

"There's my blood. Isn't that what you really want?"

"Nurse!" she screamed.

"Say it, you ball-busting bitch."

Face bloody, ablaze with anguish and fury, she was finally reached. Like the shooting blood, it came out under pressure.

"You self-centered bastard, why aren't you dead, too? Damn you to hell! You've burned my babies!"

"Ah, sure," he sighed. "Go ahead."

"I'll never forgive you, you and your miserable art. Your painting was always more precious to you than your own children, your own flesh. Why did you suddenly have to take them with you on that damned plane? Who needed you after all these years? I wish to God you'd burned up with them. Instead of them."

The dark-haired nurse, running in, had heard. Wide-eyed, her first glance took in the whole bloody scene. She quickly clamped the open vein shut and taped the tube back into place. She was furious. "Why don't you just shoot him? It's faster and a lot less messy."

Jane wept.

Gaynor lay with his eyes closed. "It's not her fault. I did it myself."

"Get out of here," the nurse told Jane. "Get out right now." She seemed ready to hit her.

27

Bloodstained, sobbing, the mother of Richard Gaynor's children fled the room.

One night, while his stitched-together body drifted in drugged sleep, the twins came to visit him . . . Tommy, with his sweet half smile and solemn eyes; Joshua, all golden and laughing. He reached for them with miraculously free arms and they were gone.

Still, it was their presence that had wakened him. And through this break in their deaths, small bits of them floated free . . . missing front teeth, high, unformed voices, the softness of infant flesh. Images of them came to punish him. They had asked so little, yet somehow it had always seemed too much. Why? It wasn't your work that made you human and whole. It was those you loved. It was how you cared for one another. He had cheated them both. He knew that now. But such knowledge comes too late. Grief sat on his chest like a dragon.

It was awhile before he was ready to speak to anyone again. When he did, it was to the dark-haired nurse who had thrown Jane out. "What's your name?" he asked.

"Kate. Kate Henderson."

He considered her, his vision tinted gray and brown by the drugs. She was small and fair-skinned, and in repose her body seemed to have the delicate, contained stillness of a Botticelli Virgin. "Will you please answer a question, Kate Henderson?"

"If I can."

"How do you keep that crazy little cap from falling off?"

She laughed. Bending her head, she showed him the bobby pins.

"Thank you." He let a few moments lapse. Then, without change of tone, in the same flat voice, he said, "How many died?"

"What?"

"The crash. How many were killed?"

She instantly turned cautious. "I'm not sure."

"In round figures. I promise not to quote you."

"Almost three hundred."

Fluids were still running in and out of his body. The

information seemed to enter through a conduit of its own, a conduit of ice. "How many survivors?"

"There were six."

The cold breath of memory moved within him. Then his mind fixed on the tense she had used. "Some have since died?"

"Yes."

"How many?"

Her expression made it clear before she answered. "All but you."

An infection set in and he suffered a relapse. Through recurrent bouts of fever he heard the doctors talking. His stomach had apparently been punctured and they were afraid of peritonitis. They were filling him with antibiotics. Once more he drifted in and out of awareness. There were different nurses in his room, but the only one he recognized during his more lucid moments was Kate Henderson. Whenever he opened his eyes, she was there. Occasionally he also thought he saw someone else, a man. But he did not recognize him. He knew he was not a doctor because he had no white coat and his hand and head were bandaged. He just stood near the door, looking at him. In Gaynor's flickering consciousness, he seemed very broad, massive, with a red face, white hair (or was it the white bandage?), and blue eyes. A patriot—red, white, and blue. Gaynor thought this was very funny. He also thought he was laughing. He wasn't. He was merely hemorrhaging. He wondered where his wife was. He thought it might be time for her to come back again. She was the only one who could make him stop laughing.

"We almost lost you," said Kate. "Everyone was very worried." She opened the blinds, and bright yellow stripes of sunlight slanted in. "Look. It's a really beautiful day."

The only thing the beautiful day did for him was hurt his eyes. He lay propped on his pillows, watching her fuss with the tubes. He felt lighter than air, almost too weak for speech. "Who's red, white, and blue?" he said.

"Is that a new riddle?"

"I thought I kept seeing a man. Red face, white hair, blue eyes. Also, he seemed to be bandaged. He just stood by the door."

"You mean Lieutenant Newman. He's a detective. He keeps asking about you."

"Why? Has he found out I blew up the plane?"

"No. But he did save your life."

Gaynor closed his eyes.

The three men from the CAB came back to interrogate him. Since he was the sole survivor, they hoped he might be able to tell them what he remembered of the moments immediately prior to the crash. They had a woman with them this time, a stenographer, who carried a pad and pencil and sat prepared to take down whatever he had to say. They stood together at the side of his bed, tall, lean men with the grave faces and dark narrow suits of professional mourners. They were very polite and solicitous, but when they began their questioning, Gaynor just lay there, coldly staring at them.

"Is something wrong, sir?" asked the tallest and gravest of the three. He seemed to be the senior member.

"Yes," said Gaynor. "My two sons and nearly three hundred others were ripped apart and incinerated, and I'm lying here like a semivegetable because you people fucked up in some way. Yet *you* come in here and question *me*. Well, I also have a question. How in the name of Christ did it happen?"

They told him what they claimed was as much as they knew so far. A private executive jet had somehow been off course and had rammed the 707 during its final landing approach. Whether this was caused by human error or faulty equipment had not yet been determined. According to the flight recorders recovered from both planes, neither pilot had indicated any advance warning of what was about to happen.

"Can you recall anything at all unusual during those final moments, Mr. Gaynor?"

His mind suddenly adrift, he was mentally painting them as three large birds of carrion, pecking apart the dead.

"Mr. Gaynor?"

"I broke the rules. It was a terrible thing to do."

"What was that?"

"I unfastened my seat belt." He was becoming nauseated and dizzy. "Do you think that could have caused the crash?"

Taking him seriously, the investigators solemnly shook their heads.

GAYNOR'S PASSION

Gaynor felt his bed, the room, and everyone in it beginning to whirl. Trembling in a cold sweat, he desperately tried to hold his stomach together. "Why?" he whispered. "Why was I the one to live?"

"It was the will of God," said the senior investigator, in need of symbols, having to say what he did not even come near to understanding.

Gaynor looked at him. Undoubtedly a very decent man, he thought and, and leaning forward, threw up all over his neat, dark suit.

He was lying alone in his room, staring his glassy, hundred-mile stare, when the man whom Kate Henderson had identified as Lieutenant Newman literally filled the doorway.

They silently considered one another. Gaynor's eyes, a deep cornflower blue at their best, were like dirty river ice. As for Newman, he had a face that, after close to thirty years of confronting junkies, larcenists, muggers, rapists, and murderers, carried few illusions. Yet it still seemed curiously searching and friendly. In fact, if Gaynor had not been told who Newman was, he would more likely have taken him for a cleric than a cop. An odd reaction, he thought, because what priest, minister, or rabbi had he ever known who looked anything like this man?

The detective approached Gaynor's bed. His forehead was bandaged, a patch of surgical tape was stuck high on his cheek, and his left hand, also bandaged, was supported by a sling. He seemed vaguely uncomfortable, an uninvited guest concerned about his reception. "I'm Jay Newman. I was the one who . . ." He hesitated.

"I know who you are."

Newman stood in silence.

"If you're waiting for thanks and a pat on the back, you won't get it from me. I wish to Christ you had let me burn with the others."

The lieutenant took out a pack of cigarettes, remembered where he was, and stuffed them back into his pocket. He looked at the back of his unbandaged hand. A meat cleaver. "Listen. I'm sorry about your kids."

Gaynor swallowed and tasted something bitter. They were the first words of condolence that anyone had offered. He was not ready to deal with them. He felt himself torn, then torn again.

"I know how you feel," said Newman.

"No you don't."

"Many years ago my wife was shot and killed. I loved her very much. They were shooting at me."

Gaynor felt as though flaming fuel were scalding his lungs each time he breathed. He shook his head slowly back and forth on the pillows. Then he kept shaking it as though palsied. "When does it start getting better?"

"I'm still waiting to find out."

They were gradually taking him off the drugs, which made it harder to find refuge in sleep. He lay awake in the night, studying the pink and white glow of the monitors on the ceiling. He had seen worse abstractions on the walls of the Guggenheim. The same murky fire still burned inside his chest. He had scattered moments of calm, but they were very delicately balanced, and he was unable to sustain them for long. Sometimes he wondered what it would be like to join his sons in whatever sweet and tender place they might finally be resting. *Goodness and mercy shall follow them . . . and they will dwell in the house of the Lord forever*. It was insanely tempting. The only true journey of love was from one pure heart to another, and those were surely a pair of exquisite hearts that had left him. He sensed lights shifting inside his brain. He heard voices whispering. He felt sick in a way that he had never been sick before. It was close to an extinction, a perfect oblivion, someplace far off from which no one ever returned. He was close, but not close enough. I'm not yet ready for that, he thought, and wondered whether he would ever be.

Kate Henderson was with him through some of the worst of it, but she may as well not have been there. Gaynor acknowledged only his ghosts. His body lay there in the bed, struggling to perform its functions, but what he might have chosen to call his soul was elsewhere in the far distances.

Kate, watching, missing nothing, finally said, "Don't you think it's time you started getting your head together?"

Eyes closed, he pretended not to hear.

"Look at me," she said.

There was enough authority in her voice to make him

obey. She stood over him in the antiseptic, harshly lighted room, her eyes bright with anger. With some surprise, it occurred to Gaynor that he was the cause.

"And you may as well stop pretending to be asleep. That's childish. You can't shut things out by shutting your eyes."

Gaynor stared silently at her.

"Your ex-wife was here to see you again. Twice. I had to throw her out both times."

"You had no right to do that."

"What do you know about rights? I thought you're only an expert in self-flagellation?"

He closed his eyes. By now it was practically a reflex. The slightest hint of anything unpleasant and his lids dropped like a pair of blinds.

"If you're that far into masochism, maybe I can find some old whips and chains and really go to work on you. Would you like that? Perhaps I can even dig up some black boots and other leather goods to go with it."

He had to open his eyes and look at her after that one. Her face was still angry. Her eyes shot sparks. Titian, during his earlier years, when he seemed to be discovering women entirely on his own, had enjoyed painting eyes exactly like that. Gaynor forced his thoughts onto the Renaissance artist who had lived and produced for all of a hundred years. Amazing. But who would want it?

"How about it, Mr. Gaynor?" Kate's voice pulled him back. "Since you seem to enjoy pain so much, let's do it right."

He closed his eyes.

His body, being a small, functioning part of the greater human miracle, continued to heal. They disconnected the tubes and deposited him in a chair for several hours a day where he sat like a propped-up corpse, his cast-encrusted leg pointing steadily north. A barber came in daily to shave him and once, also, to cut his hair. Proud of his work, the barber held up a mirror, and Gaynor saw a death's head staring back at him, a portrait painted by Goya at the end, when he was close to madness, with red-rimmed eyes, sunken cheeks, and flesh of yellow parchment. "Charming," he told the barber.

Removed from the intensive care unit, he was no longer the responsibility of Kate Henderson. For which, when he considered it at all, he was grateful. Despite her undoubtedly good intentions, she had evolved into an irritant. And a slightly crazy one at that. Who needed it? He was getting crazy enough himself. Lately, unable to read and desperate for distraction, he had started to paint imaginary pictures. He mentally painted just about everyone and everything he saw. No need for actual brushes, canvas, and oils. It was simpler and faster in the mind, and nothing to clean up afterward. Sometimes he painted as many as a dozen pictures a day. What he liked, he mentally varnished, framed, and hung. What he didn't like, he simply erased. At times he considered himself the forerunner of a unique, avant-garde art movement capable of unprecedented metaphysical breakthroughs. At other times he was quite certain he was losing his mind.

He had progressed to crutches but rarely left his room. Most of the time he just sat and painted his imaginary pictures. He was in the middle of one, a monochrome self-portrait in delicately subtle tones of green, when an important-looking hospital official appeared. The man helped him onto his crutches and escorted him down the corridor to where some specialists were allegedly gathered to consider his condition.

Entering a large, private lounge, he was suddenly blinded by television lights and seated behind a cluster of microphones. He heard the whirring of cameras and squinted dumbly into the blazing floods. A great many men and women were gathered about the room. Some held pads and pencils, others carried hand microphones and cameras, and everyone seemed to be talking at once. *They think I'm the goddamned President of the United States.*

He sat gripping his crutches with both hands and tried to focus on the questions being fired at him. It was frightening and confusing. Nothing made sense. Easy, he thought, and calmed himself sufficiently to concentrate on what they were asking.

"How does it feel to be the sole survivor, Mr. Gaynor?"

"Why was it you and not someone else?"

"Would you rather it was your sons who had lived?"

"Where were you sitting in the plane and what did you do?"

"Do you believe in God? Do you think he intervened on your behalf?"

"As an artist, will you try to paint what you feel, Mr. Gaynor?"

"Do you suffer from survival guilt?"

"How do you feel about your children dying while you're still alive?"

"Do you believe you've been spared for a reason?"

"How do you justify it to yourself, Mr. Gaynor?"

"Do you pray and give thanks to God daily?"

"Why you, Mr. Gaynor?"

Why you? Why you? Why you?

The waves of questions swamped him. His pulse beat wildly. He was drenched in sweat. He licked his lips to answer, but when he opened his mouth nothing came out. Still, the questions kept coming as though answers were neither expected nor required.

He rose on his crutches, a tall, gaunt specter with black-ringed eyes and bony cheeks. Swaying drunkenly, he lifted a crutch and swung it with all the strength he had. The cluster of microphones shrieked, fluttered, and went over. He lurched toward the nearest lights and cameras and swung again. Then he simply kept swinging the crutch in a widening arc. He had no idea what he was hitting, but knew he was hitting something. He heard shouts and cries and shattering glass. His mouth was open wide, a screaming pesthole. Fury leaked from his pores with the sweat. He swung the crutch. *Answers. He'd give the sons of bitches answers.* A fine madness entered with each breath, passed through his blood, and was breathed out again. *Whop* went the crutch, and something else flew apart.

They finally took him from the rear, but it required five strong men to do it. They held him until the last of it was spent. Then a wheeled stretcher was brought in and they pushed him back to his room. A doctor gave him a needle, although by this time it was no longer necessary. Still, it put him out. Which, considering everything, was probably just as well.

When he opened his eyes Kate Henderson was there, sitting across the private room, her tiny starched cap as ridiculous as ever.

He began painting her at once, starting with a wash of umber, then broadly brushing in the mass of dark for her hair and the purple shadows under her cheekbones and chin. Her lower lip, he decided, was extraordinary, with the kind of sensuous fullness that, under the proper conditions, could probably break a man's heart.

"I heard what happened," she said. "Those idiots should be running a circus, not a hospital."

He squinted to focus on the play of light and dark across her forehead and cheeks. Her flesh color was delicate, mostly a very pale burnt sienna and white. Still, if you looked closely, there was also a hint of cadmium red blushing from the high places. Unusual in so dark-haired, dark-eyed a brunette. He used a soft flat sable brush for that, lightly, letting the strokes follow her anatomy but still keeping strict control.

"Some of the doctors went up to the director's office and raised hell," she told him. "You don't have to worry. It won't happen again."

He stopped painting. "Why in the name of Christ did you ever want to be a nurse?"

"It's a living."

"There are easier ways."

"You're right." She shrugged. "I was main-lining it at fifteen and headed God knows where when an old black lady pulled me out. To me, she was the Virgin Mary. She also happened to be a nurse."

Gaynor highlighted her hair and added full, naked breasts with brownish purple nipples. Her body flesh was given a porcelain glow. He parted her lips slightly and painted on several touches of moisture.

"And you never got hooked again?"

"Never."

"You were really able to manage that?"

"I discovered something. What you really want to do, you can somehow do."

Working loosely, very impressionistically, he painted her stretched out naked on a hospital bed. He brushed in a man, mounting her. The man's buttocks were lean and pale, a sickly green. Gaynor painted his face the same color. When he put in the man's features, he found them to be his own.

"Remember that," she said.

He framed and hung the painting on the wall directly opposite his bed.

* * *

When he next saw her he said, "I've decided. What I really want to do is get out of here."

Her lips were slightly parted, as in the painting. "So?"

"So they won't release me."

"What does that have to do with anything?"

His personal, hand-painted pornography stared at him from the wall where he had hung it. "They have my clothes, money, and credit cards."

"I'll get them for you. And incidentally, I've had your clothes cleaned. They were a bloody mess."

"How will I get past the nurses station and out of the hospital."

"Leave that to me."

"You would do that?"

"I just said I would, didn't I?"

He was confused. "But why?"

"Because you want to get out of here and go home. And that's the first thing you've wanted."

He left that evening at the height of visiting hours, when there was a lot of traffic. Kate smuggled him down a service elevator to the Emergency Room exit. She had a taxi waiting there.

"You're alive," she said. "For God's sake, act it."

Unaccountably, he took his dirty picture with him. He discovered he had been in the hospital more than two months.

~~~~~~ **4** ~~~

Gaynor went to ground like a wounded animal in the Olympic, a dingy hotel on East Forty-first Street.

It seemed better than going home to his apartment. No one would know him at the hotel, no one would telephone, no one would come with sympathy and advice.

For two days and nights he slept, had food sent up when he was hungry, sat numbly watching a television screen, or lay on his bed painting mental pictures of whatever drifted through his mind. Sometimes, too, he just lay staring at his painting of himself on top of Kate Henderson. On the morning of the third day, he picked up his crutches and hobbled a few blocks to the main branch of the New York Public Library on Forty-second Street and Fifth Avenue. He sat reading everything he could find about the crash in the back issues of a dozen newspapers and magazines.

The accident apparently had been the single worst midair collision in the United States. A total of two hundred and ninety-seven passengers and crew members had been killed in the two planes, and an additional four victims had been killed on the ground by falling debris. Many of the bodies had been burned beyond all possible hope of identification, but an arbitrary label was established, nevertheless, for each coffin. The names of the victims were arranged in long, alphabetical lists, and Gaynor felt compelled to seek and find his sons' names. His eyes were blank. Now it was official.

There were photographs and biographies of the more noteworthy passengers, and Gaynor studied them all very carefully. There was a Nobel Laureate who had made a significant breakthrough in cancer research, a Pulitzer Prize novelist, two famous physicists from the University of Chicago, a high-ranking churchman who had spent a lifetime striving for better understanding among the world's religions, an internationally celebrated husband-and-wife acting team, an economist who had written what was generally considered the definitive work on the free enterprise system, an assistant secretary of state for Middle Eastern affairs, and at least half a dozen others whose efforts seemed to have contributed, in one way or another, to the betterment of the species.

All dead. And he lived.

Even so, Gaynor was not neglected. As the only survivor of the epic crash, he was granted his own full share of attention. There were a great many photographs of him along with reproductions of *The Philosophers*, the painting bought by the Art Institute of Chicago. In addition, the New York gallery that represented Gaynor had taken advantage of the publicity by releasing material to the media that made him seem a combination of da Vinci, Rembrandt, and Renoir, with just a touch of Andrew Wyeth thrown in for contemporary flavor.

But if Gaynor was acclaimed as the sole survivor of the disaster, Lieutenant Newman had apparently received equal consideration as its hero. Indeed, the police commissioner himself had recommended the detective for the department's highest award for valor, the Medal of Honor, a citation describing the severely burned hero's selfless act as being in the best and noblest tradition of New York's finest.

Gaynor spent the entire day at the library. Before he left, he had photocopies made of everything pertaining to the crash, including the photographs, and carried it all back to his hotel in two large folders. When he unlocked the door and entered his room, he found Lieutenant Newman looking at him from under the same turban of gauze he had worn in his news pictures. The detective also had a glass of whiskey in his hand and a pint bottle on the floor beside his chair.

"How did you find me?"

"I'm a cop. One of my jobs is finding people." Newman poured Gaynor a drink and handed it to him. "The hospital is very upset. You've become something of a national treasure. They feel responsible."

"I absolve them."

"Your wife is also upset."

"I have no wife."

"Take it easy on her. She lost as much as you."

That much was true, thought Gaynor. Squinting for lights and darks, he painted Newman in a yarmulke and a prayer shawl that seemed to go perfectly with the secret rabbi who lived in his face. "I've been reading about you. I didn't know you were such a badly burned hero."

Silently and without expression, Newman removed the bandages from his forehead and hand. The flesh beneath was unmarked.

"I don't understand," said Gaynor.

"It's simple. A wounded hero gets a better press." He carefully rebandaged himself. "Disgusting, isn't it?"

"Why tell *me?*"

"Who else? All the others are dead."

The bones in Gaynor's face jabbed his flesh. Everybody had their sores. "If it bothers you so much, why did you do it?"

"Because I'm an alcoholic fuckup. Because if I didn't, I'd have been dumped."

Gaynor looked to see if he was joking. He wasn't.

Newman sipped his whiskey and stared out the window at the early darkness. His broad face, in the glow of a dim, soiled lamp, came out yellow and red. A clown's colors. "Any more questions?"

Gaynor thought about it. "Yes. What happened to your wife?"

The detective's laugh had the sound of breaking glass. "You don't mess around. You really go for the guts." He shrugged. "Well, why not? I threw you the teaser in the hospital, so why not the rest?"

Newman took a long moment. "Except that you can't really understand what happened to Jenny unless you know something about her. You see, Gaynor, my wife always wanted to do good, to *be* good. She was no saint, but she was surely on God's side of every major human question. She was for the sick, the hungry, the abused, and for any minority you could name. Sometimes she drove me up the wall with it because she wanted me to be the same. But I was a cop. If I tried to function on her level, I'd be dead a dozen times.''

Newman paused to light a cigarette. ''So one night we were walking home from a late movie,'' he went on softly. ''The streets were empty, but as we neared our apartment house I saw a couple of guys leaning against a car. 'I don't like the looks of those two,' I told my wife. She laughed. 'Why? Because they're black?' She always teased me about my work's prejudicing me against blacks and Hispanics. Actually, I'm not prejudiced, just practical. In this town most of our felonies happen to be committed by these two groups. Facts, not prejudice. Anyway, I let her talk me out of it and we continued on. Then we were abreast of them, and Jenny saw the guns before I did because she was on the curb side. I heard her say 'Please, don't' just before the shots went off. Would you believe that? Even then she had to say please. But she still had time to move in front of me and take both bullets. Forty-five-caliber. Have you ever seen the kind of damage that size slug can do?''

Gaynor shook his head.

''I went really crazy then. I had my gun emptied before they could even get a clear shot at me. Then I reloaded and emptied it again. Six in each. The final four I put square in their mouths and took off their skulls. I'd recognized them by then. A couple of junkies I'd collared a few weeks earlier who were out on bail. I was kicking what was left of them when two patrol cars came screaming in. It took four cops to pull me away. Imagine. Two forty-five-caliber bullets. My wife weighed a hundred and four pounds. A BB gun would have been enough.''

Newman took out a battered wallet and showed Gaynor a faded snapshot of a delicate, fair-haired girl smiling in a summer sun. ''This was my wife at the age of nineteen. She hated having her picture taken, so I never had a later one.'' He put his wallet away.

Gaynor's face was rigid. ''And that's what turned you into—''

''An alcoholic fuckup? Hell no. I'd shown a talent for that long before Jenny died. I was a Harvard Jew working with street-tough Irish cops. I started on the juice to show them I was one of the boys and found I liked it. It's not hard to get hooked in this job. Do you have any idea what frustration can

41

be to a cop? So you drink or beat up your wife. Maybe someone else's wife.''

They sat silently drinking. Newman picked up the folders Gaynor had brought back from the library and glanced through the crash material. ''What are you planning to do, write a book about it? Why don't you go home?''

''To what? Reporters, phone calls, and people I don't want to see?''

''The hospital says you still have to be watched. Infection can set in. At least be an outpatient.''

''No.''

''Then I'll have to report where you are. I've got a big investment in you, Gaynor. I'm a hero only because I saved your life. If you die, where does that leave me?''

''You really are a bastard.''

Newman looked aggrieved. ''Is that any way to talk to your savior? I'll make a deal. Suppose I send a police surgeon to check you out?''

''And no one else would know?''

''Only the commissioner. He also has an investment in you.''

''Can he be trusted?''

''Christ, no. But what choice do you have?''

It was, in its own way, a kind of hibernation. Yet Gaynor was in nothing that resembled a dormant state. In fact, his mind was so hyperactive it rarely allowed him more than a few consecutive hours of sleep. Still, only a tiny corner of his brain was open to the external world. He felt no difference between day and night. All food tasted the same. And every waking thought centered about only one question: *Why me?* The assumption being that there had to be some sort of viable answer. The alternative, once admitted, that his survival had been nothing more than a reasonless accident, that there was no more plan to his having been the single person chosen to remain alive than there was to the idea of a particular leaf being the last to fall from its tree, would have been enough to send him screaming through the streets.

He had it all taped to the walls—the long lists of dead, their photographs and obituaries; the poems that had been their lives, their successes and failures, the tragic bereavement of their loved ones—all surrounded him like wallpaper from the devil's own decorator. Everything was here. If any sense was to be made of it, it had to come from within this tiny, four-walled enclosure.

The hotel room and its connecting bath were his universe. There was a double bed, a bureau, a spindly desk, a chair, a TV set, and a radio—all stained and scratched, all stamped with the same giant cooky cutter that Gaynor imagined hidden somewhere in the Rocky Mountains, turning out millions of identical articles for similar hotels around the world. There was also a ridiculous print of a naked shepherd kissing an overweight shepherdess in a field, which Gaynor finally had to hide in a closet because it was turning his stomach. He knew intimately the cracks in the ceiling, the two broken slats in the blinds, and the hooker (and her transient couplings) whose window he faced across a narrow courtyard.

It was here that he tried to justify, to explain, to put in clear perspective. He made notes, wrote little blurbs on scraps of paper, scribbling them quickly, feverishly.

What's going on? What's happening inside my head? What am I trying to do here?

Am I crazy?

Is God crazy?

If he's not crazy maybe he's left early.

Where is he?

Why me? Why me?

Reasons! There have to be reasons!

Who said so? I said so. Who the hell are you? You're nothing.

I'm not nothing. Hell! I'm a survivor.

I NEED A SIGN!

He tore up what he wrote almost as fast as he wrote it.

Although Gaynor had never thought of himself as an especially religious man, he once found himself talking to God as intimately as Tevye.

"Please. Give me a hand, Lord. I've said you do nothing without reason, so for God's sake—I mean, for *your* sake—give me a reason. You took two hundred and ninety-seven souls, including many who had in some way added to life on this earth, yet you chose not to take me. And what have I contributed? Paintings that few have ever cared about, a wife I failed to please, and two sons I loved and carried to their deaths. If you'll excuse me, Lord, it doesn't make sense. At least not to me. So I'd really appreciate a little help." As an afterthought, he added "Amen."

He was totally confused, caught up, obsessed. Eyes red-rimmed, he stared intensely at the photographs and news articles on the walls, his pale, bony face projecting all he felt. He had placed two of the articles in a most favored position directly over his rickety desk, where a small lamp cast its glow upon them twenty-four hours a day like a vigil light before an icon. He had clipped the articles from the *Times*. One was an editorial, the other, an essay written by the Reverend Clayton Taylor, a celebrated, nationally known fundamentalist minister and a frequent contributor to the op-ed page. Both pieces were carried the same day and both had to do with the crash.

The editorial, mourning the loss of so many human beings in a single terrible accident, thought it might be the proper moment to pause and ask a few questions. We flew through the air faster than sound in great monster machines, but where were we going that we had to get there so quickly? And once we were there, what would we do with the time we had saved? Rush somewhere else and save still more time? Would it not be sad, said the editorial, if in the end we finally discovered that all we had somehow managed to do was rush through life without ever really arriving anywhere?

On the op-ed page, the Reverend Taylor's concern was with God's part in the crash, in the tragic destruction of so many innocent lives. He claimed that after each such disaster, people invariably said, "God isn't fair," or "Is there a God, after all?" or "Why does he permit such terrible things to happen?" Yet it should be known that God could never stop such manmade calamities from happening without forcing men to behave according to *his* will, thereby taking from them a free will of their own. Something that God, in his infinite wisdom, would never do. Instead, his hope was to make the character of human beings more perfect so that they might create less tragedy on this poor earth. God sent his only son, said the Reverend Taylor, to lead men into the true paths. Yet he, also, men rejected and killed.

Gaynor read the two featured articles over and over like a pair of personal catechisms. Looking for what? He had never cared for Clayton Taylor. Despite the southern preacher's increasing popularity across the country, Gaynor had always been made vaguely uncomfortable by the political overtones and fundamentalist leanings of his gospel. When Gaynor thought of religion at all, he tended toward an old-fashioned view. He believed a minister of God should stay close to his flock and avoid the earthly vanities of politics, theatricality, and the media. Still, there was something in Taylor's printed message, something about God's granting to man a free will of his own, that Gaynor found oddly appealing. It somehow seemed less disturbing for it to have been man's frailty, rather than God's, that had rained those poor bodies out of the sky.

I'm going out of my head, he thought. Soon I'll be looking for heavenly signs, maybe even a burning bush.

But, as time passed, he found himself looking at the television screen instead, looking at the twenty-four-hour news channels with their continuing and repeated reports of felonious assaults, of unprovoked cruelty, of arson and murder, of rampant terror in the streets. All of which seemed to have a strangely anesthetic effect, dulling his senses in much the same way as being struck repeatedly over the head. A young mother admitted to strangling her three-year-old child because he refused to stop wetting the bed. An old man, sleeping in the park, was stabbed sixteen times by three teenagers who said they did it just for kicks. Five children and two adults were burned to death in a fire set by a jealous lover. A man machine-gunned seven homosexuals in a gay bar because he felt that such people did not deserve to live in a decent society.

Sometimes he just sat mutely in front of the screen. Other times he hobbled about the room on his crutches, a man in uncertain and erratic transit. But either way the set was always on, his companion, washing its litany of disasters over him. Human beings, every one. Like him. Like the two hundred and ninety-seven who died in the crash. And what were the reasons for these tragedies? More of man's free will? If so, maybe God should make a change. Maybe God should take over.

At one point, finally finding it too much, he twisted the dial in disgust and heard God's name spoken. Not exactly a burning bush, but perhaps a modest sign. It came from a lean, ascetic-faced man who stared into the camera with pale, clam-colored eyes and spoke quietly and unemotionally in a voice further softened by a touch of the South. It was a voice without false passion or exhortation, a voice that seemed to address God and his listeners out of reasoned and deep personal conviction, a voice surprisingly free of the stale, predictable bombast of the usual media preacher. It was a long moment before Gaynor realized he was listening to the Reverend Clayton Taylor himself.

"And so, for thousands of years," Taylor was saying, "men have lived in defiance of God's laws. Instead of following his holy commandments, they have followed the self-seeking philosophy of Satan. Our present civilization, our present way of life, has been founded upon this philosophy. It is a life built upon a desire for the material realm, for self-gain, for competition and strife. America is the greatest nation on earth today, yet because of Satan's philosophy, poverty, suffering, and inequality are still with us. Our cities are riddled with violence and crime. Our leaders, having abandoned the way of Christ, are dishonest and corrupt. And the citizens of our great nation, forgetting God's laws of truth and justice, keep electing these same leaders to ever higher office."

The pale eyes glinted in the studio spots. "Yes, Satan has organized his politics as well as his religion. He himself appears not as a devil with horns and a tail but as one who is transformed into an angel of light who preaches the easy way and the smooth answer, the eternal deceits. His ministers are transformed into ambassadors of righteousness appearing as the apostles of God. But when you hear them preach, you are hearing them preach a different Christ in the power of false spirit. They deceive men with a gospel other than the true gospel of the kingdom that Jesus brought. Satan's congregations are famous for such deception. They wear many disguises. They come from many different lands. The current state of the world—its anger, its violence and greed, its competitive principles, its corrupt and permissive political systems—is sanctified by Satan's false religions in every land. All nations are deceived. But because of America's warmth of heart, because of its free, democratic processes, because of its willingness to accept and grant refuge to those of every faith and nationality, we in this great nation are deceived most of all."

The Reverend Clayton Taylor went on, an eloquent man speaking to an unseen congregation of millions in a calm, reasonable voice. Gaynor had heard him preach on the radio several times before, but only briefly and without paying very close attention. But this time, listening intently and at length, he began to understand the insidiousness of what the man was really saying. Stripped of its rhetoric, biblical illusions, and deceptively mild tone, the underlying bigotry of Taylor's message stood naked in the light. All who were not followers of Christ were followers of the devil, and those who had not been born here did not belong here.

Lovely. And from a man of God.

Gaynor switched the reverend off and went back to his news channel, where the continuing litany of disasters, terrifying though it might be, was at least out in the open.

His telecast over, Taylor left the Washington studio where it had originated, dismissed his staff and security people for the night, and drove alone to a secluded house in a heavily wooded section of nearby McLean, Virginia. Although the name on the mailbox was Peterson, Taylor had owned the house for the past several years, a fact known only to a few close associates. A representative had bought the modest, century-old colonial for him fully furnished, complete with family portraits. Taylor was amused by, even enjoyed, his instant ancestors. Which was more than he had ever been able to say about his true lineage. Whatever else the last few generations of Taylors might have had to offer, the giving of pleasure was never included.

Melissa Bradberry's Porsche was in the driveway and in the living room, waiting, Melissa herself, a slender, attractive woman with a full figure and deceptively cool eyes. They kissed and held one another. It was several weeks since their last meeting and they both responded to it. Separation, thought Taylor. Still the most dependable aphrodisiac available. It made even the downstairs bedroom seem too far away. In three minutes they were naked on the couch.

It had been a long, tiring, tension-filled day, but her flesh pumped new life into him. For these few moments he had no brain, no plan, no wit, no care, no desire other than sexual. It was as if everything that had happened until now was just so much dead skin, waiting to be peeled away. She was another man's wife and he was no woman's husband, yet at this instant they belonged solely to each other. He had some

47

distant awareness that there might well be a world beyond the immediate reach of his body, but it held no interest for him. Then, inevitably, at the very moment desire seemed most insatiable, it was sated.

They lay together yet apart, recovering their separate territories. There were few words of love. Taylor sometimes wondered whether he even liked the woman. Cynical and worldly, a pragmatist who had never married, he nevertheless felt that if one did marry, fidelity was demanded, and that adultery remained the ultimate self-indulgence. Which had nothing to do with his concepts of God, religion, or morality. He just had a vague idea that no one was meant to have everything all ways, a belief that had never stopped him from accepting married women as lovers. Actually, he preferred them. They presented fewer problems and obligations. And often, depending upon who their husbands were, they could offer valuable side benefits. Melissa herself happened to be married to the secretary of state of the United States. No small thing. At this particular stage of Taylor's life, he tried to leave as little as possible in the hands of God.

She sat up, and looked at him, looked at the smooth tightness of his flesh, the veins like blue cord in his arms, the long, still-muscular legs. "The Reverend Clayton Taylor," she said softly.

He was not unaware that his being a minister was a large part of his attraction for her. It lent an element of grace to what might otherwise have been simple lust.

"I was watching you on TV before," she said. "I love listening to you preach. You're probably the only man alive who can make Satan and God seem sexually exciting."

"Do you think that's my appeal?"

"For women, it is. The moment you open your mouth, they can feel you between their legs."

"Madam, that's blasphemy."

"No. All I'm saying is that you speak directly to the womb, to the source of life itself. What could be better? You should teach a special course at divinity school."

"I don't think so."

He mixed a pitcher of martinis and they drank while Melissa talked about Washington. She was an easy talker, intelligent and insightful, with a wry and amusing outlook and a sharp ear for high-level political gossip. He let her voice wash over him, selecting an occasional fact for possible retention and closing out the rest. Because of his nature and circumstances, he spent very little time in positions of intimacy. When he did, even this was contrived, with everything carefully planned and fitted into his schedule. He was sometimes startled when, rarely, a particular woman seemed to arouse a spontaneous feeling of pleasure in him that was apart from the purely physical. At times he hoarded such moments. At other times they just made him more wary.

Her lips were suddenly close against his ear. "Are you listening to me?"

"Every word."

"I think I've talked long enough."

He placed his palm against her belly and moved it downward until he felt the damp warmth. "Yes."

It was almost an hour before he was able to send her home to her husband. Which was cutting it rather close because it was no more than thirty-five minutes later that he heard the first of the expected cars enter the driveway. The other four cars arrived at approximately fifteen-minute intervals, one man in each, until they were all assembled around a large oak table in the study. The five men had traveled from different parts of the country for this meeting; in wealth, influence, and prestige, they were among the leaders in their respective fields.

"Gentlemen," he said, "welcome once again to historic Virginia."

This was an anniversary of sorts, the ninth of their regular quarterly meetings. It was just two years since Taylor had gathered them together for the first time in this room, five men who previously had known one another only by reputation. Their selection had not been random but rather the final choice of a list that had originally numbered two dozen. So that by the time the five were picked, there was little about any of them that the reverend did not know. And, perhaps best of all, he knew their hates, fears, and prejudices, their consummate avarice, their vanities and small, dark spirits—in short, all of the elemental frailties that would permit them to do pretty much anything so long as it fed their egos and lust for gain. Hardly the noblest of God's creatures, thought Taylor. Still, they did meet his particular needs, and who, after all, was perfect?

Norman Garbo

Briefly, he considered them over the obligatory brandy and cigars with which each session began. Directly across the table from him sat Bill Turner, youthful, shrewd, fourth generation out of Houston, and chairman of Turner Land and Oil. Formidably aggressive in all things, he was a prodigious hunter whose greatest pleasure seemed to come from shooting holes in anything feathered or furry and helpless. Some might even have called him vicious. But to Taylor he was a treasure, a Texan who despised anyone not white, Protestant, and Anglo and who conducted himself and his affairs accordingly.

Seated beside Turner was Franklin Burns. Heavyset, enormous in stature, with an engineer's sharp, controlled intelligence, he was the West Coast master builder whose Abeco Enterprises had literally created entire cities in the deserts of Kuwait and Saudi Arabia. Because of his openly expressed antipathy toward Israel, Burns enjoyed a most favored status throughout the Arab world. Taylor could never be certain of exactly how much of the construction mogul's prejudice was economically inspired and how much was ideological, but the results were unquestioned as well as valuable.

At the builder's right sat James Billings, chief of New York's giant Galatea Corporation, which controlled radio, TV, and newspaper interests in twenty-six major cities, coast to coast. A man of poor beginnings who had fought his way to undreamed-of wealth, he had been rewarded with two wives who had betrayed him with lesser men (he was currently married to a third) and with what he called unconscionably sharp dealings and extortion by minority pressure groups. Most of his competitors endured and were grateful for the good life they enjoyed. Billings suffered the affliction of resentment and the need to justify and get even. *Good*.

Next to Billings was Reginald Stafford, their resident Boston aristocrat and the head of New England Financial, one of the oldest and most powerful investment banking houses in the country. Stafford read all the reigning philosophers and enjoyed quoting Schopenhauer. *Hatred comes from the heart; contempt from the head; and neither feeling is quite within our control* was among his particular favorites. Taylor just thought him fatuous. Still, in his cool, quiet way, Stafford was a true fanatic in his prejudice.

Then came the last of the reverend's quintet, Bob Harding, a native Georgian from his own home of Atlanta. Harding

50

was the founder of the Southern Electronics Corporation and ranked high in the Fortune 500 old-boy network. He was also the one who had done most of the screening for him when the council was first being put together. If dueling had still been considered de rigueur in the South, Taylor felt certain that Harding would be among its most enthusiastic practitioners. The man labored under the same archaic code of honor and its equally misguided sense of grace.

Taylor sipped his brandy and smiled politely at a not very funny joke he had heard several times before. His five beauties. He had known many biased people in his lifetime and plenty of them had construed for themselves the best of motives. Sometimes the nature of their hate was objective only, designed simply to do them the most practical good. *As his was.* Still, the world provided more reasons for malice than for love, so why not take advantage of it?

It was nevertheless often hard for the reverend to reconcile the prodigious brainpower that had helped these five men achieve what they had with the utter irrationality of their prejudice. But of course prejudice *was* irrational *and* a passion, not a fact. It was impervious to all reason, all experience. It was blind hate, in itself a faith so strong that it made you feel as pious as a pilgrim on a quest for the Holy Grail. Which was precisely how his five, unblessed acolytes felt. Taylor had ensured it. He had become their high priest.

He allowed them time for a few more drinks before starting the agenda. There was little actual business to be conducted in any case. The American Crusade Party's day-to-day operations were handled at the regional and local levels. Unless there were major problems or changes, the National Council, of which Taylor was chairman, dealt mainly with the latest growth figures and whatever their current projections might be for the future. These rarely proved less than encouraging. During the slightly more than two years since the party had begun operation, its growth had been phenomenal. From nothing at all, they now had 174 units in 41 cities across the country and were opening an average of 3 additional units every month. Had Taylor chosen, they could have expanded even faster. Their funds were nearly unlimited, their recruiting personnel the best, and their appeal strong in all areas. But the reverend preferred holding their growth to controllable levels. At this stage he felt it best to keep a tight rein.

They were still an underground organization. When the time came to move out into the open, the solid core that now existed would serve as an administrative and training cadre for the far greater expansion that lay ahead.

A mystique had already begun to evolve about the party, a dim suspicion that it existed on a far larger and even more threatening scale than was generally acnowledged. Its name, too, had started to be whispered about. All of which Taylor considered a definite plus. A little fear in the right places could go a long way toward achieving respect. The world respected terror. Even the Jews had finally stumbled over this fact, had discovered at last that a single Israeli soldier firing a machine gun from a tank drew a more positive world reaction than a dozen Nobel physicists. For two millennia, Jews had believed that the recital of a chapter of Psalms would do more to affect the course of events than killing their enemies. They had fought the world's evil with spiritual courage and the Bible, and they had paid in blood. Now, at last, they were using rifles and machine guns. Now they were finally seeing the blood of their enemies, not just their own. In his own way, Taylor had managed to learn from the Jewish experience. And considering his current purposes and position, there had to be a curious irony in this fact alone.

So he was not unaware of the abnormality of his life. Sometimes he wondered whether he had any place at all among other people, with their natural lives and goals. Occasionally he would have liked to believe he was one of them. More frequently, he just didn't care. He had little respect for most people and none at all for these five with whom he had chosen to ally himself. Such involvements were deforming. They twisted you out of all normal shape. In a very specific way he knew he was obsessed. But knowing your affliction was not even close to treating it.

There was a light knock on Gaynor's hotel door one morning. Expecting Room Service, he was surprised to see a woman. The hall light was behind her, leaving her face in shadow.

"It's me," said his former wife.

Gaynor tried twice to speak and somehow could not. Moving himself out of the way, he made a small, helpless gesture.

Jane came in and looked at the room, looked at the walls papered with obituaries and pictures of the dead. She sat down and stared at Gaynor with fright. "What are you doing to yourself, Richard?"

Still silent, he sat himself opposite her. She seemed older, thinner, and he recalled Newman's words: *She lost as much as you.* His face aching, he began painting her—not as she was, but as he remembered her when she was twenty-two, with springtime still in her cheeks and the hair hanging fine as silk to her shoulders.

"You look terrible," she said. "So bony and pale."

"So I look bony and pale. Is that what you came here to tell me?"

She sat stiffly, hands clasped in her lap like a child's. "No. I came to take you home."

He painted her twenty-two-year-old eyes, which were so clear and deep a green that they might have been reflecting the sea. "I don't have any home. All I have is an apartment."

"I came to take you home with *me.*"

He stared at her, his painting forgotten.

"We need each other, Richard." She gasped a little and started to weep. She pressed her hands to her face and tears flowed through her fingers. "I still can't believe they're gone. I still go into their room every morning. I want to wake them for school. I keep thinking I'll walk in and find them in their beds."

He felt, as he watched her, a terrible weight on his heart.

"I didn't mean what I said in the hospital," she said, weeping. "You wanted me to punish you so I punished you. I know what you're suffering. I never said you were a bad person. I just felt shut out. You locked yourself in your art while I waited like a beggar for you to spare me a few hours. I was desperate to change my life. I wanted to find a man to whom I'd be as important as he'd be to me."

"Did you find him?"

She brought down her hands. "Maybe I was wrong. I wanted everything and now I have nothing. At least I knew you loved me. At least you never fooled around. Maybe you didn't earn much money, but it wasn't because you didn't try." She made a soft, choking sound. "So now we'll both have all the money we'll ever need."

He frowned, not understanding.

"The insurance," she said. "Our poor babies have made us rich."

Norman Garbo

His state had been such that this was his first awareness of it. The insurance had been a kind of game. They had all taken out big, six-figure policies at the airport. He had been Tommy's beneficiary, Jane had been Joshua's, and both twins had been his. Beneficiary. One who benefits.

"Richard, please." She went over and sat on the bed beside him. "Come home with me."

"I can't."

"I hurt enough. Don't punish me more."

"It has nothing to do with you."

"Who then?"

"Me. I don't know what I am anymore. But whatever I am, I'm not what I was."

"I don't understand."

"Neither do I."

"Richard," she said, sobbing, "come home. Don't you understand? We're all that's left of them."

He started painting her again. How young she had been, he thought sadly, how loving, how filled with hope, his.

His first sight of her had been on a bright spring morning with the sun lighting her hair and something inside him wanting to kneel down. At that stage of his life, just looking at beauty was not enough. He wanted to paint, touch, and feel it close about him. With Jane, he also had to marry it. And having done all this, he finally managed to lose everything. His own fault, of course, although she suddenly seemed to be starting to claim part of the responsibility. Still, he knew better. *I don't blame you for leaving me.*

A young orphan from Indianapolis, she came to New York to seek her fortune and settled for him, instead. She came with pictures of her mother and father and the small, well-tended house where they had lived. She also came with a newspaper photograph of the mangled Chevrolet in which her mother and father had died. Gaynor burned it the first week they were married. He found her utterly unique. She had tear ducts that pumped instant floods, a laugh that erupted just as swiftly, and an off-key whistle that was fully capable of breaking his heart. And she loved him. Not just loved. Loved! *I love you more than anyone or anything on earth.* She could say things like that, usually with her eyes closed and her face lifted to God, with whom she maintained an informal but solid, working relationship. If her eyes were closed and she

54

was not in bed, asleep, Gaynor knew she probably had something going with him. He was fascinated. He had married Joan of Arc.

She had brought a new spring brightness to his winter dark. He was an angry artist, growling at the world. He was self-absorbed, intense. Painting life, he forgot about living it. She tried to show him how. She offered music and flowers. She turned food and drink into a fresh theology. No more bread and Beefaroni. In a world where hearts were cold and compassion rare, she offered space in her soul, asylum from rejection. Love shone from her eyes. She soothed him with her flesh. Jesus, he had never had it so good.

So what happened? Was it all too much for him? Did he feel he didn't deserve all that joy? No joke. He was a painter, one of a strange, historically masochistic breed. How could he produce anything worthwhile out of joy, out of a heart free of darkness? He needed the ton weight, the cold ache back in his chest. He needed his solitary struggles, his angst, his old obsessions. *Artist*, da Vinci had said, *thy strength lies in solitude*. So he began burying himself once more in what he and other fools chose to call his creative withdrawal. Fool. As if the fate of nations hung on the purity of his brushstrokes.

And what had she really asked for? No great sacrifices. No incredible luxuries. Just that he stop burrowing away like a solitary animal, that he not stare his hundred-mile stare when she or his sons begged a few hours' attention, that he show even half the interest in them that he showed in what was taking place on one of his canvases. But some men seem born to fight off the best in life until it is no longer there. Or else they pervert it into nightmares. He, somehow, managed to do both.

Still, there were times when they soared, times when there was a beatific light in his wife's hair. He saw it for sure. There were also times when she gazed at him, and in her thickly lashed eyes he saw wonders for them both despite their years of hurt and confusion. She could make him see this. She could make him feel alive. She could introduce him to hope. She could put springs in his legs that would let him leap into the future. She could make him know love.

And she could also take it away.

There came a time when more and more they began rending each other. It was a period of bloodletting and pain. A glance, a gesture, a few wrong words, could set the demons loose. He should have seen what was coming. Any fool would have. But he was not any fool. He was her husband. Also, he loved her. And regardless of whatever else might be going on, neither of these were up for grabs. At least not for him. For her, evidently they were.

"I'm leaving you," she had said. "I don't want to waste any more of my years. I want a divorce."

It was not possible. He felt betrayed, cut down. An enemy sleeping at his side all this time, dagger poised. Finally, she had stabbed him in the heart.

She was shocked by his shock. Surely he was being melodramatic, overreacting. How could he not have known, not have seen it coming? All he could do was stare at her. I'll either strangle her where she sits, he thought, or I'll cry like an idiot. He didn't strangle her. Tears ran down his cheeks and into his mouth. He tasted salt.

"I love you," he said. "Why don't you know how much I love you?"

It was enough to set her off, too. Her instant tears gushed. They sat crying together. "I know how much you love me," she said, weeping, furious at the disintegration of what she had planned as a cool, controlled scene. "But that hasn't anything to do with it."

"Then what has?"

"Living with you. I can't goddamn live with you."

And now she wanted him back. But he couldn't go back, only onward.

The police surgeon whom Lieutenant Newman had assigned to Gaynor was a gray-haired man who looked well past retirement age. He had flushed cheeks and the faint smell of whiskey on his breath. Sometimes his fingers trembled as they explored Gaynor's body. This was his third visit, and each time his narrow eyes seemed to search Gaynor's face and flesh for the signs of deception he had run into so often in more than thirty years of examining malingering police officers.

"How are you feeling?" he asked after his usual poking around.

"Terrific," said Gaynor in a flat tone.

The irony was wasted. "No complaints?"

"Absolutely none."

"Bowels regular?"

"Like a fine Swiss watch."

The doctor closed his bag. His rheumy eyes pecked at the crash material taped to the walls. "You should thank God every day for the rest of your natural life."

"You mean my unnatural life."

"What?" said the doctor suspiciously.

"Nothing."

But it was not nothing, Gaynor thought later. That was exactly it. His natural life had ended with the crash. By every law of nature and physics, he should have burned with the others. So, at the very least, whatever life remained to him now had to be considered unnatural. The question was, what would he choose to do with it?

Yet what choice did he really have? He was only a sadly limited mortal who would one day die. As did all creatures. The one thing that separated him from the rest was that in a curiously abstract, almost metaphysical way, he had already died. Which seemed to leave him indifferent, perhaps even immune (as if his survival had been a new form of inoculation), to the generally accepted dread of death. Indeed, there were moments when the prospect of dying was not without a certain appeal. In itself, disturbing. If death's threat was lost, then so too was life's joy. Finally, you felt nothing. Exactly.

He took late night walks when the streets were deserted and there was little chance of being seen by reporters. His strength was building, particularly in his arms, and he could swing along pretty well on his crutches. One night, heading back from the East River, with the city quiet about him, a man stepped from an alley and pointed a gun at his chest.

"Gimme your dough an' watch."

Gaynor looked at a tall, bearded white man in jeans and leather jacket. Now I find out, he thought. "Fuck off."

The man blinked twice. "Hey, I ain't messin' aroun'."

"Neither am I."

"You wanna get blown away for a few lousy bucks?"

"Why not?"

The man stood there. His gun began to shake slightly.

"But are you really ready to kill me for a few lousy bucks?" said Gaynor. He could see the light fade from the man's eyes.

"You're fuckin' crazy." The man hurried off toward the river.

Gaynor continued back to his hotel. He had not been afraid. Not for an instant. That much, at least, he knew.

He lay on his bed in the darkness, working on a second painting of Kate Henderson and himself. In this one their original positions were reversed, with her body now in the ascendancy and her breasts floating close above him. He painted his hands on the dip of her waist and studied the result for a moment. Then, changing his mind, he placed his hands beneath her breasts instead, cupping them lightly, his palms barely making contact, and all of it shining out of a dark umber background. He had painted their faces laughing, as though they had just shared a joke, and he wondered at this.

One night someone tapped at his door, and he jumped as though a shot had gone off. The luminous dial of his watch said it was after one.

"Who's there?"

"Kate Henderson."

He hopped to the door without his crutches.

"Don't you think I've left you alone long enough?" she said. Still in uniform, she had evidently come straight from her four-to-midnight shift.

Leaning against the doorjamb, he reached for her right there, lifting her to him easily, his mouth hard against hers before she could say another word.

She gasped. "I see you're feeling better."

Somehow, he managed to close the door and get them to the bed.

"Your cast," she warned.

He had her clothes half off. "No problem. "We'll just follow the second painting."

"What second painting?"

His mouth, going wild again, was too busy to answer. It suddenly had all these choices to make.

The shades were up, and a light from across the courtyard tinted their bodies yellow. It had been a wild, knowing, drowning experience. Better than a hundred mental paintings.

GAYNOR'S PASSION

He smiled and turned his head. "See? I told you the cast was no problem."

They laughed softly together in the rumpled bed. He watched her breasts rise and fall with her breathing. They were exactly as he had imagined them, full and firm, with dark nipples that stayed sensitive to his touch even now.

She said, "What was that about the second painting?"

He told her. Afterward, she just lay holding him.

"You don't have to worry," he said. "I'm only a little bit crazy."

"In that case, why have you got all those obits taped to the walls?"

"To try to make some sense of what happened."

"What if there is no sense?"

He took a moment to answer. "I can't let myself believe that."

"For God's sake, don't turn into one of those mystical creeps. You've suffered real pain and loss, but what you're doing here isn't going to help anyone, least of all you." She propped herself on one elbow to light a cigarette. "Do you know, you absolutely captivated me in the hospital? You were the stuff of true classic tragedy. I think I fell in love with you before you were even conscious. I used to work double shifts because I hated to trust anyone else around you."

She studied the orange glow of her cigarette. "It scares me to see what you're doing to yourself here. Listen. I know a psychiatrist who does really great work with accident trauma and survival guilt. If you'd only let me—"

"I don't need any shrink. I just need time to work things out."

"Can't you just be grateful you're alive and leave the rest alone? What you should do is start painting again. You're an artist, remember? And from everything I've read, a really good one."

"That was in my natural life."

Her eyes were black. "And now you're in your unnatural state?"

"Exactly." He smiled. "You catch on fast."

"Jesus, you do need help."

"Painting doesn't seem that important to me anymore."

"Then what does seem important?"

"I'm not sure yet. But I do know it's not just turning out a few more pictures."

Shortly before dawn he tried another rendering of them making love, but this one turned out badly and he destroyed it.

Lieutenant Newman appeared while Gaynor was in the middle of watching what had become his regular evening TV crime countdown. "Why aren't you out arresting all those animals?" Gaynor asked.

Newman settled tiredly into a chair and frowned at the screen through his cigarette smoke. "Because I'm too busy being a hero. Do you have any idea how many Rotary, Kiwanis, Elks, and Lions Club luncheons are going on in New York on any given day? Not to mention assorted meetings of the Holy Name Society, Hadassah, Knights of Columbus, and other civic and religious groups. I've figured it out. If I gave my special inspirational speech to three of these a day for five years, I still wouldn't have reached half." He poured himself a drink from his usual pint bottle. Then, as an afterthought, he fixed one for Gaynor. "Besides, it wouldn't do much good to arrest them. Most would be out on the streets again before the ink was even dry on the booking sheet. The jails are full, and the courts are mostly bleeding hearts clubs with revolving doors."

Gaynor stared silently at the TV screen, where bodies littered the street after a shootout.

"Why do you bother watching that crap?" said Newman.

"I seem to be getting addicted." The crime reports ended and Gaynor turned off the set. "Who else are you planning to send up to work on me besides my ex-wife and nurse?"

"Cardinal O'Connor. But he's been busy lately."

"You promised not to tell anyone but your boss where I am."

"Never trust an alcoholic cop." Newman smiled vaguely. "I just thought getting laid might help put things in better perspective for you."

Gaynor created an instant oil sketch of Newman in a white felt hat, ermine coat, and gold chains. "I didn't know cops pimped, too."

"Sure. We do all sorts of dumb things, Gaynor. We get ourselves knifed and shot for a day's pay. We take abuse from those we try to protect. We break our hearts doing a job we know can't be done. And sometimes we even waste good time trying to help unappreciative assholes like you get hold of themselves.''

"I never asked for help."

"I told you. You're my insurance. You're keeping me in the job.''

"I don't undersand, Lieutenant. Feeling as you do about the cops, why would you want to stay in the job so badly.''

Newman looked surprised. "I guess I've steered you wrong. There's nothing I'd rather be than a police officer.''

"Why?''

"Because I happen to suffer from what will probably turn out to be a terminal belief in the law.''

"Then you should have been a lawyer.''

"I'm that, too.''

It was not always easy for Gaynor to tell when the detective was serious. This time, evidently, he was. "Did you ever practice?''

"Only long enough to pass the bar. Then I went straight into the department. Mike Westley and I were sworn in together.''

"The commissioner?''

"None other. In fact, it was Mike who talked me into joining up. Not that he had to work very hard at convincing me. I was a romantic young man. Even then, the whole idea of the thin blue line intrigued me.''

"What's that?''

Newman lit a fresh cigarette from the remains of his old one. "The concept that only a fragile line of police officers stands between life as we know it today and bloody anarchy. And I desperately wanted to be part of that dumb but intrepid band of knights errant. I wanted to plant myself firmly before the forces of darkness and die, if need be, to hold them in check.'' Newman peered sharply at Gaynor, as if to see whether he was laughing. "I probably make it sound like *The Catcher in the Rye* with a navy blue uniform and brass buttons, but it's how I felt almost thirty years ago and it's how I still feel today.''

Gaynor said nothing. Sipping Newman's excellent sour mash, his thoughts were already some distance beyond him. He had started on a new painting. Right now it was only an immense, empty area of white in the center of his mind, but that was just temporary. In good time, he would fill it in, bit by bit by bit.

The idea, like most such notions, did not spring to life full blown in a flash of light. It evolved slowly and in gradually changing form. The thing was, God owed him a reason for his survival, he owed God a life, and somewhere between the two a proper balance had to be struck. But it was Lieutenant Newman, not God, who had inadvertently given him the first spark of the idea, and he felt himself caught up, overcome, rendered almost feverish with new excitement.

The thin blue line, knights errant, forces of darkness . . . The lieutenant's romantic images carried the rolling beat of drums and something inside Gaynor responded. Of course. This was the time for precisely such fantasies. This was the time for wild ideas and savage notions, for loud cries for justice shouted into the night. This was the time for someone oblivious to death, someone desperately in need of a mission, to take action and do something about it.

Yes, but what?

He began scribbling more of his notes.

I'm human, I'm alive, and I've got to make use of myself. I need to justify.

The essence of being decently alive and human rests on the proper use of ourselves by others and their use by us.

Suffering instructs.

No. I've really learned nothing.

But this last was not quite true. He had been learning. Hour by hour, he could feel himself getting closer to what he was after, so that one night, watching his usual televised assortment of large and small crimes, it finally broke through. Curiously enough, it had been there all along. Jay Newman had unknowingly but graciously said it: *I wanted to plant myself firmly before the forces of darkness and die, if need be, to hold them in check.*

Gaynor wanted to shout it aloud. That was it. He would be decently alive and human. He would make proper use of himself. He would plant himself firmly before Newman's *forces of darkness*. And he would do it all alone and without a uniform and brass buttons.

But of course he knew it would not be that simple. The fact was, it might not even be possible. Still, he did allow himself a small measure of faith. He had to. Mad or not, it was at least a lifeline. The only one he had.

Finally, wondering if he was, indeed, losing his mind, he once again addressed himself to God. "I'm going to try it, Lord" he said. "I really don't know what, if anything, is required of me, but I'm going to try this. I know it's an extravagant, maybe even a pretentious and mad idea, but the ordinary no longer seems possible for me. Whatever I was before, I'll never be again."

Feeling himself light with hope and dread, doubting that he even knew where he was going, he prayed that if he did at last manage to get there, something of value would be waiting to receive him. The elderly police surgeon removed the cast from Gaynor's leg and probed the pale flesh with his palsied fingers. "I think you'll do all right with it," he said without conviction. "Let's take a little stroll and see how it works."

Gaynor walked back and forth across the room several times. He felt shaky and he had a slight limp.

"How does it feel?"

"Okay."

"The limp should disappear after a while, but you'll still favor the leg. What do you do for a living?"

"I'm an artist, a painter."

"Well, you'd better paint sitting down for a time. Who knows? You may discover a whole new talent in your ass." The doctor laughed as though he had just said something excruciatingly funny.

Gaynor left his hotel room the following day. He simply peeled his crash material from the walls, placed it in the folders, and walked out the door. As he limped along the hall, his shoes making a hesitant, unfamiliar sound on the worn flooring, he felt like an overage student who had just won a degree from a special university for the insane, whose every book and lecture he had memorized word for word.

5

Lieutenant Newman sat in a rear booth at the Stuyvesant Cocktail Lounge waiting for Mary Logan, who had already called twice to say she might be delayed by as much as two hours and maybe they'd better just forget about the whole evening. Newman had told her not to worry about it, that since all the really class hookers were taken by then, he would be there whenever she arrived. The situation was not new. He was used to Mary's being late. She had an extended history of emergency cases that absolutely could not be walked away from without helpless, dependent people suffering the most dire consequences. Considering it, Newman had long ago decided there must be something about congenitally humanist women that he found impossible to resist. It was no great shame, just occasionally inconvenient.

In the meantime he waited and drank in a comfortable, dim room with a long, well-stocked bar along one wall, where the sights, sounds and smells were as relaxing and familiar to him as those of the old synagogue up the block had once been to his grandfather. A sacrilegious comparison. Or was his currently accepted God really at the bottom of a perfect sour mash?

A hard-looking detective from Newman's old precinct paused on his way to the men's room. "My hero! How's it going?"

"Hanging in. What's doing at the Ninth?"

"Same old crap." The tough face split into a grin. "Caught

a piece of your act on the news the other night. Is it going to be syndicated? You should get an Emmy.''

The detective continued on, a predator on a mountain. A thirty-second tape of Newman's address to an Anti-Defamation League dinner had been carried by a local TV station, and the response had been favorable enough for the commissioner to call him in about it. "I think you're doing well," Westley had said. "What about you? Feel any better about things?'' Newman had shrugged the question off. But giving it some thought later, he was surprised to find that despite his own initial response, as well as the mocking resentment of almost everyone he knew in the department, he was actually enjoying what he was doing. The point was, in his new capacity as a publicly acclaimed hero, he had the chance to speak out about things that really concerned him and have people willing to listen. So what was so bad? And when his bandages were finally off, even that lingering bit of rancor was gone. At least he was no longer a walking fraud.

Newman had also made another discovery. He was a good public speaker. He had a strong, unaffected delivery and enough of a feel for his audience to let him know very quickly what would and would not work. So that in addressing the ultra-liberal and Jewish Anti-Defamation League the other night, he had not only emphasized the need to protect a suspect's civil rights, but he had made sure he took some good hard swipes at the increasingly bigoted noises being made by the Reverend Clayton Taylor, who, to this kind of crowd, was already beginning to reek of death camps and crematoriums. And they had loved and applauded him. Which might not mean everything, but it was infinitely better than being despised.

He saw Mary enter the bar and stand, looking. He waved and she came down the aisle, her cheeks flushed with hurrying, her eyes bright with pleasure at seeing him. She pecked his forehead and slid into the booth.

"I'm so sorry, but this poor woman was dumped out on the street with five kids by her bastard of a landlord, and I absolutely couldn't leave until I found her a place to spend the night. Sometimes I wonder how—'' She took a deep breath and smiled. "Thank you for waiting, darling.''

He ordered her usual Scotch and water. "Okay,'' he said

when her drink had arrived. "Now tell me all about your poor, homeless lady and her five kids."

Then he just sat drinking and listening, enjoying the warm eagerness of her face, with its clear Irish complexion, saucy pug nose, and sparkling eyes, taking pleasure in the short, fluffy style of her hair and the way her breasts lifted against her blouse. Looking at her, he became aware of how much he had come to take her presence, the mere fact of her being there, for granted. It was suddenly impossible to imagine that whatever days and nights remained to him would not in some way include her. He had better be careful, he thought. There was nothing worse than a tough old ass drifting into sentimental senility.

"But enough about me," she said. "What did you do today?"

"Talked. That's what I do these days. I talk."

"Don't complain. It's the best assignment you've ever had. No midnight shifts, no one shooting at you, no captains, inspectors, or IAD on your back." She pressed his hand. "And you're really such a sweet talker, love. You should have started doing this twenty years ago."

"I didn't have my hero's credentials twenty years ago."

"And I love that part, too. I love the whole idea of your being a hero. I love having people coming over to me at work and saying they saw your picture in the paper or on TV. You've even made me a celebrity-by-proxy. Would you believe that one of the women in the Aid to Dependent Children Section actually asked for my autograph?"

"Did you give it to her?"

"Of course. I signed it 'Mary Logan, hero fucker.' "

He laughed. "You didn't."

"Celebrities-by-proxy can get away with almost as much as celebrities."

"I had no idea you were so crassly superficial."

"Fool. I just never had the opportunity before. I adore being crassly superficial. It's marvelous, much more fun than being buried in profound issues." She studied the backs of her hands. "God, how I wish I might have led a life of gay superficiality. When I think of all the years I've wasted in significant humanist works. And what have I got to show for it other than hypertension?"

"Me."

Her eyes found and held his. "Have I really?"

"Why not?"

"Do you want me to tell you?"

Newman motioned to the waiter for fresh drinks. "No."

"I think I'll tell you anyway," she said. "I don't really have you because you still carry around that dumb, thirty-year-old picture of your wife like a mooning kid. Because you still won't admit you love me as much as we both know you do. Because you still refuse to live with me on a sensible, continuing basis. And especially because you're still scared half to death of committing yourself to any relationship that threatens to make life reasonably and permanently pleasant for you."

Newman was gazing off at the far end of the room, where a homicide captain he had never especially liked had been staring at him, off and on, for the better part of an hour. It was becoming impossible, he thought, to walk into a decent bar these days without running into someone he had shared a history with in the job. Finally, he would be driven to solitary drinking.

"Finished?" he asked Mary.

"Yes."

"Well, now I know."

"You knew before. It's just that every once in a while I like to get it all properly stated and laid out."

"Okay, Madam Psychologist. So how would you label me? Compulsive death wish? Acute fear of joy? Manic-depressive? Or maybe just plain old chronic alcoholism."

"I love you, Jay."

"I can't imagine why."

The light Irish eyes went straight through him. "For a lot of silly reasons. But mostly, I suppose, because you're probably the most decent, unalterably moral man I've ever known."

"Jesus, could you get arguments on that."

As if fulfilling the prophecy, a shadow fell across the table and Newman looked up at the homicide captain, a bulky man with the glow of either high blood pressure, heavy drinking, or both on his face.

"What do you say, Newman?"

"Hello, Brady."

The captain glanced at Mary as though expecting an introduction. When it failed to materialize, he gave his full attention to Newman. "I almost didn't recognize you without your costume. What happened to all those pretty bandages you've been sporting?''

"The doctor took them off.''

"Hell. Why did he do that?''

"I didn't need them anymore.''

Brady took a long swallow of the drink he had brought with him. "I'll tell you a little secret, Lieutenant. I don't think you *ever* needed them.''

Newman said nothing.

"As a matter of fact,'' said Captain Brady, "I think your whole wounded hero bit is a fake, a masquerade perpetrated by you and your buddy, the commissioner, to turn the department clown into Prince Valiant.''

"You mean *poy*petrated, don't you?''

"I mean you're a phony, Lieutenant.''

Newman offered him the gentlest smile he had. "Why don't you tell that to the commissioner?''

"I don't have to tell him. I'm telling you. Where are your burn scars? Your face is as smooth and clean as a baby's ass.''

Newman took a moment to light a cigarette. Brady was either drunker than he looked or suffered a bleeding ulcer. "Okay, Captain. Now why don't you go back to your friends and get on with your drinking.''

"We have real heroes in this police department, Newman, cops who've suffered real wounds while performing real acts of courage. We're even graced with about a dozen a year who die doing it, God help them. And I swear to Christ it makes me want to puke every time I see you trotting out your fake little dog-and-pony act and dirtying up their bones.''

The captain turned and walked away, carrying himself a trifle unsteadily but very erect. Staring after him, Mary's face was pale. "Idiot drunk! For a few seconds back there I was afraid you were going to do something foolish.''

"Like what? Belting a superior officer?''

"You've done it before.''

"Yes. But never for just speaking the truth.''

It was well past midnight as they rode out toward the Rockaway peninsula, a long, narrow sandspit separating ocean and bay, where they both lived. Newman drove slowly and with care through the inevitable mist while Mary dozed beside him. He felt the roll of the tires, the liquor in his stomach, and the pleasant blurring of the senses that came after an evening of steady but not excessive drinking. Off to his left, a Long Island train going in the same direction passed on its midbay trestle, strings of yellow lights reflecting in the water. As a boy, Newman had gone out to Edgemere every summer with his parents and grandfather on this same line, the four of them sitting together in facing straw seats, and the smell of the sea, all that delicious salt air, coming in through the open windows. He had loved those months at the beach. It was why he had moved out there years later, although by then it was not the same.

Again, sentiment. He smiled dimly at the toylike train, remembering. It was out at the beach that he had first told his family he was going to become a police officer. Three decades ago, and their reactions were as clear to him at this moment as they had been then. His father had been furious. How could he deliberately throw away an education, a law degree, and a future of dignity, position, and money? And for what? A life of brutality? His mother, understanding neither his logic nor his needs, worried that he might be turning a little bit crazy, like her meshugana brother Marvin, may he rest in peace, who had wanted nothing but to be a fireman and who had finally died of it when a burning tenement collapsed on his head. The big surprise was his grandfather, who had simply laughed in his beard, kissed him, said it was about time the Jews started getting some Cossacks of their own to look after them, and offered his most sincere *mazel tov*. Another lifetime. How long they had all been gone.

Mary stirred against him, sighed, and drifted back into sleep. Shacks stood on stilts above the bay along both sides of the road. The marshgrass was edged in silver. They passed the stretch of Cross Bay Boulevard where the crash had occurred, and Newman kept his eyes staring straight ahead through the windshield. He still had nightmares. Mostly, the same one. The sky rained fire and bodies and he stood very still, holding an umbrella.

He drove over the Cross Bay Bridge and turned left toward Arverne through acres of closed summer bungalows and block after block of newer high-rise housing projects. The projects, mostly subsidized housing, had started out as a model interracial community but were now almost entirely black. When

Norman Garbo

Newman had brought his new wife out here twenty years ago, it had been a pleasant, well-tended neighborhood with a summer resort atmosphere all year. Little of that was now visible. Generally, what remained was a sad case of urban blight moved to the seashore. Whatever better areas were left, black as well as white, fought a losing battle for survival.

Scavenged cars littered the road. About a hundred yards off to the right, the ocean ripped along the beach. To the left, outlined by a few stunted trees, was what the locals called Three P Park, a scraggly piece of real estate long ago abandoned to the platoons of pimps, pushers, and prostitutes who hung out there. It was not a busy night, and Newman saw only a handful of regulars scattered about. Some sat on benches, others lay sprawled on the dead winter grass, while still others, mostly prostitutes, strolled along the curb looking for tricks in passing cars. Several waved to Newman as he drove by.

A few blocks farther, the detective turned right toward the beach and suddenly braked to avoid hitting something in the road.

Mary woke with a start. "What is it?"

In the glare of the headlights, Newman saw a naked black man lying face down at the end of what appeared to be a long trail of blood. Although he was not actually lying. He was crawling, dragging himself forward inch by inch like a squashed bug, while the dark, wet trail extended behind him.

"My God," Mary whispered.

"Listen to me," said Newman. "When I get out, you get behind the wheel. If anything happens, just drive away from here fast. Understand?"

Not waiting for an answer, he drew a short-barreled .38 and left the car. Stupid, he thought. The whole thing could be some kind of setup, with the blood turning out to be ketchup and long knives waiting in the shadows. And even if the blood was real, the danger of a possible ambush remained. Yet how could he risk leaving a man to bleed to death in the gutter?

He crouched in the road, peering into shadows. The street was deserted and silent. Rows of dark summer bungalows, pressed close together, stretched off toward the beach. Newman saw and heard nothing. Moving closer to the man, he touched the wetness in the gutter. It was blood, all right. He rolled the man onto his back and saw loose, bloody strips of flesh. Someone had all but skinned him, sliced him like a side of beef. The man lifted his arms to defend himself from further attack, then collapsed with a groan. Newman turned away. You thought you had seen everything, then this popped out of the gutter. He had never seen so complete a cutting job.

"Stay where you are," he told Mary.

He got an old army blanket out of the car trunk, gently wrapped the man in it, and carried him into the back seat. He held him as Mary drove toward Peninsula General Hospital. The man slipped in and out of consciousness.

"Who did it?" Newman asked when he saw his eyes open.

"White . . . dude," the man gasped. "Big . . ."

"You didn't know him?"

"I ain't . . . from 'round here. I got set up . . . a hooker. He was waitin' . . . in . . . her pad."

"Was she white or black?"

"White . . . real blond . . . with nice pink ribbons." He moaned softly. "Shit . . . Jus' wanted . . . t'get . . . laid . . ."

He was unconscious when Newman carried him into the Emergency Room of the hospital. A young intern opened the blanket and went pale. "Jesus, where did you find this?"

"In the gutter."

The doctor made a quick examination. "You could have saved yourself the trouble. He's dead."

Of a hard-on, thought Newman.

They rode away from the hospital in silence.

"Let's move to Tahiti," said Mary.

Newman shrugged. He seemed abstracted. "I have to check something out. You want me to take you home, first?"

"No."

He drove back to Three P Park, stopped at the curb, and was approached by a solitary prostitute, a lynx-eyed black woman in a red wig. "How's it going, Bertha?"

"Real slow, Lieutenant." She grinned. "You an' Mary interested in livenin' things up a little?"

"Some other time." He put a twenty into her hand. "You know a blond chick working this area? White? Maybe pink ribbons in her hair?"

"You mus' mean Rose. She does a guy they call Shimmy, a real big white mother. They new 'round here. Come outta the Bronx 'bout a month ago. What they done?"

"Set up and cut a brother."

Bertha shook her head. "Damn. That make us all look bad."

"Where do they flop?"

"Ole bungalow on Fifty-sixth. First off the beach, on left." She looked closely at Newman. "Hey, you don' work this turf, Lieutenant."

"Tonight, I do. Thanks, Bertha."

Newman drove off.

"The Hundredth Precinct is the other way," Mary said.

"I know."

"You're not really going after him yourself."

He said nothing.

"Jay . . ."

"You didn't see what they did to that guy."

"I don't care *what* they did to him."

"Well, I do."

Beach Fifty-sixth Street dead-ended in sand at the board-walk. Newman parked at the nearest cross street and got out.

"For God's sake, be careful," said Mary.

He did not even hear her. There were only bungalows on the block, and most were still boarded up from the winter. A few were burned out. Some had been fitted with heating systems and were used all year. Newman walked silently between them, keeping to the sand edging the sidewalk. He breathed slowly and deeply, the damp ocean air making his lungs ache. Primitive feathers of excitement tickled his spine, and he had the savage notion that he should dab his face with paint and go into a war dance. There had been a time when he believed exceptional things were within his reach, and at rare moments the belief seemed to return. Drawing his revolver, he half smiled. Were there violent demons in him some-where? Hell. He had become a cop, hadn't he?

Newman reached the end of the block. A heavy surf was running and the sound had grown to a steady roar. The bungalow he was looking for, the first off the beach on the left, was dark except for a single lighted window at the rear. All the other bungalows in the line were boarded up. Keeping low, Newman approached the lighted window. A shade was partially drawn, but he could see beneath it into a sparsely furnished bedroom whose walls and ceiling were covered with mirrors. A man and woman were making love on the bed. The woman had blond hair tied in pigtails with pink ribbons, the man was big and heavily muscled, and they both had white skin.

Newman felt as though he were peering, not into a room, but into a den, a lair. There was nothing tender or loving about the act being performed. These two met more like animals in a violent mood than as lovers. They tore at each other. They clawed and bit. They writhed like lizards that had crossed a burning desert to attain their moment. Flesh drove against flesh. Fingers pinched and squeezed, making cruel little forays. Mouths were hard, mean, and greedy, with all the cold slyness of city rats. Nothing here but the kind of virulent, intricate hatred that scrawled FUCK on tenement walls.

Newman left the window, kicked open a flimsy side door, and stood pointing his revolver at them before they had time to disengage.

Still, they had a certain presence. Neither cried out or showed alarm. They just lay there, staring up at Newman and being careful to keep their hands visible and not make any sudden moves. The blonde, up close, could not have been more than sixteen or seventeen, but she had middle-aged eyes that were as hard and cold as chipped ice. The man was an overgrown brute, with a scarred face and thick pads of cartilage on the sides of his temples to show that he may have once worked as a fighter.

Lieutenant Newman showed them his badge. "You're under arrest. It's my duty to inform you that anything you say may be used against you."

"What kind of arrest?" said the man. "I mean, what the hell for?"

Newman watched the glistening red snake grow limp and shrivel between his legs. "Murder."

"You're nuts. I never killed nobody."

Newman backed off, picked up jeans and a shirt, checked the pockets for weapons, and tossed them onto the bed. Then he did the same with the girl's clothing. "Get dressed."

"Hey, let's talk, Lieutenant."

The girl smiled, a cheerleader's healthy grin. "Or maybe fuck?"

"Put your goddamned clothes on," said Newman, "or I'll kick you both bare-assed into the street."

"Take it easy," said the man as he began dressing.

73

Still smiling, the girl slowly, deliberately, parted her legs and began touching herself. Newman stared at her as if she were a specimen in a zoo. A clammy odor of rut came off the bed, a thin, high smell that spoke of dirty, crowded rooms and the sewer-damp stink of sunless alleys. Breathing it, Newman never did see the knife in the man's hand until it was about to enter his stomach. Even then it was barely a glint, a quick flash of light that caught his eye and pushed him back so that the blade hooked only his jacket, ripping it straight across as cleanly as a scalpel making an incision. Then it was coming again, and this time there was no stepping back.

Newman fired without apparent aim, fired once, the explosion like thunder in the small room, and the single bullet taking away half the man's forehead. But the knife still came and Newman caught it and the man's falling body against his left arm, balancing them both in a lovers' dance as another shot went off, then a third, neither of them coming from the detective's gun but from an automatic held by the girl, who now sat upright in bed, aiming and firing at him as calmly as though she were in a boardwalk shooting gallery.

Newman, having felt the two bullets entering the man's body instead of his own, struggled under the weight of his shield. "Drop that damn gun!"

The girl responded with another shot. This one caught the top of the dead man's head and splattered Newman's face with blood and pieces of matter. "Pig bastard. You killed my Shimmy. Now I'm gonna kill you."

Newman saw her come forward onto her knees, a naked, pigtailed nymph, gripping a dark blue automatic with both hands as she positioned herself for a clearer shot at him. The whole thing was insane. He fought to hold her dead pimp for protection, but it was getting harder by the second. "I don't want to have to shoot you," he said. "Put down that gun."

She fired again, and Newman felt the dead man's shoulder take the impact. So far, she was hitting enough bone to stop the bullets. But her automatic carried a clip of ten cartridges, and one of them could hit a soft spot and get through. He was behaving like a fool. The girl was as viciously dangerous as the man had been. He should shoot her right now and put an end to it before she did. Still, he had never shot a woman in his life.

The girl crawled closer on the bed, breasts lolling, oblivious to all but her own intent. An impatient little-girl quality was suddenly in her face along with the kind of cold, animal cruelty that could let her set up a man to be sliced to pieces and dumped in the gutter to die. She knelt there, an overhead fixture lighting her hair ribbons as she aimed the automatic for her next try.

Mary Logan walked into the room.

The girl swung the gun toward her and Newman fired. She fell forward on her face. Newman let the dead man drop and went to Mary, not wanting her to see.

But she had already seen.

"Are you crazy?" he said. "What the devil were you trying to do?"

"I heard shooting. I wanted to help."

"How? By getting killed?"

Staring at the two bodies, she began to weep.

He held her. "I'm sorry. It's just that you scared the hell out of me."

"Are they both dead?"

Newman went and turned the girl over. The hard, middle-aged eyes were closed beneath her ribbons and pigtails, giving her face a look of gentle youth. The carnage was below. Newman's brain was working with difficulty. I've just killed a man and a woman, he thought. No. A man and a young girl.

"Yes, they're both dead."

"Then I suppose it's perfectly all right for you to call the precinct now," she said stiffly and walked out.

6

Going home was just about as Gaynor had expected—bad. But he had told Jane he no longer had a home, only an apartment, and that part was not entirely true. The four of them had once lived here together. The family ghosts remained, still solidly in residence. They haunted every room, every closet, every drawer. They refused to leave him alone. At times he felt he could see and touch them. They drew blood. They made his heart ache. But they also made him a kind of home.

He lived in one of those sprawling, old apartments in a once elegant but now faded building on Riverside Drive, with gracious, high-ceilinged rooms and a broad view of the Hudson. The apartment was about all he had inherited from his parents, who had died much too young and within six months of one another of cancer, a disease that no one but Gaynor had yet discovered to be contagious. Gaynor knew nothing about the practice of medicine, but he knew about cancer. It was transmitted by love. One heart drew it from another. Gaynor's mother, compelled to bury the springtime of her life, had refused to have it any other way. Having plucked her husband's malignancy full grown, like a peach, she made it her final dessert. Well, Ma, Gaynor thought, here I am. I'm back.

He allowed himself a brief settling in. You did not simply slide from one state of being to the next. A pause was needed in between. He walked, limping, from one room to another, thoughts adrift. He gazed out at the sky, at the Palisades and the river, and watched as their moods changed. He sat in the big, high-windowed room facing north that was his studio, let the familiar smells of paint, oil, and turpentine slip over him, and waited for some reaction. There was none. Nor did the sight of the canvases, hanging and stacked, finished and unfinished, move him in any way. All they offered was a greater sense of futility. An artist, if he was worth anything at all, was supposed to understand and explain things—the causes of this, the reasons for that. Yet for all those many deaths, along with his own continuing life, he still had neither understanding nor explanation. And if his soul carried its own independent knowledge of these things, it had not yet chosen to share it with him. So what kind of an artist could he be?

Gaynor's dealer, arriving unannounced on his second day home, tried to tell him.

"You happen to be the hottest artist in town right now," said Sanders, a bald, round-faced man who spoke in the kind of sincere, reasonable voice that tended to discourage contradiction. "Do you know I've sold out every canvas I had of yours in the gallery? And at double what you were getting before the accident."

"Why? Because I'm suddenly a freak?"

"Who cares about reasons?"

"I do."

They were in Gaynor's studio and Sanders was pacing nervously, looking at the paintings. "I know what you've been through, and God knows I feel for you. But this is the single positive thing that's come out of the whole nightmare and you may as well take advantage of it."

"I don't want to take advantage of it."

Bored by the entire conversation, Gaynor began a mental painting of the gallery owner.

"I don't understand you, Richard. For fifteen years you've been knocking your brains out for this. In a swamp of op and pop silliness, in a morass of fadistic expressionist nonsense, you stood like a rock. You were totally uncompromising. Now they're all but begging for you on your own terms and you shrug it off? You don't make sense."

"Stop making me sound like a monument to truth and justice. I was never that. I was just stubborn and compulsive.

It wasn't even a matter of principle. All I did was go on painting the only way I knew how."

"Thank God." Sanders began gathering up canvases from around the studio. "I have the station wagon downstairs. I'm taking these with me."

"You're going blind with greed. Most of those aren't even finished."

"Haven't you heard? No painting is ever finished. Besides, right now I can even sell your dirty underwear, and who knows how long it's going to last."

Gaynor carefully lost himself in the gallery owner's portrait, a broad rendering of heavy brushstrokes and dazzling colors in which Sanders, resplendent in bowler hat and checkered vest, was the bawling, cane-waving barker in a carnival freak show, and he, Gaynor, was the freak.

The New York City headquarters of the American Crusade Party was in the basement of a large, white Victorian house in the Flatbush section of Brooklyn. There was no visible evidence of this, however, from the outside of the building or on its upper floors. Nor could any listing for an organization of that name be found in the Brooklyn telephone book. Which meant that legally and officially the ACP did not even exist.

The basement itself was a long, rectangular room with a worn tile floor, rows of steel folding chairs, and two large flags hanging on either side of a speaker's platform. One was the American flag; the other, the party's own double-headed blue eagle. There was also a shield that carried a coat of arms showing a rampant unicorn with a coiled serpent over its head. No one seemed to know what this meant. Yet some whiff of ancient heraldry, some hot breath of forgotten gallantry or evil, must have still been coming off that mystic crest, because all who saw it felt themselves affected.

This evening's gathering was the one meeting a month reserved for the induction of new recruits, and the room was filled. The party members, all male Caucasians, ranged in age from the early twenties through the late fifties. Although they wore no uniforms as such, a quasi-military effect was achieved by their white shirts, dark trousers, and blue berets crowned with the party's double-headed eagle. Sheathed daggers were also worn, but these were just ceremonial and used only on special occasions.

GAYNOR'S PASSION

The induction rites were being conducted by the New York party leader, Thomas Mackley, a thirty-four-year-old computer technician who took his office and its duties with the utmost seriousness and who made certain that everyone else did, too. Mackley had served two hitches in the Marines and had a cold stare above a rigid military bearing that seemed to rattle invisible swords. He was also an excellent speaker, with an effortless flow of words, a cool manner, and a supreme personal confidence that the American Crusade Party held the solution to most of the country's ills. The party's supervisor for the Northeast had chosen him for all of these reasons. Although every city leader was considered important to the party's future, New York's national preeminence and particular racial and religious mix made having the right leader here especially vital. Thomas Mackley seemed perfect for his job.

Eleven recruits were being inducted this evening. As the brief but solemn ceremony reached it climax, they stood at attention on the platform, right hands raised, and repeated the party oath after Mackley:

TO FRIEDRICH WILHELM NIETZSCHE, the philosophical leader of our struggle for an idealistic national order against the forces of Zionism, race pollution, and foreign subversion, I pledge my reverence and respect.

TO THE LEADERS OF THE AMERICAN CRUSADE PARTY, I pledge my faith, courage, and obedience to all party orders.

TO THE UNITED STATES OF AMERICA, I pledge my loyalty and my compliance with its Constitution and laws until those that are unjust can be legally changed by the people.

TO THOSE UNENLIGHTENED CITIZENS who will persecute me because they have been brainwashed, I pledge my patience and my understanding.

TO THE TRAITORS TO MY NATION, I pledge swift and ruthless justice.

At the conclusion, Mackley presented each new member with a blue beret and sheathed dagger. Then he embraced and kissed them on both cheeks in the traditional French manner. This last was not an officially prescribed part of the ceremony. Mackley, however, being a longtime admirer of Charles de Gaulle, had chosen to add it himself. It constituted his personal stamp of approval.

Norman Garbo

Why did people commit crimes? What was it that made them assault, swindle, steal, rape, kill? Was it something in the genes, like a tendency in some families toward diabetes or heart disease? Or was it more the result of environment, a purely sociological problem brought on by unfortunate circumstances such as extreme poverty, prejudice, or broken homes?

Gaynor asked himself these and other questions. He was giving himself an intensive cram course in contemporary criminality. His source material came from the morning and evening tabloids and the radio and TV news reports that he kept running for hours at a stretch. He was overwhelmed by the amount of time and space devoted to crime by the media. It seemed to cast a chill blue haze over everything. In such a light there was only violence, only ill will, only bad news. And he knew he was being made aware of just the tiniest fragment of it. An infinity of snakes rustled unseen in other places. But he could deal only with what he could see, and he had to start somewhere. A beginning had to be made.

First, however, he had to prepare. It was all very new to him. There were things to be learned. He was moving into another cosmos, one without connection to either his life to date or to any of his previous concepts of reality. Instead of a normal individual's involvement with the ordinary details of daily living, he was about to cast himself adrift in a sea of violence. Still, he did have certain natural talents for whatever might lie ahead. He was, after all, an artist. Which meant he was imaginative, was trained to see with exceptional clarity, and had learned to rely on no one but himself. Perhaps he would not be setting out entirely naked and unarmed.

At no point did he try to feel himself out about the propriety of what he was planning to do. He knew it was wrong—unequivocally. The fact that he was doing it for all the right reasons—to preserve the common good, to protect the helpless, to punish the iniquitous—made it no less wrong. How many others through the years, how many saviors, how many inquisitors, how many self-appointed vigilantes, had also felt they had the right reasons while the blood ran? But he just didn't care. He had his own needs. And this seemed to be the most direct way of satisfying them. In fact, once the idea had been given birth in his hotel room, he had never questioned it.

Jane materialized at Gaynor's door one evening. She was almost hidden behind two huge shopping bags of food from the supermarket.

"Look at you," she said. "What have you been eating?"

"I forget."

"I know you," declared Gaynor's ex-wife. "You could eat bread and eggs every day for six months."

"I like bread and eggs."

"You'll die of cholesterol poisoning."

"Cholesterol doesn't poison you. It clogs your arteries."

"Then you'll die of clogged arteries." Unpacking her portable grocery store, Jane paused to look at him. "How are you?"

"Other than my clogged arteries, sensational."

"You limp," she said accusingly.

"Only when I walk."

She smiled. It was her first since the crash. Somehow it touched him more than her tears.

"What about you?" he said.

"Better. I think."

He lit a cigarette, turning slightly to keep her from seeing the unsteadiness of his hands.

"I really mean it," she said. "I even called the Salvation Army and had them take their things. Everything. I almost kept their baseball gloves. Then at the last minute I threw those in, too. I was very proud of myself."

"Have you gone back to work?"

"Yes. Almost two months ago."

"That was smart."

She worked for a large executive placement firm and was outstanding at it. In fact, she had been made a vice-president the year before. Which was when she started to earn considerably more money than he. Gaynor found it hard to believe that this had once seemed of monumental importance.

"I've also gone for help," she said quietly. "You remember Dr. Eltman. His wife bought a painting at your last showing. Anyway, he came highly recommended and I figured I had nothing to lose."

She finished putting away the groceries and he made them

both drinks, martinis—very cold, very big, very strong. Better than a shrink, he thought.

In the living room, they sat in silence.

"What about your painting?" she asked.

"What about it?"

"Have you started?"

"Yes," he said. Not really a lie. It was just all in his head.

"Marvin Sanders called the other day. He said they're grabbing anything with your name on it."

"And for all the wrong reasons."

"As long as they're grabbing, what's the difference?"

"You should know. You lived with me for thirteen years."

She sat staring into her drink. When she finally looked at him, it was all in her face. "Richard?"

Waiting, he gazed off at the darkening river.

"Please," she said. "May I just stay for dinner?"

Gaynor looked at her impassively.

"Richard, please, we're all that's left of our sons."

He wanted to weep for her.

Gaynor first saw and became interested in Ramon Escobar on the six o'clock edition of the news. Young, curly-headed, darkly handsome, Escobar was picked up by the camera as he emerged, grinning like a movie star, from a midtown Manhattan police station after being released as a suspect in the brutal mugging of an old man. The commentator said it was the sixth time in two years that Escobar had been arrested and released on similar charges for lack of positive identification and evidence. The commentator said Escobar had also been picked up and released over the years for peddling drugs, running a string of prostitutes, and buying and selling stolen articles. Something had to be terribly wrong here, declared the newsman. Gaynor tended to agree. He heard a snake rustling close by, in the darkness. It was only an imagined sound, yet it seemed real enough to set his thoughts rushing.

He went to the library the next morning. Everything the commentator had said was confirmed by microfilms of old newspapers. Escobar was indeed a very busy man. He obviously was also very clever, very lucky, or touched by the hand of God. Gaynor wondered why, with all his other, more lucrative activities, Escobar still bothered to rip off old people in the streets. Which was how he had started. Either he enjoyed keeping his hand in or was just plain mean.

That evening Gaynor went to the garage where he parked his Chevette, replaced the car's dead battery, had two nearly flat tires filled with air, and drove past the building on East Ninety-eighth Street that the *News* had listed as Escobar's address. It was an ordinary five-story tenement on a typical East Harlem block, part of an urban landscape with rusting fire escapes and stained brick parapets, faintly Venetian in style. There was broken glass in the gutters, graffiti on the walls, and people everywhere. They stood, talking, on the sidewalks. They sat on stoops and on the hoods of cars. They laughed and called loudly to one another. Gaynor drove past Escobar's house three times. He did not see Escobar himself, but he began to feel him floating in his belly juices. When he felt him almost solid enough to touch, when he sensed that he really had him, Gaynor carefully carried him home.

The phone jangled him awake and he switched on a bedside lamp. It was almost 1:00 A.M. He grunted a thick hello.

"What's wrong with you?" demanded Kate Henderson. "I was sure you'd have called me by now. Are you dead?"

He grinned. "Not now. Not anymore. Where are you?"

"About three blocks from your place. I just wanted to be sure no one was in your bed."

"Who but a crazy like you would want to be?"

"Your wife, for one."

"I'm alone."

"Good-bye," Kate said and hung up.

Gaynor felt a pleasant, irresistible force start building inside him.

She was in his apartment ten minutes later. Three minutes after that, she was in his bed. He almost tore apart her uniform in his fever to get it off. He kissed, chewed, nibbled, licked. She brought him to a pitch he had almost forgotten. He gasped. "What the devil is it with you?"

"Why?" Her eyes were all dark, pure innocence. "I just came up to see your paintings."

This time there was not even the cast to hold him back. He felt like an insatiable thief stealing pleasures.

But there was no need to steal. She offered, gave, thrust everything upon him. He seesawed back and forth, accepting first one prize, then another, then chasing after the next. And all the while in the lamplight her face, that open, caring, life-affirming, keep-nothing-back face, was both with and apart from him, was above and below, changing expressions from one minute to the next, giving and taking, whispering first to God, then to the devil, and not knowing to which it really belonged. And Gaynor, filled to bursting with her, did not especially care. Yet at one point something cold tore loose in him, as if he knew that nothing good ever came that easily, that if it was really worthwhile you finally had to pay. So that in a silent cry of dismay he searched again for what he might find in her face. But at that moment it was pure gold beneath his, her eyes alive and shining with him, and the cry faded to a whisper.

When the building had stopped moving, her fingertips traced his lips. "Now I can look at your paintings."

Wrapped in a large bath towel she went exploring, not going directly to the studio but moving slowly from one room to the next, gravely studying furniture, books, photographs, the nighttime view of the Hudson from the old-fashioned windows. Gaynor watched her. It felt strange seeing her there, felt strange seeing any woman but Jane in the apartment. He had been far from celibate since his divorce, but whatever women he had seen, he had chosen to see elsewhere. Even then, he evidently had kept a retinue of ghosts.

She was more sensitive than he would have guessed. "I suddenly feel like an intruder."

He stood silently behind her, breathing her fragrance.

"Do you want me to leave?"

"God, no."

She turned and looked at him. "I believe you. Yet you never called me. And I have the strangest feeling that if I hadn't charged up here tonight, you would have just left it at that."

He kissed and held her. What a curious young woman. He seemed to feel not one presence, but two: one, a subtly perceptive girl of cool shadows and private ghosts, and then the other, a bold and aggressive predator, the kind that regarded sex as little more than a pleasant type of physical therapy.

In his studio, she studied the tall, wooden easel, the dozens of tubes of oil paint, the work tables, the bristle and sable brushes, the bottles of linseed oil and turpentine, the drafting table under its own separate light that he used for sketches and preliminary drawings. She examined everything carefully, as though searching for possible hidden secrets. "But where are your paintings?" she said.

"My agent took them all. It seems I'm suddenly in demand. I've reversed the usual procedure. Normally, artists become famous when they die. I'm famous because I didn't die."

She looked at some rough charcoal sketches tacked to the walls. "When did you do these?"

"At different times."

"Do you always draw people so sad?"

"Probably."

"Why?"

"It's how they seem to come out."

"People do laugh, you know."

"Yes, but that's not when they interest me. Not as subjects, anyway. Laughter just briefly passes through. I like to paint what's left when it's gone. The real stuff."

"And the real stuff is always sad?"

"Isn't it?"

"Not to me." Facing him, she opened her towel and let it fall. "How does this real stuff look to you?"

Gaynor considered her, this curious girl standing naked in his studio, her flesh pure gold, all life and warmth beside the gloom of his drawings.

"Definitely not sad," he admitted. "But it's not that simple."

Moving close, she felt his burgeoning response. "Who said so?"

"You should be a debater." He sighed.

More than three billion human beings were currently alive, thought Gaynor, each with hopes and fears, each with needs, each the center of a particular microcosm, and each an expert on something. Just as he, during the better part of the past week, had become an expert of sorts on the small, terrible world of Ramon Escobar. And in a perverse sort of way, he had begun to find it oddly fascinating.

Although without legally acceptable employment, Escobar wore an impressive collection of designer clothes, drove a late model Cadillac, dined in expensive restaurants, and enjoyed the company of many women. Indeed, he cruised the city like a prince, thought Gaynor. No. A king. New York was his realm, his personal land of opportunity. He found its streets to be literally paved with gold. It was all lying there, just waiting for him to pluck it free. Which he happily did. And no one stopped him. They tried, but he was too quick, too clever. There was even a certain majesty to the way he carried himself, an air of noblesse oblige that instantly marked him as a man apart. And what did this uncrowned king do to maintain his royal state? Aside from his less visible activities in drugs, fencing, and prostitution, he knocked over the old and the infirm and ran off with their carefully hoarded, life-sustaining kale, wampum, mazuma. Gaynor now knew this part of Escobar's work at first hand. He had been watching him do it almost all week.

Escobar's method of operation in this area was basically simple, and he seemed to perform it according to some obscure but inviolate set of rules. There was even a kind of magic in it, the magic of any successfully functioning system. In this case, it turned the streets of New York into his own free-fire zone. To begin with, Escobar showed himself to be neither impatient nor greedy. He did nothing unless the conditions were perfectly suited to his needs, and he never tried to score more than once in any given night. He was, in the purest sense of the word, a specialist. He operated only after dark, only on quiet streets and in small parks, and selected only the elderly, handicapped, or otherwise helpless as his victims. Additionally, he wore a special camouflage while at work, his own protective coloration—faded jeans, black sneakers, and a dark windbreaker. So that should any of his marks later try to describe their assailant and his clothing, they would also be describing possibly a million similarly dressed, dark-eyed, dark-haired young men in the metropolitan area. Not that Escobar's carefully chosen victims ever saw very much to describe. Struck hard, fast, and always from the rear, they were usually left too shocked and befuddled even to realize what had happened. By the time they were able to pick themselves up and cry for help, Escobar and their money would be long gone.

Ramon Escobar. A name with music. It carried the grace of eagles. And the muggings were among the better things its owner did. A king with the soul of a cockroach. Gaynor carried the smooth-faced young hustler in his stomach for a full eight days. When he was able to belch him up and taste sour, he felt ready for what had to come next.

He came across the two masks in an old storage carton at the back of a bedroom closet. Identical, they had belonged to his sons, who had worn them in a series of religious tableaux put on by their Sunday school. The masks were of the rubberized stretch type that slipped over the head, with openings left for the wearer's eyes, nostrils, and mouth. Gaynor pulled one on and looked in a mirror. A bearded facsimile of one of Christ's apostles stared back at him, making him laugh. Yet the effect was so curiously lifelike that after a moment it began to seem less funny than imposing.

Once more he squinted at himself in the mirror. A living, breathing, latter-day Apostle. In a strange, aberrant sort of way, it was suddenly beginning to make a kind of sense.

Watching the late news one night, Gaynor saw Lieutenant Newman. The detective was dressed in dinner clothes and was sitting beside the police commissioner at a political fund-raising affair. The mayor was speaking and at that moment Newman's eyes were closed, making him appear to be dozing. Then there was a burst of applause, Newman's eyes opened, and he seemed to look directly at Gaynor. And the artist stared back at this strangely appealing man who had helped to preserve at least the physical shell of his old life and who had given him inspiration for his new one. Newman's face was broad, solid, strong, a possible weapon, yet his eyes were warm, even sentimental. They were human, intensely caring eyes that at that moment appeared to carry a special, almost metaphysical, message of their own. We're none of us just things, objects, Gaynor imagined their saying. We're not just articles to be picked apart, analyzed, and packaged like so many pieces of frozen meat. Bright mysteries are buried inside us. And whom could such eyes be looking at other than him, Richard Gaynor. *Ah, I'm a mystery.*

Then, having offered him this, the camera, as if legally compelled to grant equal time to an opposing view, moved to a more southerly section of the country where the Reverend Clayton Taylor was presenting something quite different to a great many listeners of his own. Here there was no love, no joy, no warmth, no hope for a future in which one might live in any other way than in fear of God's anger. Warnings were being given. All who were not true believers in Christ, all who refused to pay him his due homage, must now awake and prepare to fly from God's wrath. Let all Israelites, along with all other nonbelievers, make haste to escape while they still could, declared the calm, reasonable voice of Clayton Taylor, lest they be consumed. For it was his kingdom that was about to replace the wicked, crumbling governments of earth.

Gaynor was back in the Forty-second Street library. This time he was studying the latest crime statistics, compiled by the nation's law enforcement agencies. He was composing a letter to the media, and everything had to be properly documented. The letter itself was crucial. It had to show thought, accuracy, and, perhaps most important of all, a persuasive intellectual theory. Nothing was taken seriously anymore unless there was some sort of theory behind it. Gaynor had learned this some years before when the dean of New York's art critics declared that contemporary realist painting was not worth a damn because it lacked a persuasive intellectual theory. Although no one really seemed to know what he was talking about, Gaynor had been unable to sell a painting for fifteen months after that. In this, he intended to take no chances.

When he had armed himself with all the facts, Gayor went home and spent the next seven hours laboring over what finally took the form of a letter that he hoped would be persuasive enough to be taken seriously by the media. It said:

To the Editor:

According to the latest FBI statistics, someone in the United States is murdered every 23 minutes, is raped every 6 minutes, is robbed every 58 seconds, is burglarized every 9 seconds.

These numbers have not come about overnight. For years our criminal justice system has been acting as though criminals have greater rights than their victims. Offenders, free on bail after committing one violent crime, often commit several more while awaiting trial for the first. Each day there are reports of senseless acts of brutality while those committing them are either considered not responsible mentally or are themselves regarded simply as victims of society. Meanwhile, the statistics keep getting worse and the true victims keep paying.

Everyone knows the horrors that are going on. People no longer feel safe, not even in their own homes. The single most important duty of government is the preservation of domestic tranquillity. Law-abiding citizens have the right to be free from the fear of crime, especially the bloody, random type of crime that shatters lives in the most terrible ways. We are no longer being granted that right.

This letter, copies of which are being sent to all branches of the media, is being written to announce publicly that I, for one, intend to start doing something about the situation. I am not a crazy. I am a rational citizen of New York who hopes to advance the common good in some small way.

The truth is, I don't believe someone becomes a criminal because he was mistreated by society, or because he never finished school, or because he has no job, or because he has suffered the effects of racial or religious discrimination. The overwhelming majority of those who fall into these categories do not become criminals. So I think that those who do become criminals do so because that is what they choose to be. And as such they should be punished. Sometime during the next few days I expect to start doing what I can to foster this punishment. At the proper moment, you will be told exactly where, when, and how. I would appreciate your taking note of it. Spreading the word could prove of great value. It might even help make our common house a bit safer from tigers.

Gaynor typed a clean copy of the letter on an old portable that had belonged to one of the twins. Then he thought for a long time about how to sign it. The name suddenly seemed almost as important as the letter itself. In the end, considering the mask he intended to wear, he simply wrote: The Apostle. It felt right. It carried the required aura of mission.

The next day he had photocopies made on a coin-operated machine in a stationery store and mailed them to the *New York Times*, the *Daily News*, the *Post*, the national wire services, and to the newsrooms of the major television and radio stations. Then he went home, read the letter again, and began worrying about it. Did it echo a call to arms? Did it make claw marks on Mount Rushmore? Or did it just sound pretentious and silly? He also wondered how much of what he had written he truly believed and how much had been contrived to satisfy his own increasingly obsessive need for a worthwhile cause. Would tilting a lance at vermin really justify his survival and continued existence? He hoped to Christ it did. It appeared to be all he had.

Harry Blake was just leaving his office at the *Post* when Kelly waved to him from inside his glass cage. The reporter waved back and continued toward the elevators, hurrying even more than usual because he was late. It seemed to him that he was always late these days. Which was not really true. He just squeezed in too many things.

"Harry!"

The managing editor's shout caught him just short of an open elevator. Swearing softly, Blake worked back through the rows of desks.

"Come on, Brian, I'm up to my ears. What is it?"

Kelly handed him a copy of Gaynor's letter. "Read this."

Blake scanned it without interest. "So? It's a letter."

The editor lit a neatly sliced half a cigar. He had smoked the other half that morning. It was how he cut down. "You don't think there's a story in it?"

"Only if he does what he says." Blake looked at the typed name at the bottom. "Jesus! The Apostle, no less."

"I'm going to run it."

"Why?"

"Because it happens to fit in with a crime editorial I've got all set to go. And if the guy does come through with something, we'll be that much ahead."

"You're the editor."

Blake dropped the letter on Kelly's desk, but the editor picked it up and handed it back to him. "I've got copies. Keep it."

"What for? Its prose style?"

"It may give you ideas."

Blake stuffed it into his pocket and started out. "I doubt it."

But several hours later, during the weekly talk show he hosted for the Continental Television Network, he suddenly became aware of the letter in his pocket and pulled it out. It was pure impulse. He was stuck with a couple of dull, rambling guests and was desperate to get something going.

He read the letter on camera and it worked. Both of his previously moribund guests instantly sprang to life. One, a black educator, angrily attacked the letter as a racist indictment of the black and Hispanic communities and claimed it should never even have been given media exposure. The other guest, a liberal political writer, blasted the whole concept of vigilantes as a consummate evil that pandered to the worst of our instincts and could well threaten a return to the lynch mob psychology of the old South and West. Blake himself happily added to the heat by playing devil's advocate. Who were they more worried about, he demanded, the criminal or his victim?

They were all close to shouting when time finally ran out. Afterward, there were more than three times the usual number of call-ins. The show was judged to have been the most successful in the nearly two years that *Blake's Corner* had been running.

Gaynor lay in darkness, thinking about the twins. Instead of getting better with time, that part seemed to be getting worse. With the numbness of shock wearing off, the hurt soared free. It appeared to thrive on darkness, so he had been leaving a lamp on at night to help him sleep. Although sometimes, as now, he deliberately switched it off. He was afraid he might be cheating his sons. At least, thinking of them, they came briefly to life.

Once, when his sons had been much younger and had just discovered (in tandem) the fearful inevitability of death, they had begun to worry and ask questions about it. "Is everything just all over when you die, Daddy?" Joshua, the spokesman, had asked. And Gaynor, wanting only to offer the reassurances they needed very badly at the age of six, had tried to do what he could for them. He had told them things he did not really believe, or that he only half believed, or that he wished he believed. He had told them that nothing was ever all over as long as you are remembered and loved, that, alive or dead, as long as you remained in the heart and thoughts of even one person, you would always be blessed with life.

Yet he had felt oddly uncomfortable telling them these things. It had all seemed so childish, so filled with unjustified hope. But what else was he to have said to a pair of anxious six-year-olds? That when you died you turned to dust and that was the end of it? That there was no such thing as an immortal soul and the only things you could be sure of in this world were getting hurt and saying good-bye? Hardly. Still, he had not been able to help feeling a bit self-conscious about sounding like some sort of mystical nut who believed the spirit of love was immortal, and that all who loved could count on being granted at least a reasonable facsimile of a soul. The whole idea had seemed rather laughable.

Now, however, alone in the darkness and with his children gone, it no longer seemed quite so laughable. And he found that maybe he did believe what he had told them. Maybe he did believe that as long as he was capable of remembering, of feeling love, that some essence of his sons would remain with him. And maybe he also believed—although he might still be too embarrassed to say it aloud to anyone—that if there was such a thing as immortality, love was probably at its heart.

Gaynor had noted that off-duty police officers seemed to be involved in an inordinate number of barroom brawls during which someone would end up shot. This was undoubtedly due to department regulations, which required officers to carry their revolvers at all times in order to increase the effective police presence in the city at any given moment and make life safer for its citizens. Or at least safer for those citizens, thought Gaynor, who were either smart or lucky enough not to get into fights with off-duty cops.

He sat making these observations from a corner table of the Emerald Bar and Grill in the North Bronx. It was 1:20 A.M., and a fair number of off-duty police officers from the nearby Sixty-seventh Precinct Station had been drinking steadily and raucously since finishing their four-to-midnight tour more than an hour ago. So far, however, all had been peaceful.

Gaynor already had his selection made, a quietly bemused drinker at the far end of the bar who held himself a bit apart from his more boisterous buddies. Earlier, Gaynor had seen him drive into the rear parking lot alone, had followed him into the bar, and had been watching him ever since. The officer wore a dark blue coat-sweater that bulged significantly over the revolver holstered at his belt, a deadly baby marsupial in an off-center pouch. He had done his tour, was close to completing his prescribed postduty stop at the Emerald, and would soon be driving home to whatever it was that a few good shots of Irish whiskey would make easier for him to face. He had a big Celtic head, a thick neck, and the chest and shoulders of a onetime athlete gone to fat. Other than in his size and apparent strength, the man bore little resemblance to Newman, yet Gaynor had instantly been reminded of the lieutenant. They somehow seemed stamped from the same mold. "One good thing about being in the cops," Newman had once said. "If it doesn't bust or kill you, it calms you down. To survive, you distance yourself from people, things, and events." And evidently the drinking added to the distance.

When the officer seemed about ready to leave, Gaynor dropped a bill on the table and went out the back door to the parking lot. He felt a surge of excitement but no fear, not even nervousness. It was as if he had packed all such concerned responses away in ice, to await some future need. Or else he had killed and buried them forever.

The parking lot was large and dark, and except for the cars belonging to those in the Emerald Bar and Grill, it was empty. The other stores in the mall had been closed for hours. Before going into the bar, Gaynor had prepared for this moment by moving his Chevette close to the car driven by the cop he had picked as his man. Entering the Chevette now, he quickly slipped on one of his sons' Apostle masks and took out a realistic play pistol that had also belonged to the twins. Then he slid down out of sight and waited.

Moments later he heard footsteps approaching, heavy, a cop's tread. When he heard a car door open, he got out.

The man did not even become aware of him until he was less than ten feet away. Then, assuming Gaynor to be one of his more playful buddies fooling around, he just shook his head and grinned.

"Come on, Tony. Halloween's not for six months yet. Besides, with your face you don't need no mask."

Gaynor pointed his make-believe gun at the cop's stomach. "Put up your hands or I'll blow you away." His voice, coming out muffled and strange through his new rubber skin, was unrecognizable to him.

The officer laughed, a fat man's laugh, deep and hearty. "How? With a fuckin' toy gun?" Thumb up, he aimed a thick index finger at Gaynor's chest. "Bang! You're dead."

Gaynor stood there, his son's pistol still pointing. Terrific. To him, the gun had looked genuine, but obviously not to someone who knew guns. His mask, his threat, his whole carefully planned enterprise was suddenly turning to farce. An amateur was an amateur. But who had expected not to be taken seriously?

"When the hell are you gonna start growing up, Tony?"

Okay. So he was Tony. "Come on," said Gaynor's muffled voice. "A little laugh never hurt anyone."

"Yeah? And what if I'd had a few more belts in me? What if I'd really thought it was some crazy kind of heist and put a slug in your brain? Where would you be then?"

"Dead."

"Damn right. And I'd be up on charges. Big joke, huh?"

The officer turned to get into his car. As he did, Gaynor swung the butt of the fake pistol against the back of his head. There was a dull thud, a ripe melon being thumped. The man fell and lay still.

Gaynor stared at him through the bearded Apostle's eye-holes. It was the first time in his life he had ever knocked anyone unconscious.

He was astonished that it could be so easy. Calmly, coldly, he removed the officer's belt, holster, and revolver and carried them back to the Chevette. He took off his mask and placed it beside the toy pistol. Luckily, the gun had been made of solid, heavygauge steel rather than plastic. It paid to buy the best.

He started the car, then abruptly got out and went back to where the cop lay. He had almost forgotten to sign his work. Starting now, that was important. They had to know who was responsible and why. Gaynor took out a plain white card with THE APOSTLE typed on it, placed it in the unconscious officer's hand, and drove off. Okay. He had his required weapon, the legally constituted service revolver of an officer of the law. And everyone would know that he had it. Which was precisely what he wanted. Apart from the practicalities, it had a certain poetic appeal.

*   *   *

Two nights later, he sat parked in his anonymous-looking gray Chevette on West Eighty-seventh Street, just off Broadway. It was a mild spring evening, and the benches along Broadway's center mall were crowded with the lonely and elderly, winter-starved for human sights and sounds. Also occupying a bench was Ramon Escobar, who, though neither lonely nor elderly, had needs of his own. Gaynor was waiting for him to satisfy them. While waiting, he occupied himself with one of his most ambitious mental projects to date, a large, panoramic rendering of Upper Broadway stretching off into the spring darkness, traffic roaring in both directions like herds of steel elephants, all flashing white eyes and ruby tails. And, in midstream, trapped in the glare of the passing lights, the old people on their benches, gray heads and wrinkled skin, time-damaged faces that made metaphysical statements. Floating above, a magical lighter-than-air creature, was King Ramon himself, complete with crown, scepter and royal robes. Smooth-skinned, harmonious, Escobar gazed serenely out at the world with velvet eyes, lips parted as though for speech. So much so that Gaynor leaned forward slightly in the Chevette, as though hoping to hear some royal secret, some gemstone of philosophical wisdom that would help straighten out the con-fused pattern of his life. But at that moment the true, real-life Escobar rose from his bench, and any such knowledge was lost forever.

Ramon crossed Broadway through the rushing traffic and headed west on Eighty-seventh Street. A short distance in front of him, a heavy-legged old woman waddled arthritically in the same direction.

Gaynor started the car, drove past Broadway, and slowly followed, stopping from time to time to maintain a safe interval. It was much darker on the side street, with no traffic moving and only an occasional pedestrian visible. Tall, gray apartment buildings crowded together on both sides, forming the walls of a tunnel. A wind came off the Hudson and scraps of paper flew. They might have been white doves. Gaynor carefully kept his distance. Knowing it would come any moment now, he felt his blood pumping and smiled. Apart from everything else, it was fun, an exciting kid's game.

Seconds later Escobar suddenly sprinted forward, a dark streak in the night, his muted working clothes making him barely visible. He reached the old woman, snatched the purse from her hand, and roughly shoved her to the sidewalk. She cried out, but Escobar was already dashing down the street, and there was no one to hear her except Gaynor. And Gaynor was unable to stop. He was too busy following Escobar, who had rounded the corner and was now flying uptown on West End Avenue, the old woman's purse safely out of sight inside his windbreaker.

Two blocks farther, Escobar got into the white Cadillac that Gaynor had seen him park at the curb less than an hour before and drove toward the Hudson. Staying a full block behind, Gaynor followed the Cadillac north on Riverside Drive, then under the Henry Hudson Parkway and into a section of Riverside Park that ran along the edge of the water. When Escobar swung off to the left and stopped, facing the river, Gaynor continued around a curve and out of sight behind some trees. He parked, left the car, and began circling back on foot.

He was still limping, but he had been exercising regularly with weights to get his strength back and he felt reasonably in control of his body. Dressed very much like Escobar, he wore a loose-fitting gray windbreaker, jeans, and dark running shoes. He was learning. In front of him, trees and bushes hung suspended in the dark. Behind flowed the Hudson, opaque as tar. There had once been lights along some of the paths, but vandals had kept knocking them out and the city no longer bothered to replace them. The park was empty now, an abandoned battleground. Even lovers desperate for their own private dark were afraid to enter.

Gaynor stopped when he saw the white Cadillac through the trees. Quickly, he slipped on his mask and a pair of black leather gloves and took out his newly acquired .38-caliber Smith & Wesson revolver. Keeping low, he approached the Cadillac from the passenger's side, stuck his gun through a partially open window, and aimed it at Escobar's head. "Freeze or you're dead."

Escobar stared dumbly at the rubber face of the Apostle. His mouth opened and closed twice. Floating out of the darkness as it did, the mask seemed to startle him more than the revolver. He had been going through the old woman's purse and its contents lay spread out beside him: cash, checks, bankbooks, charge cards, keys, letters—her entire stock of valuables. In his hands were earrings, a bracelet, and two rings, items apparently too precious to the old woman to be left behind, unguarded, in her apartment.

"Put the rest of that stuff on the seat," said Gaynor.

Escobar was still staring at the mask.

"Do it!"

He obeyed.

"Now get out of the car."

"Hey, you ain't gonna take my wheels, man!" Panic had abruptly given him back his voice. "Okay. Take this other shit. But I bought this Caddy all straight and legal, all with my own bread. You ain't takin' this baby."

"Move or I'll blow your brains out." Gaynor was beginning to feel like a poor man's Clint Eastwood.

"Hey, gimme a break."

"Sure. I'll give you a break. Which is more than you gave that old lady. If you move out of there real fast, maybe I'll even let you live."

"Shit. I sweated blood for this car."

"Get out."

Escobar shook his head. The injustice was simply too great. It paralyzed him.

Gaynor held the revolver with both hands, as he had seen cops on TV do, and aimed it squarely between Escobar's eyes.

"You've got till the count of three," he said and began counting. "One."

Escobar stared into the muzzle of the gun.

"Two."

Escobar moistened his lips. Otherwise, he did not move.

"Three."

Gently, Gaynor began squeezing the trigger. He felt the pressure build. He saw Escobar's eyes, desperate, searching, pry deep into his. Something of his own, some part of him, flew out to meet them. Gaynor felt it go but did not understand it. Escobar did. He got out of the car.

Keeping the gun aimed at Escobar's head, Gaynor walked around to his side of the car. "Turn around."

"What you gonna do now? Shoot me in the back?"

"I said turn."

"You're bad. Whatever I done, least I never killed nobody." Standing, Escobar's legs had begun to tremble.

He turned then, and Gaynor clubbed him with the gun butt and watched him fall. He was right, he thought with vague surprise. He knew it before I did. I was ready to kill him.

Using prepared lengths of nylon cord, Gaynor tied Escobar's ankles and wrists, gagged him with his own handkerchief, and stretched him out on the back seat of his Cadillac. He left the contents of the old woman's purse clearly visible in front and attached one of his Apostle calling cards to Escobar's windbreaker with a safety pin. On an impulse, he went through the glove compartment and found a revolver, a silencer, and an assortment of fake or stolen IDs and credit cards. He put them in his pockets to consider later. Then he locked the car, placed the keys on the ground behind a tire, and walked back to his Chevette.

Ten minutes later, he called the Thirteenth Precinct from a public phone and spoke to a Sergeant Warneky. "Listen carefully," he said, using a handkerchief to muffle his voice. "I'm going to say this just once. About half an hour ago an old lady was knocked down and had her bag snatched on West Eighty-seventh Street. It was done by a punk named Ramon Escobar, whom you can find, all nicely tied up, in a white Cadillac near Ninetieth Street and the Hudson River. Everything he stole is laid out on the front seat. The car keys are behind the left rear tire." He paused. "Have you got all that straight?"

"Who the hell are you?"

"The Apostle," said Gaynor and hung up.

Driving around to different pay phones, he made similar calls to the same newspapers and broadcasting stations to which he had mailed his announcements several days before. Now the letters would have to be taken seriously. Now proper attention would have to be paid. Or so he believed.

Yet what did he really know about what anyone else would or wouldn't have to do? He was not even sure about himself. With all his sincerity, with all his sublime motivation, with all his thought and planning, the whole concept of what he was doing sometimes seemed little more than an adolescent fantasy. The planet hurtled through space, millions labored, suffered, and died while he busied himself behind the false face of a Sunday school apostle.

Still, as of tonight it had stopped being merely a fantasy. A beginning had been made. And walking home after parking his car, Gaynor breathed the cool brackish air sweeping off the Hudson and began to feel better. A hazy moon shone, and the West Side of New York suddenly seemed oddly frail and appealing in its dim, blue-gray glow. The light filtered through the cables of the George Washington Bridge. Pieces of it gleamed from apartment house windows. Pools of it washed the tops of the sycamores along Riverside park, where he hoped that by now battalions of cops and reporters would be in the process of dealing with Ramon Escobar. And Gaynor felt, finally, that perhaps he was being put to some worthwhile use.

~~~~~~~~~~~~~~~~~~~~~~~~~~~~~~~ **7** ~~

This isn't me, thought Newman. I don't belong here.

Seated beside Michael Westley in the plush, soft gray interior of the commissioner's chauffeured limousine, he felt himself an imposter, an intruder into one of the most sacred vales of the powerful and privileged. There was even a hint of perfume in the air, faint as a ghost, as if someone unbelievably lovely had passed through moments before. Not really too terrible. It was just that it was too late for him to get used to such things. They made him uncomfortable. Westley, on the other hand, suffered no such compunctions. Elegant, poised, relaxed against the rich upholstery, he gazed benignly out at the sunlit vistas along Fifth Avenue, a wealthy land-owner taking a soul-satisfying afternoon inventory of his possessions. Half turning to speak to Newman, his eyes held it all.

"It was really a great talk, Jay. One of your best. And I especially liked that point you made about the police as whipping boys." As usual, Westley's voice was so soft as to be barely audible. "I know the cardinal was also impressed. As was everyone else. You could feel it in the room. You had them with you all the way."

They were on their way downtown from a Knights of Columbus luncheon at the Waldorf at which Newman had been the featured speaker. Indeed, he had chosen the point Westley referred to very carefully. With an audience of Catholic hard-liners, you were all but forced to take a strong law-and-order approach. Especially if you were a Jew. So he had told them that the police had become an absolute blessing for liberal politicians and judges, because all the repressiveness needed to keep society from ripping itself to pieces these days was shoved off on those whose job it was to enforce the law. Which meant that the cops were labeled fascist, cruel, and worse, and all the pious, self-righteous officials were spared any possible taint. Hence, cops as necessary whipping boys for an ultra-liberal society in which few citizens were as ready to admit their illiberal attitudes as they once were.

"Glad it went okay," he said.

A streak of late sun, slanting through the limousine's windows, gilded the commissioner's face. "More than just okay. The fact is, you've been doing an absolutely superb job all around lately. Better than I could have hoped for when I shoved you into it."

"Thank you, Mr. Commissioner."

"You don't have to get on your high horse. All I did was say something nice."

"And all I did was thank you."

Westley's smile narrowed his eyes to moist diamonds. "What's the matter? Can't you deal with approval?"

"I've forgotten how."

"Would you rather be getting reamed?"

"No. But it's become more my natural condition."

The radiophone buzzed at Westley's elbow, and he picked it up and spoke quietly for several moments. Newman stared thoughtfully at the back of the driver's head. It was true. In an odd, almost perverse sort of way, Westley's approval made him feel even more like an imposter. So was he a fool or just a little crackbrained? It was becoming increasingly hard to tell.

Westley put down the phone, and Newman thought it best to shift the conversation to something other than himself.

"How does this Apostle business grab you? Any feeling about it yet?"

The commissioner stared blankly at him.

"Both the *Post* and *News* carried his letter."

"I read the *Times*. What are you talking about?"

Newman had the newspaper clipping folded in his wallet; he gave it to Westley. Apparently the office of the commissioner was above such minutiae.

Westley glanced through the letter and returned it. "Another vigilante nut. So?"

"I don't think this one is a nut."

"They're all nuts."

"The letter is too good. It's too well written, too logical."

"Some of our worst psychopaths are the most literate." Westley lit a cigarette. "When was the letter carried?"

"About a week ago. Two nights later, the Thirteenth Precinct gets a call from the same character describing a mugging that has just taken place and telling where the perpetrator could be found. He was there, all right—bound, gagged, surrounded by his loot. A neighborhood pimp, pusher, and A and R man with a history of six collars and no indictments."

"And?"

"The punk claimed he was framed, set up by enemies. When the victim, an old lady, was unable to pick him out of a lineup, he was released for the seventh time."

"That's all?"

"Not quite. An off-duty cop from the Sixty-seventh got creamed in a parking lot and had his piece lifted. At first he said he was hit from behind and never saw his assailant. Then he read the letter in the paper, began to worry, and confessed his gun had been taken by a guy in an Apostle mask who left his calling card."

The radiophone buzzed again. Westley took the call, then slid open the glass partition behind the driver. "Get us to Twenty-second Street between Eighth and Ninth. Fast. Use your siren and party hat."

The limousine leaped forward, siren wailing and roof light whirling and flashing. Traffic parted to let them through.

"Another nut," said Westley. "Only this one is tossing his kids out of windows."

They were there in minutes. The streets were blocked off by two patrol cars, but the limousine jumped the curb and went around them. Newman followed Westley out. Small groups of people stood staring upward, gripped by a pack sense of smell. Death was in heat. Newspapers were spread over three small shapes in the gutter, but the blood ran out from underneath. A bullhorn roared half-intelligible words. Newman gazed up with the crowd. On the sixth floor of an old tenement, a man, a woman, and their remaining child were framed by an open window in a horrifying tableau. The child was little more than an infant, and the man was trying to pull it from the woman's arms. They swayed back and forth, moving stiffly, spastically, like figures in an ancient Punch and Judy show. Neighbors shouted and screamed from surrounding windows. On the sidewalk directly below, clusters of men held blankets spread out in a pathetic and obviously hopeless effort to catch whoever came down next.

"Where's the goddamned fire department?" Westley asked a harried-looking sergeant.

"On the way, sir. And I've got some men up there now, trying to bust in the door."

Indeed, a huge hook-and-ladder truck did come screaming into the block almost at that moment. Newman turned away and tiredly climbed back into the limousine. He had no desire to watch what he knew was about to happen. Bad memories sifted through his brain. His eyelids felt heavy. He closed them and waited.

A long sigh rose from the crowd, then a scream. A few seconds later he heard the other, more terrible sounds.

Ah, God.

He did not move or open his eyes until Westley was in the car and they were once more riding downtown.

The commissioner looked at him. "What's the matter?"

"Nothing."

"You sure?"

"I've seen these things before. They don't get any better with repetition."

They rode in suddenly heavy silence.

102

"I spoke to some of the neighbors," said Westley. "The man had a long history of mental disorder. In fact, he spent the last six months in Bellevue specifically for threatening to kill his family."

"When did the genius shrinks let him out?"

"Three hours ago."

"Jesus Christ!"

"Don't worry. They won't sweep this one under the rug so fast."

Newman stared broodingly at the shadowy streets of Lower Manhattan. "I'll take *my* nut anytime. He's practically benign by comparison."

"Who's that?"

"The Apostle."

"You make it sound as though we're being offered some kind of metaphysical choice."

"Maybe we are," said Newman.

But, in considering it, he really had no idea what he meant.

The lieutenant concentrated on holding himself motionless against the curved warmth of Mary's body. Unable to sleep, he lay breathing the vaguely erotic scent of her perfume. Then, afraid he would only end up waking her, he quietly slipped out of bed and went into the kitchen, carrying her fragrance with him. He also carried the Apostle's letter.

He was reading it for the fourth time over his second glass of brandy when Mary appeared, squinting against the fluorescent glare.

"Have you given up sleep entirely?" she said.

"How brilliant a psychologist are you?"

"Reasonably brilliant. Why? Do you want me to treat your insomnia?"

He slid the newspaper clipping across the table. "Tell me what sort of a man would write a letter like this?"

"Are you serious?"

"At three in the morning everyone is serious."

She sat down, took a sip of his brandy, and rubbed her face more fully awake. "Just remember. Psychology is still more of an art than a true science."

"I promise not to tell anyone."

He watched her as she read, chin propped on one hand, brow furrowed, mouth set in concentration, jaw clean and sharp as a carving. She had slender fingers and a dancer's long, graceful neck. Her head, a lily on a stalk. Mary.

"All right." Finished reading, she considered him gravely. "But first, has anything happened since the letter was in the paper?"

Newman told her about the cop's stolen revolver and the captured mugger. "So?" he said. "How does the guy sound to you?"

"Frankly, darling, a lot like you."

"Very funny."

"It's true. There are things in that letter that I've heard you say a hundred times over the years." She smiled sweetly. "Are you sure you're not really the Apostle?"

Newman lit a cigarette, blew smoke, and waited.

"Except, of course, that you have an almost obsessive belief in the law and you're not crazy."

"Then he's bananas?"

"I'd say there has to be *something* a bit strange about him. Things may not be all that great these days, but they're certainly not bad enough for a new Messiah to come leaping out of the woodwork."

"You mean he thinks he's another Jesus?"

"It wouldn't have to be that extreme. Although calling himself the Apostle might show a leaning in that direction." Her eyes, fully awake now, glinted in the kitchen light. "What I really mean by a Messiah is someone with an unnatural need to feel himself a guardian of society."

"What would make him like that?"

Mary lifted her head and stared at the ceiling as though invisible answers were hidden there. The movement hollowed her cheeks, showing the bones beneath. "A lot of things. Anger . . . depression . . . a violent shock of some sort . . . any real or imagined trauma. But whatever the reason, it would have to be very strong, very extreme."

"What about fear?" Newman swirled his brandy in slow circles. "The guy is putting himself up against dangerous criminals and an army of cops. Wouldn't that normally be enough to scare the hell out of someone?"

"Yes, but the man you're talking about wouldn't care about danger. He'd probably welcome it. Martyrdom, death in a just cause, might even be what he's after."

Newman finished his drink and sat smoking quietly. He

seemed wholly relaxed and at ease, yet a large blue vein pulsed heavily in his temple.

"No more questions?" Mary asked.

"Not at the moment."

She leaned across the table and kissed him. "I did good?"

"You did very good."

"Then let's go to sleep, darling. I have a long, hard day of further good-doing tomorrow."

But, lying once more in darkness, she seemed as little ready for sleep as he. "The man has barely started," she said. "How could you be so hooked on him? I don't understand."

"Yes you do. You saw it right away. The poor schmuck is me, gone a little ape."

At seven-thirty the next morning, Newman called the police commissioner at his private home number.

"What's wrong?" Surprise and concern strained Westley's voice.

"Nothing is wrong. I just wanted to talk to you before you got jammed up at the office." Newman saw that Mary was up and watching him from bed, a muted figure in the misty dawn light. "I hope I didn't wake you or get you at a bad time."

"Stop being so ingratiating. That worries me even more. What the devil is it?"

"I'd like to take advantage of my current state of grace to ask a favor. There's an assignment I want."

"You already have an assignment. The best of your career. And you're doing marvelously at it." Westley paused. "Ah, I see. That's what's bothering you. You feel a pressing need to return to your more natural state—unalloyed disaster."

"This won't interfere with my speechmaking. I just want you to give me the Apostle investigation."

"There *is* no Apostle investigation. I didn't even know about the man until you brought him to my attention. The fool isn't worth taking the time to look for. That kind falls down all by himself."

Mary sat up in bed, naked. Newman stood leaning against the wall, solemnly considering her breasts. "Not this one," he told the commissioner. "Anyway, all I'm asking is that I be notified and given support by all precincts if there are any further developments. If you're right and he trips over his own feet, or if nothing more happens, then of course that's the end of it and there's no big deal.''

Westley breathed slowly, heavily, through morning-clogged sinuses. "What I fail to comprehend is why you're so interested in this silliness.''

"Let's just say the guy piques my imagination.''

"But he's almost childish in his simplicity.''

"So am I, Michael.''

"That's probably what concerns me.'' Westley's breathing was still labored. "All right,'' he said. "But bear this in mind. No lapses in your public relations effort. Not even a hint of a letup. I want your word on that.''

"You have it.''

Newman was smiling as he hung up.

"You sold him?'' said Mary.

"Not really. But I think he loves me enough these days to give me just about anything I want.''

"I feel the same way. But who can ever tell what you want?''

He climbed back into bed and kissed her breasts. "If you don't mind being a bit late for your good works, I'll show you.''

An all-points bulletin went out from New York Police Department Headquarters at 1:00 P.M. that same day. It was addressed to all precincts in each of the five boroughs and stated that from this time forward, Lieutenant Jayson Newman would be in command of any and all investigations into the identification, whereabouts, and possible apprehension of the suspect known as, and using the alias of, the Apostle. The bulletin additionally stated that any information relating to the aforementioned suspect was to be immediately passed on to Lieutenant Newman at Police Headquarters and that under no circumstances was any action to be taken, either directly or indirectly, until it was first cleared with Lieutenant Newman as officer in charge.

The bulletin was signed by Michael Westley as commissioner of police. It had, however, been composed and dictated by Lieutenant Newman.

Newman was up in the North Bronx, not far from the Yonkers line. He was reading a newspaper at an empty desk in the Sixty-seventh Precinct's squad room. The place smelled heavily of dust, stale sweat, and disinfectant, and he chain-smoked to sweeten the air. When the four-to-midnight tour came off duty, a uniformed officer approached. "Lieutenant Newman?"

The detective nodded.

"I'm Reagan. The desk sergeant said you wanted to talk to me."

Newman pulled over a chair and held out his cigarettes. The officer, a big, paunchy man with a weathered face, accepted both. "How did it go tonight?" Newman asked.

The cop shrugged. He was impatient, edgy. He wanted no small talk. "What's up, Lieutenant?"

"Not much. Just a few questions about the other night."

"Hey, come on. I already went through all that shit."

Newman gave him a moment. The man was embarrassed. He felt emasculated. For a cop to have his gun taken was like watching his wife being raped. "Relax, Reagan. That kind of thing can happen to any of us at any time."

"Not to me. Not before this, anyway. Not in nineteen years. And it wouldn't have happened this time if it wasn't for that goddamned fake gun. That's what threw me off, what made me turn my back on him. I figured no real A and R man would be dumb enough to heist a cop with a cap pistol. I figured it had to be one of the guys from the Emerald, fooling around."

"Emerald?"

"The Emerald Bar. We usually stop there for a couple after a tour. It was in the back parking lot that he hit me. I still can't believe it. A fucking toy gun."

"Forgetting the mask, how would you describe him?"

"Tall. Maybe a bit over six feet. Well set up in the shoulders." Reagan squinted at the lieutenant through drifting smoke. "Built a little like you. Strong." The cop sat morosely, in silence.

"Do you remember what he said when he pointed the gun at you?"

Reagan thought for a while. "He said, 'Put up your hands or I'll blow you away.' He probably heard it in a movie somewhere. Even that should have told me something. Imagine. He tells me to put up my hands in a damn parking lot."

"How was he dressed?"

"Dark windbreaker and jeans. Like a couple of the guys in the bar that night."

"Age?"

"No telling. Though not too old from the way he put me out."

Newman took out a pad and pencil and made some notes. "How did he come across? Did he seem nervous, panicky, excited—anything like that?"

"That was another crazy part of it. He was none of those things. I mean, the guy didn't know his ass from his elbow, yet he waltzed through it like he did it twice a day and didn't give a damn one way or the other."

Indifferent. Mary had hit that one right on the nose. Newman wrote the word on his pad. Then he carefully underlined it.

Reagan sat hunched over, elbows on knees, staring at the backs of his hands. "The thing is, I feel like such a damn jerk. But what really bugs me, Lieutenant, is that whatever the sonofabitch does from here on in, he'll be doing it with *my* piece."

Newman was still surprised by the amount of mail he received after each radio or television appearance. He found it a continuing source of wonder that large numbers of people, complete strangers, would not only find something of value in what he had to say but would take the time and trouble to write to him about it. He felt curiously moved. Of course, not all the mail was laudatory. Opposing views were also expressed, including a fair number of outright attacks. But the response was overwhelmingly in his favor, and he began setting aside a portion of each day for personally replying to letters of particular interest. The remainder was answered with Xeroxed form letters sent out by a secretary.

One afternoon he opened an envelope bearing the return address of the American Fundamental Church in Atlanta, Georgia, and found a letter from the Reverend Clayton Taylor. It said:

Dear Lieutenant Newman,

I have on several occasions heard you interviewed on network news programs and each time was impressed by what you had to say on the subject of law and order.

These are trying days in which we live, days in which

the basic rights of American citizens are being threatened by a savage minority. It is reassuring to discover that there are still men like yourself, men in positions of public trust and service, who are fighting the apathy and indulgence that are gradually undermining this great country.

As you may know, I myself have been doing all I can in this same battle.. To this end, it has become important that I ally myself wherever possible with those who feel similarly. And particularly when they are respected opinion-makers such as yourself.

When I am next in New York, I hope I may arrange a meeting with you that could well prove of value to our common cause.

The letter was signed CLAYTON TAYLOR in a broad, bold, yet precisely controlled hand.

"I'll be a sonofabitch," said Newman softly.

He answered the letter at once.

Dear Reverend Taylor,

The mere fact of your being impressed by anything I might have to say on any subject whatsoever is enough to scare the hell out of me. It also makes me wonder where I could have gone so wrong. Because the truth is, the only common cause we could possibly share is our mortality. In time, like all members of our species, we must both die. Yet although the prospect of living forever is about as unappealing as any I can imagine, I would gladly accept even this if, in so doing, I could cancel out the sharing of anything at all with you.

Just one final point of information. The name Newman is not, as you undoubtedly assumed it to be, German. In my case it happens to be Jewish.

Sorry, Reverend.

Newman signed the letter. And just to ensure its getting off without delay, he walked down to the corner and mailed it himself.

The lieutenant had just finished a live, six-minute segment on the Channel 10 *Evening News* when a production assistant handed him a message requesting him to call the Thirteenth Precinct immediately and ask for Sergeant Rozelli.

He made the call from the producer's office.

"We just got something on this Apostle business," Rozelli reported from the other end.

"I'll be there in fifteen minutes."

He actually made it in ten.

Four minutes after that, he was sitting alone with Ramon Escobar in a locked interrogation room, a square, windowless cubicle that held only their chairs, two green-shaded overhead lights, and a wooden table with a bulging plastic bag on it. The two men sat looking at one another: Newman, dead still in his chair; Escobar, shifting nervously, hands and eyes never quite at rest. They could not have been more different. It struck Newman instantly. The big ol' hound dog and the shining-eyed ferret. He took out a pint of whiskey and put it on the table.

"Have a drink, Ramon."

"What good's a drink? That ain't gonna help me none."

"What do you figure will?"

Escobar's face was morose. "Nothing."

"It can't be all that bad."

"No? I got some choice. I either go into the can for five to ten or I end up dead."

"Maybe not. Let's hear about it."

Escobar changed his mind and took a long swallow from the whiskey bottle. "Aah, the guy's nuts. You know about the first time he hit me?"

Newman nodded.

"I thought I came off pretty damn good then. I mean, you guys really had me cold. There I was, all tied up and delivered like a chicken on the back seat of my Caddy, and I faked my way out, didn't I?"

"You sure did. You're one slippery kid, Ramon."

"So I figured that was the end of it. I figured the creep would just go on to whatever other flaky things creeps like that go on to. But I figured wrong." Escobar shook his head, an unjustly persecuted innocent mourning the inequity of his portion. "And what happens is, he's waiting for me again last night just as I'm getting into my Caddy."

"You mean right after you pulled another job?"

"Yeah. And a damn good one, too. More than a hundred in cash, a beaut of a watch, credit cards—the works. And this time he jams his piece square in my goddamn ear and says,

'You got one more chance, Ramon. Either you turn yourself in tomorrow with whatever stuff you got from this and any other jobs or you're dead.' ''

"Those were his exact words?"

"Yeah."

"And you think he meant what he said?"

"Why else would I have walked my ass in here?" Escobar opened the plastic bag and dumped an assortment of loot onto the table. "You know what kind of rap I'm gonna have to take for all this shit?"

Newman nodded, rocking sympathetically, an old Jew at the wailing wall.

"But it still beats getting my brains blown out." Escobar took another solid shot of whiskey. "Listen, Lieutenant. I been working the streets since I'm nine and I don't scare easy. But I swear to Christ, this flake's got me spooked. There are guys who talk and guys who do, and this guy's a doer."

"How do you know?"

"Because I know. Because he was just a hair away from burning me the first time. He counted to three, and when I didn't do like he said, when I didn't move fast enough, he was gonna blow me away right there. I swear to Christ I tasted it in my mouth. In my business you get to know these things or you don't last a week. I guess in your business, too. Understand what I mean, Lieutenant?"

Newman understood. They shared a specialized line of knowledge. Cops and criminals. Were they tied by a psychic bond? In a sense, he felt closer to this habitual thief than to the average law-abiding citizen.

Escobar misread his silence. "I guess to you I'm just some kind of animal. Or maybe not even that. But I got as much right to live as anybody. So why does that clown have to pick on *me?* How the hell did *I* ever hurt him? Does he think he's God or something?"

"That's what I'm trying to find out." Newman watched Escobar absently pick among his collection of stolen treasures, his dark eyes puzzled, hurt. "How did he act, Ramon? Was he cool? Was he excited? What?"

"The first time he was cool, all right. Ice. Not last night, though. Last night he was sore as hell at me for wasting all his hard work and not staying in the can where I belonged.

111

And he tells me right out that if I don't get in here and make it stick this time, I'm as good as dead. He says there ain't no way I can hide because he knows me and I don't know him, so I'll never know when I'll get hit or from where it'll come. But he says I can sure bet my ass it'll come."

"You never thought about trying to get out of town and losing him?"

Escobar smiled without joy. "Sure. I even packed a bag and tried it one night. Only I never got more than a few blocks before he hit me. When I came to, there was this card pinned to my jacket. It said if I tried running out again, I'd get a bullet. And you know something? I think he was hoping I'd try it."

Harry Blake, of the *Post*, caught Newman as he was about to leave the precinct house. "Anything more on the Escobar kid, Jay?"

"How much have you got?"

"Just that he turned himself in and signed a confession because the Apostle threatened to kill him."

"Then you've got everything," said Newman.

"What about the Apostle?"

"What about him?"

"Do you have any plans?"

"Sure. I'm going to find him."

"And then?"

"I'm going to put him away with Escobar," said the detective.

A flashbulb exploded as he went out the door.

Newman's picture was in that evening's final edition of the *Post*, along with Blake's story on Ramon Escobar and his career to date. Beneath was a paragraph to the effect that Lieutenant Newman had been personally selected by Commissioner Westley to direct an intensive search for the individual calling himself the Apostle and that a hotline had been established to receive calls from anyone with information about the case. It was also briefly mentioned that Lieutenant Newman was the officer whose heroism resulted in the rescue of Richard Gaynor, the famed artist and sole survivor of the most disastrous single air crash in commercial aviation history.

* * *

Newman was preparing for bed when the telephone rang.

"Is this Lieutenant Newman?" asked a muffled male voice.

"Yes."

"This is the Apostle."

Newman took a long, slow breath.

"It said in tonight's *Post* that you've been selected to direct an intensive search for me. Is that true?"

"It is."

"Well then, congratulations."

The detective was trying to decide whether it was really the man himself or someone's idea of a joke.

"I just hope you won't make your search too intensive, Lieutenant. Remember. We're on the same side."

Whoever it was, hung up.

~~~~~~~~~~~~~~~~~~~~~~~~~~ 8 ~~~

Walter Hanson usually came home between 2:00 and 3:00 A.M., so Gaynor parked his Chevette a few blocks away at 1:45; ten minutes later he was in position and waiting.

Gaynor's latest subject of interest, Hanson was an investment counselor who maintained an office but was suspected of making his real money dealing in heroin and cocaine. Although this suspicion had existed for years, it was only a few months before that a grand jury had finally been able to indict him on a drug charge and bring him to trial. Before the two major witnesses against him were able to testify, however, they had the bad luck to die in separate accidents that occurred within a twelve-hour period. One was struck by a speeding hit-and-run driver as he was going for his morning newspaper. The other was electrocuted when a portable heater fell into his bath water. As a result, Hanson was acquitted of all the charges against him. And when an outraged newscaster was just a bit too zealous in implying that the two accidents did seem incredibly coincidental and fortuitous, Hanson promptly slapped both the newsman and his network with a ten-million-dollar slander suit. If nothing else, Gaynor was impressed with how high the cost of balm for offended innocence was running these days.

An elegant, polished man, Walter Hanson had held a crowded news conference to announce the lawsuit. "He that filches from me my good name," he quoted in rounded Shakespearean accents, "robs me of that which not enriches him, and makes me poor indeed." Observing his performance on TV, Gaynor was fascinated by the man's arrogance. It had to represent the absolute ultimate in chutzpah.

Gaynor stood in a dark areaway between two converted loft buildings, the SoHo street in front of him shadowed, quiet, and empty other than for an occasional passing car. High up in what had once been a row of factories and warehouses, a few scattered lights burned as the artists who now lived and worked there struggled through the night to achieve what they may have failed to accomplish during the day. Watching, Gaynor saw dark figures drift, in silhouette, across pale yellow windows and felt a stab of envy. Somehow the nights had always been the best. There was just you, the canvas, and whatever it was you happened to be after, and the rest of the planet was either off somewhere or nonexistent. Yet these were the least lonely moments of all. You needed no one. Understandably, it was at night that Jane's resentment had been strongest.

At exactly 2:24, a taxi pulled up in front of the building to his right and Walter Hanson got out.

Gaynor slipped on his mask.

Hanson was tall, lean, slightly stooped, and carried a cane and an attaché case. He paid the driver and watched the cab take off down the empty street and disappear around a corner. Then he crossed the sidewalk, leaning lightly on his cane for support, and unlocked the building door. As he went in, Gaynor left the areaway and came up behind him.

He pressed his revolver against the back of Hanson's neck, the gun lengthened now by Escobar's silencer. "Don't turn around and don't talk. Just keep moving straight ahead."

Hanson stiffened for a moment and froze in place. Then he did as he was told. An elevator was waiting. It was surprisingly well appointed and luxurious for that area. As was the entrance lobby. Living here had already passed beyond the reach of any working artist, thought Gaynor. He pressed a button and they moved slowly upward. Hanson stood staring straight ahead, his face a sharp wedge in the pink-tinted overhead light. The elevator stopped at the fourth floor, and they got out facing a single metal door, decorated and enforced with baroque wrought-iron scrollwork.

"Open it," said Gaynor.

Three separate locks clicked and the door swung open. Gaynor prodded Hanson inside, touched a light switch, and locked the door behind them. The converted loft was huge, evidently covering an entire floor of the building. And except for some abstract paintings, everything was white—couches, chairs, rugs, cabinets, tables, lamps, walls, ceilings, floors. All white. It might have been a landscape of sculpted virgin snow. Or pure, uncut heroin, thought Gaynor.

"May I turn around now?" asked Hanson.

"Very slowly."

Using his cane as a pivot, Hanson came around in small, measured steps. When he saw the mask, he shook his head at what appeared to be a mixture of amusement and disbelief. "Well . . ."

"You know who I am?"

"I've read about you. You're God's self-appointed missionary. His personal avenging Apostle." Hanson still held the attaché case along with his cane. An expensively tailored trenchcoat was belted over a dark, pinstripe suit. He might have been a visiting prime minister. "But why should *I* warrant your attention? What could you possibly want of me?"

Gaynor pointed to a couch with his pistol and Hanson sat down. Easing into a facing chair, Gaynor said, "You mean because your life to date has been so pure and blameless?"

Hanson said nothing. He had a narrow, aristocratic face, so lean that the skin seemed translucent. An ax blade.

"I'll tell you what I want," said Gaynor. "First, I want

115

you to show me where you keep your drug inventory. Then I want the names and addresses of your suppliers and dealers. Last, I want a detailed, handwritten confession of how you murdered, or arranged for the murders of, the two witnesses who never got to testify at your trial.''

Hanson smiled. It seemed to split his face.

''Apart from everything else, I must say your presumption is boundless. Especially since a legally constituted jury found me innocent on all counts. And there's no evidence whatsoever that those two witnesses died in any way other than by accident.''

Gaynor just looked at him.

''As a point of information,'' said Hanson. ''Why on earth would you expect me literally to destroy myself by doing what you've asked?''

''Because if you don't, I'm going to kill you right where you sit.''

Hanson's laugh didn't seem at all forced. ''You talk very easily about killing. Have you ever killed anyone?''

''No.''

''But you're ready to start with me?''

''If I have to.''

''In cold blood? Even though I'm sitting here unarmed and defenseless?''

''Yes.''

''I'm sorry, but I can't believe that. If killing was your trade, if you were a professional hit man, or if you were some hophead desperate for a fix, I admit I'd be very frightened at this moment. But from all the reports I've read about you, even from your own original letter in the newspapers, you impress me as a rather naive but high-minded type who isn't about to take a human life just to make a point.''

Gaynor was mildly surprised. A semiliterate street kid like Roman Escobar had been able to sense more about his potential for killing than this obviously intelligent and worldly man. But of course Hanson was thinking logically. Which, in this case, could be fatal.

''I've been reading about you, too,'' he said in his mask-muffled voice, ''and you disgust me. You're nothing but elegant filth. You peddle dope to school kids, murder with a shit-eating grin on your face, and haven't even the poor excuse of being disadvantaged or in need. You're the absolute bottom, the worst—an educated, privileged man without heart or conscience. That's why I picked you. And that's also why I can shoot you and not feel a thing if you don't do as I say."

Without changing expression, Hanson's face seemed to tighten. He nodded slowly, a careful man giving due consideration to a suddenly serious problem. His hands, pale as cream, rubbed the smooth, graceful curve of the cane resting between his legs. He half smiled, but this time the small show of amusement was less convincing.

"I must admit you do make me sound rather disgusting."

Gaynor looked at him and waited, wishing he could manage to light a cigarette while aiming the revolver.

"But it's not really all that simple," said Hanson. "Nobody sets out to be a villain, a miscreant, what you so self-righteously describe as elegant filth. I certainly know I didn't. But things happen. It's odd, Mr. . . ." He laughed. "Apostle? There was a time when I was quite pleased to regard myself as a distinctly high-minded, even a heroic, figure in the general scheme of things. I came out of Vietnam with so many medals my hometown gave me a parade. But I also came out riddled with iron and so much pain that I needed a continuous supply of drugs just to get me through a day. It seems to happen one small step at a time. First, it's just yourself. You're just desperate to take care of your own needs. You don't plan any further than that. Then someone asks—"

Hanson stopped and shook his head. He almost seemed embarrassed. "Ah, but you're not really interested in my poor little soap opera, are you?" he said, and he came up out of the couch swinging his cane.

Gaynor squeezed the trigger. There was a soft *whoosh*, and Hanson fell back as though struck by a club. He looked startled. A small hole had appeared in the upper left sleeve of his coat. It slowly reddened about the edges. Then a trickle of blood appeared and ran downward in a thin, wavering line.

"I'm only going to ask you once more," said Gaynor.

"Don't be a fool. What good is killing me? It won't change anything. Nobody hooks junkies. They hook themselves."

"Not twelve-year-olds. They need help from pricks like you."

Hanson fought off a rush of pain. His face had turned

waxen. "Be sensible. I'll give you a quarter of a million. Cash. You can walk out of here rich."

"You refuse to understand a damn thing, don't you?" Gaynor raised the revolver until it pointed squarely between the wounded man's eyes. "You've got ten seconds."

Hanson's breathing deepened. A tremor swept through him. Then he sank back into the couch and seemed to continue sinking beyond even the couch and himself. "All right."

"Where do you keep everything?"

"I'll have to show you." With great effort, Hanson raised himself to a standing position. There was a black hole in the white cushion behind him. "Tell me. How do you get so damned self-righteous? There's a whole system functioning out there. With or without me it won't vary a hair. Whom do you think you're helping?"

"Me." Gaynor motioned him on with the revolver.

Moving stiffly, leaning heavily on his cane, Hanson led the artist into a large, high-ceilinged bedroom. This area, too, was done completely in white except for the paintings, huge abstractions of raw color full of savage smears and drippings. Gaynor gave the pictures only a brief glance, yet they cut at him with a sharp maniacal edge. High twentieth-century art. Hanson worked his way to one of the paintings and pressed a corner of the thin molding around it. Instantly, a section of white paneling slid downward, revealing the dials and steel facing of a massive wall safe.

Hanson stood there, his back to Gaynor. His body suddenly went slack inside his clothes, and he seemed to diminish. His coat might have been hanging empty inside a closet. He swayed slightly and leaned against the wall. "You know, one way or the other you're ending my life." He spoke facing the safe, his voice without strength or timbre. "A bullet might even be kinder than forcing me to do this."

"That's up to you."

In the following silence, waiting, Gaynor saw the signature W. HANSON on the painting above the safe. Everybody an artist. He felt enormously depressed.

"What the hell," said Hanson and seemed to rally. His body straightened and he went to work on the dials.

Gaynor stared at the man's painting directly above him. It was an abstraction, little different from the rest of the canvases in the room, and he realized they had all been done by

118

Hanson. No wonder they had cut at him. They were as cold, sharp, and lethal as their creator. If an artist did, indeed, paint what he was, then where was the hope of redemption for this one?

He heard the safe click and saw the door swing open.

"Well, here's what you wanted," said Hanson softly. Turning, he fired as he came around. There was no explosion, only the same quiet *whoosh* as before. This bullet, too, was silenced.

Feeling a sting in his right cheek, Gaynor slipped to one side and pulled the trigger. He started to aim and fire again, but there was no need. As Gaynor stared over the gun barrel, Hanson dropped, knees and face forward, onto the floor. His cane fell beside him. He was holding a revolver that looked exactly like the one in Gaynor's hand. Gaynor stood looking down at him. The bullet had angled upward and removed a small section of Hanson's skull. Gaynor did not bother to turn him over. He had no wish to see any more of the damage. Taking a deep breath, he waited for some sort of reaction to set in. He felt hollow. That was all. A moment later, he went to work.

Inside the safe were four large plastic bags of fine white powder and dozens of smaller packages of the same substance. There was also an account book with names and addresses and several thick bundles of cash in bills of large denomination. Gaynor counted the money. It added up to slightly more than $475,000.

His cheek burned. He touched the spot and felt a small tear in his mask. When he looked at his fingers, there was blood on them. Close.

He put everything back into the safe but did not lock it. Then he took out one of his cards and printed a brief message to the police in slanting block letters. It said: "For the record, Hanson fired first. The gun he used is in his hand, the bullet, in a wall somewhere. P.S. I counted the money."

Gaynor dropped the card beside Hanson's body and left the apartment. The elevator was still there. He removed his mask and reached the Chevette without seeing anyone. At Canal Street, he stopped at a pay phone and called the Nineteenth Precinct. He gave Walter Hanson's name and address to the desk sergeant and told him what he would find there. Before hanging up he said, "Please don't forget to notify Lieutenant Newman." This made him smile.

Driving uptown, he used three different telephones to call the media. Then he headed home, went to bed, and, as the sky was just beginning to turn pink, had no trouble falling asleep.

He awoke slowly, reluctantly, using the old trick of keeping his eyes closed and trying to fool himself into believing he was still asleep. The trick failed. And inevitably the unpleasant knowledge intruded that he had killed a man. Or had he merely dreamed it? Then, waking further, he recalled the details one by one, and any possibility that it might have been a dream disappeared forever.

Back in the world, he had a deep headache behind his lids that promised to get worse as the day wore on and a burning sensation along his right cheekbone. When he finally opened his eyes and looked at the time, it was close to 2:00 P.M. He had never slept that late before in his life. But he had never killed anyone before, either.

He waited until he knew the early edition of the *Post*, New York's only evening newspaper, would be on the stands, then went out and bought it along with the *Times* and *News*. Carefully not looking at them, he carried all three newspapers back to the apartment.

It was on all the front pages. The *Post* and *News* carried it in screaming headlines above pictures of Hanson taken outside the courthouse at the time of his trial. APOSTLE KILLS DRUG KINGPIN, said the *Post*. NARC CZAR BLASTED BY APOSTLE, declared the *News*. The *Times*, being of a more conservative bent, headed its account with far smaller type that simply said: VIGILANTE FATALLY SHOOTS ALLEGED NARCOTICS DEALER. Beneath the headlines, the stories themselves offered varying descriptions of Hanson's narcotics trial, of his having been acquitted of all charges, and of the coincidental deaths of the two major witnesses. The stories also reported that the police had found almost half a million in cash in Hanson's wall safe along with a supply of heroin and cocaine that carried an estimated street value of four million dollars. Additionally, there were accounts of the Apostle's message to the effect that Hanson had fired first, that an expended bullet had indeed been dug out of a wall by the police, and that no determination had yet been made as to whether the bullet had actually been fired from the revolver found in the alleged drug dealer's hand.

Gaynor listened to a recital of similar stories that evening on television and radio. In most instances, it was the lead item. One network sent a reporter, camera, and microphone out into the streets to get the reactions of passersby. They were overwhelmingly in the Apostle's favor. Only one news commentator, in reviewing the story of Hanson's life and death, mentioned anything at all about his having been a severely wounded, much-decorated hero of the Vietnam War.

"What happened to your cheek?" asked Gaynor's former wife.

She had not noticed the wound until they were in the living room, having a drink. It was late, after 11:00 P.M., but Jane had taken to dropping in at odd hours whenever she felt the need to talk, and Gaynor had nowhere near the heart to turn her away. Once she had even appeared in the middle of the night when Kate was in the bedroom. Unaware, she had talked steadily for an hour before Gaynor finally threw on some clothes and took her home.

"I cut it shaving," he told her now.

No one's beard grew at that spot, the wound was obviously not a razor cut, and Jane knew he used an electric shaver. But her thoughts were elsewhere.

"I'm afraid I'm not doing very well," she said.

"What does the doctor say?"

"Not much. Mostly, he just listens." Gazing out at the lights along the New Jersey shore, her face had the tight, pinched look of controlled pain. "Nothing seems to mean anything. Not my work, not the people I see, nothing. I feel empty, joyless. It's as though I died when they did. The only person I have any real desire to talk to is you, and I can't even fool myself about that. It's because I know you hurt, too. I've gotten so awful. I'm so selfish, so self-pitying. I *want* you to hurt. I *want* you to share it with me. If you didn't hurt, I couldn't bear to look at you."

He reached for her hand where it lay on the couch between them. Her flesh felt cold, her bones fragile.

"It's just so unfair," she said flatly. "I keep thinking of all the things they never had a chance to do, all the things they might have become. I keep imagining impossible deals to make with God. Like giving them each twenty or thirty more years of life and taking the time from us, instead.'' She paused and looked at him. "Would you be willing to agree to that?''

"Yes.''

"Of course. I know how you loved them. And Lord, did they adore you. Which is another thing that keeps stabbing me . . . how I pulled you apart. The divorce. All that. I stole your time with them.''

"I stole it from myself.'' If there was going to be a pouring on of ashes, he could outpour the best of them. "I was a madman. I had the insane idea that my work was more important.''

She sighed. "At least you've still got that.''

The implication was so obviously that it was far more than she had that he couldn't let it go. "No I don't. I haven't been able to pick up a brush since it happened.''

"But you said . . .''

"I said a lot of things.''

She looked up past her drink at him, seeking his face. "I don't understand. Painting was your whole life.''

He was silent.

"So what do you do?''

"Something better. At least that's what I keep telling myself.''

Being puzzled darkened her eyes. "Please, Richard. I'm really not very good at games these days.''

"I'm sorry.'' Then he thought, Why not? Why the hell not? If it could help him, why not her? He abruptly rose and went into his bedroom. When he returned a moment later, he was carrying an opaque plastic shopping bag inscribed with the Henri Bendel logo.

He sat down beside her once more, carefully keeping the bag between his knees. "I'm not sure how you're going to react to this, but I've got a strong feeling that you, of all people, might be the one person who should know about it.''

"Know about what?''

Reaching into the bag, he took out, in order, the Apostle mask, the revolver and attached silencer, and finally a cluster of white calling cards on which was printed THE APOSTLE.

"This," he said, and he arranged everything on the coffee table in front of her like the loveliest, most valuable of gifts.

Her eyes, still darkly puzzled, seemed to see only the mask. "That belonged to the twins." She frowned, as though wondering why he had chosen so cruel a way to punish her. "I remember when I bought it. It was for the Sunday school play . . ."

Gaynor watched as she slowly picked up the mask and slipped it over her hand. A fingertip broke through where Hanson's bullet had creased the cheek. Gravely, she wiggled it, her thoughts still in the past. Then, staring at the revolver and the cards, she seemed to become aware of them for the first time. "Did the gun belong to them also?"

"No. The revolver is real."

She picked up the cards. "And what are these?"

"My identification."

Even then it did not break through all at once but came, rather, in a slow progression, a gradual adjusting in space, with her eyes shifting back and forth between him and the objects he had laid out in front of her.

At last she whispered, "Is it really true?"

"Yes."

"But why?" Her voice was odd, groping, not her own. "How did you ever come to such a thing?"

He shrugged. A haze filtered over his lids and turned faintly red. "I was desperate. I needed some kind of reason, something that might make even a little bit of sense."

"My God, and this was what you came up with?"

He looked helplessly at her as she suddenly began to weep. He blinked, insanely close to tears himself. "It's that awful to you?"

"No." Jane pressed her face to his neck, hiding. "It's just so . . ." She gasped, groping. "It's just so . . . terribly sad."

They sat holding one another.

The idea was just too tempting for him to resist. There was even a kind of titillation in it, the crazy excitement of leaning just a bit too far out of a high window and sensing the fall. Finally he put through the call to Police Headquarters one morning.

"Have you completely forgotten poor old Gaynor?" he said when Newman got on.

"Well, I'll be damned."

"No need to go that far. But when you save a man's life, don't you automatically take on some responsibility for it?"

"You're right. At least, to a point."

"If you've got some time later today," said Gaynor, "I'm absolutely loaded with Jack Daniel's."

There was only a slight pause. "I'll be there at six."

"I'm at a Hundred and Ninth Street and Riverside Drive. South corner."

"I know where you are." Newman hung up.

Gaynor opened the door for the detective almost exactly on the hour. They shook hands and stood staring at one another. Gaynor sensed, almost felt, a curious wave of energy flow between them. The last time he had seen Newman was in his burrow at the Olympic Hotel.

"You look pretty good," said the lieutenant. "Like you might even make it."

"I decided to protect your investment."

Newman lit a cigarette, and in the glow of the match his eyes held Gaynor's in some deep authority of feeling, grave and bewildering but with just a hint of mockery buried inside for a joker. "I guess I've neglected you. It hit me when you called."

"Hey, you're not responsible. I was only kidding on the phone."

"Psychologist I know says nothing is ever really said in jest."

"Screw your psychologist."

"I do," said Newman. "As often and as thoroughly as I can."

Gaynor led him through the foyer, down a short hallway, and into the living room.

"What did the doctor say about your limp?"

"It should disappear in time," said Gaynor. "Is it really that bad?"

"No."

"Still, you noticed it fast enough."

"I'm a cop. Noticing useless things gets to be automatic after a while." Gaynor put some ice and Jack Daniel's into two glasses and handed one to Newman. Well, there it was, the opening salvo from the opposition. He could feel it go through him like a tracer of light. Still, it was not all that unpleasant. And what else, besides his limp, had he failed to consider?

"I frankly never expected you to come out of it this well," said the detective. "And I don't just mean physically. You've got more guts than I thought."

"Hell, I was left alive, so here I am. I get up in the morning, eat, go to the can, and fall asleep at night. It's no big deal."

"Come on. We both know it's not that simple." Newman lifted his glass. "Anyway, here's to one day at a time."

They drank for a while in silence, and Gaynor felt an almost electric sense of loss. They might have been sitting at a wake.

"You've been doing pretty well yourself. I've been reading about you. Even saw you a few times on TV. How do you like being a celebrity?"

"More than I thought I would. It sure beats getting kicked in the ass."

"I also read where you've been stuck with this Apostle thing."

"I wasn't stuck. I asked for the job." Newman swung his eyes about the comfortable, old-fashioned room like two gun turrets. "I'm going to enjoy putting this particular little momzer away."

Gaynor showed surprise. "Why? All the guy is doing is helping you clear the streets of a few extra vermin."

"Do you know what would happen if five thousand more good-hearted killers decided to pick up guns and start helping us?"

"You think he's a killer?"

"Try asking Walter Hanson that question."

"It said in the paper that Hanson fired first."

"It wasn't Hanson who said it."

"But the man was a drug pusher and a murderer."

"Not according to the law." Newman took a long pull of bourbon and savored it as it went down, a deep religious experience. He shook his head impatiently. "People don't understand. You can't turn the law on and off like a faucet.

125

It's either there or it's not there. And imperfect as it is, the alternative is chaos.''

"I'm still rooting for the Apostle.''

"So is everyone else," said Newman dryly. "You should see the mail pouring in. He'll never make it to Election Day, but if he did, he could be president.''

"You expect to get him that soon?''

"I give him two, three months on the outside.''

"How can you be so sure?''

"Because he's an amateur, a novice. He'll make mistakes." Newman squinted at the rows of books that covered the far wall. He might have been trying to memorize the titles.

Know a man by the books he reads, thought Gaynor.

"But I may not have to wait that long," said the detective. "If I seem to be having too much trouble, he'll help me himself.''

"You think he wants to be caught?''

"Maybe not consciously. But he's already called me on the phone and I'm sure he'll keep calling. That's all part of his game. It adds to the excitement. It makes him feel superior and in control. Finally, as he grows bored, he'll start tossing me specific clues and hints.''

Gaynor added more bourbon to their glasses. Then he ran off a quick mental sketch in which Newman, dashing in the familiar deerstalker cap favored by Sherlock Holmes, sat smugly puffing on a curved meerschaum as he outthought his evil opponent.

"Well, at least you seem to be enjoying yourself.''

Newman laughed. "I am. I just hope I don't find him too quickly. I want it to last.''

The detective rose and walked over to a framed snapshot of Jane and the twins. The picture had been taken two years earlier at Jones Beach, and the three of them looked tan, smiling and happily immortal in a golden summer sun. "I meant to ask. How is your ex-wife doing?''

"Not as terrifically as I.''

Gaynor was reading the *Times* over his morning coffee when he came to a full-page advertisement in the form of an open letter. It was printed in large type and addressed to "The Individual Known as the Apostle.'' It read:

The Bible tells us, *Vengeance is mine, I will repay, saith the Lord*. Yet there are times when even the patience of saints would be tried, and alas, we are none of us saints. I pray that you may be forgiven for daring to seek this terrible vengeance of your own.

But if blame must be placed, let it be placed not only on your poor shoulders but on the shoulders of those holding political office whose policies of indulgence toward savagery and lawlessness are steadily destroying our American heritage.

So we must all take heed. We must be vigilant. We must raise united voices against the forces of darkness. And when someone such as yourself, who has so prophetically assumed the name of the Apostle, is sadly driven to violent and lawless action, we must accept our fair share of the responsibility. We have remained silent too long.

God bless and forgive you,

Clayton Taylor (Rev.)

There was an inscription a the bottom of the page stating that the space had been paid for by the Friends of the American Fundamental Church.

He received an urgent call from Marvin Sanders at the gallery.

"You won't believe this, but I'm out of paintings."

"What about those pieces you took when you were here?" asked Gaynor.

"I just sold the last of them. I told you. You're hot as a pistol these days."

Gaynor found the simile curiously apt.

"Do you have anything at all I might have missed?" said Sanders.

"Just some studio sketches. And I'm not about to give you those."

"What have you been working on?"

Gaynor took a long moment. "Nothing."

"What are you talking about? What do you mean, nothing?"

Gaynor was silent.

"Are you serious, Richard?"

"Very."

"You mean you've done nothing since—" Sanders was unable to say it.

"I'm afraid not."

"Oh, Christ." The gallery owner's voice softened. "I'm sorry. I had no idea. I feel like a damn fool."

The line stretched silently between them.

"Do you want to talk about it?" asked Sanders.

"Not really."

"Are you getting help?"

Gaynor stared at a hairline crack in the wall. The inevitable question. What had people asked before Freud? "Yes," he said to forestall any pressure.

"An awful lot of people paint for therapy, you know."

"Yes, but not when they're artists."

"Of course. I'm an idiot. I'd tell a writer with writer's block to treat himself by writing."

Gaynor smiled. Poor Marvin.

"Listen," said Sanders. "Despite an unfortunate amount of evidence to the contrary, I'm not just a money grubber. I do care about you. And I certainly believe in your work."

"I know that."

"I'll be in touch. And if there's anything at all I can do, please let me know." Sanders sighed, the sound drifting, deep and tragic, over the wire. "It's a crazy thing. You know who I keep thinking about since you said you weren't painting?"

"No."

"Your father."

Gaynor carefully hung up the phone.

His father? Yet it was not really so crazy. Deeply, inextricably involved with his son's painting as long as he drew breath, Tom Gaynor had been fiercely proud of every brushstroke even when there was pathetically little reason for pride. His son the artist. Dying, he refused to leave for the hospital unless his four favorite canvases went with him. Gaynor had ached to roll them up in his coffin, this man who peddled insurance seventy hours a week to eke out a bare living, yet once happily swore to support his son for as long as he lived if he just kept on painting. The minister at his funeral, not having known the deceased, asked Gaynor to tell him a few things about his father. "He loved my mother and me very much," Gaynor had said. "He never hurt a living creature. He never did a petty, mean, or dishonest thing in his life. He saw the face of God in every lousy picture I ever painted.''

After the funeral, Marvin Sanders had taken Gaynor aside. ''There's something your father made me swear never to tell you, but I'm going to tell you now,'' he said. ''Do you remember the only three paintings we sold at your first show?''

''How could I forget? The money kept me going for a year.''

''It was your father who bought them.''

A strong west wind drove bursts of rain against the windows as they lay naked in the shadowed room. The curtains were open, and Gaynor could see the late afternoon sky, lowering and gray, over the Palisades. An electric clock hummed softly.

''When do you suppose I'll start getting bored with the unblemished perfection of your body?'' he said.

Kate nibbled idly, contented as a cat, at his earlobe. ''Dummy. You never get bored with an addiction, just more strongly addicted.''

''I think you're right. You're habit-forming.''

Eyes closed, he ran a hand lightly, exploringly, over her body, touching the high and low places, missing nothing. A blind man, he thought, memorizing his world.

''Keep doing that,'' she purred, ''and I'm going to have to put you to work all over again.''

''Hey, you can't get blood from a stone.''

''You're no stone and it's not your blood I'm after.''

Slowly, gently, she moved to him.

She had the lips of a virtuoso, soft, clinging, filled with promise. They breathed new life into him. They brought him unexpected gifts. Finally, they slipped him free of himself.

''Jesus Christ,'' he said when he was able to speak, ''there should be a law against you.''

''There is. It's just very hard to enforce.''

The rain was hitting more softly now against the windows. Far off, on the river, a ship's horn blew, its sound mournful and deep in the quiet room.

''What a lovely cocoon.'' Kate sighed. ''I hate to leave.''

''Then don't.''

She kissed him and rose, reluctantly, from the bed. "I'm on shift in an hour. You're not my only patient, love."

"With that treatment, you must be in great demand."

She smiled and went to his closet for a bathrobe. When she turned, she was holding a shopping bag marked HENRI BENDEL. "Aren't you a darling. You've bought me a little surprise from Bendel's."

"Hey, give me that." Gaynor abruptly sat up in bed. "It's not for you."

"Who then? Your wife?"

"No. Of course not. It's just something for myself."

"Really? From Bendel's?"

"Why not?"

"No reason. Not if you're going in drag these days. It just happens to be a women's store."

"Ah, you've found me out." He slid off the bed and started toward her. "Now be a good little girl and give me that bag."

Teasing, she backed away from him. "Not until you tell me what's in it. You're suddenly making me very curious."

"Okay. It's something for Jane. You were right. I was afraid you might be jealous, so I lied before."

"No. You're lying now."

He made a sudden lunge for her. Anticipating the move, she dodged to one side, ran giggling into the bathroom, and locked the door behind her.

"Kate, please don't open the bag," he said through the door.

She laughed. "You kidding? How could I not? I'm a woman."

Gaynor slowly went back to the bed. He lit a cigarette and lay there, waiting.

It took her a long time to come out. When she did, her eyes were flat. "I'll tell you something crazy. Somehow, I'm not that surprised. There's even a weird sort of logic to it." She spoke coldly, matter-of-factly. "What really bothers me is that I should turn out to be such a lousy nurse. Stupid. Here I thought you were coming along so well, that you were getting better by the day."

He lay watching her from the bed. He was fascinated, even admiring. How composed she was, how beautifully controlled. With a bit of training she could be an outstanding neurosurgeon. He began a portrait of her at work, eyes cold and commanding above her surgical mask, brow pale and cool, scalpel poised. Surgeon of the Year. She would be a cinch for the cover of *Time*.

"Jesus, do you need help," she said.

He smiled.

"What's so funny?"

"I hear tell that everyone needs help."

"Some more than others." Kate stood there very stiffly, staring at him. "My God, you actually killed a man the other day, didn't you?"

He said nothing. His terry robe, much too large on her, slipped open, and he saw her breast tremble with her heartbeat.

"Tell me. How does it feel to kill?"

Gaynor remained silent. He was still working on that one himself.

"Aren't you at all afraid?"

"No."

"You *want* to die. Is that it?"

He considered the question. "I think it would be more accurate to say that I'm indifferent to the possibility."

Without warning, she hurled the shopping bag at him. It struck the wall above his head and fell on a pillow. So much for the neurosurgery, he thought sadly, and began brushing out the unfinished portrait.

"Damn you!" she swore. "If you're so hot to die, then die. But why did you have to drag me in on the program?"

"I'm sorry. I didn't mean for you to find out."

"Didn't you?" Stepping close, she hit him across the face. "Then why did you leave that damn bag right in front of the closet where I was sure to see it?" Pale with anger, she went back into the bathroom to shower and dress.

When he swallowed, he tasted blood.

It was four days after his last telephone conversation with Marvin Sanders that he started working again. There was no conscious premeditation. He just walked into his studio one morning and began fooling around with a pad and piece of charcoal. Nor was he aware of any particular ideas struggling for expression. His thoughts seemed blank, without direction. Once, however, he did briefly find himself thinking of his father. All right. So it was a filial act of contrition. Which in itself was not important. All that mattered was that his hand felt alive and moving again.

He watched his apparently random strokes grow and spread until they covered nearly a dozen sheets. It was only then that he saw the first faint hint of something. Strangely, it bore no resemblance to anything he had ever done before. And when he tried to push it further, tried to give it more specific form, it disappeared entirely. Yet it had been there.

9

A ringing telephone woke Newman at 2:10 A.M. He was alone in bed in his apartment. The caller turned out to be the desk sergeant at the Eighty-first Precinct in Brooklyn.

"You said to call the minute we heard anything, Lieutenant. We just heard."

Newman was still only half awake. His eyes searched the shadowed darkness—chair legs, a bureau, carelessly tossed clothes. Nothing human, nothing warm. "What is it this time?"

"According to the Apostle, attempted rape. He said he had to tie up the woman, too. Seems she was scared and wanted to beat it. He said they're right off the Belt Parkway, under the Verrazano Bridge."

Newman shook his head to clear it. The action soured the whiskey in his stomach, nauseating him. "Get one radio car over there, no more. And they're not to go any closer than fifty yards. I want the Apostle's footprints, not those of cops. Also, put in a call to Headquarters for a forensic team.''

He was out of bed with one trouser leg on when he hung up the receiver.

It took him half an hour to reach the site. He drove under the curving bridge ramp, swung onto the grass, and parked behind a patrol car. A hazy moon shimmered over the narrows and a light fog hugged the ground and cut off the tops of trees. A few early morning trucks and cars whispered past on the parkway.

"What have you seen?" he asked the two cops waiting for him.

"There's a car behind that second row of bushes," said one of the men. "No sound or movement. The sergeant said not to go any closer than this."

Newman took a flashlight and walked toward the bushes. The two officers waited behind. The ground was soft and spongy, with scattered patches of bare dirt surrounded by rings of winter-dead grass. Newman stepped carefully, trying to keep to the grassy places. When he passed the first line of bushes, he was able to see the bodies.

Picked up by the flashlight's yellow beam, a man and a woman were stretched out on the ground. They lay within a few feet of one another. Their wrists and ankles were bound, they had gags in their mouths, and their legs and lower torsos were exposed. The woman's dress, a blue waitress's uniform, was ripped open from top to bottom, and her undergarments appeared to have been cut away. The man's trousers and briefs were tangled about his feet. The woman was black, the man white. They were both fairly young and their eyes, blinking against the flashlight's beam, were frightened. One of the Apostle's calling cards was pinned on the man's jacket. The woman was making soft, whimpering sounds behind her gag.

"It's okay," Newman told her. "There's nothing to be afraid of. I'm a police officer."

He put down the flashlight and took the gag from her mouth. Then he untied her, helped her to her feet, and covered her with his coat. "Are you hurt, miss?"

Shivering with the cold, she shook her head.

Newman did not even look at the man. Leaving him lying

there, he took the woman back to the car and started the engine and heater. He told the two cops to watch for the forensic team and wave on any rubbernecking traffic.

"You want a drink?" he asked the woman.

"Jesus, yeah."

He had a pint of whiskey in the glove compartment and gave it to her. She drank quickly, without breathing, as if trying to get the alcohol straight to her stomach. "That dirty creep," she said softly. "He should have his balls cut off."

"Can you tell me what happened?"

She hugged the bottle for security. "He was hiding in the back of my car, I guess on the floor, when I got off work. I didn't even know he was there till I was on the parkway. Then he grabbed my hair, put a knife to my throat, and made me drive under the bridge here. I tried to run when we stopped, but he was on me and started ripping and cutting my clothes." She took another swallow of whiskey. "Jesus, how do guys get like that? All they gotta do these days is ask nice and they can have all they want."

"He didn't actually rape you?"

"He sure tried, but this dude in the Apostle mask came up in back and really whopped him before he could."

"How did the Apostle get here?"

"Damned if I know. I heard a car drive off later, but it was on the other side of those bushes there and I never saw it. He had me all tied up by then anyway." She stared off at the bridge lights, each with its own nimbus of fog, looping gracefully to Staten Island. "Aah, I was stupid. I never should have told him I wasn't about to hang around waiting for no cops. I should have kept my mouth shut, then just taken off. Telling him only got him mad and yelling at me."

"What did he say?"

"That I had to stay and tell what happened. That I had to press charges or that animal would just be running loose, doing his thing again. You know, all the usual bullshit."

"It's not bullshit. That much, at least, is true."

"Hey, come on, man. You know better than me what happens when a chick yells rape. Everyone acts like it's her fault, like she went and asked for it. And if she happens to be black and the dude is white, you can forget it altogether. I mean, what the hell kind of chance has she got then?"

She began shivering and sucked at the bottle again.

"What can you tell me about the Apostle?" asked Newman.

"That I love him," she said flatly. "That he saved my ass. That if I ever see him again I'll kiss him."

The forensic team arrived in a van followed by an unmarked radio car. Newman left the remains of his bottle with the woman and had one of the specialists drive her to Coney Island Hospital for the required examination. Then he took the sergeant in charge of the team over to look at the failed rapist, still lying bound and gagged.

"I don't understand, Lieutenant. You've got this guy cold with everything but a hard-on. Why did you get us down here? What else are you looking for?"

"Signs of the Apostle," said Newman. "The woman said he had a car parked behind those bushes. See what kind of tire marks and footprints you can pick up. And go over this jerk with a fine tweezers. The Apostle tied him up and handled him. I know you can't get any prints off clothing, but he may have left something—hairs, fibers—who knows? I also want a complete set of pictures."

"You mean you want a full four-star production?"

"All the way."

The fog drifted in layers as they went to work.

The background reports on the would-be rapist were thorough but offered Newman no real surprises. Identified as Frank Galt, the man was twenty-seven years old, lived alone in a furnished room in a blue-collar, South Brooklyn neighborhood, and worked sporadically as a warehouseman and lower-level club fighter. In the past five years, he showed a record of eight arrests and no convictions on an assortment of rape charges. In each case, his alleged victim was a black woman. Just ten days before, Galt's most recent arrest and release had been the subject of an angry editorial in the *News*. In it, the writer attacked a system of justice that permitted an obviously chronic offender to go unpunished repeatedly because his victims were either too ashamed or too intimidated by police cynicism to press charges. The *News* could offer no solution to the problem short of changing laws, court procedures, and rules of evidence. Nor, after reading the article himself, could Newman. But inasmuch as he was more interested in the Apostle right now than in general reform, he found himself considering other possibilities.

* * *

He had a detailed forensic report in his hands within five hours of the attempted rape.

Impressions left by the only unidentified tires in the area carried no distinctive marks other than an embedded nail and glass fragment in the right front tire. It was the size and type of tire that had been used as standard equipment on three different compact car models produced by General Motors in 1978 and 1979. The footprints that carried the possibility of being the Apostle's were made by a size eleven shoe with a broad, rounded toe of loafer or moccasin design. They had been worn by a man of approximately six feet in height and weighing a hundred and eighty pounds. There were no discernible fingerprints on any part of Frank Galt's clothing nor on the clothing of the victim, Geneva Desmond. There were, however, three strands of hair that belonged to neither of these individuals and that were typed as being straight, medium brown, and Caucasian. The cord used to bind Galt and Desmond was an ordinary grade of number 4 white nylon, identical to that used in tying up Officer Reagan and Ramon Escobar. An internal medical examination of Geneva Desmond conducted at the Coney Island General Hospital revealed that she had engaged in sexual intercourse sometime during the previous three hours. An examination of Galt revealed severe swelling and lacerations of the right rear portion of the skull, indicating a blow struck by a right-handed assailant wielding a hard, blunt weapon. There were also traces of dried semen on Galt's trousers and briefs.

He was dozing in the chair outside the commissioner's office when something woke him. He blinked several times, then looked up into Michael Westley's eyes.

"Come inside and sleep," said the commissioner. "It's quieter and less public."

A Seth Thomas clock read 8:30 A.M.

They were alone with the big double doors closed behind them. "My grandfather died at the age of ninety-three," said Westley, "after a long, debilitating illness. But even before embalming, he looked better than you do now."

Newman rubbed his face with both hands to get the blood moving. "Did you listen to the news on the way down?"

"If you mean the bit about the Apostle's latest, I listened. I assume that's what kept you up all night."

"Read this." Newman handed him the background material on Frank Galt. "I need your okay to try something."

Westley glanced over the single typewritten sheet. "Very inspiring. So?"

"I figure if we let the prick go, he'll be out there dropping his pants again within the week. And I also figure the Apostle will soon be right behind him, more worked up than ever. Then all we'll have to do is keep a few good sidewalk artists watching Galt's back. I don't see how it can miss."

Westley took a long, dark cigar from the humidor on his desk but did not light it. "We can't just let the man go. And certainly not if his victim presses charges."

"Galt is white and the woman is black. She knows what she'll have to face in the courtroom. The Apostle had to tie her up to keep her from taking off in the first place. That part won't be any problem."

"The media will kill us. They'll scream to high heaven. Especially the professional minority sympathizers."

"Screw the media. They'll scream no matter what we do. They're just whores turning their daily quota of tricks. I certainly wouldn't let them affect how we handle this."

The commissioner made a small ritual of lighting his cigar. "What do you say, Michael?"

"I can't help recalling when you first brought this Apostle character to my attention and I dismissed him as just another nut. You were obsessed with him even then, weren't you?"

Newman said nothing. He was very tired and needed a drink badly. He stared at a mahogany liquor cabinet in a far corner of the office. It was suddenly hard to think of anything else.

"Obviously you were right and I was wrong," said Westley. "He is clearly not just another nut. He is a nut with style, good instincts, and enormous appeal. He puts on a rubber mask and proceeds, in the full glare of the media, to act out every man's fantasy. My wife, my entire family, adore him. So do all my friends. They can't wait to hear about his latest exploit. He's Robin Hood, Zorro, and Spiderman rolled into one. He cuts through all the nonsense and does whatever has to be done. I swear, sometimes I'm jealous." The commissioner smiled rather wistfully. "Naturally, he's a menace to the established order and must be stopped. And of course he will be. But the day he is, I think it might be best for us both to disappear for a while.''

Newman could not take his eyes from the liquor cabinet.

"All right, do whatever you have to," said Westley. "And for God's sake, get over there and take a drink. You look awful."

The victims of rape and attempted rape were generally held by municipal hospitals for a twenty-four-hour period of observation, a precaution that considerably lessened the chance of latent symptoms and claims and further lawsuits.

Driving to Coney Island General, Newman passed the place beneath the Verrazano Bridge where he had been just a few hours before. Things looked different in the sunlight, less menacing and ugly. His heart was stirred by the bright sky, the sparkling water, the open horizon. Still, you had to be foolish to let your guard down. Darkness always returned.

Even young, reasonably healthy people looked frail and sickly in those terrible hospital gowns and Geneva Desmond was no exception. How small she is, thought Newman, how sadly vulnerable. He took her to an empty consulting room and gave her a cigarette. "So how do you feel?"

She managed an unconvincing smile. "Like I almost got raped."

"You look fine."

"I look like shit. It's a funny thing. It gets to you."

He lit her cigarette and she coughed up smoke.

"Last night I just wanted to run off and forget it," she said. "I mean, nothing really happened to me, right?" She shook her head. "Wrong. Today I discovered plenty happened to me."

"What do you mean?"

"This." She held out her hand, which was trembling violently. "But even more important, I got mad as hell. Who does that mother'n creep think he is to stick a lousy knife to my throat? To knock me down on the ground. To rip my clothes. To try and shove that thing of his inside me. Hey, I'm not dirt, man." She drew nervously at her cigarette. "You wait and see. You can forget those things I said last night. I'll be the best damn witness you ever saw. All I want now is to get that sonofabitch put on ice for a thousand years.''

"I'm afraid it's not going to be that easy, Geneva. In fact, I think it would be smarter for you not to press charges at all."

Dark eyes wide in a smoothly beautiful tan face, she stared at him. "You kidding me or something?"

"No. I wouldn't kid about something like this. It's actually for your own good. Much as I hate to say it, you were right last night. You'd be better off forgetting the whole thing. I'm telling you this as a friend."

"Don't hand me that friend shit." She was so angry she inhaled too strongly and began to choke. "You're no friend of mine. I'll bet if the colors ran the other way, if he was black and I was white, you wouldn't be telling me to forget a damn thing, would you?"

"This has nothing to do with color."

"Like hell it don't." Her eyes flashed, her head was high, her arms were folded tight as a locked door. "Well, you're not talking me out of it. I'm not letting that rat run loose."

"I'm sorry you feel that way. But you'd still make out better by dropping all charges." Newman sighed. "You're married, aren't you?"

She looked suspiciously at him. "Yeah. What about it?"

"Where's your husband now?"

"On the road somewhere. He's a long-haul trucker."

"When did you last see him?"

"About three days ago."

"Have you spoken to him since this happened?"

She shook her head. "What's this got to do with my husband? Why are you asking me all these questions?"

"Because those are the questions a defense attorney is going to ask you if this goes to trial."

"So?"

"So your examination last night showed evidence of recent sexual intercourse. It had nothing to do with the attempted rape. Is that what you want your husband to hear in a courtroom?"

Her eyes went even darker. "You got no right . . ."

He said nothing.

"I'm a person, too, damn it!"

"I'm sorry, Geneva. I really am."

Norman Garbo

"Bullshit!"

Newman looked helplessly at her.

She started to cry, the tears running unchecked down her cheeks. "Fucking Jew bastard."

Naturally, he thought.

The Eighty-first Precinct was one of the oldest in Brooklyn. You could smell its senescence. Underground streams flowed nearby and the walls oozed damp. They might have been shedding tears, and Newman guessed they probably had good reason. He followed a guard down a flight of stone steps and past a row of holding cells in the basement. They were all empty except for the last. This one held Frank Galt.

Newman gave the guard his revolver and went in. The guard locked the cell behind him. He told the detective to yell when he was ready to come out. Then the guard walked away.

The cell had a stained sink, a toilet, and a narrow bunk with a bare, mildewed mattress. Gault had been stretched out on the bunk, but he sat up now. Newman stood against the cell bars, considering him. Even sitting, Galt looked big. He had washed-out blue eyes and the flattened nose and facial scars of a fighter who had never been great on defense.

"It looks like your luck is holding," said Newman. "The woman isn't pressing charges."

Galt blinked several times. Then he just sat there, grinning. It did nothing especially good for his face.

"You think that's funny?" asked the detective.

"Shit, man. It ain't luck. I mean, luck ain't got nothing to do with it. Why do you suppose I pick niggers?"

"Real smart." Appearing to share in the amusement, Newman moved away from the line of bars.

Galt rose from the bunk and swaggered over. He looked about as happy as his nature would ever allow him to look.

"You're really a sweetheart, aren't you?" said Newman and hit him in the stomach with his full weight behind it and his feet firmly planted. As Galt doubled over with a grunt, the detective followed up with a carefully measured right to the jaw. Galt dropped to his knees, fell sideways, and threw up on the cement floor.

"Guard!" called Newman.

140

The officer reappeared and unlocked the cell door. He stared through the bars at his prisoner.

"When he's feeling better," said Newman, "have him sign the usual release forms and let him go."

Time had taught Newman not to love surprises, not even good ones, and this was not a good one.

All he had known was that he was to be appearing on a live half-hour segment of *Blake's Corner*, that the subject of discussion was "the new vigilante," and that there would be another guest as well. What he had not known was that the other guest, evidently a last-minute replacement, would be the Reverend Clayton Taylor.

Nevertheless, it had seemed a curiously fitting climax to what had been one hell of a day. *And* two nights, he thought, inasmuch as it had been night when it started and was night again. Yet carried along by a heart-pumping crest of adrenaline and whiskey, he felt less tired now than when the Brooklyn precinct sergeant's call had pulled him out of bed some twenty hours before. Even at this moment, with the blazing television lights stabbing at his eyes and Harry Blake's deep, mellifluous voice injecting all the hyped-up drama of a championship fight into his introductory remarks, Newman felt an extra surge of energy that hit him very much like the start of a dangerous hot pursuit.

They had met only ten minutes before in the ready room. Taylor had arrived late, sweeping in like a front-running presidential candidate with an entourage of bodyguards, reporters, and public relations people. They had shaken hands, passed through the usual amenities, and been ushered onto a set where they were seated and fitted with lapel mikes. It was the first time Newman had seen Clayton Taylor other than on the TV screen; the clergyman looked taller in person, more physically impressive, with not a spare ounce of flesh anywhere and pale, steady eyes that took your measure like a steel tape. Still, they were eyes that carried crinkly laugh lines at their corners, and these gave off a distinct air of fortified good humor. On selected occasions, Newman imagined, they could probably be disarming. "Lieutenant Newman and I have never met," Taylor had drawled, smiling, on introduction, "but I suppose you might say we fall under the heading of old pen pals."

Norman Garbo

A very funny man.

Newman had appeared before on *Blake's Corner* and knew pretty much what to expect. The show's format consisted of generally free-swinging conversation centered about a subject currently in the news, with Blake acting as moderator. Since this week's subject, "the new vigilante," had been inspired by the Apostle's growing notoriety, Newman was there as the officer in direct command of the New York Police Department's efforts to apprehend him. As for Taylor, his more or less sympathetic attitude toward the Apostle was already known through his open letter to the *Times* and similar statements.

Blake made a few introductory remarks, then asked his guests to state briefly their positions on that evening's topic.

Newman went first, speaking quietly but forcefully, piling his arguments like rocks. It was all self-evident, he told the gleaming red eye of the camera. Civilization, the very fabric of society, depended upon the law for its continued existence. Without the law, the strong would prey on the weak, might would be the only accepted right, and the principles of the jungle would prevail. Certainly many laws were faulty, and their enforcement too often limited and frustrating. But what was the alternative? Everyone making his own judgment of right and wrong and enforcing it with guns? To accept the Apostle's right to act outside the law, to accept his right to kill, would be to accept in principle the right of every other citizen to do the same. And what chaos and terror would result.

Newman felt reasonably pleased when he finished. He had not become emotional. He had not attacked his opponent. He had not personalized what was essentially an impersonal, academic question of right and wrong. Mary would be proud of him.

It was the minister's turn. Smiling benignly at his unseen audience, he declared that the Apostle existed today because there was an unfortunate need for him to exist. He was symptomatic of all that was wrong with American society, threatened as it was by rampant crime and godlessness. Indeed, our real danger lay, not in the misguided actions of this single individual, but in our refusal to open our eyes and act ourselves. If anything, the Apostle had to be regarded less as a threat than as a warning and a symbol. In cases of morality and survival, Taylor stated reasonably, God's laws must sometimes be given preference over man's. If we refused to believe this, then good Christian Americans would be doomed to go on seeing their homes and lives violated, their police cut down for simply doing their jobs, their children corrupted by drugs and pornography, and dark and foreign elements taking over their land.

There was barely a pause as Blake attacked. "What dark, foreign elements, Reverend? Kikes, niggers, and spics?"

Taylor's faint smile remained unaffected. "Those words aren't mine, Harry. They're yours. I don't go in for crude name-calling."

"Forgive me, Reverend. Crudeness is one of my problems. But it sometimes helps cut through the pompous rhetoric."

"I'm a minister," said Taylor. "Take away my pompous rhetoric and you render me mute." He turned to Newman. "Despite what you've said here tonight, Lieutenant, I still feel we're kindred spirits on the subject of terror in our streets. Haven't I often heard you attack the indulgence of our courts and penal system?"

"Yes, but I still believe in the law."

"So do I," said Clayton Taylor, "until it fails us. Then I can at least begin to understand the emergence of someone like the Apostle."

"I can't."

"You're a police officer, Lieutenant. You wouldn't allow yourself to admit it publicly, in any case."

Blake broke in. "Can you also begin to understand the emergence of lynch mobs, Reverend?"

"The Apostle is no lynch mob."

"In principle he is," said the reporter. "All you have to do is multiply him by five hundred."

"You oversimplify it."

"I'm just trying to follow your personal style, Reverend. Reduce everything to a simplistic exaggeration and attract the lowest and broadest common denominator."

Taylor looked straight through him.

"You know what I mean, Reverend," said Blake. "Blacks are criminal and shiftless, Hispanics immoral and dirty, and Jews a worldwide Zionist conspiracy."

"I think you're obsessed with some of our less happy minorities, Harry."

"No, sir. You are." Blake's smile was pure river ice. "Or

wasn't it you who only last month said in a California speech—
and I quote—'History has already begun to vindicate many of
the Third Reich's more extreme racist policies.' "

Newman wondered what any of this had to do with "the
new vigilante." Still, he found himself taking a nervous sort
of satisfaction in it. He had never been a particular fan of
Blake's sensationalist approach. Nor did he care for some of
his more dubious journalistic ethics. Yet tonight, for some
reason, Harry Blake was on the side of the angels. Not that
Taylor appeared in any way disturbed by his host's nipping
and scratching. Barely aware of the jackal at his heels, the
great lion of Christ remained serene and untouched.

The show ended moments later with each guest making a
few brief, final remarks. Blake, not looking happy, thanked
them both for appearing.

Newman left the set as quickly as he could. There was a
bad taste in his mouth and he suddenly felt exhausted. He
picked up his coat from the ready room and started toward the
elevators.

"Lieutenant Newman?"

One of Taylor's entourage was hurrying down the corridor
toward him.

"If you have a moment, sir, the Reverend Clayton Taylor
would like to talk to you."

Reverend. Worthy of reverence, deserving to be revered,
used as a title of respect for a clergyman. "He just talked to
me," said Newman and continued on.

The man came after him. "Please, sir, I believe it's
important."

"Not to me."

The man stared helplessly at him. He seemed frightened.

What the hell, thought Newman. "Okay. Take me to your
leader."

The messenger's gratitude was almost pathetic.

Taylor was alone in a large, VIP dressing room. He was
sipping from a snifter of golden Napoleon. "Brandy, Lieutenant?"

"Why not?"

Taylor poured a generous measure and handed it to him. "I
appreciate your coming. I frankly didn't think you would.
What was it? Curiosity?"

"Compassion. I was afraid you might shoot your messenger. Besides, I needed a drink."

Taylor laughed, an easy, relaxed sound. A gunfighter, thought Newman, with his guns checked for the evening.

"What do you want from me, Reverend?"

"I thought I'd made that abundantly clear in my letter. Quite simply, Lieutenant, I want you on my side."

"I told you how I felt about that in my reply. Didn't you read it?"

"Of course I read it." Taylor's smile was as disarming as his laugh. "And it was a masterpiece. I don't think I've ever been inveighed against as poetically. I keep it on hand in case I should ever suffer from the sin of arrogance. But just to keep the record straight, I was well aware of your being Jewish long before you pointed it out to me. You've obviously been misled by my public rhetoric."

Newman looked at him. "Misled? What's that supposed to mean?"

"It means I don't believe that anti-Semitic pap I occasionally spout any more than you do. I'm not a fool, Lieutenant. Nor am I lacking in education. My Doctor of Divinity was earned at Yale University. Do you really believe I don't know what the Jews have contributed to the best of the world's ethics, culture, and religion? Do you really believe I'm ignorant of the true tragedy of these extraordinary people over the past two millennia? Do you think there's even the smallest possibility that I could seriously sanction the bestial murder of six million Jews in what was without doubt the single most horrendous human aberration in recorded history?"

Taylor paused and waited, as though for Newman to attack, but the detective remained silent.

"You don't really know me, of course," the reverend went on, his voice quiet, controlled, and infinitely plausible in the plush, pale yellow dressing room, "but there's very little I do in life that isn't done with some ulterior purpose in mind. And my purpose in coming across as one of our less appealing bigots happens to be twofold. First, because there's no faster or more effective way to get the media's and the public's attention. And second, to help me appeal to our unfortunate human need for scapegoats. People need clear, definable enemies to hate. They need someone other than themselves to dump their guilt, failures, and frustrations on.

So I'm busy providing a few of those. And it works. Adolf Hitler was a true monster, but the man should be on the cover of every political textbook ever published. He won an empire and almost won the world by institutionalizing the big lie, by telling the Germans they were a superrace and that the rest of mankind were lower animals."

Taylor's laugh echoed pleasantly. "You see, Lieutenant, despite my divinity degree I'm essentially a politician, and lies are the prime tools of the political trade. If a politician lacks the talent to create effective lies, he should go into some other line of work."

If it was intended as a joke, Newman failed to smile. "What office are you planning to run for?"

"No office. All I'm trying to do right now is break loose from my southern taproots, gain some national attention, and build a broad enough following and power base to carry a little electoral weight here and there. I want people in public office who feel as I do about the vital elements of American life." His eyes found Newman's. "As I know you feel about them, too."

Newman picked up the dark green bottle of Napoleon and poured himself another drink. With enough of this stuff, he could listen to anything.

"Please, Lieutenant. At least credit me with not being a complete fool. Why would I have bothered writing to you, why would I have wanted you with me in the first place, if I didn't believe we were in accord on the basic issues? Whether it be our runaway crime rates, or the destruction of our inner cities, or the collapse of our moral standards and family units, or the loss of faith in our country and those who run it. And what is perhaps saddest of all, even the loss of our sense of tragedy. Good Lord, man, I've heard your voice thicken with emotion when you've said it. 'What's happening to us?' you've asked. And in my own voice, in my own way, I've asked the same thing."

"But why me? What's so special about a lowly Jewish cop?"

"Don't be so humble, Lieutenant." The reverend gave Newman a long, hard stare that could have measured him, struck a balance, and buried him without blinking once. "You happen to be an extremely articulate, intelligent, heroic police officer with fast-growing appeal and influence. And as far as I'm concerned, your being a Jew would just be an additional asset. It could help you reassure the Jewish community. You could let it be known that my occasional anti-Semitic rantings are really only a temporary political expedient and that no Jew has anything to fear from me. As a Jew yourself, they would listen to you."

"You want me to be your Judas goat."

"Sweet Jesus, no. You'd actually be doing your coreligionists a favor. You'd not only be sparing them unnecessary concern, but by helping me, in the long run you would also be helping them. Since American Jews, as a group, are essentially law-abiding, responsible, city dwellers with a strong regard for order and property, with an ingrained respect for human dignity and life, they're the ones who always suffer the most during periods of high crime and social upheaval. You're a New York City police officer. Do I have to tell you what our inner cities are today? They're open cesspools. They're junkies with knives, defecating in hallways and gutters, and everything burned to the ground. They're prostitutes and faggots with VD. They're throats slit for a Timex watch and eighty-two cents in change. They're armed camps under siege. They're barbarian hordes and the fall of civilization. But if I get what I want, Lieutenant, your Jews will get law and order, renewed urban growth, and freedom from fear. Not too bad a bargain, as I see it."

Newman fought an impulse to move in close and strangle him, he was that furious. Awesome, the man was absolutely awesome. He could make a platform of supreme intolerance sound like an irresistible mix of needed social reform and the Sermon on the Mount. "You're either mad or you think I am."

"But of course not knowing this," continued Taylor as though Newman had not spoken, "the Jews are fighting me with all of their considerable resources. And that sort of misguided action can only end up being counterproductive to everyone concerned. Which means all of us." He offered the detective his most ingenuous smile. "The fact is, Lieutenant, the only issue you and I have not been in full agreement on tonight is that involving our friend the Apostle. And despite your public arguments to the contrary, I have a strong feeling we're of a mind on that, also."

147

One of Clayton Taylor's staff knocked and came in to say that it was time for them to leave for the airport.

The reverend stood up. "I know I dumped a lot of heavy material on you tonight, Jay, so I don't really expect any instant miracles. All I ask is that you give what I've said some consideration."

Jay, thought Newman as he hurriedly finished his drink. He did not call the man Clayton.

Mary had fallen asleep in his bed with the television going. A Vietnam War movie was on, and her face looked soft and vulnerable in the reflected light of exploding shells and burning villages. Newman's bedroom echoed to the thunder of battle, to the terrible cries of the wounded. When he turned off the set, the sudden silence woke her.

"Ah, I tried to wait up for you. I guess I didn't make it." Her voice was heavy with sleep, her hair fine gold where a bedside light caught it. "What time is it?"

"About two." He kissed her and went into the bathroom to undress. "How did you like the show?"

"God, that minister is really something. I was watching your face. At one point I was afraid you were going to hit him right on camera. Then I was almost disappointed when you didn't. I don't know how the FCC sometimes lets him say what he does over the air."

"It has something to do with the First Amendment. I believe it's called freedom of speech."

"The ignorant sonofabitch abuses the privilege."

Newman came back into the room without his clothes. He sat on the edge of the bed and lit a cigarette. "Maybe a sonofabitch, but not really so ignorant."

He repeated some of the things that Taylor had told him afterward.

There was no sleep left in her eyes when he finished. "Talk about your megalomaniacs. The man is a walking case history."

"It's not that simple."

"No one ever said megalomania was simple. All sorts of hallucinations are involved."

"You think he's hallucinating?"

"What I think, darling, is that he suddenly sounds even more frightening than before."

Newman stared tiredly at the floor.

"Ah, come to bed, love."

He put out his cigarette and crawled, shivering and exhausted, between the sheets. Mary tried to warm him with her body, which she did. But she also managed to arouse him and they ended up making love, performing the act almost reflexively and without preliminary. That sweet, familiar flesh. And how reassuring. All complexities reduced to the single-minded, homespun purity of pursuing the orgasm.

But in the following darkness he lay sated yet somehow sleepless, and all the same anomalies were there, just as disturbing as before. Sexual solutions were as temporary as any other. "Don't worry, boychik," his zayde, his grandfather, had once told him at a moment of seemingly endless childhood hurt. "Everything passes." True enough. But since the good would thereinafter have to pass as well and as quickly as the bad, where was the profit in knowing this?

And how would his zayde have reacted to the Reverend Clayton Taylor? No problems there, thought Newman. His grandfather would have had to ask only one question: *Was the man Jewish?* And since the answer in this case was obviously no, he was clearly the enemy. If not specifically in the past, then probably the present. If not in the present, then surely sometime in the future. There were no exceptions.

His zayde had carried two thousand years of Jewish pain and blood in a special pouch to support his theory. It was a history lesson that ran down into shadow and up into fear. Yet it was never abstract, never anything but deeply personal. His grandfather, Israel Newman, had survived his own private pogrom at the age of seven. Israel's mother and father had not. They had been ripped with pitchforks by Russian peasants and fed to the village pigs. After two days and nights, Israel had come up out of a cellar with his baby sister. What remained of his parents lay in the gutter.

The detective remembered when the Catholic church had announced, with great fanfare, that it had decided that the Jews should no longer be forced to carry the blame for killing Christ. His grandfather was close to death when he heard, and very weak, but he had still somehow managed to spit.

Newman finally slept deeply, heavily, through the night and into the morning. Eyes still closed, he reached for Mary and found her gone. He wondered how late it was. Then he opened his eyes and saw the man.

The man sat watching him from a bentwood rocker in the far corner of the bedroom, and Newman instinctively reached for the gun he kept in his night table.

"I already have it," said the man and held up the detective's off-duty revolver. "It's all right, Lieutenant. I'm a friend. It's just that I worry about surprising someone with guns around."

Being careful to keep his hands visible, Newman slowly sat up in bed. The man spoke English fluently but with the faint suggestion of an accent and the extra precision of a learned language. He was dark-haired, over forty, and sat with the easy grace of someone who kept in shape.

Tough, thought Newman. "Who the hell are you?"

"My name is Zvi Avidan. I'm an officer in the Mossad."

"In the *what?*"

"The Israeli Intelligence Service."

Newman stared at him.

The man tossed over a plastic ID bearing his picture. He apparently held the rank of major. "If you would like confirmation, please call the Israeli Embassy in Washington and ask for Colonel Yaakov Netter, the military attaché. When he gets on the line, let me speak to him."

Newman picked up the phone beside his bed, dialed Information, and was given the embassy's number. He made the call and asked for Colonel Netter.

"Who's calling, please?"

"Major Avidan," said the detective.

When the colonel got on the line, Newman gave the phone to Avidan, who spoke briefly in Hebrew and handed the receiver back to him.

"Lieutenant Newman?"

"Yes."

"I am confirming that the man I just spoke with is Zvi Avidan. He will answer whatever questions you have. I sincerely hope you will be able to help us."

"How can—" began Newman.

"Thank you," said the colonel and hung up.

Newman put on a robe and went into the bathroom. When he came out, Avidan returned his revolver. "Sorry."

"Let's get some coffee. Then maybe you can tell me what this is all about."

Mary had left a pot going on the stove. Newman poured a double shot of whiskey into his cup. Avidan took just coffee. They sat considering one another.

"Is this how you guys normally do business?"

The major shrugged. "Unfortunately, certain precautions are necessary. If the threat wasn't always so real, it would be our national paranoia."

"Okay. So?"

"We need a favor from you. We don't like to ask these things, but sometimes circumstances leave us no choice." Dark eyes flashed a kind of whimsy. "It concerns the Reverend Clayton Taylor, who seems to have become a fan of yours."

Newman just looked at him.

"The fact is," said Zvi Avidan, "we have been keeping an eye on the reverend for some time now. Not only has he been reaching a growing audience with his far right, racist overtones, but he seems to be building a political power base that could eventually reach far enough to threaten Israel's security."

"Why Israel?"

"Because our military and economic well-being still largely depends on American support. If a hostile majority in Washington suddenly decided to end that support, if it decided to favor the Arabs and the multinational oil interests, our survival could easily be threatened." The major smiled with a teacher's patience. "So you see, Lieutenant, we're forced to have more than a casual interest in the American political scene."

"I still don't understand what any of this has to do with me."

Avidan lit a cigarette and drank his coffee, a man accustomed to his own pace. "Taylor made you an unusual offer last night. What did you think of it?"

"How did you know about that?"

"We left a microphone in his studio dressing room and turned lucky. Usually his security people pick up everything we put in. This time they were either careless or didn't expect him to be in the room long enough to warrant that careful a search."

Newman shook his head. Emptying the coffee from his

cup, he refilled it with whiskey. Avidan watched without expression, but Newman could almost feel him taking silent inventory. Fine. He could carry the latest intelligence on the alcoholic Jews of the Diaspora back to Jerusalem.

"So?" said Avidan. "What did you think of Taylor's proposition?"

"The man must think I'm an idiot."

"No. He's very impressed with you."

"Then *he's* an idiot."

"I'm afraid not." The major glanced briefly, wistfully, around Newman's kitchen, at the assortment of sparkling American appliances and at the sun streaming brightly through the windows. "Actually, Lieutenant, what we would like you to do is accept his proposition."

"What?" said Newman dumbly.

"When he next contacts you, we'd like you to talk further with him, listen carefully to all the specifics of his offer, and finally agree to what he asks. It would be most valuable to us. We would at least have a chance to learn what he is up to."

"You can go fuck yourself."

Avidan looked mildly reproachful.

"Listen," said Newman. "Where the hell do you get off coming to me with your meathead ideas? Why me? I'm no goddamned Israeli."

"But you *are* a Jew."

"I'm an American."

"You're a Jew first."

"Like hell I am. Jesus, that's exctly the kind of Zionist conspiracy shit that creeps like Taylor feed on. And apart from everything else, you're asking an American citizen to spy for a foreign government. And that's goddamn treason."

"Israel is America's closest Mideast ally, not its enemy. And keeping a watchful eye on Clayton Taylor is far more likely to turn up some kind of hatemongering, fascist subversion than any kind of classified military information."

"I don't care what you call it. It's still working undercover for a foreign power."

Avidan exhaled slowly. He suddenly looked tired. "I cannot understand how any Jew, anywhere, could regard Israel as a foreign country. We have five thousand years of blood flowing in the Jordan. Our entire heritage lies buried in Jerusalem."

"My entire heritage lies buried on the island of Manhattan. Get someone else to play spy for you."

"There *is* no one else who has your opportunity."

They sat in silence. Through an open window, Avidan watched the sun sparkle on the Atlantic. Overhead, a plane headed south from Kennedy.

"I'm sorry," said Newman. His anger spent, he was able to be more sympathetic. He actually had warm, deeply rooted feelings for the Israelis, even a certain pride. In a hostile world, they had proven to be this century's survivors. He felt sure they would manage to go right on surviving without him.

Zvi Avidan shook his hand at the door. "Maybe I came at you too hard, too abruptly, with this. In a few days you may feel differently. If I may, I'll contact you again."

10

Gaynor struggled through four drafts of a letter to the Reverend Clayton Taylor. Considering it one of the more significant statements he had ever tried to make, he wanted it exactly right. In its final version, it said:

Reverend Clayton Taylor:
I watched your televised discussion with Lieutenant Newman the other night and found your subtly implied racism even more offensive than usual. You call yourself a minister of God, yet you preach hate instead of love, lies instead of truth. I not only reject your approval of what I

am doing, I resent it. There is not a single substantive issue that we could possibly be in agreement on. I despise everything you stand for. It's hard to believe that any civilized human being in this century would dare voice praise for the racist policies of the Third Reich, the creator of man's ultimate abomination, the Holocaust. Yet, as I understood it the other night, you have evidently managed to do even this. You are a malignancy under God.

He signed the letter THE APOSTLE and mailed copies to the *Times*, the *Post*, the *News*, the Associated Press, and to the major radio and television networks.

"I don't like that clown in his silly mask calling you a malignancy under God," said Melissa Bradberry. She had clipped a summary of the Apostle's letter out of the *Washington Post* and brought it with her to the Virginia house. "It's offensive and humiliating."

"Actually, it shows a rather nice turn of phrase."

"I don't understand how you can take this sort of thing so lightly, Clayton."

They were in an upstairs bedroom. The heavy breathing was over, and a late afternoon sun filtered through light blue curtains.

"I'm a man in public life," said Taylor. "I attack individuals, groups, and sacred institutions. It's only logical that I should be attacked in return." He looped an arm about her breasts and felt the flesh quiver. "Besides, there are undoubtedly as many who would agree with the description as not."

"They're fools."

Eyes half closed, he was perhaps as close to relaxation as was possible for him. He lived as a stranger in an alien land, the self-determined head of a shadowy cabal, secure nowhere. Despite almost constant security, he knew he could be shot down at any time in any crowd and the police would have the blood hosed off the pavement and the traffic flowing before you could say a fast amen. And who would really care? His parents were long gone, and he was without family or close friends. Which was exactly as he had chosen it. Still, at occasional rare moments it was not unpleasant to hear a few words of unquestioned support, even if they came from another man's wife.

"I wish Dexter had your ability to shrug these things off," Melissa said. "He's impossible to live with when he or his policies are under attack."

"Then he never should have accepted an appointment to the State Department. The world being what it is, he's sure to be damned regardless of what he does." The reverend paused. "How did his Mideast trip go? There was very little in the media. I assume the Arabs and Israelis are being as frustrating and deadly as ever."

"Evidently not. In fact, Dexter came back happier than I've seen him in a long time."

"What did they do, send him home with a belly dancer?"

"Better than that." She hesitated, but only briefly. "There suddenly seems to be a possibility of real peace in the area. Dexter was able to get the promise of key concessions all around. He's absolutely thrilled. He feels it's a triumph for exactly the kind of quiet, personal diplomacy he's been pushing from the start."

Taylor's eyes were blank. "That's certainly marvelous news. I'm delighted to hear it."

"Only the president and a few of his top advisers know. I don't think Dexter would have told even me if he could have resisted bragging. There's a lot of talking still ahead and any leak could be dangerous."

"Then maybe you shouldn't have told me."

She kissed him. "Dear Christ," she whispered. "If I can't trust *you*, then who does that leave?"

"God."

When Gaynor heard the news reports of Frank Galt's release, he took the subway to a public phone booth in Times Square and put through a call to Lieutenant Newman at Police Headquarters. When the detective answered, he covered his mouth with a handkerchief.

"This is the Apostle."

The wire just hummed.

"Did you hear me, Lieutenant?"

"I heard you. It's your dime. Go ahead and talk."

"I had hoped for better from you, Lieutenant. I went to a lot of trouble to give you Frank Galt, and all you did was put him right back out on the street."

"Sorry about that. But unfortunately the victim refused to press charges."

"That's what it said in the papers. Only it doesn't happen to be true."

The wire hummed once more. Waiting, Gaynor stared off at the Times Square traffic, pressing in all directions.

Newman finally spoke. "Why do you say that?"

"Because I called the woman and that's not what she told me." A lie, but a little fishing couldn't hurt.

Newman broke into a sudden spasm of coughing. It took him several moments to recover. "Goddamn cigarettes. They'll kill me before you do." He breathed deeply. "Okay. So what was her version?"

"That you pressured her into not pressing charges."

An operator cut in to ask for more money; Gaynor put another quarter in the slot.

"She must have been afraid to tell you the truth," said Newman. "Just as she was afraid of having to go into a courtroom and accuse a white man of attempted rape." He paused for several beats. "Anyway, why would I do something as pointless as setting Galt free if I didn't have to?"

"To set him up as bait for me."

Newman laughed. "Hey, I wish I was that smart."

"You are."

"Is that what you called to tell me?"

"I didn't want you to waste all that time watching Galt."

"What else have I got to do?"

"Go on TV and say nasty things about me."

Newman did not respond.

"I saw you on the show with Taylor," said Gaynor through his handkerchief. "It was crazy. All I had on my side was that hatemongering sonofabitch."

"Maybe that should tell you something."

"It tells me there's a certain kind of insanity loose."

Newman broke into another fit of coughing. Then the operator again interrupted to ask for money and Gaynor clanked another coin into the box. Crowds hurried past the booth where he stood. Theater marquees flashed lurid ads for sex shows. Cops patrolled in pairs. A bearded prophet carried a sign announcing the end of the world. A bag lady stopped to rummage among her worldly possessions. Far off, a siren wailed.

"I must be allergic to your voice," said Newman, recovering.

Gaynor stood watching the bag lady. The things that could finally happen to people.

Newman said, "It's characteristic, you know."

"What?"

"That you should be calling me. Teasing the hunter adds to the fun and games. Or does it just make you feel untouchable and superior?"

Gaynor turned away from the bag lady and saw the two patrol cars working their way through the traffic. They came in silence, without their sirens going. His brain seemed to react like a faulty machine. How about that? he thought, and he was out of the booth and pushing through the crowds before the first of the cars was able to reach the curb. He turned west on Forty-third Street, staying close to the building line. He felt his heart pump as he ran and heard his breath rush out. Then his bad leg gave way and he fell, hitting heavily on his elbows and rolling. Several passerby helped him to his feet. Keeping his head down and averted, he grunted a kind of thanks and moved on. He no longer ran, but walked very quickly. He glanced back. There were no cops behind him. Reaching Eighth Avenue, he walked uptown for two blocks. Then he stopped a cruising taxi, rode it to about a mile from his apartment, and took another cab the rest of the way.

Breathing normally again, he felt curiously exhilarated. That was some Newman. He found himself grinning. Maybe only a small victory, but a victory nonetheless. In his mind, he painted a huge spider lurking in its web. It wore Newman's face.

Gaynor had pushed as far as he could with the charcoal and was now working with oils. He had stretched a huge, rectangular canvas, taller than he. Why not? If you can't paint good, paint big. Still, just handling, just breathing the paints almost seemed enough for now. As though the touch and smell of the pigments alone might in some way seep through his pores and turn him into an artist again, albeit a different one. And he did feel as though he were beginning over. Whatever he had been, he was not anymore. He had learned that much just from the charcoal.

He was working broadly, wet in wet, the entire canvas

brushed in and flowing. He was still chasing ghosts, their forms barely discernible in the same amorphous brightness he had first envisioned back in his hotel room. Phantoms rising. Gently, he dragged them with a dry sable brush, feeling the tug of pigment on soft hair, seeing the forms merge even more. But not too much, he told himself, not so much that they'd be lost entirely, none of that fading into the abstract. Although for the first time he could actually feel the temptation. How much simpler just to let it all blend together and let everyone see what they wanted. Everyone a shareholder. Except that he wanted no shareholders. This was all his. He was the one who had suffered for the knowledge. He was the one who knew. And whatever was going to come would have to come through him.

Yet in certain parts, painting, he felt much as he always had. He sensed that important lessons were to be learned here, that deep secrets were about to be revealed. He still responded with the same reverence for the whole business, still felt awed by the process itself. Pure wonder. A brush moved, paint swirled, and what had been nothing became something. Typically, too, he was still impressed most by what he understood least. And his newly pursued ghosts, those few faint images floating out of their pale mists, were cryptic enough to overwhelm.

He stopped work only after the last of the light had gone. As if once having started again, it would have been an unforgivable breach of contract to quit an instant sooner. *Why?* He asked the same question he had always asked but still had no answer. And when his wife and sons had asked, he'd had no answer for them, either. And they had deserved one because it was from them he had stolen the time. A minute here, an hour there. Bits and pieces that had finally added up to their lives. Jane had once called him the most selfish man she knew. She had later recanted but was probably right. Denying it then, he admitted it now. Self-indulgence came with the territory. It was as essential to the calling as paints and brushes.

It had not been worth it.

Jane arrived, bearing fillet of flounder. She insisted on cooking dinner for him. "You eat too much meat," she said.

"Last time you said I ate too much bread and eggs."

"That, too. You've got to eat more fish."

"I don't like fish."

"Nonsense. It's all in your mind."

Eating together, it felt absolutely natural having her in the apartment, as though she had never left. Except, of course, that there were just the two of them.

"The fish was very good," he said afterward. "I must admit it."

"It'll keep you living forever."

"That's hardly an inducement."

It was his first slip of the evening. To cover it, he told her about Newman holding him on the phone while he had the call traced and radio cars dispatched. He told the story lightly, making the incident seem more amusing than it had actually been. Still, there was pleasure in simply being able to share it.

Jane nodded and smiled. She was a superb listener. It was one of the reasons for her success. "You certainly make it all sound very jolly. But what would have happened if you hadn't seen those police cars in time?"

He laughed. "Then my old buddy Newman would have gotten a big surprise."

"And you'd go to jail?"

"What else?"

"On what charges?"

"I imagine they'd have quite a variety to choose from by now."

"Like murder, for shooting that drug dealer?"

"No doubt."

"And that doesn't bother you?"

He watched the deliberate way she smoked. She smoked even more than he did, which was a lot. "In my place, would it bother *you?*"

"No." She smiled. "We're really quite a pair, aren't we?"

He stared at himself in a mirror on the opposite wall. Who was this man?

"Richard?"

He knew what she was about to say before she said it.

"May I sleep with you tonight?"

Ah, he was becoming psychic.

It was like being with another woman, not the woman he

had married and lived with for all those years, not the mother of his children, not the wife who had left him because he had failed to provide what she had wanted and needed. Taking her clothes off was like peeling away layers of memory. Once she was naked, they had no past.

It was the same for her.

"Ah, God, look at you," she whispered when she saw the network of scars she had never seen before. She hugged his head between her breasts. "I have marks, too, darling. Only mine don't show like yours."

His arms went around her. This poor broken vessel. For a while, at least, maybe he could hold the pieces together.

Gaynor's thinking was becoming so convoluted that he no longer recognized it as his own. Whose then? Newman's? Or maybe it was just long overdue training in reality. But was the reality also Newman's?

What he was trying to do was think the way the detective might be thinking. Since the Apostle had called to say he knew Frank Galt had been released purely as bait, it seemed logical to assume that even if Newman had intended such use for the rapist, he would have dropped the whole idea. Why waste time on a trap that had no chance of working? And if this were the case, Gaynor wanted a second try at Galt. Only this time he would make it stick. The man was a chronic, unregenerate offender. He had no business being loose on the streets.

Still, there was no sense in being careless. There was always a chance that Newman did have someone watching Galt. So Gaynor thought it best not to use his own car. Just a glimpse of his license plate and the Apostle would be undone. But leasing a car was also out because he would have to show either a driver's license or a credit card. Which left him with only one option. He would have to steal a car. The idea alone made him laugh. Evidently once a line of reasoning was accepted, everything else became not only possible, but logical. And considering all he had done so far, grand theft, auto, should offer no great problem.

Not so. Special skills were required for every line of work, and he turned out to be less than qualified as a car thief. It always seemed easy enough when he saw it done in the movies, but he had no way of getting a set of master keys, and he knew absolutely nothing about how to jump wires. But after a bit of thought, he came up with what seemed like a viable alternative.

Early one evening he stood across Sixth Avenue from the Hilton at the height of the check-in rush. He watched guests driving up, one after another, unloading their bags and leaving their cars double-parked at the curb until the attendants could park them. At one point, Gaynor counted eleven cars in line, with three men working. He waited until all the attendants were out of sight, then quickly dodged across the avenue and slid into the last car in line. It was a blue Pontiac with Ohio plates and the keys in the ignition. Calmly, Gaynor started the car and pulled out into the uptown traffic.

An hour later, having replaced the Ohio plates with a New York set he had lifted in a Yonkers shopping plaza, he was ready for his second try at Frank Galt.

Certain hours were reserved for the twins. It was not unpleasant. Conjured up at will, they brought a sweet, aching sadness that was almost pleasurable. When his sons were very young, perhaps three or four, on Sunday mornings he often took them to Riverside Park, where they enjoyed shooting their toy pistols and playing cowboys and Indians with him. They had not yet discovered it was the Indians who were really the good guys, so they were always the cowboys and he was always the Indians. The game would finish up the same way every time, with Gaynor stretched out dead on the grass and the twins singing a mournful cowboy lament at his side. His only possibility of revival was to receive ritual kisses from them both, one on each cheek. Then, like Lazarus, he would rise from the dead.

But one Sunday, lying there like a good dead Indian and awaiting his life-renewing ritual, the kisses failed to arrive. Peering out of one half-open eye, he saw his sons watching him from behind a tree. Evidently, this time they had decided to let him stay dead. Good-bye, Daddy, and off they went through the bushes. Gaynor lay very still. Ah, they were on to him at last. They knew what a terrible father they'd been stuck with and were dumping him once and for all. Abandoned by his own flesh and blood. Yet who could blame them?

After a few moments he saw them returning. They came

slowly, whispering together in their big cowboy hats. Would they revive him or let him stay dead forever? They stopped a few feet away while his fate hung in the balance. Then, apparently deciding that a lousy father was better than no father at all, they knelt and kissed him.

Gaynor wished he could have offered them the same miracle. But what had there been left for him to kiss?

By eleven-forty of the third night, he was almost sure Galt was about to try again. The rapist had already taken on a clearly definable shape for him. They all seemed to, finally. If you watched you saw it. And he had been watching.

Tonight, parked in his stolen Pontiac across from a large diner in South Brooklyn, he could see Galt eating alone beside a window. A waitress stood talking to him, laughing at something he had said. She was pretty and she was black. For the past half hour Gaynor had been observing them as he might have observed two performers in a silent film. Those two sad actors. There was something almost indecent about watching people who did not know they were being watched. But while he was watching, who was watching him?

He had, of course, taken every precaution. He had kept very long intervals between Galt and himself. He had watched his own back at every possible moment. He had never parked anywhere near where Galt had parked. Still, it was impossible to know such things with certainty. Which was probably just part of the excitement. That much he had learned about himself. The very nature of what he was doing was intended to expose his person, to make himself vulnerable. If he wanted to be safe, he had only to stay at home.

Near midnight, Galt spoke once more to the waitress, paid his check, and left. He stood casually in front of the diner for a moment, looking about. Then he walked around to a back parking lot and out of Gaynor's sight.

Gaynor waited. It was a Saturday night, and even at this hour there was a lot of traffic on Flatbush Avenue. A few miles south, over the Atlantic, the lights of a late plane could be seen drifting down toward Kennedy. Gaynor stared off at it. Just a speck in the night, yet intense human actions were going on within. The sky was pure, without threat. Still, something was always there, waiting.

The waitress came out, lighting a cigarette. Finished for the night, she wore a tightly belted raincoat over her uniform. Raising her collar against the chill, she, too, walked around to the parking lot and disappeared.

Moments later, Gaynor saw her drive out in a yellow Toyota and head southeast along Flatbush Avenue. She appeared to be alone in the car. Gaynor sat there for another few moments. When no one followed the woman, he turned on his motor and started in the same direction. He checked his rearview mirror. Nothing looked suspicious at his back, just a normal flow of traffic. The Toyota was now more than two blocks ahead but was easy to keep in sight because of its color. When it reached Avenue U, it turned east along a line of small-boat marinas edging the waters of Mill Basin. Gaynor followed. No one made the turn behind him.

It was a clear, starry night, and Kennedy's lights gleamed brightly from across Jamaica Bay. This was the closest Gaynor had been to the airport since the crash, and he could feel it reacting on him. His heart pumped faster and his breath raced to keep up. Which suddenly made the nature of his condition seem so curious, even ridiculous, that he was forced to see it as though for the first time. What was he doing here, driving along the back roads of Brooklyn in a stolen car? He had to be comical, dangerous, and crazy all at the same time. Or was he simply bewitched, filled with demons? Either way, he saw little possibility of a cure.

There was very few cars on this road, only two, now, between Gaynor and the Toyota. In back, he saw no cars at all. The area was one of small docks and boats, of wetlands and marshgrass and scattered houses built close to the water. The Toyota turned left, away from the bay, onto a narrow trail. The car behind it kept going straight. Gaynor slowed. When he came to the intersection, he drove a short distance farther, cut his lights, and stopped a few feet off the road in the marshgrass. A moment later he saw the Toyota's lights go out also. Taking his mask, his revolver, and some lengths of nylon cord, he left the car and started to walk.

He was on an unpaved, sandy road with bulrushes crowding in. There were no houses here, only an occasional fishing shack. The smell of low tide hung heavy. When he had walked about three hundred yards, he stopped to put on his mask and check his revolver and silencer. Then he moved forward once more.

Gleaming like an oversized toy in the starlight, the Toyota sat parked in a small, cleared area to the right of the road. Gaynor quietly approached. He looked through the rear window and saw two half-naked bodies thrashing about on the back seat. The woman was pinned on her back with Galt astride her. Eyes wide, she stared fixedly at a long hunting knife he held in one hand. The pale halves of his buttocks heaved and thrust. The act of love.

Gaynor checked the rear door lock on the side behind the rapist's back. The latch was up. Moving quickly, he yanked open the door and rammed his gun against Galt's naked backside.

"Freeze or you get it straight up the ass."

Galt grunted and stopped in midthrust. The woman's eyes blinked over his shoulder at the Apostle mask.

"Drop the blade," said Gaynor.

The knife fell.

"Now back out of there. Slowly. And just remember. I owe you one from last time."

Galt slid out. With his pants tangled about his ankles, he looked much less threatening than ridiculous. Fear had already shriveled him in front. He started to turn, but Gaynor stopped him with the revolver against his neck.

"Hey, gimme a break," he complained. "Shit, man, she's only nigger cunt."

Gaynor was tempted to squeeze the trigger. This creature was less than human. Instead, he reversed the gun and swung the butt hard. Galt fell without a sound.

"You really the Apostle?" The waitress had adjusted her clothing and climbed out of the car. "I mean, no fooling?"

Gaynor nodded. He had put away his gun and was tying Galt's ankles and wrists. "He didn't cut you with that knife, did he?"

"No."

The woman took two quick steps and kicked Galt hard between the legs. Gaynor winced. She tried it again, but he caught her ankle. "Easy. We don't want to mess up the evidence."

"Come on. Let me fix him good."

"You can fix him good in court."

"Don't you worry. I'll do that, too."

"I hope so. The last woman was afraid to press charges."

"Well, that ain't this woman." She peered closely at his eyes through the mask holes. "Hey, what do you look like under there?"

"Like an Apostle of God."

She flashed a grin. "You think I don't believe that? I bet you do."

He suddenly straightened up, listening.

"What's wrong?" she said.

Gaynor was still listening when a voice came out of the bulrushes. "This is the police. There are three guns on you. Put up your hands."

Well, thought Gaynor. He felt absolutely nothing. Slowly, he raised his hands. Off in the darkness, he heard water splash. Then he saw three men in plainclothes coming toward him with drawn revolvers.

"Hey, you guys got it all wrong," said the woman. She was very excited. "He just saved me. The dude you want is all laced up there on the ground."

No one paid attention to her.

"I'd swear on a Bible there was no one behind me," said Gaynor, speaking to the closest detective in his mask-muffled voice. "How did you do it?"

The man's face was shadowy in the darkness. "We were watching Galt. When we saw him slip into the back of the Toyota, we just stuck a beeper under the bumper and followed its signal."

Electronics. Gaynor was waiting for one of the cops to come over and remove his mask, but no one appeared to be in any particular rush. Newman would have had it off the first minute.

"You cops are really something!" yelled the woman, growing angrier by the second. "I get raped by a honky with a knife, and all you give a damn about is sticking it to the guy that helped me."

"Easy, sister," said one of the detectives. "We'll get to you in a minute."

"Who you calling sister? I ain't your sister."

The other cop grinned. "What's the big deal? You never got laid in a car before? I don't see no blood."

She went straight for his face with her nails. The force and unexpectedness of the attack sent him stumbling backward. The cop next to him grabbed for her arms. When the third

165

plainclothesman turned to watch what was happening, Gaynor started for the bulrushes.

He had to cover about twenty feet of open ground, and he ran crouched over and weaving. There was a shot. He heard it at the precise instant he felt the bullet hit his arm. It threw him off balance, but he kept moving. There was a second shot. This one missed him entirely.

He heard a shout. "Stop that goddamned shooting. The lieutenant wants him alive."

Then he was in the bulrushes. He ran as fast as he could, head down, pushing his way through the tall, brackish-smelling weeds. At first he ran without conscious direction, just wanting to lose pursuit. When he felt his feet splashing through cold water, he began circling back toward where he had left the car. He was breathless but moving well, and the bulrushes and darkness made a perfect screen. Bless that woman, he thought, and for the first time realized that she had attacked the cop just to help him make a break for it. Well, he would send her flowers.

Behind him, he could hear the three detectives calling to one another as they thrashed through the high, spiked cattails. The darkness was confusing, and for a moment he was afraid he might have been running the wrong way. Then the ground began to rise slightly and he was on the road and saw the Pontiac. Twenty yards away was another car, the one the police must have arrived in. Gaynor punched holes in two of its tires with a pocket knife. Then he cut the radio microphone free and tossed it into the weeds. Seconds later he was driving away. When he glanced around, he saw that none of the detectives had reached the road.

He drove back to Flatbush Avenue, swung left onto the Belt Parkway, and headed for the Brooklyn-Battery Tunnel. His wounded arm felt numb but maneuverable, and he hoped this meant no bones were broken. From what he could tell, there seemed to be little bleeding. He had always been a good clotter, anyway. Driving, he felt pleasantly in control. That great icy feeling. Still, this had been the closest yet. An electronic beeper, of all things. He had a lot to learn but doubted he would have the time.

In Manhattan, he stopped to call Kate at the hospital. "What time are you off your shift?"

Her voice was cold, distant. She was still angry with him. "Why?"

"I need you."

"Well, I don't need you."

"I mean professionally."

There was a pause. "Goddamn you. I knew it. I'll bet you've been shot."

"Only a little bit."

"Where?"

"In South Brooklyn."

"If you dare make jokes I'll hang up."

"Upper left arm. The bleeding has stopped, and I don't think any bones are broken."

"Do you feel cold?"

"No."

"How far are you from home?"

"About fifteen minutes."

"Go home and get into bed," she said. "Shock can surprise you and it's dangerous. I'll be there in forty minutes."

She hung up.

He parked the stolen car on the street a few blocks from his apartment and walked the rest of the way. By the time he got home, he was no longer feeling so great. The fine icy feeling remained, but now he was shivering with it. There was also a slight dizziness when he bent or turned too quickly. Remembering Kate's warning, he undressed and got into bed.

The wound itself looked worse than he had expected. There were actually two wounds, one going in and one coming out, surrounded by spreading purple aureoles. They were in the fleshy part of his arm, just below the shoulder, and they were starting to hurt a great deal. I've been shot, he thought, and for some reason he found himself grinning like an idiot.

Kate came with a black leather medical bag and her most frigid, no-nonsense manner. He lay back happily, feeling like an ailing child whose mother has just arrived, taken over, and relieved him of all concern. He kissed her cheek. "Mommy."

She examined his arm. "You're lucky. If the bullet had hit a bone, you'd be headed for the hospital right this minute."

"I couldn't do that. Gunshot wounds have to be reported to the police."

"Too bad. Then you'd have lost your arm and probably died."

167

With brisk efficiency she cleaned and bandaged the wound, gave him a painkiller and an antibiotic and settled him warmly under the covers. "How did it happen?"

He told her.

"So you're not as smart as you thought you were," she said.

In bed, with Kate ministering to him, he almost felt himself back in the hospital. "I never thought I was smart."

"Well, you're not. How you could even have conceived of this whole Apostle stupidity is beyond me."

"I'm very creative."

"You're a jackass."

He grinned.

"Stop grinning. Throwing away your life is nothing to grin about. I haven't been able to get it out of my mind since I found out. In a single instant you changed everything for me."

"I'm sorry."

"No you're not. You're enjoying my involvement almost as much as your planned martyrdom." She took a long, deep breath. "All right," she said more calmly. "Clinically, I suppose it's understandable. You've gone through a frightful ordeal. You've suffered terrible physical and emotional trauma. Life has lost its appeal. You feel a need to justify your survival by sacrificing yourself in a noble and worthy quest. But what I *can't* understand is the utter silliness of how you've chosen to do it. You're stamping on cockroaches. Do you really think squashing a few measly bugs changes anything?"

"Listen. A few here, a few there."

Face set, she leaned toward him. "You were dead for me from the moment I saw that mask and gun. The only thing I had to decide after that was whether to say good-bye and start blocking you out right then or stay with you to the end."

"And what did you decide?"

"That I loved you," she said quietly. "That whatever crazy thing you felt you had to do, there was no way I could leave you to do it alone."

He was touched and it embarrassed him. He said nothing.

"Which doesn't mean I've stopped being furious at the petty waste of what you're doing. Still, that part can be corrected. And since I'm now involved, I've found a way to do it.''

"You're not a nurse. You're a director. Who said I wanted it corrected?"

"You don't know what you want. You're in extreme psychic trauma." Digging in her bag, she took out a newspaper clipping and handed it to him. "Here's what you want, dummy."

It was a *Times* report on his letter to Clayton Taylor. He stared blankly at it.

"You still don't know what you've got there, do you?"

"I guess not. What have I got?"

"Your quest. Your worthy cause. Your crusade. Whatever."

He gazed at her through a thickening haze of medication.

"Your letter said it all. Superb. When I first saw some of the quotes, I was so excited and proud, I wished everyone could have known it was you who wrote them. They said everything about Taylor that needed to be said. And for the first time I began seeing a chance for something more in your Apostle's future than just this pathetic and terminal vendetta."

"What did you see?"

"The Apostle taking on the devil. All out. This man is evil, Richard. He's all the hosts of darkness. Squash him, and you'll be doing far more than just squashing a few bugs."

Gaynor smiled. "That's a job for Billy Graham. The Apostle is no evangelist."

"The Apostle is anything you choose to make him. He has the media's attention. People listen to what he says."

The drugs were making his eyes droop.

"Don't you dare fall asleep on me now."

He opened his eyes but seemed to be looking at her underwater. He said, "Words aren't the Apostle's appeal. He has to do more than write letters. He has to act. He has to pose a threat."

"Okay. Let him act. Let him pose a threat to Taylor."

"How?"

"Let him say Taylor has to stop peddling his lies and hate or . . .''

"Or what?"

She stared at him as if trying to stamp his image on her brain. Sitting on the edge of the bed, she was a white-clad mystic.

"Well?" he said.

"You mean the Apostle would have to threaten to shoot Taylor if he refuses to stop?"

"What else? Excommunicate him?"

"Do you think that kind of threat would scare him off?"

"Probably not."

"Then what?"

"Simple. The Apostle either goes through with it or backs off."

She sat there in silence. Go on, he thought, just a little more and you're all the way home. To keep himself awake, he began painting a midnight swamp of rotting mangroves and deadly southern snakes. Zephyrs of gray gas rose, barely visible in the darkness.

A look of hers went straight through him. Suddenly he was no longer alone. He had a partner.

11

The Nineteenth Century Club was housed in an aristocratic old limestone building that did its architectural best to help its longtime tenant live up to its name. Indeed, from the moment Newman followed Michael Westley past the club's worn, neoclassic façade on East Forty-third Street, he felt himself adrift in an earlier time. And the dark mahogany walls, high-ceilinged rooms, and faded furnishings only added to the illusion. Even the exclusively male, dinner-suited membership, unsullied by any hint of a female presence, seemed to project an aura of carefully preserved hard-line chauvinism. Looking about, Newman was sure he must have seen these same sharp, patrician faces in paintings by Stuart and Copley. He was also sure he was the only Jew in the place.

Still, it was he who was presented as the main speaker of the evening, and it was these same austere gentlemen who listened to him with interest and applauded loudly when he was through. Afterward, the commissioner took special pains to introduce him to no less than three past or present United States senators, an associate justice of the Supreme Court, a former governor, and the chairman of a multinational banking institution whose assets were greater than those of many sovereign nations. "You've become my star," said Westley. "I really enjoy showing you off." It had only been that evening that Newman had learned that Westley was not only a long-standing member of the celebrated club but was also its current president.

When most of the members had left, the police commissioner took Newman upstairs to a private lounge on the second floor. There was a good fire going, and portraits of America's early leaders lined the paneled walls. They sat quietly, drinking and smoking. My grandfather should see me now, thought Newman, and wondered when, if ever, he would stop thinking like an immigrant Jew. How many generations did it finally take? Or was it less a question of time than blood?

"I received a letter from Clayton Taylor this morning," said Westley. "Oddly enough, much of it concerned you."

Seeming to come from nowhere, the remark hung in the room like cordite after an explosion.

"He was very complimentary. He wanted me to know what an exceptional spokesman he thought the department had in you."

"Sure," said Newman. "I'm his favorite Jew."

"What's that supposed to mean?"

The detective repeated parts of his conversation with Taylor at the television studio.

"Interesting." Westley sat considering it. "Have you heard from him since?"

"No."

"Well, when he does approach you again, I'd like you to do me a favor."

"Kick him in the ass?"

"Nothing so simple. What I'd like is for you to indicate you might be willing to go along with some of the things he asked."

Newman, finding his mouth open, quietly filled it with brandy.

"Don't seem overly eager," said Westley. "The man is no fool. At first just tell him you'd like to know more. Then you can agree to at least give it a try."

"But why, for God's sake?"

"Because I'm about to enter my political phase and both of you can be very helpful to me. Taylor, because he's become the major spokesman for all the splinter groups that make up the growing conservative movement in this country. And you, because I need someone I can trust to let me know what he may really be up to." Westley seemed vaguely amused. "Don't look so astonished. Did Teddy Roosevelt stop at police commissioner?"

The lieutenant stared at him. He had no idea what to say. About to mention Major Avidan's similar request of the other day, he thought better of it and remained silent.

Westley lit a fresh cigar. "These are troubled times, Jay. Even the liberals are afraid to walk the streets at night. A far right law-and-order backlash has been building for years. You've seen the reaction yourself whenever you've spoken. Quite frankly, I've been using your public appearances as a kind of litmus test, and the results have been very encouraging. And not only with the general public. The group you addressed tonight represents about as concentrated an amalgam of political sophistication and power as you'll find anywhere, and they bought every single concept we were selling."

We, thought Newman. Of course. Suddenly it all made a weird kind of sense. "I'm really pretty thick, aren't I?"

"How could you have known? I gave you no hint. I wanted to be sure the timing was right and I had the necessary backing."

"And now you're sure?"

Westley turned toward the fire, his face reflecting its glow. "There were men here this evening who not only want me to be governor of New York but who can literally ensure that it happens. As these things work, the final counting of votes becomes little more than a formality."

"Why only governor?"

The commissioner's smile was as controlled as his voice. "I know you think you're joking, but with the right combination of circumstances anything is possible. That's why I'm so interested in Taylor. He's been attracting a lot of attention lately on the national scene. And you never can tell in politics." He pointed to twin portraits of the second and sixth presidents that hung side by side over the mantel. "My mother's name was Adams, in case you didn't know."

Newman hadn't known.

"All of this really shocks you, doesn't it?" said Westley.

"A bit. Though I suppose it shouldn't. You do have all the credentials—looks, temperament, background, religion. Everything for the perfect candidate. But if this was what you wanted, why did you spend almost thirty years in the cops?"

"Because until now that was where I wanted to be. But nothing stays the same. Now I want different things. I also have different things to offer. Besides, where can I go from police commissioner if I don't go into politics? To a corporate law practice? I have to feel committed to something important. I have to take sides on significant issues." He fell silent. "Will you help me, Jay?"

"You know I will."

Westley touched Newman's arm. It was an awkward, self-conscious gesture from a man who had done few such things in his life.

It was only as they were leaving that the commissioner asked, "What's happening with your Apostle campaign?"

"I almost had him last night."

"Almost?"

"He took our bait like a hungry fish. Three detectives stood pointing their pieces at him. Then the woman he'd helped suddenly created a distraction, my men turned into Keystone Kops, and he got away."

"They never saw his face?"

"No."

"My wife will be happy to hear it."

Half an hour later, Newman was driving home on the Belt Parkway when he glanced at the car in the next lane and saw the tough, unsmiling face of Major Avidan. Somehow, he was not surprised. He pulled into a parking area that faced Mill Basin and waited for the Israeli to join him.

"What took you so long?" he said.

Avidan considered his dinner suit. "You look very nice, all dressed up. Very high class."

"Hell. I'm a high-class cop." He offered Avidan a cigarette and lit it for him. Then he lit one for himself.

"You're being much more friendly tonight," said the major. "Does that mean you've reconsidered?"

"Yes."

"May I ask what changed your mind?"

"I heard someone whistling 'Hatikvah.' "

Avidan shrugged. "Whatever your reason, we're grateful."

They sat looking at the water. The lights of a fishing boat coming in drifted slowly past.

"Okay," said Newman. "What now?"

"It's as I told you last time. Wait until Taylor contacts you. Listen to his proposals and finally agree to go along with them. I'll be in communication at regular intervals. If you should ever need me, call Colonel Netter from a public telephone. He'll let me know."

"That's all?"

"For the time being."

"What am I supposed to be looking for?"

"There's no telling."

"Then how will I know whether I've found it?"

"You'll know," said Avidan.

The lights of a second fishing boat slid past, following the first. Its engines chugged softly, and their sound mixed with the hum of traffic from the parkway.

"I'm afraid I don't have any more information," said the major. "If I did, I'd give it to you."

Newman doubted that. A sabra, he thought, probably from one of the border kibbutzim. Most of the native Israelis he had met appeared to have a style all their own. There seemed to be nothing traditionally Jewish about them. Their parents were sensitive, nervous, highly strung, with awkward bodies. *Their* nervous systems were forged of copper wire, their bodies those of a new tribe of Hebrew Tarzans roaming the hills of Galilee. Where their parents were intense, warm, and communicative, they were tough and remote. Maybe that was exactly what we finally needed for survival, but its ultimate effect was to make him feel he had more in common with any black man off the streets of Harlem.

"Good luck," said Zvi Avidan, "and thank you again." He went back to his car and drove off.

A detailed map of the City of New York covered almost an entire wall of Newman's office. On it, the detective had pinned red flags to indicate the exact points at which the Apostle had surfaced. Newman spent hours studying the flags, trying to put together some sort of pattern from their locations. As far as he could tell, they might just as easily have been tossed in at random.

The latest flag had been added only that morning. It was on West 103rd Street, just off Riverside Drive, and marked the precise spot at which a stolen out-of-town automobile had been picked up. The car was a dark blue Pontiac with switched New York plates and had been quickly identified as the automobile used by the Apostle on the night of his abortive capture. When Newman had Forensics go over it, they found bloodstains on the front seat.

He questioned Detective Mulcahy, the man who had done the shooting. "How many rounds did you get off?"

"Two."

"Where were you aiming?"

Mulcahy hesitated. He was very young and he looked worried.

"Torso? Legs? What?"

"It all happened so fast, Lieutenant."

"But you still had time to get off two shots, right?"

The cop was silent. He sat chewing his lower lip.

"Is this the first time you've ever fired at a suspect?"

"Yeah."

"Listen," said Newman more softly. "Most cops serve their full stretch and retire without shooting anyplace but on the range. If you're not a little psycho, it's upsetting to fire at another human being. I understand that. So just take it easy. All I'm trying to find out is where you might have hit the guy."

"I don't know. I was excited and rushing, so I probably jerked the damn trigger. But when I fire offhand at the range, I usually wind up high and to the right."

"Okay, let's look at it. If you got him in a leg, he couldn't have run fast enough to get away. If he was head-shot, he couldn't have run at all. And if he caught one in the back, he'd have been down within yards. Also, there wasn't very much blood in the car, and what was there was on the right side of the driver's seat. So I'd say you probably got him someplace around the right shoulder or arm.''

Mulcahy still looked unhappy. It was enough to make Newman question the other detectives for the third time. "We're leaning toward a right arm or shoulder wound. Would you two be willing to go along with that?''

They looked at one another.

"I guess so," said Robbins.

"What the hell does that mean?''

"It was dark, and there was a lot happening," said Loretti. "We wouldn't want to swear to it.''

"Well then, what would you swear to?'' asked Newman. "That he made the three of you look like a bunch of first-class schmucks?''

Still, he had more to work on than he'd had only a few days before. He sent people to check all the hospitals for possible unreported gunshot wounds, and he turned Forensics loose on the blue Pontiac. Going a step further, he told his detectives to fan out from the spot where the car was discovered and see if any bloodstains could be picked up within a radius of six blocks. "Check all sidewalks, gutters, building entrances, steps, and lobbies," Newman ordered. "I have a feeling he lives pretty close to where he dumped that car. I doubt whether he'd have taken a cab at that hour. The cabby might have remembered him. And he certainly wasn't about to go for any long walks with a bleeding bullet wound. So let's focus on that six-block area and see what we come up with.''

Newman could feel himself beginning to sniff out the warm, sweet scent of the man. And were the upper reaches of his right arm actually starting to ache a bit? He laughed. Voodoo. Nevertheless, it took nearly half a bottle of Jack Daniel's before he could rid himself of the phantom pain.

Alone and half dozing, Newman became aware of Clayton Taylor staring at him from the television screen opposite his bed. He heard the minister preaching one of his regular thirty-second spots, sponsored by the American Fundamental

Church in its effort to bring God back into the American home.

"The sad truth of it is," the Reverend was saying, "that, left to our own resources, we poor humans have no higher principle in our hearts than self-love. We are wholly given over to it. Nothing we do has any higher origin than self-interest. We are so put together that it is against our nature to desire anything but our own advantage and our own glory. We are less benevolent than animals, who never ask anything more than to live from day to day. We are, in fact, fiercer than the lion and the tiger in the jungle. So much so that armies of police are required to keep us from tearing one another apart. Only the benevolence of Christ can save us from ourselves. His arms are open to us. Let us not deny Him . . ."

"Let's go see my blue-eyed brother," the detective told Mary when she got home.

He meant Paul Newman. He had never met the actor but had always felt a strong affinity for the cool, free-wheeling type of character that Newman portrayed so convincingly on the screen. Besides, they shared not only the same family name but the same birthday. Undeniable bonds. To the point where once, passing by the film star on Fifth Avenue, the lieutenant had felt a very real sense of shock that the man could actually look straight at him and not even know who he was.

Tonight, watching his larger-than-life namesake as a failed, boozy lawyer, desperately fighting for personal and professional redemption against the combined forces of a powerful law firm, a corrupt judge, and a traitorous lover, Newman clutched Mary's hand and suffered two hours of tension and almost palpable pain before Paul, truth, and justice finally prevailed.

Driving home, the detective felt limp but exalted. "Christ, that was good. It really tore me up."

Mary leaned over and kissed him. "I adore going to the movies with you. You're wonderful, like a kid at a Saturday matinee. You love, believe, and are moved by everything."

"You didn't like the picture?"

"It was okay, a pleasant little fairy tale. The best part was watching it with you, feeling your involvement. That's one of the things I love most about you. You've spent a lifetime working in a sewer, and you still have faith in the triumph of good over evil."

"You're making me sound naive."

"No. Pure."

"There's a difference?"

They were driving over the Fifty-ninth Street Bridge, and the metal grillwork hummed beneath them. Ahead, in the distance, a giant Pepsi-Cola sign cast a red glow over the darkened factories of Long Island City.

"A big difference," she said. "Naive is simply not knowing how bad things really are. Pure is knowing the worst but believing it doesn't have to be that way."

"You mean I can't even learn from experience?" He laughed. "I guess what I really liked tonight was the idea of Paul being a boozer and still coming out on top."

"Naturally."

He had Mary pull a pint bottle and two paper cups out of the glove compartment and pour them drinks.

"To old Paul and Jay," he toasted. "Up the boozer brothers."

"May you both prevail."

They drank solemnly. Newman drove one-handed. Leaving the bridge, they passed beneath a rattling elevated train and swung onto Woodhaven Boulevard.

"Who do we drink to next?" he asked.

She gave it careful thought. "How about the Apostle?"

"What about him?"

"May he also prevail."

"Impossible. How can we both win?"

"I thought we decided you're one and the same."

Newman held out his cup for a refill.

"It's kind of a cute idea," she said.

"But not very logical. You once said he was crazy and I wasn't."

She poured more whiskey into their cups. "Maybe I was wrong."

"About who? Him or me?"

"Maybe a bit of both."

"Thanks a lot."

She laughed. "The word 'crazy' doesn't really mean anything to psychologists, you know. It's a legal, not a medical, term. Actually, we're all a little strange."

The traffic pressed together and crawled to a halt. Newman sat drinking his whiskey and staring at the taillights of the car in front. "It wasn't reported in the press, but the Apostle was shot the other night."

"My God!" Mary spilled some of her drink. "What are you telling me? He's dead? You killed him?"

He looked at her. Then the traffic moved and he started to drive once more.

"Jay! For God's sake!"

"I didn't shoot him. I wasn't even there when it happened. And he wasn't killed. He escaped. So he probably wasn't hurt very seriously."

Mary gulped the remains of her drink and poured herself another.

"I didn't know you felt that strongly about him," Newman said.

"Neither did I."

They crawled along, bumper to bumper.

"Does this mean you may be getting him soon?" she asked.

"Who knows? Maybe seeing some of his own blood will scare him off. Maybe he'll quit."

She studied her cup. "Why don't *you* quit?"

"Quit what? The case or the cops?"

"You're a lawyer. You keep talking about your belief in the law. Why don't you really practice it?"

"You mean I could be a boozy shyster like brother Paul?"

"You could be anything you want."

"I think I'd rather be a boozy cop."

He braked for a light. The car behind, riding too close, hit his bumper. Mary almost went into the windshield.

He swore softly. "You okay?"

"Yes. But what a waste of good whiskey." Both their cups had emptied over the dashboard.

Newman leaned out of the window. "Get off my damn tail," he shouted at the car in back.

The driver pointed a stiff middle finger at the sky.

Newman shifted into Park and got out.

"Jay!" Mary called after him.

He approached the other driver, a young man in a stretched

Mercedes. A curly-headed blonde sat close beside him, and there was another couple in back.

The driver lowered his window. "Fuck off, jerk, you're holding up traffic."

Newman reached in and grabbed his throat. The man's eyes widened. He fought to pull free but was unable to move. Everyone in the car started to yell. Newman half lifted the driver from the seat. The traffic light had turned green and horns were honking.

"Let him go, Jay." Mary was standing beside him. "That's enough. Let him go!"

Newman looked at her. He looked at the young man's frightened, bulging eyes. Then he let go and walked back to his car.

"Crazy animal!" one of the girls yelled after him.

Driving once more, he smiled dimly. "An overreaction, huh?"

Mary said nothing.

"I think I'd have been very happy to kill the bimbo at that moment. Do you know that?"

"Yes," she said. "Now let's see if you're sober and rational enough to figure out why."

"That's easy. He gave me the finger, he called me a jerk, and he told me to fuck off."

"And?"

"He was young."

"What else?"

"He was driving a thirty-thousand-dollar automobile created by the same lovable folks who gave us Auschwitz and Dachau."

"Very good," she said quietly, the patient teacher encouraging her less than brilliant pupil. "Now what do you say we get to the real heart of it."

"There's more?"

"Give it some thought, darling."

He was silent.

"Well?"

"If you think you're going to get me to say I'm a burnt-out, short-fused boozer who'd be less dangerous practicing law than enforcing it, you're not as smart as you look."

She sighed. "Neither are you, love."

He sat beneath the big map, going over his latest investigative reports.

A few small bloodstains had been found on the sidewalk between the 103rd Street location where the Pontiac had been found and 104th Street and Riverside Drive. The blood was the same type as that of the samples taken from the Pontiac's upholstery, which meant that in all probability the Apostle had been heading west and uptown from the car rather than east and downtown. This considerably narrowed the search area, but it still left quite a few blocks of very large apartment houses to be checked.

He called in Mulcahy, Robbins, and Loretti and crayoned a red circle on his map. "The chances are pretty good that the Apostle lives someplace in this area," he told the detectives. "Now all we have to do is find him."

"How?" said Loretti.

"By trying to act like reasonably competent police officers."

Robbins coughed. It was what he did when he was nervous, a tic. "Do you know how many apartment houses are in that circle, Lieutenant?"

"Yes," said Newman. "Seventy-two. And the number of individual apartments comes to exactly fifty-four hundred and ninety-three."

"You mean we have to check them all?" said Mulcahy.

"Not necessarily. You can always go into some other line of work."

They sat regarding him unhappily.

"But we've got nothing to go on," complained Loretti. Thin and sallow, he looked tired in advance.

Newman groped through a desk drawer, felt several hidden bottles, and settled for a fresh pack of cigarettes. "We've got more than you think. To begin with, you'll get tenant rosters from all the buildings and go over them with the supers or doormen. You'll find out the number of people in each apartment, their sex and their general age category. This will cut out all women, children, and probably males over fifty. I take it you all agree that the man you saw was on the youngish side."

The detectives nodded.

"And tall, well set up, wide in the shoulders?"

The three men agreed once more.

"So that narrows it still further." Newman paused to light

181

his cigarette. "And of course we've still got a bullethole in him somewhere. Check that out with the doormen and janitors. Any known injuries in their buildings? Anyone breaking normal routine and not going out? Check neighborhood drugstores for sales of gauze and antiseptic. And if we ever get to the point of needing final verification, we've got the cast of a shoeprint he left under the Verrazano Bridge."

Robbins coughed. "What about fingerprints in the Pontiac?"

"He either wore gloves or wiped the car clean."

"I was thinking." Mulcahy flushed as everyone looked at him. "Doesn't the Apostle seem like the kind of guy who'd be living alone? I mean, I can't picture some working stiff with a family knocking himself out at all crazy hours with this kind of stuff."

"Good. That gives us another possible category. Men under fifty, living alone."

Loretti said, "We're talking like he's got to be in that circled area. How can we be so sure?"

"We can't," Newman admitted. "All we can do is take an educated guess and hope we get lucky."

After the others had left, he felt oddly depressed. He had lost even the exhilaration that illusory progress sometimes brought. He tried a few quick shots of bourbon, but even that failed to give him a lift. He wondered just how badly the Apostle had been hurt and suddenly wished he would call. But when his phone did ring sometime later, it was Clayton Taylor.

"I'm an irrespressible optimist, Lieutenant. I'll be at the Waldorf overnight and was hoping we might get together this evening and talk."

"What time?"

"Would eleven be too late?"

"I'll be there."

Newman hung up the phone. The price of friendship.

The suite was on the thirty-first floor and facing west over Park Avenue. The towers of Manhattan glittered through the windows and the sky glowed, but Newman somehow felt locked inside a cave. Still, he smiled as he shook the cleric's hand and accepted his ceremonial snifter of Napoleon with the humble gratitude of a deserving pilgrim.

Taylor had opened the door himself and they were alone.

He wore a maroon silk robe over formal trousers, and Newman found the effect oddly reminiscent of the urbane and elegant sophistication of a Noel Coward play. Some redneck preacher.

"I hope your being here means a positive response."

Newman gazed at him across a white Louis XV table. "It means I'm willing to listen."

"Good. I ask no more. Incidently, I've already written your boss to tell him what a superb job I think you're doing for the department's image. A little stroking in high places never hurts." He paused. "Did you know I expect to be one of his major supporters?"

Newman looked blank.

"I thought you might have heard. Westley's about to announce for next year's gubernatorial race."

The detective managed to show surprise. "Does he stand a chance?"

"He can't miss. He's exactly what the times call for. A law man."

"Well, good for him." The room was quiet. The walls and carpeting were thick, and all street sounds were very far away. "Now let's hear exactly what you want from me. And please. No crap. No campaign rhetoric. Just the facts."

Taylor called forth a reasonable facsimile of a smile. "You don't fool around none, do yuh, Lieutenant?" The drawl was pure country southern, a brief lapse. "All right. What I want is for you to help me in the big cities, the major urban centers. I want you to be my unacknowledged voice. I want you to say all the things I'd like to say but can't. I want you to let the Jewish community know my true intentions. I want you to speak to their leaders and opinion-makers. I obviously can't expect their open support, but at least they can keep their media from screaming about gas chambers and crematoriums."

"What am I supposed to tell them?"

"Everything I told you at our last meeting. That my occasional anti-Semitic comments are just a temporary expedient. That those I help put in office—and Westley can serve as a perfect typical example—will only ensure better, safer lives for their people. That I'm willing to give them written guarantees that no Jew will ever suffer the slightest indignity or harm from me personally or from those I endorse." He studied Newman as if measuring his response so far. "And you can also tell them that I'll contribute a million dollars a month to the UJA, or any other fund they choose, for as long as they don't actively come out against me.''

Newman stared out over the floodlit spires of the city.

"How does it sound?" said Taylor.

"Like the Jews are suddenly very important to you."

"Not suddenly. Practical politics aside, I'm a Christian minister who believes in and loves Jesus, and Jesus was a Jew. An awkward historical fact that too many so-called Christians try very hard to forget.''

"A nice bit. But you haven't come to *my* gift yet. Since you're such a practical politician, I can't wait to hear what you're going to offer *me*.''

Taylor laughed. "I must remember never to underestimate you. It could prove a fatal mistake.''

"So what do I get?"

"How about police commissioner?"

"Of what? Oshkosh?"

"No. New York."

Despite himself, Newman was affected. It went straight from his head to his stomach. "You could really do something like that?"

"It's nothing but local, pork barrel politics. If I couldn't handle that, I might as well have stayed home in Atlanta.''

The detective carefully kept his mouth shut. Two airplanes fall out of the sky, he thought, and I'm goddamn struck by lightning.

"I'm actually just looking out for myself, little brother," said Taylor, again slipping into his soft, down-home accents. "What could be more soothing to the largest, most influential Jewish community in the world than having a Jewish police commissioner as my spokesman?"

"You make Machiavelli look like a bum. Do you do as well with God as with politics?"

"I hope so. I try, anyway."

"That part never bothers you?"

"Why should it bother me? I've always done his work wherever I found it.''

They sat drinking in the quiet room.

"Well?" said Taylor at last. "Is there some hope for us?"

"Why not?"

"Good." He reached over and shook Newman's hand. "I'm sure it'll work out for everyone."

Newman was sure of nothing.

To Thomas Mackley it was like being a Marine again, back in Nam. The sense of mission, the feeling of imminent danger, the quality of being part of something greater than yourself, were all sensations he had missed for more than fifteen years. Even the name of the exercise seemed perfect. Operation Tomahawk. Christ! You could almost hear the fucking howitzers.

Just fifteen minutes before, at exactly 0200 hours (the jump off time assigned by the American Crusade Party's regional headquarters), Mackley and his carefully selected team of three had left the Flatbush section of Brooklyn in a 1982 Ford station wagon for Jamaica, Queens, and their first target of the night.

They rode without speaking; the streets were deserted, the city dark and quiet. The beast slept, thought Mackley. His men were as tense and expectant as he. There was real risk ahead as well as fear of failure. This was more than just another outing. It was the ACP's first attempt at a nationally coordinated action. At this very moment, in fifty-three cities and towns across the country, similar strike teams were en route to objectives of their own. The selection of the targets themselves had been left to the individual unit leaders. The only requirements were that the intended victims be among the party's regularly targeted minority groups and that every reasonable effort be made to avoid casualties. This was in the nature of a test. ACP headquarters was simply checking out its planning and organizational capabilities on a national scale. If all went well, stronger, more significant action would follow.

Mackley drove cautiously, staying within the posted speed limits and braking at all red lights and stop signs. He was taking no chances of drawing the attention of a stray patrol car. His future in the party looked especially bright at this point, and he wanted nothing to jeopardize it. Which was why the three men he had chosen to be with him tonight were his best—devoted to the cause, but not crackpots.

All sorts of creeps were attracted to stuff like this, and Mackley prided himself on his ability to spot them before they caused any trouble. He himself bought little of the party's official line. He was too smart to really believe that all the country's troubles were caused by its blacks, Hispanics, and Jews. That was just for simpletons, those who needed a nice, clean-cut enemy to hate, someone to blame for their own failures. But he well understood the party's need for the line. Hitler had won an empire and almost the world just by promising to institutionalize the pogrom. There was always a future in carefully directed hate.

Their Jamaica target was in an old section of rundown stores and warehouses that were part of a black ghetto near York University. Mackley parked in an alley. Then he waited in the station wagon while one of his men stood watch fifty yards away and the other two pried open a warehouse door and disappeared inside. He checked the time: 0253 hours. They were right on schedule.

Moments later, when the warehouse doors again opened and closed, Mackley glimpsed the incipient flames inside. Fine. A little disciplined exercise in organization and public relations. Apart from its more practical physical results, fire had mystic overtones. It went all the way back to the public burnings of the Middle Ages. People might shake their heads in apparent horror and sympathy, but the thrill would still be there, the subconscious association made. Ghettoes and fire, fire and ghettoes. Mackley half smiled.

His remaining two targets for the night were an ancient kosher restaurant on the Lower East Side of Manhattan and a bodega up in Spanish Harlem. Both actions were carried out as smoothly and without incident as the first.

When the fire marshals later sifted through the ashes, they found (as intended) plenty of evidence of arson, all pointing directly to the occupants themselves.

It was several days before the overall results of Operation Tomahawk filtered down to Mackley's level. Of the 159 targets chosen to be hit nationwide, 137 were totally destroyed, 14 suffered at least 50 percent damage, and 8 attacks were aborted for reasons of security. According to the media, only 7 deaths were reported, well within the acceptable range for that size operation.

12

Gaynor had just finished changing the dressing on his wounded arm when the doorbell rang. It was late afternoon, and his ex-wife often dropped by at this time. Still buttoning his shirt, he opened the door and looked into the dark eyes of Jay Newman. *Aah, it's all over. He knows.*

It was a curious feeling to see the detective's face staring back at him, inquisitive, at that moment far more predator than rabbi. Gaynor could almost sense the beating of the man's heart. And there was an intimation of something more, as if, alone in a locked, windowless room, he had watched a gust of wind blow some dead leaves from a table.

"I was in the neighborhood and suddenly remembered my responsibility," said the detective. "Or maybe it was just your Jack Daniel's I remembered."

Gaynor shook his hand. "Either way, it's good to see you."

In the living room, Newman chose the same chair he had sat in before. People seemed to do that, thought Gaynor. He poured two generous shots of bourbon and added a touch of water. "Still chasing your friend, the Apostle?"

"That's why I'm here."

Unaccountably, Gaynor found himself smiling as he fussed with the drinks.

"We're pretty sure the guy lives in this general area," said

187

Newman. "I was just checking some leads and thought of you."

"As a possible suspect?"

Newman laughed.

Gaynor handed him his drink and sat down with his own. "You sound as though you're getting close."

"Close enough to have put a bullet in him. Not me. One of my men. We found a stolen bloodstained car on a Hundred and Third Street near Riverside Drive. So at least we know he's hurting, needs treatment, and can't be too far away."

"Poor bastard. He could be dead or dying somewhere."

"No. We think he just caught one in the arm."

Gaynor felt an insane urge to touch the wound. It had suddenly begun to ache, then itch. Watching Newman, he saw him absently rub his arm at the exact place.

"To hell with him," said the detective. "Let's hear about you. How are you managing? Okay?"

"Sure. Absolutely great."

"I mean really. Without the bullshit."

Gaynor concentrated on his drink. It occurred to him that he had left his doctoring materials—gauze, antiseptic, surgical tape—on the bathroom sink, but he seemed to be without enough energy or interest to do anything about it.

"I've started to work, but it's mostly groping."

"Anything I can look at?"

"Not really."

"I guess it's still pretty rough for you."

The expressed feeling, the empathy, brought a sudden soreness to Gaynor's heart. It rose from his chest and clotted in his throat.

"For Christ's sake, spit it out. Keep it inside and it just turns rotten." Newman's eyes were black. They reflected bereavement. "Didn't I once tell you I know how it is?"

"You also told me it doesn't get any better."

"So? That doesn't mean you have to curl up and stop living."

"Who's stopped living?"

Newman looked at him with his bereaved Jewish eyes.

"Self-pity is digusting," said Gaynor. "I despise it."

"So do I. But I must admit I've always found it very comforting, even enjoyable. Like crawling into a nice warm bed when you're cold and tired. Along with a bottle, there's hardly a thing can match it. I swear, sometimes it beats getting laid."

"You don't feel that way anymore. Not now."

"What do you know about how I feel now?"

Gaynor shrugged. Even the slight motion brought a twinge to his arm. "A lot of good things have happened to you lately. You're not what you were before the crash."

"Do you really think going around making asshole speeches can change me where I live? Do you think I'm that much of an idiot?" There was sudden anger in Newman's face and voice. The warmth, the reaching out of a moment before, had vanished in a squall of self-contempt.

What did I say? Gaynor wondered. "I've heard you speak. You're saying important things."

"Important, shit. I'm a goddamned fake."

Gaynor looked away from the detective's eyes. He found them too disturbing. This was a lofty, prideful man. Self-esteem was what made him run, was probably what had driven him to the bottle in the first place because he could never squeeze out enough to meet his needs.

"You're not a fake, Lieutenant."

"If you compromise, you're a fake. And I've sure as hell compromised."

"Who hasn't?"

Newman threw back his head and emptied his glass in a single gulp. "The Apostle."

Gaynor sat listening to a vague humming in his ears.

"There's a momzer who doesn't even know what compromise means," said Newman. "He believes and he acts on his beliefs. He doesn't just talk. He *does*. No accommodations, no adjustments, no concessions. And the fact that it's all going to end up killing him doesn't even enter into it."

"That's good?"

Newman rose, went for the bottle, and poured them fresh drinks. "It's good for his soul. But isn't that what we're talking about? The rest, of course, is pure disaster. The rest makes him a walking time bomb, potentially the most danger-ous man in the city."

"Why is that?"

"Because he's a fanatic. Because he's lost the necessary restraints of fear. I'll tell you something, Richard. The guy was shot the other night only because he walked into a setup, a trap he had called to tell me he knew about. How would you say that sounded?''

Gaynor decided not to say.

"And I'll tell you something else," said Newman. "I'm absolutely goddamn fucking jealous."

He's forgotten all about me, thought the artist.

Waiting to heal, healing, Gaynor was pleased to accept the Reverend Clayton Taylor as his new preoccupation.

He spent day after day in among the old newspapers in the main library, researching the cleric's life, reading whatever he could find that had anything to do with him—biographical details, published writings and speeches, stated beliefs on God, sin, politics, and the processes of life and living. Who was he? What was he after? How was he going about getting it? It was no longer enough simply to listen to Taylor's demagogic preaching. Since it had suddenly become quite possible that this was a man whose life he might soon be making serious threats against, he had to be very sure the whole thing made sense.

Sense, he thought. What strange state had he reached that he could honestly consider even an outside possibility of assassination a rational concept? Yet he did not feel strange. The fact was, he had been moving toward this point for so long and in so gradual a progression that his finally having arrived there seemed nothing less than reasonable. And the additional circumstance that it had turned out to be Kate herself who had inadvertently given him the idea added its own special symmetry. The human soul had more sides than he would ever live to uncover.

So now he was learning about Clayton Taylor. Now he was doing his best to find out what had twisted and bent the man's life into its present curious shape. Didn't you have to study the past to discover present and future relevance? Yet what could be considered relevant to the making of a southern hatemonger? As it turned out, Taylor was no Georgia cracker, no backcountry farmboy, no sharecropper's embittered son— none of the usual stereotypes. The product of several genera- tions of distinguished scholars and academics on his father's side, he emerged as a Phi Beta Kappa out of Clemson Univer- sity and a Doctor of Divinity out of Yale. Out of his maternal line flowed a steady stream of hard-to-count millions from tobacco and oil. So what was there to be angry about? What reason did he have to hate?

Yet Taylor apparently did hate. It was in everything he said and wrote. It even seemed to be in his face (in an old photograph) at the early age of fourteen, before time and experience had taught him to put a proper cover on such things. There he was, posing beside a flowering magnolia, a lean, fair-haired adolescent with frail, bony arms and dark shadows under his cheeks and eyes, clear signs of a need to punish. In beautifully tailored summer whites, he already revealed the disdainful pride of the child who has suddenly come upon the awareness that it was never very hard to hurt people, that it was in fact the root of all winning and power. The ability to cause catastrophe was the force and authority to rule. That kid knew more at fourteen, thought the artist, than I'll know when I die.

Still, Gaynor had his own diseases, and it made him feel no better to discover different infections in Clayton Taylor. All it did was help him occupy his empty hours and days. Which, too, was undoubtedly important. It afforded the chance to survive until it was time to make a contribution of true significance. Or was he merely aspiring to new heights of presumption and self-deception? Who was it—Rousseau?—who had said, ''I know my heart and I know all men.'' Yet how many ever really knew their own hearts? All Gaynor knew for sure was that he was trying. And the results to date? So far he had just managed to squash a few cockroaches (according to Kate's accounting) and get himself a neat .38-caliber hole in his arm.

In books and magazines, in Xeroxed letters and articles, Gaynor carried Clayton Taylor home from the library. Studying to become an authority on the minister, he found the essence of the man stubbornly escaping him. He had great bundles of facts but no understanding of what they added up to. If anything, they clotted his brain, made him feel dense. Struggling to work them through, he also struggled with his painting.

He was working on half a dozen compositions now (as if being totally committed to one might prove fatal), but it was still his big canvas that held and challenged him. Maybe it was because the people in his other, smaller paintings were coming so much more easily. With their wild faces, their grossness, their bent bodies, it was as if Goya himself, in his last, tormented years, was personally guiding the brush. His big one was something else. Nothing came easily here. He normally liked to know where he was heading with each stroke, but in this he was stumbling like a blind man.

Yet, bit by bit, something did start to evolve. At first it was little more than a mass of swirling color, all blues and grays (its original brightness having long gone), a dark abstraction out of some nightmare vision of hell. Then he was able to pick out that first floating eye, so pale, so perfectly cold and evil, that he faltered before its stare. But it was, after all, only an eye. So he added another to make them a pair, and he and the emerging face were on their way, with a crazy beak for a nose and a black pit below that had to be the mouth.

Stroking with care, he laid on blue blood and gray mud like ribbons pinned to the chest. Then a slash of darkness went in over the mouth and sucked the face in backward, as though with the punch of a bullet. The expression was that of an old man, sly and toothless, with a splash of pain across the lips. A single arm took shape, grew, but remained alone, its mate having been blown away or erased or simply lost somewhere.

Whap! went the brush, and a fresh hole appeared where the heart should have been. Yet the face above seemed to grin, as if there were pleasure even in this. Cut out the heart, it said, and hurt went too.

But did it? And if it did, was it all accident, a blind groping, nothing more? Or were there moments when the blue thing really spoke to him? At times it seemed so. Not that he understood. It was enough that he would feel lights moving between them, as if the pale eyes were begging him to attack, to rend, to mutilate further. Until there came a moment when he could no longer face the eyes, for now they held it all—the blood, the carnage, the screams that never sounded. And again he faltered and had no stomach for the rest. Covering the blue thing with a sheet, he turned it to the wall.

Though still lacking the clarity of focus on Taylor that he would have liked, Gaynor nevertheless took his next step. He composed his second open letter to the Georgia cleric.

GAYNOR'S PASSION

To the Reverend Clayton Taylor:

For reasons I can't pretend to understand, you are doing everything possible to spread the evils of prejudice throughout this basically decent land. Any man who preaches the hatred of other men because of their race or religion is appealing to the worst of all human failings. You are a minister. You were ordained to preach the word of God, which is love. I therefore beg you. Please. Fulfill your mission. It is the most noble calling a man can have. If you refuse, you will force me to fulfill mine.

When the message was typed clean, Gaynor sat staring at it. Was it right? Did it say everything he wanted to say? Was the implied threat clear enough? He had reached the stage of wondering why he had written it at all. He began to think he was simply trying to sell himself on an idea that he was not even convinced was right. He read the letter again and this time found it irritatingly presumptuous. What made him think that this man, this reverend, this nationally acclaimed demagogue, would in any way be affected by an anonymous threat? Privately or publicly, he would just laugh. And then what? More and increasingly shrill threats? Or would the Apostle simply kill him? Unless, having once entered the realm of absurdity, there no longer were any logical solutions. Perhaps the usual standards could no longer be applied. Maybe there just was no right way to compose such a message.

Finally, having Xeroxed the proper number of press copies and signed them THE APOSTLE, he mailed the letter exactly as he had written it.

Two hours later, carrying a Samsonite one-suiter, he arrived at La Guardia Airport in time to catch the 1:00 P.M. Delta flight to Atlanta.

The decision to go had been an impulse. He had only the vaguest idea of why he was going and what he expected to accomplish when he got there. He hoped that once on the plane, he might be able to understand more. A futile hope. He flew the whole way in a cold sweat, chewing at his lip, all thought frozen in the past. It was his first flight since the crash, and his mental condition was such that this fact did not even occur to him until he was on the plane and belted into

Norman Garbo

his seat. Despite the hour, he drank steadily all the way. His flight attendant kept smiling pleasantly at him, but he found it impossible to look into her pretty, smooth-skinned face. When the plane touched down in Atlanta about an hour and a half later, he walked off as stiffly as a poorly programmed robot.

Using one of Escobar's forged credit cards, he rented a gray Ford from Hertz and bought a guidebook and a detailed map of the city. Then he checked a few addresses in the telephone directory, found and marked them on his map, and drove away in the warm Georgia sunshine.

He drove south on Route 85 and got off just past Red Oak. Spring seemed to have arrived early and the fruit trees were well into bloom. In the distance, the hills were a soft, misty purple. Rolling yellow clouds hung low. He began a dozen paintings as he drove. He finished none.

Gaynor saw the White Christ when he was still more than a mile away. It stood on the crest of a hill, arms outstretched in blessing or supplication, a dazzling alabaster against the sky. According to the guidebook, the huge statue was eleven stories high, sixty feet wide, and was built of steel-reinforced concrete. At night it was floodlighted and visible for miles, dominating the surrounding area and serving as an inspiring checkpoint for planes passing through the darkness overhead. For visitors, the spiritual atmosphere was further heightened by the sound of recorded hymns drifting from strategically placed loudspeakers. The White Christ had been erected by the American Fundamental Church within the vast parklike setting of its national headquarters, and it was said to attract as many as five million pilgrims and tourists a year. The guidebook credited the Reverend Clayton Taylor himself with the statue's original concept and design, going on to describe the burial crypt at its base where the church leader's remains would eventually be laid to rest.

About a quarter of a mile past the White Christ and sprawled across a verdant hilltop of its own was the headquarters of the American Fundamental Church. Also white, also huge, its three soaring cement towers seemed less an architectural statement than a special blend of religious dogma. For the payment of a two dollar "donation," escorted tours were offered; Gaynor made his contribution and joined a group of other visitors. They were led by a pretty blond guide in a navy blazer and gray skirt whose soft drawl seemed to give off its own scent of jasmine. The building's centerpiece was an immense, ten-thousand-seat tabernacle with vaulted ceilings reaching for God. About it were arranged the church's radio and television studios, a publishing division with its own computerized printing presses, and a two-hundred-thousand-volume library that boasted one of the most complete collections of religious writings in the world. Also included in the complex were the classrooms, laboratories, and lecture halls of Clayton Taylor University, together with its medical school and teaching hospital.

This man had done it all. Gaynor's brain struggled to make somethng coherent of it. Narcissism masquerading as God's work?

The tour ended in an auditorium where other groups had already gathered. Moments later the lights were lowered, and a film was shown illustrating the American Fundamentalists' efforts to do good in a wide variety of areas, culminating in a brief recorded sermon by the church's leader. Then it was announced that since it was a long-established custom of the Reverend Taylor, when in residence, to grant a few private audiences to visitors, those interested would be able to pick up a qualifying questionnaire on the way out.

Why not? thought Gaynor.

The questionnaire asked for the applicant's name, age, address, religious affiliation, and reason for requesting the audience. It was explained that inasmuch as it was possible for only a limited number of audiences to be granted, selections would be made almost entirely on the basis of the applicant's stated need. Gaynor considered it. Then he wrote: "My two children, my entire family, died in an accident that I somehow survived, I no longer care about living." He made up a name and address and handed in the form.

Half an hour later the name he had chosen, Ralph Kimball, was among the five selected. Shortly thereafter, he was searched by two men for possible weapons. Then he was shown into a large, austerely furnished study where the church leader himself was seated behind a bare, polished desk.

Taylor rose and came forward to shake his hand. About the fine-grained, paneled walls were photographs of the minister standing with the president in the Oval Office, heading a delegation of clergy at the United Nations, speaking from the pulpit of his tabernacle, and digging a ceremonial shovelful of earth for the foundation of the White Christ. Curiously, there were no windows in the room. Recessed spots beamed down, spreading a dramatic, almost beatific, light.

"Please sit down, Mr. Kimball."

There was a black leather couch against a long wall, and Gaynor settled into one corner. Taylor took the other angle. His pale eyes rested for several moments on his visitor.

"Your face looks familiar. Have we ever met?"

Gaynor shook his head. He had never even thought of it. Right after the crash, his picture had been on the front page of every major newspaper in the country. But that was months ago, and it seemed unlikely that Taylor would be able to place him. Still, the man did have good eyes. In a curious way, the possibility of recognition was not unappealing. All his responses seemed to be completely and dependably backward.

The pale eyes appeared to soften. Or was it just part of the overall lighting effect? "My heart goes out to you, Mr. Kimball. To bury one's children is to bury the springtime of one's life. I can think of very little that is worse."

Gaynor stared fixedly at a wall.

"Do you believe in God?"

"Sometimes. At least I try."

"If God chose to spare your life, don't you think he may have had a reason for sparing it?"

"So far he hasn't told me what it is."

"We're just poor humans. It's never easy for us to understand his reasons. Often, we must accept them on faith alone."

"I'm afraid my faith isn't that strong, Reverend."

Taylor looked searchingly at him. "Why are you here? Why did you ask to see me? Did you think I could pluck a reason out of the sky and hand it to you?"

Gaynor did not answer. He was surprised to find that he was actually listening to the man.

"What did you expect?" Taylor persisted. "A blaze of light and a five-minute miracle?"

"I don't know what I expected. I'm not always rational these days. You're a minister of God with an eleven-story Christ and cement towers reaching for heaven. Maybe I thought you knew something I didn't."

"We all know the same things. The only real difference between us is that I don't believe God moves by accident."

196

"My kids were ten years old, Reverend. The worst they ever did was sometimes forget to brush their teeth. That's not enough reason to kill them." He focused on the clean, spare line of Taylor's jaw. "Nor can I see my own death as causing any real loss to anyone or damaging even the tiniest part of God's master plan."

"You have no family?"

"No."

"No wife?"

"We're divorced."

"Your work, whatever it is, offers you no reward, no sense of fulfillment?"

Gaynor shook his head. "All I can think about is that I'm alive and my kids are dead."

They sat in silence in their separate corners of the black leather couch. Gaynor felt his heart beating quietly alone. In a demented kind of way, he could also feel Clayton Taylor giving deep, serious thought to his problem. It was as if here, in this place, Taylor could behave only as a minister of God, with all the rest temporarily held in abeyance.

"I won't insult you by attempting to minimize your pain, Mr. Kimball. But unfortunately the only thing grief does is aggravate the loss. In these few moments allotted us, I wish there were some way for me to pick up a hypodermic needle and give you a quick, emergency shot of faith to make your ordeal easier to bear. Belief in God, the acceptance of his will, is all that any of us have to lean on in our anguish. Without faith, we're forever locked inside our poor suffering skins. There's no way out. And finally, as you've discovered, we find we've lost all reason for living."

"When I was very young I believed." Gaynor's voice sounded distant even to his own ears. "But as I grew up it began to seem childish."

"Believing *is* childish. That's why religious people always act a lot younger than their ages. God is their good fairy. But when the alternative is either despair or the abyss, what real choice is there?"

"What about you? Are you childish?"

"To God, we're all childish." The minister smiled. "No. That's too easy. You deserve more than pious platitudes. Yes, I *am* childish. God *is* my good fairy. I *do* believe it is he who gives me what I ask. If I ever stopped believing, if he were ever taken from me, if I were ever left solely dependent on my own limited strengths, I'd be bereft and frightened indeed.''

A buzzer sounded.

''Aah.'' Taylor sighed and spread his hands helplessly. ''Our time is almost up. These brief talks are so frustrating. What can a few moments accomplish? Sometimes I think I should stop them entirely. Yet I haven't the heart. Deep down I suppose I do secretly believe in the blaze of light and the five-minute miracle. What do you think, Mr. Kimball? Have I been able to offer you anything at all?''

''As much as anyone, Reverend. At least you took me seriously. And you seemed to be honest. Which I appreciate.'' Again he felt his heart beating but less quietly this time, as if it were sending panicky signals to the void. Thoughts of death came, so joyful they almost made him dizzy. ''But I must admit it has made me curious.''

''About what?''

''About how you could speak to me as you're doing now, yet preach the kind of venom I've heard from you on TV.''

Taylor stared at him until the silence had no air left. Then his long, bony face broadened into a joyous grin. A tragic El Greco priest of a man. Gaynor wondered whether he might have pushed him too far.

''Not an especially happy choice of words, Mr. Kimball, but I understand what you're implying. In response, I can only say that you're talking about two very separate areas of my life, politics and God.''

''Can they really be kept separate?''

''They have to be. There are more than twelve million unemployed in this country today. Not even God would dare to appear to a hungry man except in the form of bread. There's no theology, no Jesus Christ, in the indignity and bitterness of poverty. When I get those twelve million souls back to work, I hope I'll be able to get rid of what you so unkindly refer to as my venom.''

The buzzer sounded again, this time more insistently. Taylor rose and Gaynor stood up with him.

''Just a final thought, if I may, Mr. Kimball. God does his best for us all. But if he somehow fails to provide acceptable answers for you, I hope you'll make a real effort to find them for yourself.''

"I'm trying, Reverend."
They shook hands.

Two hours later, Gaynor was parked off a quiet, wooded road in the Forest Park suburb of Atlanta. An orange ball of a sun was sliding behind the trees and dusk was settling fast. From where he sat, he could see a small, one-story cottage with vines screening the porch and a red brick chimney at each end. High weeds flourished on what had once been a lawn, and gaunt, half-dead pines leaned at unlikely angles. A rusted iron table and some chairs lay sprawled to one side of the entrance path, lending a final touch to the general air of neglect. The house was the only one in sight. It was lived in, but at this moment it was empty. Gaynor had called from a roadside phone a few minutes before arriving. The phone number and address were among those he had looked up in the directory at the Atlanta airport.

It was not quite dark when an ancient Plymouth rattled by and turned into the rutted driveway that ran along the near side of the house. A small, elderly woman got out. Despite the mildness of the air, she wore a hat, coat, and gloves. Leaning heavily on a cane and carrying a paper shopping bag, she started toward the house. Because she was badly crippled, it took her awhile to get there. When she finally reached and opened the front door, Gaynor came up behind her.

"Mrs. Forsythe?"
She turned and stared at his Apostle mask.
"Please don't be frightened. I just want to talk to you. I'm sorry about the mask, but I'm afraid I can't let you see my face."

"Why? Are you so homely?"
Up close she had wet, sparkling eyes, two round spots of color high on her otherwise pale cheeks, and an unexpectedly youthful line of gray bangs showing from under her hat. Whatever else she was, thought Gaynor, she certainly wasn't afraid. "Don't you know who I am?"

"Should I?" Squinting through old-fashioned, silver-rimmed spectacles, she peered up at the mask more closely. "Of course. I've seen pictures of that false, rubber face in the newspapers. Are you really the same person? What is it you call yourself?"

"The Apostle."

"Ah, yes. One of Christ's disciples. But what could you possibly want with me? Has my time finally come? Are you here to escort me to my maker?"

"May I please come in?"

"Who could deny an Apostle entry? And such a polite one." Her voice, pure Dixie, was almost coquettish in its inflections.

Switching on a light, she led him into a room crowded with books, faded furniture, and the accumulated clutter of a lifetime. Two cats lay motionless on a couch, and a fat old basset struggled up from the hearth, waddled over for a welcoming pat, and went back to his place. The old woman removed her things, limped into the kitchen with her shopping bag, and returned with a wine bottle.

"This is my first apostolic visitation. I do hope you drink sherry." She filled two glasses and handed Gaynor one. Then she sat studying what she could see of his eyes through the mask. "I'm trying to recall some of the things I've read about you. If I remember correctly, I believe you fancy yourself a latter-day knight errant, a self-styled righter of wrongs. Undoubtedly very noble, but also very presumptuous. Do you really feel qualified to play God?"

Gaynor tried sipping a bit of sherry through the mask's mouth opening. The drink tasted rubbery. This was some old lady. "No, ma'am. I'm just trying to give him a little hand here and there. Which is why I've come to Atlanta. I'm hoping you might also be able to help."

"That's fine with me. I have a seventy-five-year collection of wrongs that badly need righting. Did you bring an extra mask?"

"I'm afraid all I brought are some questions about your husband and Reverend Taylor."

The humor drained from her face. "My husband is dead. And as far as I'm concerned, so is Clayton Taylor."

"Well, you see, ma'am, I've been going over some old newspaper articles about your husband, about how he worked with Taylor in the American Fundamental Church and—"

"My husband, the Reverend Hanson Forsythe, *founded* the American Fundamental Church," the old woman cut in stiffly.

"Yes. So I read. And I also read about his tragic and untimely death. It must have been a great loss for you."

"It was a great loss for many more than just me. It was a

great loss for the church. Hanson Forsythe was a man of God, sir, not an ecclesiastical fascist like Clayton Taylor. But my husband has been dead for twelve years. I'm sure you didn't travel all this way just to pay a belated condolence call. Exactly what is it you want?''

"The truth about your husband and Taylor."

Delicate muscles worked in her face. "I've been telling the truth for years. People think I'm paranoid, a silly, hallucinating old bore. No one will even listen to me anymore."

"I'll listen."

"What's the use? It won't change anything."

"Please. Just tell me."

The old woman stirred in her chair. The slight movement hardly disturbed the dress draped about her bones. The dog on the hearth moaned in his sleep. The smell of damp ashes drifted from the fireplace. Above the mantel, an oil portrait of the late Hanson Forsythe showed the narrow, ascetic face and distant gaze of a man whose eyes seemed to be set on nothing mortal or even of this planet. It might have been painted, thought Gaynor, by no less than the left hand of God.

"You hear that, Jimmy?" Mrs. Forsythe spoke to the dozing basset. "The Lord's own helper has come all the way to Atlanta just to hear the truth. Shall I give it to him?"

The hound, hearing his name, wagged his tail twice and went back to sleep.

"Well, why not? I suppose I should be grateful to find someone who is even interested after so many years. Though to me it doesn't seem that long ago. When you reach a certain age, your concept of time changes. The years start running together and the distant past seems closer and more meaningful than the present."

She paused to collect her thoughts, and her hands, pale as sunlight, grasped her cane and sherry glass as though guarding two of life's more delicate points of balance.

"It's really not a long or complicated story. At least not in the actual events. Hanson, my husband, founded the American Fundamental Church about thirty years ago because he chose to interpret the Bible much less literally than other Baptist congregations in the area. He was a loving, deeply spiritual man who believed all people were equal in the eyes of God, and he lived and preached accordingly. When Clayton Taylor joined him as assistant pastor some years later, he seemed to think very much as Hanson did. In those days Clayton was warm, brilliant, charming, and, despite his family's great wealth, seemed to have a genuine calling for the ministry. Neither my husband nor I could possibly have guessed what was to come later.''

A car was suddenly passing on the road in front and she tilted an ear toward it. A fly buzzed against a dusty window. One of the cats changed its position on the couch. The house groaned as it settled.

"The process was so subtle, so gradual, so insidious, that I suppose Hanson was never really aware of what was happening until it was almost too late.'' She drew her lips up in a wistful smile. "Or maybe he was just human enough not to want to be aware because of all the other things.''

"What other things?''

"The church's flourishing religious and social programs, the enormous growth in the congregation, the money pouring in from the Taylor Foundation, the exciting building program. It was all quite dazzling to a poor preacher who had spent much of his life struggling to keep his roof from leaking and his congregants from slipping away. But when Clayton's increasingly offensive bigotry and political chauvinism reached the point where it could no longer be ignored, my husband ordered him to end it or leave the church. This was no idle threat. Hanson still had enough influence with the trustees to force him out. And he would have if Clayton hadn't had him murdered.'' The old woman sank back into her chair, her face suddenly slack. Tears ran, and she turned her face to one side in shame.

"Twelve years,'' she said fiercely. "Twelve years and I still weep like a fool whenever I talk about it.''

Gaynor waited, his face rigid and sweaty under the mask. "One would think I'd have gotten over it by this time.'' She wiped her eyes and made an impatient gesture. "But you didn't come here to watch a sentimental old lady cry, did you? I apologize,'' she said more calmly and continued. "It was less than a mile from this house that it happened. We were driving home late one night when a man pulled alongside in another car and there was a shotgun blast. It took away most of Hanson's chest, a small part of mine, and sent us down into a ravine. My husband was killed instantly. I was badly hurt and left crippled. But I had seen the gunman's face. He was so sure, so arrogant, that he had not even bothered to wear a disguise of any sort. He was a close friend of Clayton's who also worked for him as a combination speech-writer, public relations adviser, and bodyguard. The police arrested him on my identification, but he turned out to have an unshakable alibi. Clayton himself swore under oath that the man had been at the church with him at the time of the shooting. So of course the police had to let him go.''

Mrs. Forsythe stared flatly at the Apostle's unchanging, bearded face. "So there's the truth you wanted, Mister Christ's helper. Does it shock you?"

"No, ma'am. I read pretty much the same thing in those old articles. That's why I'm here. I wanted to hear it from you."

"And now that you've heard?"

"I believe it."

"No one else does. I've told that story so often I've driven even my friends away with the telling. Everyone is properly sympathetic, of course. After all, my husband was killed, and I was crippled and left for dead. It's a very sad story. And everyone did love Hanson. But how could they possibly accept the idea of Clayton Taylor bearing false witness under oath? It would be like accusing the pope himself of lying. Besides, if they did accept it, they would also have to accept the idea of Clayton being an accomplice to cold-blooded murder. Good Lord. They would sooner die.''

"Does the man you say did the shooting—William Reese, I think the articles said his name was—does he still live in the Atlanta area?"

"Of course. He's a very high-ranking member of Clayton's political entourage." Her eyes, misting over, turned very tired. "Why shouldn't he be?"

"Is he married?"

"Not anymore. Not at the moment. Two wives have divorced him. Now he lives alone. Just he and his lovely memories.''

Gaynor finished his sherry and stood up, suddenly more exhausted than he could have imagined. The old woman's cane had fallen to the floor, and he absently picked it up and handed it to her. "How do I get to his house from here?"

"Save yourself the trouble, Mr. Apostle. It won't do any good.''

"You never can tell."

Mrs. Forsythe tried to smile, but her lips only trembled. "I suppose you must be very young behind that mask," she whispered. "Exactly how old are you?"

"Thirty-five."

"Thirty-five," she said reflectively. Slowly, she put out her hand and touched Gaynor's. "Sometimes I feel so old I forget what world I'm living in. I speak to my animals or to the walls and see faces that have been dead for a dozen years and I think I'm speaking to them."

Leaning on her cane, she abruptly rose from her chair. "Ah, God. I've always despised whining, nostalgic old ladies. Now I find I've become one of them. Let me get a sheet of paper and a pencil. It's not easy to find William Reese's house if you're not familiar with the area. I want to write down the directions for you."

The house was in a heavily wooded ravine about a mile from College Park. Gaynor again had called from a roadside phone and again had received no answer. This time, however, he chose not to wait in his car. Instead, he put on his mask and gloves, parked the car off the road behind some trees, and circled the grounds on foot. Iron coach lanterns lighted a pillared entrance, and lights were on in several rooms. But they were evidently controlled by an electric timer because the rooms were empty. Gaynor opened an unlocked kitchen window, cut a hole in the screen, and climbed through. Then he chose a large, comfortable chair in a study off the entrance hall and settled into the darkness to wait.

Almost instantly, he felt himself starting to doze. He fought it for a while, then gave in and drifted into restless, haunted sleep. He dreamed he was running along a white, sunlit beach with the twins in some sort of wild game of tag, the three of them splashing through the water's edge and laughing so hard, so convulsively, that they could barely catch their breaths. Then the slam of a car door woke him with a start, and he hurried to a window and saw a tall, heavyset man approaching the house.

Moments later, William Reese came into the study and turned on the light. Gaynor aimed his revolver at him.

Reese silently leaned back against the wall. He looked at the Apostle mask, the gun, the attached silencer. The quick hazel eyes were the key, the identifying mark. In all other respects, the man looked pretty much like any other ex-athlete gone to fat, with a red, drinker's face, rugged, out-of-focus features, and a body that was still hard beneath the excess flesh. But the eyes carried the real threat. They were those of a combat infantryman. They had no pity.

"Take off your jacket," ordered Gaynor's muffled voice. "Slowly."

Reese did as he was told. Under the jacked he had on a filled shoulder holster.

"Remove the gun. Use only the tips of two fingers. Drop it on that chair."

This, too, was silently done. Gaynor took the revolver, a snub-nosed police special. He nodded at the chair and Reese sat down. Gaynor sat down eight feet away. He could almost sniff suppressed anger coming off the man like an animal scent, dull and powerful.

"Well?" said Reese at last. "Are you going to tell me what it's all about?" It was another native accent, deep Georgia, and heavy enough to trip over. "Or am I supposed to sit here and guess?"

"It's about a twelve-year-old murder."

"Is that some new kind of riddle?"

"I'll make it plainer. Twelve years ago you killed the Reverend Hanson Forsythe. I figure you've gotten away with murder long enough. Now I'd like you to write me a little confession."

Reese shifted his mammoth shoulders. He was a fortress. He looked impregnable. "I thought you only played these games of yours in New York. What are you doing in Atlanta?"

"I'm branching out." Gaynor took out pen and paper and placed them on a small table. "Start writing."

"What do you suggest I say?"

"Nothing elaborate. Just the basics. Just that it was you who killed the old man on Clayton Taylor's orders. Then you can sign your name and date it."

"That's all?"

"Yes."

Reese settled back with an air of exaggerated ease, a conceit of many big men who assume their strength and power are boundless. "Why are you being so unfriendly? Don't you know the reverend loves you?"

"Well, I'm afraid I don't love him."

"That's too bad. But as it happens, sir, Reverend Taylor and I didn't have anything to do with killing Hanson Forsythe. You've probably been talking to his poor, dotty old wife. She's been telling that same crazy story ever since her husband died. Nobody around here believes her."

"I'm not from around here. I believe her. And I want that confession from you."

Reese sighed. "Now let's stop being foolish. I've got no intention of writing a confession to something I didn't do. So if that means you're going to shoot me, then go ahead and shoot."

"Is that your final word?"

"It is."

Gaynor raised his revolver and sighted at a point directly between the man's eyes. There was getting to be a sameness to this. Could it be that he was growing bored? Very gently, he started to squeeze the trigger. Reese watched his finger. He did not even blink.

Gaynor lowered the gun until it was pointed at Reese's chest. "Don't you care about living?"

"As much as anyone. But if I wrote what you're telling me to write, I'd be dead anyway."

"You mean Taylor would see to it?"

"I mean I'd be dead."

Using one hand, Gaynor stuck a cigarette through his mask opening and lit it. An idea had begun to form, and with it, a curiously pleasurable excitement. "All right," he said, "I'm going to offer you a deal. You'll put nothing in writing, nothing you could be held to. I just want you to say it. I just want to hear you tell me straight out that you killed Forsythe, answer a few questions, and you get a chance to walk away from this clean."

"What kind of a chance?"

"A good one. Better than you deserve. Two guns on the floor and we go for them at the same time."

The gray eyes were suspicious. "Why would you do that?"

"Because I may be a little crazy," said Gaynor, "but I'm not crazy enough to enjoy shooting anyone, even you, in cold blood."

And you've also got a recorder planted somewhere."

"There's no recorder. If you don't believe that, you can

disguise your voice with a handkerchief so it can't be recognized. Fair enough?''

Reese's gaze turned raw. Things were being weighed inside his head. Gaynor waited. He still felt oddly joyful, as if the possibility of death right now would be an exciting experience that might not be available again. His eyes passed over a large gun cabinet. It had a great many weapons on display—rifles, shotguns, pistols—all carefully oiled and polished, all neatly arranged in rows. Southerners and guns. A lifelong love affair. Or were they forever preparing for another civil war?

"Okay," said Reese abruptly. "If I can muffle my voice."

Gaynor tossed him a handkerchief. "Go ahead."

Reese bunched the square of cloth and covered his mouth. "I did the shooting," he said. Even with the handkerchief, his voice was easy, matter-of-fact. He might have been saying, I did the singing. "I shot Hanson Forsythe."

"Did Taylor tell you to do it?"

"Yes."

"Why?"

"He needed the old man out of the way. Forsythe was pressuring him with the trustees."

"How was the killing done?"

"From a moving car."

"What was the weapon?"

"A twelve-gauge shotgun."

"Why didn't you kill Forsythe's wife, too?"

"I thought I did. That was my big mistake."

Gaynor nodded. He appeared satisfied. Watching Reese, he went over to the gun cabinet. "Stand up and face the wall. Lean against it with both hands, legs back and spread."

The big man very slowly did so.

Gaynor chose two identical .38-caliber revolvers, found the proper ammunition, and loaded them. "Let's go to the basement."

Downstairs, there was a long, clear area with a cement floor and exposed foundation walls. The utilities were off in another section. The only sound was the soft hum of a water heater.

"Here's how it's going to work," said Gaynor. "I'm going to place these two guns twenty feet apart on the floor.

You'll stand behind one and I'll stand behind the other. At the count of five we go. Understood?''

Reese just looked at him.

"You have a question?"

"Yes," said Reese. "Why are you doing this? I don't understand. I mean, if you're too damn holy to finish me off cold, why don't you just go home and forget about it? Why risk getting killed when you don't have to?"

"Because now that I know for sure, I can't quite let you get away with murder."

"But if you end up dead, I'll be getting away with it anyway."

"Yes, but then it won't be my choice anymore."

It was still beyond Reese's understanding. Doubt shadowed his eyes. "Then since it looks as though one of us is going to die very soon, at least let me see your face. I'd like to know who might be killing me."

Gaynor thought about it.

"How can it hurt?" asked Reese.

Beginning to feel that he himself was willing this one step at a time, Gaynor removed his mask and put it in his pocket.

Reese stared, frowning. "Who are you?"

"My name is Richard Gaynor."

"Should that mean something to me?"

"There was a plane crash some months ago that killed almost three hundred people. I was the only survivor. You probably read about it."

"I'll be damned." Reese suddenly seemed to be trying to enter Gaynor through his eyes. "But what did that have to do with this whole Apostle business?"

"A lot of good people died that night. Somehow, I didn't. I'm just trying to even the score a bit, make a kind of payment."

"How? By playing Jesus Christ with a gun for the rest of your goddamned life?"

Gaynor felt oddly exposed without his mask. Still, there was a new kind of intimacy. "What would *you* have done?"

"Who the hell knows? But nothing that crazy. Maybe spend a few months just drinking and screwing."

Priorities, thought Gaynor. "And after that?"

"I'd have forgotten it by then."

"I doubt it. Not if your kids had died on the plane."

"I don't have any kids."

"I did."

"Aah." It was probably the softest sound the big man possessed. He smiled, and one of the fluorescent lights overhead seemed to twinkle about his face. "So that's it. You just don't give a damn. You *want* me to blow you away, don't you?"

Gaynor stood silently pointing his revolver. He felt cold, as if an unseen window had suddenly been opened.

"Okay, so be it," said Reese. "But since we suddenly seem to be letting it all hang out, you might as well know something, too. I lied before. It was my own idea to kill that old man. Reverend Taylor never even knew about it till it was done. Then he went wild. He wanted to tear me apart. The only reason he saved my neck with that fake alibi was because he knew I did it for him."

"I don't believe you."

"Why in the name of Christ would I lie now?"

Gaynor had no answer.

"What's the matter? Can't you stand the idea that the reverend might not be as much of a sonofabitch as you've set him up to be?"

Apparently not, thought Gaynor.

"That's the trouble with you walking Jesus Christs," said Reese. "You need your certified Satan of the Month like a junkie needs his fix. And if you can't find one, you make him up."

"I couldn't make Clayton Taylor up. I wouldn't know where to begin."

"Damned right you wouldn't. He'd be too much for a death-hungry sickie like you even to begin to understand. But in the meantime, he's given more hope to more people than I could ever add up. That's why I had to get rid of Forsythe. He was going to put the reverend down. And if I had to, I'd do it again for the same reason." He looked almost sadly into Gaynor's eyes, then shrugged. "Ah, this is a waste of time. You don't even know what I'm talking about."

"I'll ask once more. Will you sign a confession?"

"Come on, little Jesus. Put the guns on the floor and let me blow you to heaven like you want."

Under the bright fluorescent lights, there was an almost ceramic clarity to the cellar scene. It might have been a snowscape, thought Gaynor, and he put together an instant painting of pale blues, grays, and whites, with a jet black crow swooping low across the foreground and the bare bones of winter trees in the distance. As an afterthought, he added a few touches of crimson directly beneath the bird. It had to be blood. But whose?

"Put your hands in your jacket pockets," he said.

When Reese had obeyed, he placed one of the revolvers on the floor a few feet away from him and slowly backed off. His own gun still pointed at Reese's chest. At twenty feet, he placed the second revolver on the floor. The two men stood facing one another behind the guns. Gaynor laid his own revolver on a nearby shelf. Then he put his hands in his jacket pockets as he had ordered Reese to do.

He began the count. "One. Two."

He saw Reese smiling slightly. His eyes glinted. His face was flushed, and he seemed like some sort of large, exotic animal.

"Three."

Reese jumped the count and moved for the gun. Hands free of his pockets, he went forward and down, reaching, a giant crow in a snowy landscape. The sonofabitch, thought Gaynor without surprise, and he stood very still, a mildly interested spectator at a late shooting match. His eyes, flat and colorless, showed no emotion. They might have been glass. Waiting until Reese had the gun in his hand and was bringing it up, Gaynor fired through his jacket pocket. He fired twice, one shot instantly following the other, the explosions ricocheting back and forth off the concrete walls like a machinegun burst. Reese's momentum carried him onto his knees and face. His hand, reaching, still held the revolver.

Gaynor turned him over. Both bullets had caught him in the upper chest. He was dead. The hazel eyes bored into the ceiling. They looked as hard as ever. Gaynor forced them closed. Then he concentrated on what needed to be done. He had worn his gloves during the entire time so there were no fingerprints to worry about. He retrieved his own revolver from the shelf and left behind the weapon he had fired. It was the snub-nosed police special that Reese had been carrying. He remembered the handkerchief he had given Reese to disguise his voice and found it in the dead man's shirt pocket. Preparing one of his usual Apostle calling cards, he printed:

IN MEMORIUM, FOR THE REVEREND HANSON FORSYTHE. He placed the card beside the body and left the house.

There were many pious people, he thought, who managed to find a satisfactory level of justice in the ordinary ways of the Lord. Things surely couldn't happen in this world without divine intention. Still, a bit of mortal help now and then couldn't hurt. Glory be to God.

13

News of the apostle's warning letter to Clayton Taylor and his shooting of William Reese arrived too late to make the morning editions but were carried by all the wire services—first as a flash bulletin, then as the lead item on regularly scheduled radio and television newscasts. Featured at this stage were simply the facts that, not only did the Apostle appear to be threatening the life of the nationally known church leader, but that he had underscored the seriousness of this warning by actually killing one of the minister's closest aides.

Later, however, as the police and media were able to examine the circumstances surrounding the shooting more closely, other details were revealed: namely, who Reese was, why he had been singled out for punishment, and the meaning of the cryptic message on the Apostle's calling card. In conjunction with this, the press ran photographs of Hanson Forsythe taken just prior to his murder along with quotes from his widow to the effect that as far as she was concerned,

Reese's death was merely a fortuitous combination of justice deferred and God's will. There was also a dramatically moving Associated Press picture of the old lady, eyes closed and hands extended in benediction, as she silently blessed the anonymous Apostle for having finally granted payment to her martyred husband after twelve long years of waiting. When asked for her reaction to the Apostle's warning letter to Clayton Taylor, Mrs. Forsythe was reported to have declared that although she had never been one to believe in violent solutions to life's problems, the nature of today's world was unfortunately such that the gentler alternative of turning the other cheek was just likely to result in one's being struck twice.

The Reverend Clayton Taylor himself was portrayed as griefstricken at having lost his longtime associate and shocked and bewildered by the Apostle's commission of so reasonless an act. He reminded the press that twelve years earlier William Reese had been declared innocent of the crime for which the Apostle had allegedly punished him, and that no new evidence to the contrary had been introduced since. When questioned as to how he felt about the Apostle's taking the law into his own hands, about whether he now would not perhaps choose to reconsider his former endorsement of such tactics, Taylor replied that one unhappy aberration, regardless of how tragic the result, should not be used to negate all the potential benefits of what must still be considered a basically positive concept. As to the warning letter and its possible effect on his future actions, Taylor stated that in due course he would offer a carefully considered reply through the media. In the meantime, however, he hoped that it was generally well enough known that in matters of morality, ethics, and personal behavior, he answered only to God.

What's he trying to do to me? wondered Newman.

It seemed in no way strange that he should be taking the Apostle's latest exploits personally. Indeed, it struck him as entirely logical, as though the two of them were connected by an intricate network of invisible strings. Jiggle one and the other shook. So that since he himself had suddenly entered into a significant new relationship with Clayton Taylor, wasn't it only logical that the Apostle should be establishing one of his own? But what did strike Newman as rather curious was that after almost two days, the Apostle had not yet felt compelled to call and talk about it.

No more than an hour after this last thought, however, the call did come in.

"Miss me?" asked the familiar, muffled voice.

Newman found himself grinning at the phone. "You're absolutely intuitive."

"What are you grinning about?"

"That's pretty good. Are you psychic, too?"

"It's all in your voice. Besides, I feel the same way."

Newman chose to remain quiet on that one.

"And you needn't bother stalling with the long silences. I've learned from last time. I'll never hang on long enough for you to get a trace again."

"How is your arm?" asked the detective. He knew from the lack of a quick response that he had hit it right. "Don't neglect it. Gunshot wounds infect easily."

"You're pretty cute, too."

"Not as cute as you. Atlanta was murder number two. Are you starting to enjoy it yet?"

"Just to keep the record straight," said the camouflaged voice, "it wasn't murder. I put two guns on the floor. Reese had the same chance as I."

"Terrific. I'll recommend you for the Fair Play of the Year award. And now I suppose it's Taylor's turn to get shot because you think he ordered the Forsythe killing."

"No. That was the big surprise. At the end, Reese admitted Taylor knew nothing about it. Taylor was actually angry when he found out what Reese had done."

Newman sat staring blankly at a peeling cabinet. He was not even trying for a trace on the call. Apart from everything else, he was too interested in the conversation to risk losing it. "Then why did Taylor perjure himself by making up an alibi to save Reese's neck?"

"Loyalty to a devoted disciple. It almost makes him lovable, don't you think?"

"I'm curious," said the detective. "Why this sudden absorption with Clayton Taylor?"

"Didn't you read my letter in the *Times*? Or do cops only read the *Daily News*?"

"I read it. And I thought it was a pretentious piece of crap. I'd like to hear your real reason for going after Taylor."

There was no answer. The silence dragged.

"Are you still there?" Newman again found himself smiling. "I hope I haven't hurt your feelings."

"What do *you* think my real reason is?"

"Simple. You're after a big, grandstand play, and Clayton Taylor is perfect for your needs. You're getting bored with the local talent and want to go national. So you wrap yourself in self-righteous rhetoric and ride the reverend's reputation onto the front pages of every paper in the country."

There was a smothered laugh at the other end of the line. "You really see right through me, don't you, Lieutenant?"

It was not the response Newman had expected.

"But I'm sure you're excited by the whole idea," said the voice. "As I become more famous, so do you. And isn't that really what we're both after? Fame?" The laugh was repeated. "I think my safe time is about up. Speak to you soon, Lieutenant."

The wire went dead.

Harry Blake brought the managing editor into his office, closed the door, and sat him down facing a large form draped with a sheet. Kelly chewed his half a cigar and waited, his expression that of a tolerant adult indulging a hyperactive child.

"Okay. I give up. What is it?"

Blake lifted the sheet, exposing a life-size mannequin like the ones used in window displays. The dummy was dressed in a dark windbreaker, faded jeans, and running shoes and on its head was a bearded Apostle mask. The effect was so lifelike the Kelly just sat staring.

"What do you think?" said Blake.

"He's almost frightening."

"I'm going to make him a regular feature on my show, work out imaginary interviews with a taped voice, that sort of thing. I want to create a visual persona to go with the mystique I've been building in print. The reader response has been tremendous. Have you been checking the mail lately?"

The editor nodded. He still seemed transfixed by the dummy, a mute apostolic vision in twentieth-century street clothes.

"I just wish I knew who the guy was," said the reporter. "I'd like to kiss him on both cheeks. Do you realize what he's done? In two months, he's turned a vague biblical image into everyman's fantasy. He's become a living legend, a one-man force for good and justice in a cynical, unjust world.''

"He's also killed two men," said Kelly flatly.

Blake waved his hand disdainfully. "They deserved killing."

"And how about threatening to assassinate a minister of God?"

"Clayton Taylor? That's some minister of God. Besides, there was no mention of assassination in the letter.''

"The threat was implicit." Kelly worked his mangled cigar. "I'm afraid we're going to have to take it a little easy, Harry.''

"What easy? I thought we were going all out on this?''

"We are. Within reason."

Blake looked closely at the editor. "What are you trying to say? You suddenly sound like a fucking lawyer, Brian. Are you weaseling on me?''

"It's not a question of—"

"Bullshit! I know you. Jesus, you're suddenly running scared.''

"Be reasonable, Harry. The publisher has been on my back all morning. Our hero has made an abrupt change. He's no longer what he was two days ago. Attacking muggers, rapists, and pushers is a lot different from killing a man like Reese and threatening the life of a powerful national figure like Taylor. A newspaper simply can't appear to be endorsing this sort of thing.''

"I'm not a newspaper. I'm Harry Blake.''

"All I'm asking is that . . .''

But Blake, no longer listening, had picked up his customized Apostle and was carrying him out of the office.

The dummy appeared on *Blake's Corner* two nights later. The talk show's featured guest, he sat imperturbably opposite Harry Blake and answered questions in a taped voice that one of the studio engineers, using echo chambers, had given the portentous tones of a biblical prophet on an embassy to Mount Sinai. The questions covered a wide range of topics, and the dummy's opinions coincided, naturally, with those of the show's host. These included everything from Blake's feelings about major political candidates to the current breakdown in morality, to racism, to foreign affairs, to the state of the nation itself. When the subject of the Apostle's recent killing of Reese and his threat to Clayton Taylor was broached, the dummy said, "Whatever I may have done or yet threaten to do, I follow my own conscience, which remains clear. And that, to me, is sweeter than love."

Blake liked that last line he had placed in the dummy's mouth and chose to end the show on it. Indeed, his column the next day, a heated polemic on man's never-ending quest for a higher justice, was titled "Sweeter Than Love."

The dummy Apostle proved an instant success. *Blake's Corner* was a network show, and the responses came in from all over the country. There were even calls from the campaign managers of two senators up for reelection, asking that their candidates be granted the opportunity to open a dialogue with the surrogate Apostle on the next available show.

The American Crusade Party's National Council was gathered once again in the chairman's Virginia retreat. It was not one of their regular meetings, but an extraordinary session called to discuss three recent happenings: the ACP's first nationally coordinated strike, the killing of William Reese, and the Apostle's implied threat to Clayton Taylor himself. Taylor also had a fourth item for the agenda, but none of the others knew about it yet.

The successful national operation was examined first, with each of the council members—Turner, Burns, Stafford, Billings, Harding; the reverend enjoyed likening them to the ultimate WASP partnership—contributing the details pertinent to his respective region. The seven deaths were discussed briefly and with the cool detachment of generals, themselves safely removed from the scene of battle, considering the latest casualty counts. The dead were, after all, only numbers. In their meeting room was a large map of the United States pinned to the wall, with acetate overlays, colored pins to indicate particular points of action, and red and black crayon markings to lend an orderly and formal look to the entire operation. They all seemed to have studied the same financial and political manuals, and several had written books on the changing power structures within a variety of democratic and totalitarian systems. Time also was spent working on the plans for National Operation II, which was scheduled to take place soon. This action, however, would be primarily political, with the targets selected from among the lower echelons of municipal and state government.

Taylor, as chairman, did the summing up. "Just one point, gentlemen, that I know we're all aware of but that still bears mentioning. We're entering the phase of operations in which more and more blood is likely to be shed. This is unfortunate but necessary. Because we're all compassionate human beings, there may be moments when we'll be both frightened and horrified by much of what we see happening. That's precisely when we must be strongest. Let's be sure to bear this in mind during the weeks and months ahead."

His brief statement completed, Taylor found himself more amused than concerned. There was little chance of compassion interfering with the plans of these five men. If they felt anything at all, it was probably the beginning of dread. His sleek, well-fed power brokers were still barely on the fringes of what awaited them. With the first mention of blood, the reverend could almost smell the burgeoning fear, could almost feel all that was bright and green among them draining away. In a sense, it was an extinction. If they lived another twenty years, or even forty, they would remember that this was the moment that death began.

The fear was further compounded by the discussion of Reese's death and the threat to Taylor. The reverend was learning more and more about wealth and power. Mostly, they made the fear of dying that much greater. And suddenly there was this Apostle, this anonymous killer, this madman, this avenging angel who had already killed twice and now was threatening to kill their leader.

They all had suggestions.

"You'd better start toning down your speeches," Frank Burns told the reverend. "You've got to go easy until we at least get a fix on this crazy."

Stafford's advice was for Taylor to double his bodyguards and stay away from unprotected public places.

"Our number one priority must be to find this man," said James Billings. "We must hire our own investigators. The police are incompetent. They're doing nothing."

Turner, from Houston, suggested the posting of a million-dollar cash reward for information leading to the Apostle's capture or death.

The councilman from Atlanta, Bob Harding, drawled, "Why

not just play possum with him, Clayton? Why not agree to what he asks, work out some kind of meeting, and grab him?''

The reverend listened without comment until they had finished. ''I appreciate your concern, gentlemen, but I don't share it. In fact, with the proper handling, all this publicity can be priceless to us.''

''What good is the publicity if he kills you?'' said Burns.

''He won't kill me, Franklin. Not in cold blood, anyway. This man is not an assassin. The men he's killed so far, including Bill Reese, were armed and trying to kill *him*. He won't risk losing his precious saintly image by murdering an ordained minister of God.'' Taylor smiled faintly. ''And that's regardless of how much he feels I'm subverting the Lord's word.''

''Then what do you plan to do?'' asked Stafford.

''Open up a dialogue,'' said Taylor and left it at that.

It was only then that he considered them ready to hear what he had learned about the secretary of state's recent Mideast tour.

Newman drove slowly along the narrow, one-way street, moving west toward the Hudson. It was dark, and the building numbers were hard to read. Also, it was after midnight, he had better than half a pint of bourbon sloshing around inside him, and his eyes were not at their best. His eyes actually had not been at their best for ten years and he owned several pairs of glasses, but he never remembered to carry them. Besides, a cop with glasses was ridiculous. Then he saw Mulcahy step out from between two parked cars and he stopped just past the entrance to what he assumed must be number 659.

Mulcahy slid in beside him. It was a cool night, but the young detective's forehead and upper lip showed small beads of sweat.

''He came in about an hour ago. I called you right away.''

''Was he alone?''

''Yeah. I swear to Christ I think it's him, Lieutenant. I think we've really got him this time.''

Newman lit a cigarette to cover his bourbon breath. He was less hopeful than Mulcahy. One or another of his men had already come up with a fair number of false leads. Still, you never knew what was going to come flying out when you went around beating bushes, and despite himself Newman felt on edge, even nervous. Over what? he wondered. That it would or wouldn't be him?

"All right, let's hear it from the beginning."

"The guy seems to fit on all counts," said Mulcahy. "He lives in the right area. He's about the right height, build, and age—between thirty and forty, I'd guess. He lives alone. I checked with the janitor and he's divorced. And listen to this. About a week ago, he bought a load of antiseptic and surgical gauze and tape from a drugstore on the corner of Broadway and a Hundred and Eighth. The druggist remembered him because he was asking a lot of questions about how to treat a knife cut. He told the druggist the cut was in his kid's arm. And it turns out he has no kid."

"Did you get a key?"

"Just to the downstairs lobby. An apartment key wouldn't do us much good, anyway. The tenants all add their own inside chains and deadbolts. He lives sixth floor rear, facing north. It's an old building, so there's a line of fire escapes."

Newman put out his cigarette and opened the car door. "Okay, let's go."

There was no doorman, so they let themselves into the lobby and rode an elevator down to the basement. From there, they worked their way out to the back of the building and found the line of fire escapes leading to the suspect's apartment.

"I'll take the fire escape," said Newman. "You go upstairs and in exactly five minutes ring his doorbell. When he asks who it is, identify yourself and tell him there's been a robbery down the hall and you want to ask him a few questions. Be polite, quiet, and unthreatening. Don't disturb any neighbors. And be sure to keep to one side in case he panics and fires through the door. Remember. He's already killed two men, so it's not just fun and games."

Mulcahy's face looked blue and drawn in the starlight. He chewed his lower lip. "Think maybe we should call in for some backup, Lieutenant?"

"We don't need a platoon for this. It could still be nothing. Either he'll check your badge and open the door or he'll go for the fire escape. Either way, we can handle it. If he does let you in without a fuss, cover him and unlock the back window for me. Do nothing else by yourself. Understand?"

Mulcahy nodded.

"Then let's do it."

Mulcahy boosted Newman to the first-floor fire escape ladder, then disappeared into the basement. Newman silently climbed the ladder. Far off, the lights of the George Washington Bridge were framed between the walls of two buildings. A salt breeze lifted off the river. The lieutenant stifled a cough and tasted tobacco smoke. Six floors up, he peered into a darkened bedroom. Reflected light filtered in from another room. He drew his revolver, stepped to one side of the window, and knelt on the slatted iron flooring. He was sweating now and could feel his shirt, wet and cold, sticking to his back. Christ, he was more nervous than Mulcahy, but for different reasons. Glancing up, he saw a low bank of cumulus, glowing orange from the city's lights. A moment later he could hear the faint ringing of a doorbell.

He squatted. At first there was nothing. Then the dark shape of a tall man appeared in the doorway and entered the bedroom. Newman watched as he went to a closet and came out slipping an envelope into his pocket. The man seemed to move calmly and unhurriedly, with no wasted motion. Newman heard the doorbell ringing steadily and insistently. Then the man approached the fire escape window, unlocked and opened it, and looked straight into the muzzle of the lieutenant's revolver.

"Police," said Newman. "Step back and put up your hands."

The man dove instantly, straight out. One hand grabbed the revolver, the other tore at Newman's face. A skull like a boulder smashed into his chest. Still squatting and off balance, he was slammed back against the fire escape rail. His gun clattered against steel. Seconds later, he heard it land in the courtyard. Schmuck! He swore at himself. Twenty-two years a cop and then this. He struggled to get up, but the man was all over him by then and he felt a stab of pain in his groin. The Apostle, he thought, and he had visions of celestial lights while a fist hammered his nose and throat and a solid kick caught him in the stomach. He doubled over. Whatever breath he had left was sucked out. Then a dead cold chop struck him in the back of the neck and cut off a small forest of nerves.

Dimly, he could feel himself being lifted. Anguish so intense it was almost pleasurable seemed to push into him. It changed at once to shock. This momzer was trying to kill him. Another few seconds and he'd be in the air, flying without wings. Pressure was building behind his head. He felt betrayed, as though a solemn if unacknowledged pact was being violated. He wanted to scream out *Hey, what's going on? This is me, Newman. Since when do we kill each other?*

As of now, evidently.

But even that was somehow wrong. And without knowing anything more, he knew this could not be the Apostle. He knew it the way a Jewish kid wakes up one morning and knows he is different from practically all other people on the planet. Pressed hard, bent backward over the rail like a reluctant lover, he squeezed a knee between the man's legs and drove it straight up with all his strength. The man cried out. He released his hold, and Newman hooked an arm about his head. He tightened the arm, putting pressure on his throat and cutting off his air. The man was strong, and for a moment Newman was worried that he might not be able to keep his grip. For about ten or fifteen seconds they swayed together on the fire escape, the two of them straining in balance. Then Newman sensed the man's strength starting to ebb and he gained control, locking a hand about his own wrist, slowly choking him into unconsciousness. When he felt the man's body begin to go limp, he knew he could kill him. He wanted to. He was that irrational with anger. There was a murmur in the man's throat, no more than a whisper, and he coldly listened to it. Hatred passed through him in waves. *Jesus, what's wrong with me?* he thought and released his hold just in time. The man fell at his feet like a bundle of rags. Newman dragged him off the fire escape, into the bedroom. Then he went to the front door and let in a very pale, panicked Detective Mulcahy.

The man revived in a few minutes with little more than a sore neck and throat. His name was Arthur Condon, and he had approximately three quarters of a million dollars' worth of uncut diamonds in the envelope Newman had seen him put in his pocket. The stones were later identified as having been taken from a courier at gunpoint several weeks before. Condon did have a self-treated wound in his arm, but it turned out to be a knife cut from a fight with a confederate who had apparently fingered the job for him. The diamond thief was sure it was this man who had turned him in when he failed to get what he felt to be his fair share of the loot.

Newman wrote a recommendation that Detective Mulcahy be cited for exceptional police work in breaking the case. Considering the possibilities, the lieutenant felt it had all turned out incredibly well.

Newman was speaking to a national convention of Reform rabbis at the Americana Hotel. That's what I do, he thought. I speak. I'm transmogrifying into a disembodied voice.

Still, he was not that different, not unique. In one way or another, everyone had their own propaganda. You had a belief, a hope, a line of reasoning, and you projected it. You spread it about. If you were lucky and good enough, you were able to move those listening to you to feel and believe as you did. And tonight, for his own part, Newman, a lieutenant of detectives, a propagandist for himself and the New York Police Department, a nonpracticing Jew, was trying his best to make it known to these several hundred leaders of Reform Jewry that in a curious way the Reverend Clayton Taylor could actually prove to be a blessing in disguise to the American Jewish community.

Newman did this subtly, of course, giving the whole premise a light, amusing twist and tacking it on like a tail to his usual law-and-order proselytizing. You had to be careful with this crowd. They were smart. They could sniff out a phony pitch from its opening sentence. But this was what he had committed himself to do, and he was doing it.

So he tread cautiously projecting the concept that, ridiculous as it at first might seem, Taylor's artful anti-Semitic insinuation could in the end work in their favor. Consider. It was difficult for anyone to explain why, after the almost forty years of general tolerance and understanding that followed the Holocaust, many nations and individuals now seemed to have done an abrupt about-face. The only logical answer seemed to be that Jews were acceptable only as victims, and when their collective condition in the world changed so that they no longer appeared to be victims, then the non-Jewish population of the planet found this so offensive to their delicate, goyische sensibilities that they felt forced to start turning them into victims again. Accordingly, if the rest of the world could only be made to believe Clayton Taylor's rejuvenated lies about the Jews, then they might again consider them properly returned to their perennial status and learn to love and embrace them once more.

Everyone laughed. Fine. Laughter was a good beginning. It was effectively disarming. It also had the ability to turn the ugly and fearsome into merely the banal.

But upstairs later, at a private meeting with the group's president, Dr. Morris Sokolsky, there was little evidence of laughter as Newman told the rabbi about Clayton Taylor's assurances and offer. To Newman's surprise, Sokolsky himself had turned out to be a fairly elderly man with long, white hair and a thin, bearded, ascetic face. In his mind, the lieutenant had always associated Reform Judaism with a youthful, clean-shaven image, and the rabbi seemed oddly out of character in the role, as though an error had been made somewhere back at central casting, and an old Orthodox type had been sent over by mistake.

Dr. Sokolsky listened gravely and without interruption until Newman had finished. Then, squinting narrowly at the detective, he said, "Let me see if I understand all this properly. You're telling me that Taylor claims his anti-Semitic innuendoes are only a temporary political expedient, that the Jewish condition will actually improve because of him, and that he'll contribute a million a month to the UJA or whatever for as long as we, the Jewish community, don't actively campaign against him and those he supports. Is that correct?"

"Yes."

"And what about you? How do *you* feel about it, Lieutenant?"

"I wouldn't trust the man as far as I could throw him."

"Then why are you even bothering to offer me such a proposition?"

Newman felt strangely foolish. "Because someone from Israeli Intelligence has asked me to get close to Taylor, and this is the only way I can do it."

"Aah." The rabbi interlaced pale, delicate fingers and rocked gently in his chair. He seemed to be praying.

"If you want to check, I can tell you who to call at the Israeli Embassy."

"You're spying for Israel?"

"I guess that's what it comes down to."

"That's against many of our laws, you know. You could get into serious trouble."

"So what else is new?"

"What are you supposed to be looking for?"

"They say they don't know."

Dr. Sokolsky sat rocking silently for several moments. "As it happens, I once worked with the Israelis myself. I helped get arms to them in forty-eight, when they were granted independence, then denied the means of keeping it. It was very complicated. Money had to be raised, weapons found and purchased, transportation arranged, officials bribed, papers forged, borders crossed. That was also against our laws. But, in retrospect, it was perhaps the most satisfying accomplishment of my life."

"Then you'll go along with it?"

"It's not that simple. To begin with, whom may I tell what you've just told me?"

"No one. My neck is way out as it is."

"Then it's impossible," said Dr. Sokolsky. "Certain top organizational leaders would have to be told. Otherwise, there's no way I can convince them to accept such a deal."

Newman said nothing. He seemed to be sliding in deeper by the minute.

"Consider, Lieutenant. Once I agree to such a proposition, I'm as exposed as you. You'll just have to rely on my discretion. I assure you, I'll tell no one who doesn't absolutely have to be told."

"All right."

"Good. That should take care of our key leaders. But we're all going to need at least the illusion of logic to persuade our congregations that we suddenly haven't taken leave of our senses. How do you propose to handle this in your own public statements?"

Newman shrugged. "For me, it's not that difficult. The people Taylor is endorsing are actually those I'd back myself. They're all strong, conservative, law-and-order candidates, which is what I happen to believe this country needs right now. American Jews have been knee-jerk liberals too long, anyway. It's time they started reacting to practical need rather than aesthetically satisfying humanist theory."

224

"That's all very fine, but we can't tell our people that."

"You don't have to. Taylor's not asking us to love and endorse him. He just doesn't want us attacking him from the pulpit and through the media."

"You make it sound almost reasonable," said the rabbi flatly. "And think of all the Jewish lives we can improve, perhaps even save, for a million dollars a month."

"Who knows? Maybe I can even get him up to two million." Newman gazed into the old man's eyes, pouched in waxen wrinkles. "The growing cost of anti-Semitism. If we make it expensive enough, maybe we can eliminate it entirely."

It was only the beginning of their discussion. They talked far into the night. Apart from everything else, there were some very real problems involved in simply trying to work out such an agreement. To begin with, no single organization was qualified to speak for the country's approximately six million Jews. The most that could be hoped for would be a consensus among the leaders of the three major rabbinical confederations—Reform, Conservative, and Orthodox—and those of the Anti-Defamation League and the United Jewish Appeal. The directors of the last group could be especially helpful in contacting the various division heads responsible for fund-raising in their respective professions and industries, with the major emphasis here on the media.

It was close to 3:00 A.M. when Newman rose to leave.

"I'll be honest with you, Lieutenant," said Sokolsky, shaking his hand. "If anyone but you had come to me with this proposal, it would have made me very uneasy. But I respect your judgment and trust your instincts. You're not only one of us but you've spent a lifetime as a police officer. Which means you're far better versed in the practicalities of day-to-day survival than we in the rabbinate. We're too much mystics and dreamers."

"You weren't too much of a mystic and dreamer back in forty-eight."

The old man reluctantly let go of Newman's hand. He stood there, blinking. For a moment he seemed to forget where he was and to whom he was speaking.

"Please" he said tiredly "be a nice-careful little spy. For all our sakes."

* * *

When he got home, he discovered Mary asleep in his bed. She often did that, sometimes surprising him in the middle of the night as she crawled in beside him. "I suddenly needed to feel you" would be her only offered explanation. "Yes, but what if you slid in and found another woman with me?" he once asked. To which she replied, "So? I've always wondered how it would be with three, anyway." He believed her. At times she had an almost clinical, probing, mentally acquisitive attitude toward sex that could either amuse or irritate him, depending on his mood. Tonight, welcoming him beside her, she was all warmth and tenderness in her lovemaking, as though saying, *Come in, darling, don't you know you're my life?* This room, he thought, this bed, this canopy of darkness. Sometimes his, sometimes hers. Increasingly, it seemed to be where they really lived.

Still, at the end, as always, she was unable to let him immediately drift off into sleep. The urgency of passion— lust, she called it—relieved, there was always something she was anxious to have him tell her about. Tonight, she had to hear all about his meeting with the rabbi. Listening, she lay with her head on his chest in her undisputably favorite listening position, feeling his breathing as he talked, his voice soft, mellow, and losing itself quickly in the silent room.

"Is it okay if we go to sleep now?" He sighed when he was finally through.

She did not answer.

"What is it?"

"I suppose you didn't tell the rabbi that Taylor was going to reward you with the police commissioner's desk?"

"Ah." He lay breathing the sweet, just-washed smell of her hair. "Is that really how much you think of me?"

"I didn't mean . . ."

But they both knew she did.

"I told him," Newman said.

"How did he react?"

"He thought it would be wonderful. My God. A Jewish police commissioner of the world's greatest city. If anything, it was this that reassured him about Taylor's intentions."

"I'm sorry." She kissed him. "Forgive me?"

"I forgive you. But how could you have even thought something like that?"

"Because I'm stupid."

"Whatever else you may be, you're sure not that. Try another reason."

"Then because I happen to be a professional psychologist," she said quietly. "Because I happen to know how vulnerable the best of us can be when we want something badly enough. And . . ."

"Go on."

"And I've never known you to want anything as you suddenly seem to want to be police commissioner of New York."

Newman was finding himself overwhelmed by a sudden influx of confessions. People were coming into Police Headquarters, asking for him by name and refusing to speak to anyone else. They claimed they were simply following the Apostle's orders. Newman was so swamped with paperwork that he had to requisition two additional clerks to handle it.

They all came in with the same story. Each of them had received a letter followed by a telephone call. Both messages came from the Apostle. The letters were typewritten. The calls were described as sounding weirdly muffled, as though the caller, a male, was speaking through a crumpled handkerchief or cloth of some sort. The messages themselves, also apparently identical, alluded to crimes allegedly committed by the individuals called and for which they had somehow managed to escape punishment. First among them was a pyromaniac accused of incinerating a dozen people in a tenement fire but against whom the police had never been able to collect enough hard evidence to get an indictment. Then there was a husband whose long-abused, cruelly battered wife was too intimidated to press charges, a gang leader who had been extorting protection money from neighborhood shopkeepers, a child abuser who preyed on victims too young to bear credible witness, a fast-talking swindler who had defrauded a great many elderly people out of their life's savings, and several chronically drunken drivers who had never received anything more than token fines. These, along with others, streamed into Newman's office like eager penitents seeking absolution from their parish priest.

The Apostle's messages were brief and to the point. *Report to Lieutenant Jay Newman at Police Headquarters,* he told his chosen sinners. *If you refuse, you will die. This is not a*

*joke. I have already killed two men. You have twenty-four
hours to get your life and affairs in order.*

Now he's really going off the deep end, thought Newman.

But that was not what he truly believed. The more he
considered the Apostle's latest burst of activity, the more sane
it appeared. The man had established a reputation. He had
been credited with two widely publicized killings. The deaths
ensured his being taken seriously. All he had to do now was
put his two corpses to work for him. Which was precisely
what he was doing. In the meantime, of course, he was
helping to clear the city of a great many vermin, a fact far
from lost on the police commissioner.

"What we obviously need," he told Newman, "are a few
more Apostles. I hope you're not getting too close to picking
him up."

"Very funny. I assume that's supposed to be a joke."

"Only partly. This is one of those situations with built-in
ambivalence." Westley fitted a cigarette into his holder and
lighted up. "How is your investigation going? I haven't heard
anything on it from you lately. Or have you been too busy
taking confessions?"

"We're inching along. It's mostly pick and shovel work at
this stage."

The commissioner closed his office door and sat down at
his desk. "I've been meaning to talk to you. Quite honestly,
the one disturbing element in this entire Apostle jamboree is
his sudden threat to Clayton Taylor. Do you think he's serious about it?"

"He just killed one of Taylor's top aides. How much more
serious can he get?"

"That's what's starting to worry me."

"I didn't know you cared about the good reverend that
much."

"Don't be childish. What has caring got to do with it?
Since you're now entering the devious realm of power politics, you're going to have to start thinking a lot differently
than you have in the past. Without Taylor, I have far less
chance of being governor, and you have no chance at all of
being police commissioner. Which makes the state of the
man's health of more than passing interest to us both. Hasn't
that even occurred to you?"

"My mind doesn't work that way."

The commissioner looked mildly pained. "Now you're being superior. And that's another thing you're going to have to start adjusting. You can no longer float so supremely above the battle. You can no longer just say fuck you to one and all. You can no longer afford that particular luxury. Which may yet turn out to be the single greatest price you're going to have to pay for your latent ambition."

Newman was silent. Suddenly, everyone seemed to be lecturing him on the temptations and pitfalls of aspiring to high office.

"But getting back to the Apostle versus Taylor," said Westley in his soft, whispering voice. "Since our local masked avenger felt compelled to kill this man Reese for that old Atlanta murder, must we now assume he'll also feel justified in killing Taylor himself for ordering it?"

"No. Before Reese died, he apparently told the Apostle that the reverend had nothing to do with the murder, that he was actually furious when he found out and only alibied him out of some misguided sense of loyalty."

"What are you talking about? Where did you pick up that information?"

"From the Apostle. He called soon after the shooting."

Westley stared at the detective. "You mean you've actually spoken with him?"

"Several times. It's a little game he seems to enjoy playing. He likes to bait me. He muffles his voice to disguise it and calls from different pay phones. Once, I even managed to hold him on long enough to get the call traced, but he slipped away. Now he's gotten smarter."

"Interesting." Westley leaned back in his chair, the cigarette holder at a jaunty angle in a corner of his mouth, his custom-tailored suit creasing gracefully across the chest. "Why do you suppose he feels the need to do that?"

Newman shrugged. "I guess it adds to the kicks, personalizes it. Who knows with this kind of joker."

"Did it ever occur to you that he may be someone you know?"

The detective shook his head.

"Is it so impossible?"

"No. But I can't really buy it. It's too neat, too simplistic."

"Why would he bother disguising his voice if he wasn't afraid you might recognize it?"

"That's just part of his schtick, like his mask and gloves. He does it with everyone, even those he's sending in to confess. They all describe the same, muffled telephone voice." Newman grinned. "I appreciate your trying to help, Michael. But didn't you just say you hoped I wasn't getting too close to picking him up?"

"That was before I really began considering his potential threat to our mutual godfather."

The commissioner's chiseled, much-too-perfect face was helped, even humanized, by the faint suggestion of a frown. It was still there and growing stronger when Newman left.

Exactly one week after William Reese was killed and the Apostle's warning to Taylor was made public, the minister's widely awaited response to both was carried by the media as a full-page ad in the form of an open letter. It began with a brief, fragmentary quotation from *The Book of Common Prayer:*

> Our Father, who art in heaven . . . forgive us our trespasses, As we forgive those who trespass against us.

This was followed by a second quote, this one from Virgil:

> A sudden madness came down upon the unwary lover— forgivable, surely, if Death knew how to forgive.

The religious and poetic tone of the letter having thus been set as one of forgiveness and the Apostle himself granted no less than the mantle of Orpheus, the reverend continued in his own words:

> I pray, dear Apostle, that these past few days have given you sufficient time to reflect upon and repent of the tragedy of your recent actions. May God grant you absolution for what has to be described as a calamitous error in judgment. As for your poor estimate of all that I am attempting to do, I can only say that it saddens me deeply. I, like you, am merely seeking what is best for the majority of our countrymen. I feel righteous in my heart. I pray that I am also righteous in the eyes of God. For only the Lord has the power to turn me from my path.

Newman read Taylor's message in the *New York Times* while drinking his morning coffee. The response held no surprises for him. There was nothing else that he could reasonably have expected the minister to say. Still, it somehow filled him with sadness, as though some inexplicable, undefined hope had suddenly died for all time. Love, he remembered having once read, was the word of God and it allowed for no division, no pettiness, no selfish practicalities of judgment. At some point, everyone had grown up being told to love his neighbor as himself and his enemy as his brother, and when did they all start believing otherwise?

Well, he would see what happened next.

What happened next turned out to be a brief postscript to Clayton Taylor's earlier response. Newman saw it as an ad in the *Times* two mornings later. Addressed to the Apostle, it said:

I have been doing some thinking. I have thought, if only there was some feasible way for us to meet and to talk. I believe with all my heart in communication. I believe there is nothing on God's earth that cannot be worked out by two well-intentioned human beings sitting down together and talking about it. Is such a thing at all possible for us? The nature of your unique personal situation puts it up to you to decide, to know, to figure something out. I cannot easily accept our being locked forever in our present adversarial position. If a meeting is in any way attainable, please call me. I will try to agree to whatever terms you offer.

Better, thought the detective, much, much better.

14

Gaynor had not worked on the big, blue canvas in days. He had not even taken off the sheet and looked at it. Just being in the same apartment with the painting and thinking about it seemed to sicken him in a new way. Creatively, it had as good as left him for dead. The vengeance of those maniacal eyes was complete. Nothing productive or decent seemed to remain in him.

Then the stubborn part of his brain took over and he tried to hold on to himself. You can't quit now, he thought. You haven't finished your work. And he went back to the canvas to do what some part of him had known all along had to be done.

He was interrupted late that afternoon by an unannounced visit from his dealer, whom he was careful to keep out of the studio. He had no intention of letting Sanders see what was happening there. How could he possibly begin to explain? To this end, Gaynor thought it best simply to say that he still wasn't working.

Fresh out of sympathy and understanding, Sanders instantly attacked. "Enough is enough," he said. "This is ridiculous. I'm sorry, but now you're just wallowing in it. Now you're just indulging yourself. I'm really disappointed. This isn't like you, Richard."

Gaynor smiled.

"You're amused?" The gallery owner's round, florid face

was even redder than usual. "You do have certain obligations, you know."

"To who? You and my public? I'm sure you're all managing okay."

"I mean to yourself and your talent. God gave you a priceless gift. To waste it is the worst kind of sacrilege."

"Do me a favor, Marvin. Don't invoke God. It worries me when people do that. It's a sure sign they've run out of logic."

Sanders waved a plump hand. "And you think sitting around, feeling sorry for yourself, is logical? What the hell do you do all day?"

"Indulge in wild sexual fantasies."

The gallery owner shook his head in frustration, a mourner grieving for the newly dead.

"From time to time I also paint these fantastic mental pictures," said Gaynor. "But since I'm the only one who can see them, I'm afraid you'd have trouble selling any. Right now, for example, I'm working on this very imaginative piece, all soft, misty pastels, of you and God taking a stroll together, trying to figure out what to do about me. There's just the two of you in a flat, lonely landscape, barren of life. All that's visible in the distance is the smoke from—"

Sanders swung around. "A burning plane?"

"Naturally."

"And what do you have God looking like?"

"Beardless and bald. I know it's a pretty radical concept, but I really don't think he should be hiding behind all the foliage. There's a certain elemental purity in naked skin. Don't you agree?"

"Sure. That's why I keep waiting for a bald president. We haven't had one since Eisenhower. Maybe that explains a few of our recent problems."

They stood looking at one another.

"Ah, it's just that I mourn for you, Richard." The soft, gentle face held about as much distress as there seemed room for. "You knew so early what most artists are never able to learn."

"What did I know?"

"That a sense of the wonder of life is infinitely more important to painting than the whole complicated business of making a picture."

"Yes, but it's still only a painting."
"And that's not enough?"
Gaynor shook his head.
"Why not, damn it?"
"Because it can't breathe."

"The eternal spiritual light is what we must watch for," said the reverend's tape-recorded radio voice, "for it shines from the universal holiness of life. It reaches our heart and changes our nature so that we can accept total belief in the teaching of Jesus Christ. It is a glow that illuminates God's worthiness to be served. It presses and encourages our hearts in a sincere love of God, which is the only principle of a true, gracious, and universal obedience to his divine will. And finally, it is a beatific light that convinces us of the reality of the glorious rewards that God has promised to those who devote their natural lives to serving and obeying him."

Now there's a man, thought Richard Gaynor, listening in wonder, who can get his mouth to say just about anything.

Jane brought over an old photo album along with that evening's fish, and after dinner they sat looking through it. The pictures covered the period from their first date through their courtship and into the early years of their marriage. At that time the twins had not even been conceived, yet Gaynor could feel them hovering over each snapshot, trying to reach him, their sweet breath close enough to mist his eyes and warm his cheeks. Unborn, they came to visit.

The photographs might as well have been of two strangers. Who were those two lovely young people, holding hands under a tree, smiling in the sunlight, strolling along some forgotten beach? Could they be Jane and him? He knew why she had brought the album, but it failed to work. To escape it, he took her to bed and they made love. His opiate. Hers, too. God, he could be grotesque. Sometimes his lust was comical, the silliest kind of human struggle. Yet what would he do without it?

So he lay back as she romped above him. Dark-tipped in the lamplight, her breasts swayed, teasing his lips. Her body a powdery gold, his own an empty battlefield marked by bombardment, its latest gouging still under gauze. Earlier, seeing his new wound for the first time, she had stared, suddenly worried and afraid. Minor, he assured her, but she was not convinced. The same bullet might have killed. Of course, but so what? Now, performing wildly, pouring out certain unfamiliar bursts and acts of passion, she tried to show him *so what*. There was none of this good stuff for the dead. What had she been doing since she left him, he wondered, and with whom? Somehow, he failed to care. Her fear became rapture, her guilt, happily remembered love. Or was that only how it seemed?

"Why don't I come home?" she asked when things had quieted down. "Why don't I just move right back in?"

He took refuge in a cigarette.

"Don't you feel anything at all for me anymore?"

"You were the one who left," he said.

They were at the kitchen table and Jane was pouring coffee into two mugs. Gaynor surveyed what he could see of his apartment—the dining room, the entrance foyer, half of the living room. The furniture was Jane's. At least she was the one who had shopped for it. Walking out, divorcing him, she had chosen to leave everything behind. As though fearing further contamination, he thought.

Feeling an ache in his chest, he wanted her to hurt a little, too. "Just out of curiosity, how many guys have you slept with since you flew away?"

Like someone slapped, she blinked several times. There were faint purple circles under her eyes.

"Roughly, three hundred and fifty. Give or take a dozen."

"You've learned a few things."

"So have you." Her voice was very flat, very dry. She was, sitting there, an extremely grave woman. "Who's been doing the teaching, your li'l ol' nurse?"

He was surprised. "What do you know about Kate?"

"I saw her leaving one night. No wonder she was so quick to throw me out of your hospital room." Jane toyed with her coffee. "Is she really that great in bed?"

Gaynor launched a full-color rendering of the three of them in a round robin. He stopped when he couldn't decide who should be doing what to whom. There were too many possibilities. It was too confusing.

"Do you love her?" Jane asked.

"How could I love her? I don't even love myself."

"Does she know about you? I mean, the Apostle?"

"Yes." Then, seeing her expression, he sighed. "I didn't tell her. She found my mask and stuff in the closet. Besides, what difference does it make?"

She looked up, seeking his face. Her eyes rested there, lightly, ready to fly off if she saw any sign of attack.

"Will you ever really be able to forgive me for leaving you?"

"What's there to forgive? People walk out on each other every day. That's not our problem."

"It might help us both if I came back. Can't we at least give it a try?"

"There's no point."

"Why not?"

He looked helplessly at her. "Because I have no future."

"Neither do I."

To get away from her eyes, he rose for more coffee. She still doesn't really understand, he thought.

It was easier with Kate. At least she understood, or seemed to. Sometimes he wondered whether he himself fully understood. But since it was Kate who had inspired the whole idea, she at least had a proprietary interest. And it gave them something to talk about when, briefly, they'd had enough of each other's bodies. Her voice made dead space come to life.

"So what are you going to do about it?" she said. "Are you going to meet him?"

They were discussing Taylor's recently published invitation.

"What could it accomplish?"

"You never know. Aren't you even curious to hear what he has to say?"

"I've already heard."

"I mean privately, one on one. Without all the garbage for the media."

"I've talked with him privately, too."

"Atlanta doesn't count. He didn't know who you were?"

Gaynor studied her face. It seemed changed since they had met, somehow thinner and more fragile. It made her eyes look larger. "He could be setting me up, working with the cops. Maybe Newman even gave him the idea."

"I don't think so. It's not his style. Besides, he'd be crazy to want you caught. You're giving him more publicity than money can buy. I'm sure he'd rather just gentle you along, get all the mileage he can out of your threats. Having you picked up would only end it all."

Gaynor laughed. "You're really having a ball with this, aren't you?"

Her eyes seemed to go dark. "How can you think I'd have a ball at something that's going to bury you?"

He put out his hand and touched her cheek. "All I meant was that you seem to be putting the same zest and enthusiasm into this Clayton Taylor business that you put into everything else. Is that so terrible?"

"Yes. Because that's not how I should be doing it. If anything, I should be doing it reluctantly, with sorrow and regret." She shook her head. "Lordy, lordy. Zest and enthusiasm. For an act of suicide."

"Hey, come on. That's what I love about you. You're no crepe-hanger. You know how to take life as it comes."

"I know how to take death, too," she said flatly.

"You're a nurse. You can't avoid it."

"Hell, I go chasing it." She made a strange, awkward gesture, hands and shoulders lifted. "I assume you don't know I was once married."

Gaynor looked at her. She suddenly seemed transparent. He felt he was staring right through her.

"He was one of my first patients. Acute leukemia. The doctors gave him six to nine months. So naturally I had to marry him, right? He actually lived for a year and a half, so I guess my zest and enthusiasm paid off a little." She forced a smile. "So you see? You're not my first terminal involvement."

"Did you love him?"

"Sure. Why not? I love anybody who seems certain to die soon. That's why I can deal so well with you." She chuckled softly. "And the only time it hurts is when I laugh."

Okay, she understood, he thought dully. Marvelous. To get her out of it, he said, "You may be right about setting something up with Taylor. It might be fun, at that."

"Fun? You're getting like me."

"But we've got to arrange it so I won't be a sitting duck. Even if Taylor is sincere, Newman could still have cops watching his back. It's going to take some figuring out."

"What else have we got to do?"

*   *   *

They worked on it for most of the following week. Once more going to the library, Gaynor poured through assorted CIA and FBI manuals on surveillance techniques and how to escape them. All of which he found curiously intriguing. There was an entire secret world out there. It was like placing a drop of swamp water under a high-powered microscope. Teeming battlefields became visible. Nothing was as it seemed. Every word, every act, was suspect. And this was how the intelligence community lived out their lives. It suddenly seemed as if everyone was determined to improve life on this earth. But each in his own way. Even if he had to kill to do it. Just like me, Gaynor thought.

When he and Kate had it figured out, when all the projected arrangements appeared as foolproof as they could make them, Gaynor went out to a Broadway telephone booth and put through a call to Atlanta.

"Reverend Taylor, please," he told the person who answered.

"Who's calling?"

"Just tell him it's the Apostle."

"I beg your pardon, suh?"

"Apostle," Gaynor said through his handkerchief. "Like those good people in the Bible who spread the word of Jesus."

"Yes, suh."

Several moments passed. Then Clayton Taylor said, "Is it you?"

"In person."

"This is strange. How can I know for sure?"

"You can't. You've just got to have faith, Reverend."

"I hope this call means we're going to meet."

"If you'll agree to my conditions."

"I'll certainly try. What are they?"

"First, that you come to New York," said Gaynor. "Second, that the meeting itself takes place late at night when very little traffic is moving. And third, that you use public transportation to get where I tell you to be."

"No problems there. When shall we make it?"

"How about three nights from tonight? On Wednesday."

"I can manage that," said Taylor. "Where and at what time?"

"I'll tell you that in New York. Where will you be staying?"

"At the Waldorf."

"I'll call your room at exactly one o'clock A.M. on Wednesday night. But if I read, hear, or even suspect you've told anyone, it's off." Gaynor hung up.

Wednesday night drifted in cool and clear, with a brilliant show of stars and a crescent moon hanging low.

At exactly one o'clock, Gaynor called the Waldorf-Astoria, was connected with Taylor's room, and heard his voice. "Welcome to New York," he said. "I'll be giving you instructions one step at a time. Some of the procedures may seem strange, but they've all been carefully laid out for my protection and must be followed to the letter."

"I understand."

"There's a public phone on the northwest corner of Lexington Avenue and Fifty-fourth Street, about six blocks from where you are now. I'll call you there in precisely twenty minutes. And don't take a cab. Walk," said Gaynor as he put down the receiver.

He had a walkie-talkie in his car. Moments later, Kate was on it.

"He just came out of the hotel," she said. "There's no one behind him. Not walking, anyway. It's hard to tell about the cars."

"Keep a full block back. Watch for the same cars reappearing from different directions. And make sure this talking machine stays in your bag whenever you're visible."

When he called the Lexington Avenue number, Taylor answered at once, sounding slightly breathless.

"There's a subway entrance at Fifth Avenue and Fifty-third Street," said Gaynor. "Take a downtown train and get off at the Forty-second Street station. At one forty-five I'll call you at one of a bank of three phones on the northeast corner of Forty-second Street and Third Avenue."

"Which of the three phones?"

"The one that rings."

Kate reported in. She was about to follow the minister down into the subway.

When Gaynor called Forty-second Street at the designated time, there was no answer. He called again and heard Taylor say, "The train was very bad. It kept stalling."

"Tell the mayor," said the artist through his handkerchief. "The Harley Hotel is right near where you're standing. Go up to Room Fourteen Sixty-five. The door will be unlocked."

"May I ask how long this goes on?"

"No."

Kate called to say that no one had followed Taylor into the hotel and that she was in position. Moments later, Gaynor had Room Fourteen Sixty-five on the line.

"Reverend, do you see the connecting door between your room and the next?"

"Yes."

"Well, now we come to a rather delicate part. First, you're going to have to remove all your clothing, including your underwear, and pile everything on the carpet beside that door. Then you'll raise your arms and turn completely around while someone observes you from the next room to make sure you're not wired. After that, you'll go into the bathroom and close the door so your clothing can be checked. You're not to come out until the phone rings again." Gaynor paused. "If all this is getting to be too much for you, Reverend, you can quit now. But I'm afraid these safeguards are necessary."

"If I were wired," said Taylor, "this room would already be surrounded. But since I've come this far, I'll go all the way."

It took eight minutes for Kate to report in. "He's built very nicely. There was nothing on him."

Gaynor called Taylor back. "You can get dressed now."

Wearing his mask and gloves, the Apostle entered the room a short while later. Taylor was fully dressed and waiting, a composed man with much on his mind. Gaynor drew up a chair and sat down facing him. His eyes flicked past the connecting door. It was open just a crack. Kate was listening. "All right, Reverend, now what did you want to tell me that was important enough to make you put up with all this nonsense?"

"It was interesting." Taylor smiled thinly at the Apostle mask. "But I must admit your disguise does take some getting used to."

Gaynor sat waiting.

"To begin with," said the minister, "I wanted you to know I'm no cynosure of evil. Nor am I prejudiced against any human being because of race, religion, or national origin.

The hate you accuse me of preaching, I preach not out of personal belief, but simply as a means to a political end.''

"You'd better explain that one to me.''

"The fastest way to bring people together en masse is by carefully manipulated prejudice. You can't shape history with declarations of benevolence. That has to be left for later.''

"When later? After your carefully manipulated prejudice sends rivers of blood flowing through the streets?''

Taylor sighed. "You're being melodramatic. Any blood you see in the streets is more likely to come from the same criminal violence that you yourself have been fighting than from anything I say. Whatever emotions I arouse will be safely released in the voting booth.''

"I don't believe that.''

"Then why didn't you shoot me when you were in Atlanta and shot William Reese?''

"Because it wasn't you who murdered Hanson Forsythe.''

"That wasn't the reason. It was because you haven't quite figured me out yet. And that's also why you agreed to this meeting. Before you can commit yourself to killing me, you need to be absolutely sure I deserve it.''

Gaynor stared hazily out from behind the Apostle's rubber flesh. The minister seemed far off in the distance, obscured by mist.

"For a hypermoral type like you,'' said Taylor, "to kill unjustly would be the ultimate horror. And despite all your angry name-calling, you're not really convinced I'm the villain you claim. You saw all I've done in Atlanta—the church, the university, the hospital—and that sticks in your craw doesn't it? You can't quite swallow all that.''

What am I doing here? Gaynor wondered. What do I want him to tell me? What am I waiting for?

"I'm sorry about your children,'' said Taylor quietly, "but killing me isn't going to bring them back.''

Gaynor just looked at him.

"It really wasn't very difficult to figure out. How could you be in Atlanta and not try to see and talk to me? I'd have done the same in your place. So after Reese was shot, I went through the tapes of all the interviews I'd granted that day. Your Mr. Kimball's speech pattern was the only one that was unmistakably New York. I listened to it again and again.

When you finally called, I knew instantly it was you. Muffled voice and all."

"Congratulations." Moving deliberately, Gaynor took out his revolver, screwed on the silencer, and pointed the weapon at Taylor's chest. "But why did you tell me?"

"To establish trust. We have to be able to believe one another. Don't worry. If I was able to turn you over to the police, or if I'd even wanted to, I'd have done it by now. Besides, the fact that I saw your face doesn't tell me who you are."

Gaynor gestured impatiently with his revolver. "Exactly what do you want?"

"To arrange a deal."

"You're crazier than I am."

"There's nothing crazy about a deal. It's what makes life manageable. I want, you want, we do for each other."

This was an impossible conversation, thought Gaynor. There was no logical way for it to be happening. The whole discussion had to have taken some sort of mad, metaphysical turn.

"I've been piecing things together," said the minister. "I'm beginning to understand your needs. Your children are gone, your life is empty, and you have to justify your existence with good deeds. Fine. Wonderful. In a short time you've captured the imagination of a great many people. You've become like a mythical figure, a symbol of right and justice in a society rendered catatonic in these areas. All of which can have enormous value to me politically. The Apostle's endorsement of a candidate would be an instant seal of integrity."

"And of course you'd choose the candidate."

"We'd do it together."

Gaynor's laugh was smothered and hollow behind his mask. "We'd never agree. I happen to love Jews, blacks, and Hispanics."

"Please . . ." The minister shook his head wearily. "Please forget my public rhetoric. I've told you. That's not me." He paused for a moment. "Perhaps this may help convince you. Recently, through Lieutenant Newman of the New York Police Department, I arranged to contribute two million a month to the UJA as proof of my good will. I also offered a written pledge that American Jewry will never suffer either from me personally or from any official I help place in office. If these people are willing to accept my good intentions, I'm hoping you can, too.''

Initially disbelieving, Gaynor decided it had to be true. It could be checked too easily. But what arrangements had he made with the NAACP and the Hispanic Development Association?

"I suppose this was another of your deals?'' he asked.

"It's the only civilized way for human affairs to be conducted.''

"What do you get out of it?''

"No attacks from their pulpits. No vilification from their media.''

"But how did Newman get involved?''

"I approached him. He's a police hero, he's a Jew, and he believes as I do about law and order. I felt he'd be the perfect spokesman for what I'm offering.''

With some surprise, Gaynor found he was still pointing his gun at Taylor's chest. "And what's your deal with *him?*''

"He'll be police commissioner.''

Gaynor needed a moment to digest it. "And what about the commissioner we've got?''

"Westley will be announcing for governor next week. And I can assure you he'll go a lot further than Albany.''

His new coldness slipped over Gaynor like a coat. The faces and deals of Clayton Taylor. If a deal could grow bones and flesh, it would look exactly like the minister. It would wear the same perfectly tailored suit, it would comb its thick, dark hair the same way, it would have the same tightly drawn skin shaped into the same expression of absolute sincerity. What I should do, thought Gaynor, is blow him away right now. It would all be very simple at this moment. Once I let this moment pass, it will never be simple again.

Taylor must have seen something of it in Gaynor's eyes because he suddenly stiffened. It was pure reflex; his body was preparing for a bullet. Even so, he smiled.

"You're close. But I can't quite believe you'd be able to do it like this.''

Gaynor was close to proving him wrong. A heavy whiff of the minister's death clogged his throat and cut off his breath. And what sickened him most was that he knew he could do it.

"Now listen to me,'' he said, and his voice, though muffled by the mask, was trembling with where he had been. "It was you who asked for this meeting, so you must have thought you had something wonderful to offer. Well, you were wrong. I think you and your deals stink. You corrupt whatever you touch. You appeal to people's worst instincts—their greed, their cruelty, their need to hate. And what makes you even more contemptible is that you *do* know better, you're not just some ignorant, hatemongering redneck acting out of stupidity and anger. Jesus, you're even worse than I thought. You're the most cold-blooded self-seeker I've ever known. How dare you play God with people's lives?"

"How do *you* dare?" Clayton Taylor's face was set, devoid of emotion. "I think you've really started to believe this Apostle role you've taken on. It's actually carrying you along now, isn't it? Who appointed *you* God's messenger on earth?"

Gaynor rose and jammed the muzzle of his silencer against Taylor's forehead. "I appointed myself. And you'd damn well better remember that."

He drew back his gun, leaving the impression of a small, perfect circle in the center of Taylor's forehead.

"You're making a terrible mistake," said the minister.

Gaynor ripped the telephone receiver from its wire and left the room. The hotel corridor was empty. He took off his mask and gloves, put them in his pocket, and headed for the elevator. Behind him, he heard Kate's door opening.

From a black Chevrolet parked near a Georgetown street corner, two men sat watching the house at 36 Cedar Mews, where the secretary of state lived with his wife and two servants. It was 6:35 on what promised to be a warm, clear morning, and there was no traffic. The men's names were Simmons and Garrison, but they carried no identification to indicate this, and the car had been stolen less than two hours before. They were charter members of the American Crusade Party's Washington, D.C., unit, which had been among the first three such units to be established nationwide.

Simmons was at the wheel, a young man with the scarred hands of a construction worker. Garrison, seated casually beside him, held a Uzi submachine gun across his knees. He was a bony man with a pug nose whose nostrils cut the air so broadly, his intelligence seemed concentrated there. Neither man spoke, nor did they so much as glance at one another. Each might have been sitting alone. Yet the sense of total rapport they communicated was such that even their breathing appeared synchronized.

At 6:45 an official State Department limousine turned the corner and parked in front of number 36. Two men in dark suits got out and stood talking on the sidewalk. Simmons started the Chevrolet's engine, its sound lost in the roar of an early takeoff from National Airport. Several moments later, the door of number 36 opened and Secretary Bradberry appeared, a tall, sun-tanned man in a navy blue suit. Simmons put the engine in gear and the car slid forward. The secretary paused on his front steps to light a pipe. The car picked up speed as it approached.

There were two short bursts of machine-gun fire. The first sent Bradberry tumbling down the steps and riddled the front door. The second cut down the two men on the sidewalk. One of the men, however, did manage to get off three shots at the rear of the departing Chevrolet before it turned a corner and disappeared. The entire episode had taken exactly sixteen seconds.

The secretary of state suffered shoulder and chest wounds that required three hours of emergency surgery and left him in serious but stable condition. His chauffeur was dead on arrival at the hospital. The Secret Service agent assigned to the secretary died less than four hours later.

Credit for the shooting was claimed by a group calling itself the Palestine Liberation Movement. In three separate telephone calls to the media, the PLM condemned Secretary Bradberry for having initiated secret negotiations among Israel, Egypt, Lebanon, and Jordan to further betray Palestine's three million refugees with a peace treaty in which they would have no voice. Although the White House denied that any such talks had taken place (as did Israel and the Arab countries named), Washington rumors were quick to assert otherwise. At Walter Reed Army Hospital, Secretary Bradberry remained unavailable for comment.

15

Newman awoke earlier than he would have liked with a cracking headache, a bitter-tasting mouth, and the cold certainty that nothing good could possibly lie ahead for him. What had he been drinking last night? He found an almost empty quart bottle of vodka in the kitchen and poured its remains over some ice. The drink tasted rich, burning on its way down, and did its work. Now I'm alive, he thought.

He shaved, put on some coffee, and brought in the two morning papers from outside his door. In the unfailingly precise, dignified language of the *Times,* a report on the bottom of the front page warned that the old were growing in numbers and impact. *Warned?* It made them sound like a new kind of plague. Which was pretty much how they were starting to be regarded. Better not to get too old. Maybe his liver would at least save him from that.

Another heading caught his eye: SELF-STYLED APOSTLE SETS JULY 4TH DEADLINE. Beneath it was a brief description of the Apostle's latest open letter to Clayton Taylor, in which Independence Day had apparently been set as the date for Taylor's acceptance of his earlier warning.

The lieutenant put down his coffee with a not yet steady hand and spent the next five minutes searching for his glasses. Finally locating them in the bathroom, he turned to the *News,* which not only carried the same announcement in banner headlines, but also ran the Apostle's complete letter on page 3:

246

To the Reverend Taylor,

Since you've rejected my earlier warning, since you're still spewing your messages of hate, I'm giving you final notice. If you haven't ended these ridiculous incitements by midnight of July Fourth, or declared your intention to do so, I shall do it for you.

My choice of July Fourth is no accident. It's a date symbolic of all the decent, humanist principles upon which this country was founded and which you seem determined to destroy.

The Apostle

Newman read the letter twice more, but that failed to make it better. He glanced up at the date.

It was June 7. He had twenty-seven days.

"I'm expanding the search area another five blocks north," said Newman. "That will bring us uptown to a Hundred and Twelfth Street, from Riverside to West End." He crayoned in the new parameters on his wall map. "Continue with the same method and line of questioning you've been using."

None of the three detectives said anything. They just stared at the map of Manhattan's West Side. From their expressions, it might have been the western edge of Siberia.

"What's the matter?" Newman looked at them. "If something is bothering you guys, let's hear it."

Robbins's cough showed his nervousness. "It just seems like such a waste of time, Lieutenant. Nothing but dead ends. Maybe we should try something else."

"Like what?"

"How about watching Taylor's back, putting him under twenty-four-hour surveillance? The Apostle might be following him around right now, looking to pick his spot."

"We're New York cops," said Newman, "not federal agents. We can't operate interstate or even outside our own city limits."

He leaned wearily against his wall map. "Any other ideas?"

The office was silent. Outside, a teletype and a dozen typewriters were clacking.

"I was just thinking, Lieutenant . . ." It was Mulcahy. He flushed as everyone looked at him. "Why couldn't we set something up? I mean, like we did with that rapist. What if the reverend sent the Apostle one of his messages through the newspapers? What if he said, 'Okay. I'll do what you ask. I'll stop saying all those things about the Jews, blacks, and Hispanics. But I want a meeting. Just the two of us. I want to talk things out, face to face, with no one else around. You call and tell me where and when and I'll be there. Alone.' "

The young detective nodded to himself, working it through. "Then we put real tight surveillance on the reverend and move in at the right time. How does that sound?"

"Lousy," said Loretti. "The Apostle's no dummy. He'd see through that in a minute. Besides, Taylor would never agree."

"It would also have to be here in the city," Robbins added. "Otherwise we'd be outside our jurisdiction, like the lieutenant said."

"The Apostle would want New York, anyway," said Mulcahy. "He knows the town inside out. It's his turf. And as far as the reverend goes, he's already said he'd agree to anything to arrange some kind of meeting."

Newman let them argue it out.

"It's a possibility," he finally said. "It's certainly worth thinking about. In the meantime, we'll push on with our extended pick and shovel work."

Mulcahy looked down at the floor.

Newman called Clayton Taylor in Atlanta, was told he had a speaking engagement in Kansas City, and at last reached him at his hotel there.

Taylor's voice came across lilting and cheerful, his mood, expansive. It was not the sound, thought Newman, of a man with twenty-four days to live. Three of the original twenty-seven had already passed.

"How are things back in New York, Lieutenant? No problem with the check, I hope."

"The check was fine." It was the first of the two-million-dollar payments to the United Jewish Appeal. "Came in right on schedule. Certified. The director asked me to convey his appreciation."

"Ah, but I'm sure that's not why you're calling."

"I haven't spoken to you since your days became numbered. What are you doing about it?"

Taylor laughed. "Making sure I savor every moment to the fullest."

"What about security?"

"No more than usual."

"Do you think that's smart?"

"According to the terms of my final warning, there's no need to worry until midnight of July Fourth."

"He might change the terms without notice," said Newman.

"Not our Apostle. Too much moral superiority."

"Have you sent your reply yet?"

"I'm working on it."

Newman stared across his desk at the broadening line of markings on his wall map. "Before you give it to the media, there's something I'd like you to consider." He told the minister about Mulcahy's idea.

Taylor heard him out. "I'm really not interested, Lieutenant."

"I admit it's a long shot, but if you played it right, there's still a chance he'd meet with you."

"I know that," drawled Taylor from a thousand miles away. "In fact, I've already met with him. But I don't especially want to do it again."

Newman slowly straightened in his chair. He wished the minister was sitting across from him at that moment. He would have liked to have seen his face. "What do you mean, you've already met with him? When was that?"

"One night last week. At the Harley Hotel in New York. It was all very complicated. I tried to reassure him about my intentions and offer him a deal, but it was a waste of time. Apparently Christ's Apostle is above such things."

"We could have picked the guy up. I don't understand, Reverend. Why didn't you let me know?"

"Because I didn't want him picked up. And I still don't. He's of much greater use to me this way, sending threatening messages and staging ultimatums. The truth is, he's getting me more media coverage than the pope and the president combined."

"He's also about to get you a thirty-eight-caliber bullet in the head," said Newman.

The minister breathed deeply, long distance. "I don't really believe that. He had a perfect opportunity to kill me the other night and he didn't take it. We were alone, no one knew about it and he had a gun on me. All he had to do was squeeze the trigger. The Lord's Apostle doesn't commit homicide. It simply isn't in line with his image of himself."

"It's a nice theory, but I doubt whether the two men he's already killed would be impressed."

"You worry too much, Jay."

"Naturally. I'm a Jew."

The minister chuckled softly. "Talking about that, how have you been doing with your chosen brethren?"

Newman filled him in with a carefully edited version of what was actually happening. It had not been simple or easy, but so far, he claimed, he was giving Taylor his full two million worth. Traditionally, a consensus of ten Jews added up to ten different opinions. Which was pretty much the initial response he was getting from the groups and committees he addressed on the minister's behalf. Still, his own stature and reputation seemed to be such that his personal assurances were generally accepted in the end. That, and the two million a month, he thought with not unreasonable cynicism.

Yet he found himself curiously affected, even toched. His word, his integrity, were being accepted without question. It was a new experience for him, particularly as a Jew. He had never felt or projected this sort of image before. Despite his undeniable background, he had always lived pretty much alone, as an ethnic outsider. The only group affiliation he had ever allowed himself was his six months with Alcoholics Anonymous, and that had proven a dismal failure. Ironically, his dealings with Clayton Taylor seemed to have done more to involve him with the Jewish community, to make him feel more like a Jew, than anything since his bar mitzvah.

By the time Newman was ready to hang up on the minister, he felt tempted to say *shalom*.

It was beginning to seem like too much of a coincidence. Suddenly, all this ethnic involvement.

It started with an early evening call from the Apostle—this one terse, all business, no fooling around.

"An Orthodox rabbi on the Lower East Side was beaten up, robbed, and had his beard cut the other night," reported the muffled voice. "You know about it, Lieutenant?"

"I heard something."

"I've got the two creeps who did it. They're down by the South Street Seaport Museum, under the East River Drive. I left them tied up behind some construction material. And do me a favor, Lieutenant. Handle this one yourself, personally."

The line went dead.

Newman called the Fourteenth Precinct and had the desk sergeant send two patrol cars to the designated spot. Then he drove down in his own car to meet them.

It was all routine enough. A couple of young, Hispanic street gangsters who got off their *cajones* by beating and robbing the few elderly Jews still remaining in the once predominantly Jewish area. Mutilating the rabbi's beard was what made this one just a bit meaner. A knife in the gut, thought Newman, might not have hurt nearly as much. The Apostle apparently had found the two suspects by shoving his pistol into the mouth of another gang member and threatening to blow the top of his head off. Not an especially subtle means of interrogation, but who could argue with the results?

With the two young hoods dispatched to precinct headquarters, Newman went looking for their victim. *And do me a favor, Lieutenant. Handle this one yourself, personally.* What kind of favor?

The crumbling, Lower East Side neighborhood was not unfamiliar. His grandparents had lived there. So had just about everyone else's, the Emma Lazarus dream carved on their brows with a kitchen knife. Trade in your kishkes for a chance to be free and rich in the land of opportunity. The Tenth Ward was known as the typhus ward. Tuberculosis was called Jewish asthma. To the west were the goyim, to the north, America. Still, his grandparents had both had soft eyes, a special kind of velvet.

He parked his car and wandered through the streets. Most of the old landmarks were gone—the kosher butchers and restaurants, the aromatic delicatessens, the bakeries with the golden challahs in the windows. In their places were bodegas and storefront social clubs with Hispanic names and Latin music blaring from loudspeakers. The people on the street, sitting in front of the stores and tenements, looked at him as at an alien creature. They saw a big, wide-shouldered man with a heroic head staring up at windows and down into cellars, barely seeing the dark faces about him. He might have been a tourist, a foreigner, an extraterrestial. What did he know about sweat shops, drug busts, macho knifings, six kids in two rooms? What experience could he have had with the minute-by-minute problems of real life?

He found the rabbi's synagogue on a narrow side street just off Delancey, a tiny, decaying building squeezed between two nineteenth-century tenements. Inside, the evening services were going on. Newman stood in a narrow vestibule, listening to the Hebrew chanting that came from behind a pair of battered doors. On an impulse, he took a skullcap from a cardboard box and went in.

About two dozen men in yarmulkes and tallithim were praying. Most of them were quite old, but there were also a few younger men. Upstairs, in a little balcony, an elderly woman prayed alone. The rabbi Newman was looking for, Duv Glickstein, stood on the bema, a slender, unexpectedly youthful man with a turban of bandages under his yarmulke, very thick glasses, and the remnants of a mutilated beard. Newman breathed deeply. The air held a dimly familiar and unmistakable smell—the mixed aromas of bodies, old clothing, worm-eaten books, rubbed wooden benches. A century-old stink. The odor of piety? It intrigued him that in the more than forty years since he had been in one of these old shuls, the perfume had remained essentially the same.

He stood, sat down, and stood along with the others. Almost unconsciously his lips moved, remembering a few ancient Hebrew words. *"Schma yisroyail adonai Ailohainue . . ."* Near the end of the service, when the recently bereaved rose to recite the kaddish, he, too, got up and recited with them: *"Yisgadal v'yiskadash shr'me rabbo . . ."* So he remembered. Yet what could it mean? All it did was summon his dead.

As the worshipers folded their prayer shawls and left, he approached the bema. The rabbi stared half blindly at him through his lenses. "You're the speachmaking cop, Newman, aren't you? I heard your nonsense at the UJA dinner the other night." The rabbi touched his bandaged head. "I suppose you've come about this."

Newman suddenly wished he hadn't.

Exchanging a few words with his congregants, Glickstein led the detective to his study, a cluttered cubbyhole with a single window looking out at a brick wall. Stacks of books were everywhere, overflowing shelves, chairs, tables, desk, and much of the floor. The rabbi cleared a seat for Newman. Then he took a medicine bottle from a desk drawer, removed his glasses, and put a few drops of fluid in each eye. Gasping, he screwed up his face. "Burns like Hades. Acute glaucoma. Sometimes I think the treatment is worse than the disease. Still, I'm not blind yet. Ever think about being blind, Newman?"

The lieutenant shook his head.

"I do. All the time. Helps me appreciate the miracle of sight. An astounding capability. Yet I always took it for granted. But not anymore." He replaced his glasses and blinked rapidly at Newman. "I noticed you still remember a few prayers."

"I guess it stays with you."

"How did it feel?"

"Like it was coming from someone else's mouth," said Newman. "How does your head feel?"

"Like it should be on someone else's neck."

Neither man smiled.

"We think we've got the two who did it," said Newman. "You'll have to stop by the precinct."

"What's suddenly got into you people? How did you do it so fast?"

"We didn't. This was one of the Apostle's."

"Aah." The department's lack of achievement seemed to please him. "I'm no novice as a victim, you know. This was the third time for me in six months. I'm thinking of getting a steel yarmulke. Though it was a first for my beard." Long, aesthetic fingers probed and confirmed the damage under his chin. "We're just about finished down here. When the last of our *altes* die out, that will be the end of it. Too bad. This was our entrance to America. We rose in it like yeast. Now it's drugs, knives, guns, anger, hate. A battleground. Soon it will be a cemetery. And for some reason you seem to be trying to help it along."

Newman stared dumbly.

"You're surprised? I don't know why. I listened to you speak to all those UJA *machers* the other night, all those big-shot, fund-raising geniuses, and I wanted to jump up and shake your teeth loose. Are you crazy, Newman? What are you trying to do to us? One Holocaust wasn't enough? You're trying to light a match to another?"

"Wait a minute!"

The detective started to get up, but Glickstein leaned forward and pushed him back. "No. *You* wait a minute. I can't turn on a radio, go to a meeting, or read a newspaper these days without running into more of your foolishness. Now, for once, *you're* going to hear *me*."

Looking at the frail, bandaged, half-blind rabbi looming threateningly over him, Newman had to smother a grin.

Glickstein was not amused. "How can you do it? A lying chalyera like Taylor should be spun over an open fire, slowly, and you tell us to hold our tongues? What's wrong with you?"

"I explained the other night how . . ."

"Yes, yes. I heard all that rubbish." The rabbi dismissed it with a flick of his wrist. "I heard about the assurances, about the two million a month, about how we'll benefit in the end. And all I wanted to do was vomit my roast beef. Do you know why? Because it's all so contemptuous of us. It buys us so cheaply. It exploits our congenital need to be victims. It proves we're always ready to begin a fresh march toward the oven for whatever reasons the goyim happen to think up between their first and third martinis."

Martinis, thought Newman dully. What could this poor angry man possibly have against martinis?

"Those animals who took me apart the other night," said Glickstein, "Those voncen who scrambled my brains and desecrated my beard. Who do you think teaches them? They're not born hating us. They learn it from the lies of vermin like Taylor." Myopically, he rummaged through the clutter on his desk, found a half-ripped news clipping, and waved it under Newman's nose. It was the Apostle's recent threat to the minister. "Here is someone who understands. Here is a man who knows there's only one effective way to deal with such danger."

"You approve of murder, Rabbi?"

"That shocks you, doesn't it? You ask, how could a spiritual leader, a man of God, sanction the taking of human life? Truthfully, I wonder myself sometimes. I become ashamed. I think perhaps I should give up the calling, go into some other line of work. How did I get this way? I ask. Yet it's no great mystery. All I had to do was think about babies being thrown alive into the ovens at Auschwitz."

Glickstein stared blankly at the torn clipping. "Let me tell you something, Mr. Big Shot Policeman. There's a dream I keep having. It's January 30, 1933. I'm in Germany. Adolf Hitler has just been elected chancellor and he's telling his famous lies about the Jews. I'm upset, frightened, but friends tell me not to worry. They point out that the Germans are a highly civilized, highly cultured people who have always treated their Jews decently. They tell me that no one of any intelligence could possibly believe such lies. My friends also tell me that not even Hitler believes them, that he is only using anti-Semitism as a temporary political expedient. I believe that's the correct expression? Nevertheless, I'm worried and I'm afraid."

The rabbi paused to glance at Newman's face, a lecturer on genocidal dreams making sure of his audience's attention.

"Then one night I find myself alone in a forest with Adolf Hitler. There's just the two of us, and I have a loaded gun aimed at his head. I have only to pull the trigger and the threat to me and to those I love will be ended. Still, I hesitate. I am not, after all, a murderer. I believe in the sanctity of human life. Also, none of my people have yet been harmed. So far there are just the lies, the threats, and some inconveniences. Yet I feel in my heart that I'll never have this chance again, that if I don't act now, the sky could turn black and the earth could open."

Glickstein fell silent, dying eyes still focused on Newman. There was a quiet air of expectancy about him that the detective found impressive.

"What did you do?" Newman asked.

"I don't know. It's always here that I awaken."

Newman somehow felt cheated. Around him, the smell of centuries seemed to rise from the clutter, from dusty books that might have been passed down through forgotten shtetls, their yellowed pages preserved through fires, pogroms, and the clubs, swords, and guns of angry Christians.

"What if it was your dream, Lieutenant? Tell me. What would you do with that gun?"

"Hell, it's easy enough to be brilliant with hindsight."

"If you're going to hide behind platitudes, try this one." Glickstein blinked as if trying to see more than he could. "Those who refuse to profit from the past are doomed to repeat its disasters."

Newman did not bother correcting the misquote. Incredible. A rabbi preaching politics by assassination. His grandfather should hear Glickstein talk. Still, his zayde had been tough, a survivor, a broad, thick-chested immigrant with fists like sledgehammers, who never forgot who the enemy was and who had, in his day, broken his full share of goyische bones. Maybe Israel Newman might not have been so shocked by Glickstein after all. Given the chance, he might even have pulled the trigger himself.

The rabbi suddenly seemed almost smiling. It was the closest he had come. "I was just wondering, Newman. What's your honest opinion? Do you think the Apostle could be Jewish? I'd like to think so. It would help make up for Jews like you."

Saturday dawned bright and warm, so Mary packed a picnic lunch and they went to the beach. Newman stretched out in the sun while Mary, with the fairest, most delicate of Celtic complexions, hid under a beach umbrella and warned the detective about skin cancer.

Another new idea, thought Newman. When he was a boy, his mother used to scold him for not staying out in the sun long enough, for not soaking in its health-giving rays, for not getting more color in his sallow cheeks. Did he want to fade away and die of consumption? In those days, sun and fresh air were the cures for everything from asthma to TB. Now, somehow, they just managed to kill you. In fact, there were now so many new killers around, they had to wait in line for their turn. Baking in the hot sun, feeling the sweat literally pour out of him (all the bad, all the poisons, leaving), Newman dozed.

He awoke with a cry. The sweat had turned cold, and there were floating red spots in front of his eyes.

Mary knelt beside him "What is it, darling?"

"Nothing." He pulled himself up, his body soaked, sand sticking to his flesh. "A bad dream."

"I warned you about lying in the sun."

"You warned me about cancer, not dreams."

"What was the dream?"

He shook his head.

"Tell me. If you don't tell someone, it just keeps recurring. That's the only way to get rid of bad dreams."

"Is that Freud's theory or yours?"

"We sort of collaborated."

She wiped him dry with a towel and pulled him to safety under her umbrella.

"If your theory is right," he said, "I know a killer-rabbi who got rid of this little beauty by slipping it to *me*."

"If you don't tell me this minute, I'll push you back into the sun."

"All right," he said and repeated Glickstein's nocturnal fantasy of aiming a gun at Hitler's head.

"And that's what you dreamed? That's what the rabbi has you working on now?"

"It seems so."

"It's an interesting concept," she said. "What did you do in your own version?"

"I'm not an assassin."

"Not even asleep? In a dream?"

"I wasn't even tempted."

She looked at him curiously. "Then why did you wake up in a cold sweat, crying out?"

"The sun. It either gives you cancer or makes you crazy."

He escaped into the ocean for a cure. His mother would have approved. Salt water, she had believed, was even better than chicken soup.

They stood rimmed by moonlight, the stereo playing softly from the living room, the phosphorescence of the Atlantic reflecting blue-white through the windows. Naked, they touched one another: she, still tentative, still half shy even after so many years; he, still marveling that the wonder of it remained possible for him. Their flesh was warm, responsive, extra sensitive from the hours of sun and water. A bonus. What had they done to deserve it? No longer young, they continued to be exquisite in what they offered and grateful for what they received. Violet shadows lived in their eyes. Newman had never moved so easily, so well. It was impossible to do anything wrong.

The phone shrilled beside his ear.

He groaned. There was a luminous clock on the night table. Its hands pointed to one-fifty.

"Don't answer it," she whispered.

For a moment he was tempted. But the run was spoiled then, anyway. He picked up the receiver.

"I couldn't sleep," said the muffled voice. "I thought maybe you couldn't either."

Newman sighed. "Have a heart. It's almost two o'clock." Drawing Mary closer on the bed, he shared the phone with her.

"My father used to say we'd be a long time dead, so why waste your life unconscious in the dark."

"Was your father a philosopher, or an insomniac trying to make the best of things?"

"Half and half, I guess. But isn't that what philosophy is? Giving yourself reasons for not really wanting what you know you can't have anyway? The thinking man's religion, indispensable in the absence of God."

"That's what you called to tell me at two in the morning?"

There was a silence. "I called because I'm disappointed and puzzled about something, and these things always seem worse in the middle of the night," said the muffled voice. "I was hoping you might be able to clear it up for me. I was hoping you might be able to explain how someone like you, someone with a lifetime of integrity behind him, could sell out everything, including his birthright, for a stupid bauble like a political appointment."

Newman swallowed dryly. He said nothing.

"Taylor told me about your deal," said the voice quietly. "I assume it's true."

"Assume what you want."

"But how could you do it?"

Newman did not answer. He felt Mary's body beside him, her breath warm on his cheek.

"Forget what I just said about selling out. I don't really believe that. I'm sure you honestly feel you're doing the right thing. Which is what I find so frightening. If that devil's preacher can fool you, he can fool a hell of a lot of others."

"But not you, of course."

"And not Rabbi Glickstein."

It figured, thought Newman. No wonder the guy never slept. He was too busy talking to everyone on the phone.

"I had hoped Glickstein might be able to shake you a little, help bring you to your senses."

"Please," said Newman tiredly. "Stop worrying so much

about me. Worry a little about yourself. There's more need for it there.''

"Why do you want to be police commissioner so badly?"

"For all the same reasons I wanted to be a cop."

"I'm sorry. But if it's going to depend on Taylor, I'm afraid you're not going to make it."

"Why? Because you're going to shoot him?"

"If he makes me. And it looks as though he's going to do just that. The man carries the threat of demons.''

Newman pushed himself up in the sex-rumpled bed. "I've got bad news for you, son. You're not shooting anyone because I'm going to nail you first. Do you know why? Because you're the one who's the real threat, not Taylor. You poor schmuck! It's sickies like you who buried Lincoln, Kennedy, King, and God knows how many others. And all of you so sure of your virtue, all of you spitting bullets and tearing flesh, all of you with your shining visions of the ultimate good. You may be the first of the bunch to call yourself the Apostle, but you're straight out of the same stinking hell as the others!''

Breathing heavily, Newman slammed down the receiver.

Clayton Taylor's response to the Apostle's ultimatum came over the radio as the lead item on the morning news. Newman heard it as he was driving along the Belt Parkway on his way to work. Eyes fixed on the road, he listened closely, hands gripping the wheel tightly enough to turn his knuckles white. During the past several days, awaiting the minister's reply, he thought he had envisioned pretty much the way it would finally be. He had expected nothing startling. So of course he was about to be proven wrong.

Addressed simply to the individual known as the Apostle, the broadcast reply stated:

"Though I read your latest ultimatum with great sadness, I cannot honestly believe you have it in you to harm me. I cannot believe that someone with your need to do good could turn into a cold-blooded assassin.

"To show my faith in this judgment, I intend to address a public rally at New York's Yankee Stadium on the night of July Fourth.

"I, too, am impressed with the symbolism inherent in this

day. To which end, I expect to use the occasion publicly to reaffirm my belief in an America dedicated to the health, prosperity, and general well-being of all true, Christian Americans.

"I pray you will be present to bear witness to this reaffirmation. Perhaps it will help you understand that with the Lord at my side, I need fear nothing. May he be with you."

Newman stared off at the road. Pure and simple, it was an invitation to a double killing. Which meant there wouldn't be half enough seats to go around.

Zvi Avidan was waiting for him in his kitchen when he returned that night.

"Don't you ever enter a premises or talk to a person like everyone else?" asked Newman.

"I'm afraid I've forgotten how."

"How did you know I wouldn't be coming home with someone?"

"Your lady friend is out of town on a case and you're notably faithful."

"Jesus!" Newman brought out some Jack Daniel's and two glasses. "No wonder you guys have never lost a war."

The major smiled. "Well, neither have you people."

"Not for the same reasons. Besides, we lost Vietnam."

"Only because your hearts were never really in it."

Newman poured the bourbon and they sat drinking.

"I just heard about this stadium business," said Avidan. "What is Taylor up to?"

"He didn't tell me."

"What do you think?"

"Just a lot more hype."

The Israeli frowned.

"Drum beating," explained Newman. "Publicity. He feeds on it."

"He could also die from it."

"That's a risk he's evidently willing to take."

The fluorescent light shadowed Avidan's cheeks. "We made an interesting discovery the other day. We think Taylor may be conducting a liaison with the wife of your secretary of state."

Conducting a liaison, thought Newman. How much lovelier and more elegant than just getting laid.

"You writing a capitol gossip column, too?"

"That attack on Bradberry worried us, so we started watching those close to him. We overheard his wife calling the reverend in Atlanta."

"Maybe she's just concerned about her soul."

"It wasn't that kind of conversation."

"So?"

Major Avidan shrugged. "A basic intelligence rule is never to trust coincidence, and there were simply too many of them here."

"I still don't understand."

"Consider," said the Israeli. "The secretary was involved in a Mideast peace initiative whose success depended upon personal diplomacy and secrecy. He somehow was shot within days of its expected completion, exposing and aborting the entire plan. Which, incidentally, would have been very favorable to Israel. Mrs. Bradberry happened to be one of the few people who knew about all this, and she, it now turns out, was involved with the Reverend Mr. Taylor, whose feelings about Israel are only too well known."

Newman stared at the Israeli officer. "But she may not have told him."

"Ah, but she did. You see, Lieutenant, that's one of the things we learned from her telephone conversation with Taylor."

"And what about that Arab group claiming responsibility for the shooting?"

"A lie. Pure cover. Our sources confirm it. The PLM didn't even know about the peace plan at the time of the shooting."

"But *Taylor?*" Newman shook his head. "Whatever else he may be, I can't believe . . . ."

Avidan smiled somewhat sadly.

16

The sonofabitch was clever, thought Harry Blake. In a single master stroke, Taylor had managed to turn the whole thing into exactly what he wanted—the ultimate media event. Indeed, within thirty-six hours of Taylor's announced plan for his July Fourth rally, there was more outright hype going on than for the last three Super Bowls combined. Blake was fascinated, angered, and depressed all at the same time. Incredible. One man publicly threatens to kill another, the intended victim hires a giant sports arena for this occasion, and the citizens of the most literate, most highly developed, most avowedly pious nation on earth go wild with anticipation. The reporter was sure there had to be significant moral lessons to be learned somewhere in all this, but he was afraid to search them out.

Still, he was a journalist. So that, having words and a voice, he used them. Where was the shock? he demanded. Where was the horror, the outpouring of rage at the whole concept of a life-and-death issue being turned into a public spectacle? Had they become a nation of perennial voyeurs? Had all empathy, all compassion, finally been buried in the artificial turf of their playing fields?

He asked his questions in print and on television but liked few of the replies. Besides, words were not even close to being flesh. They had no real substance, no blood or fiber.

They could never begin to hold back death. Yet they were **his** metier, his chosen line of work.

Big deal.

"What's wrong with us, Brian?" he asked his editor. "What's happened to our fucking sense of tragedy? Don't we give a shit about *anything* anymore?"

Kelly had no answers for him. Nor did Blake expect any. And all the pious editorials, all the fine-sounding protests being run in their own and other allegedly more reverential, more publicly concerned journals, meant absolutely nothing. Finally they would all, including he, exploit it to the fullest.

Cloaked in a mantle of righteous fire, Clayton Taylor was still confining his preaching to radio and television. This time, however, it was live.

"Those of you who are out of Christ, beware," he was saying with a gentleness that belied his words. "Worlds of misery, rivers of burning brimstone, are awaiting you. There are the glowing flames of God's wrath, there is hell's gaping mouth open, and you have nothing to stand upon and nothing to take hold of. There is nothing between you and hell but the air. It is only the power and the pleasure of God that holds you up.

"Of course, you don't know this. You can't see the hand of God. You look at other things. You look at your good health, at your friends and family, at your worldly goods. But these things are nothing. They can't protect you. If God should withdraw his hand, you would fall screaming into the flames, you would fly down into the bottomless gulf. Your wickedness would make you heavy as lead and you would sink and keep sinking.

"Those of you who deny Christ, those of you who persist in worshiping your false gods, should know this and be warned."

Melissa Bradberry called immediately after his broadcast. It was the first time she had been able to reach him in almost a week.

"Where are you calling from?" he said, instantly cautious. Despite his reminders, she tended to be careless about security when thwarted.

"I'm at a pay phone at Walter Reed. You needn't worry,

Clayton. I have as much at stake as you." Her voice was cold, stiff. "It's been one devil of a week."

"I can imagine. How is Dexter?"

"Out of danger, but utterly miserable. All his hopes, all his work, lost. Not to mention the lives."

"I'm so very sorry. We're all praying for a lasting peace in the Holy Land."

"As if this wasn't enough, now I've got you to worry about." She sighed and her voice softened. "I don't understand. Why in God's name would you risk your life in a stunt like that?"

"I'd hardly call it a stunt."

"Really, Clayton. If ever there was a grandstand play, this is it. Which is all very fine, but hardly worth dying over."

"Believe me. I have no intention of dying on Independence Day."

"Who's going to protect you? God?"

The reverend smiled. "Ye of little faith."

"It may happen that he's a little busy that day."

"In that case we can always fall back on two thousand police, the FBI, and my security people."

His manner was able to reassure her at least partially. He had been somewhat less successful in calming the ACP's five National Council members, who had been calling in all week. They were very much concerned about his safety. In fact, they were almost manic on the subject. How dare he risk his neck when they had so much time, effort, and money invested? Such depth of sentiment. Nevertheless, he did his best to explain.

"Please try to understand," he told them at a precisely arranged conference call. "This was far from a rash act on my part. I've thought everything through very carefully. Life is as important to me as it is to the rest of you. Assuming this Apostle person shows up at all, I'll be better protected in that stadium on July Fourth than I could possibly be anywhere else. Remember. Under these conditions, *I'm* the one selecting the time and place, not my would-be assassin."

In discussing it with Gaynor, Kate had very much her own reaction. "The man is diabolic, the devil himself. I swear, he's simply not human."

"Come on. He's smart. Give him credit."

"Credit? You want me to give him *credit?*"

Just off her shift and still in uniform, Kate glared at him across the table of a small bar in his neighborhood. It was something of an occasion, one of the few times they had ventured out of Gaynor's bed and apartment together.

"You've got to admit it was an inspired move," he said.

She was too contemptuous of the whole idea to answer.

"You're losing your humor," Gaynor told her.

"You think it's funny?"

"In a way. What I don't think is that we should get all worked up and emotional about it."

Kate finished her martini and signaled the waiter for another.

"You have to look at it coldly," he said. "It's classic. It's quintessential Machiavelli. The old prince himself couldn't have worked it better. He took my threat, my ultimatum, my deadline, wove them into a net, and trapped me inside it."

"Well, no one says you have to stay trapped."

He smiled.

"I'm serious."

"Okay. You're serious. How do I get out?"

The waiter brought Kate's fresh drink and she sipped it slowly, carefully, with all due reverence. After eight hours of intensive care duty, a dry, well-chilled martini was about as close to a religious experience as she seemed able to get these days.

"Of course, the best and safest way out," she said, "is to just quietly retire the Apostle and leave Taylor standing in the middle of Yankee Stadium with nothing but his cock in his hand."

"Very visual. I'll do it as a large-scale mural one of these days."

"But you're not interested?"

He lifted her hand and brushed her palm with his lips. It smelled faintly, sweetly, of soap.

"No harm in trying." She sighed.

"What else?"

"Arrange another meeting with him."

"And?"

"Accept his deal. It wasn't all that bad. As he said, you could swing a lot of weight in the right direction, maybe even pick our next president."

"I wouldn't know who to pick."

"I'll tell you," she said.

He sat listening to a jukebox pounding. At the far end of the bar, a solitary man moved closer to two women and started a conversation.

"What else have you got in your little bag?" he asked.

Kate took down half her martini in a single swallow. She seemed paler, more tired, than usual.

"Well?"

"Hedge," she said. "Keep a dialogue going through the media. As July Fourth approaches, find a common ground. Work out some sort of compromise. I'm sure he'll grab for it."

"You really can get your mouth to say just about anything, can't you?"

"Yes. If there's a chance it might keep you alive."

He ordered another double brandy. It was his third. They were just starting to do him some good.

"All right," she said and retreated to her fall-back position. "Then I suppose you have no choice but to kill him." She used the word like a club, watching his face for its effect. There was none. "But at least do it on your terms, not his."

"What are my terms?"

"A time, place, and method of your own choosing."

"What does that mean? Blowing up his house in the middle of the night? Sending him poisoned mushrooms? Cutting his throat in an alley? What? Tell me."

"I'll tell you what it doesn't mean," she said. "It doesn't mean letting him set you up like a clay pigeon in Yankee Stadium. It doesn't mean two hundred police sharpshooters waiting for you to make your glorious gesture. It doesn't mean going out like Butch Cassidy and the Sundance Kid, with not enough of you left to bury."

He watched the two women and the man at the bar, talking and laughing like old friends. The mindless, instant mating ritual. How fast these things happened. He felt oddly jealous.

"I never said I was going to make any glorious gestures."

"Oh, Richard."

Now she sounded like Jane, he thought. Why did women always end up sounding like your wife?

The jukebox banged on.

"Try to understand," he said.

"I do understand. Too well. That's my problem."

"I've been publicly challenged. There's a hard-earned image to be protected. The Apostle can't just go skulking off into the dark with his tail between his legs."

"Why the hell not?"

He looked at her.

"Oh, God!" she said. "Now you've even started believing your own hype."

"I always did."

"And you accuse *me* of losing my humor. Don't you hear yourself? You sound like a fanatic."

"Of course I sound like a fanatic. I *am* a fanatic. What else could the Apostle be? But at least I can still see and enjoy the whimsy in what's happening."

"Wonderful. Congratulations. So you'll die laughing."

They sat drinking in silence for a while, not quite looking at each other.

"I thought you understood all that," he said wearily.

"I do. But that doesn't mean I have to cheer you on."

"Remember. Taylor was your idea, not mine."

"Don't remind me. Anyway, who could have expected it to end up in a turkey shoot at Yankee Stadium." She fussed with her drink, moving it in small circles on the table. She seemed suddenly separate in her loneliness, her eyes angry and sad. "It's sickening. They're turning it into a Roman circus. Can't you see they're nothing but a pack of apes out there? They smell death in heat and come sniffing around for a piece of it. Take away their clothes, slogans, and theories, and you'll find you're throwing away your life for a bunch of baboons."

"Well, they're our own species."

"I'm not proud of it."

The trio at the bar left together and Gaynor stared dimly after them. The Apostle and the apes. It did have a certain ring. Considering the possibilities, he turned it into one of his wilder canvases, a full-color oil of them all swinging through the trees, tails high, with the Apostle himself in the lead. Deciding on a last-minute correction, he painted out the Apostle's mask and brushed in his own face. It seemed to fit. He did not see Newman come in or even notice him approaching until he stopped at their booth.

"What's the matter?" said the detective. "Have I changed that much?"

Kate grinned. "Hey, look who's here."

Gaynor stood up and shook Newman's hand. There was a sudden fluttering in his stomach, but it was not unpleasant.

"Are you on duty or can I buy you a drink?"

"What's one thing got to do with the other?" The detective sat down beside Kate and ordered a double bourbon. "Nice to see you two still getting on. Anything serious yet?"

"Just fooling around," said Gaynor. "You've got to be crazy to get serious with a nurse. They undress guys."

"Chivalry is dead." Kate made a face at him.

Gaynor smiled and decided it might be fun to go straight for the lion's beard. "Except for the Apostle. Now there's a true, old-time chevalier. Right, Lieutenant?"

"Right now he's just a true, old-time pain in my ass."

"How is the chase going?" Kate cut in. "I haven't been reading much about it lately."

"That's because there hasn't been much to read." Newman devoted a long, solemn moment to his bourbon. "Fact is, I've just had another lead wash out three blocks from here. I came in to console myself. Running into you two is a bonus."

"Cheer up," said Gaynor. "One way or another, you've got to have him in nineteen days. That's not so long to wait, is it?"

The detective looked at him with his dark, rabbi's eyes, his expression strangely blank. Almost deliberately so, it seemed to the artist.

"I'm talking about July Fourth," said Gaynor. "All you have to do is wait for him in Yankee Stadium."

Kate was nervously working her martini, her eyes flicking first at Gaynor's face, then at Newman's. She might have been watching a tennis match in which only one of the contestants knew he was playing. She tried to catch Gaynor's eye, wanting to warn him not to get too cute with his baiting, but he was apparently enjoying himself too much to notice.

"It's not that simple," said the detective. "I have to get him before the Fourth. If I don't, all I'll probably get is a double killing." He shook his head in irritation. "The trouble is, everyone thinks they're so damned clever. This whole stadium idea is the worst thing Taylor could have conceived. Yet I can't get him to call it off. He's fallen in love with it. He thinks the whole concept is brilliant. But it's the kind of operation in which it's impossible to guarantee his safety."

"Why not?" asked Kate. "You've got enough cops."

"In a place like Yankee Stadium there's no such thing as enough cops. You're talking about fifty thousand people milling around. And we don't even know what the guy looks like. If a man has a gun and doesn't mind dying himself, he can kill just about anybody under those conditions."

Kate licked her lips. "You think the Apostle wants Taylor badly enough to commit suicide?"

"Of course. There's probably nothing that would make him happier than murdering this fake monster he's created and martyring himself doing it."

"You surprise me," said Gaynor. "If I remember right, you not only once thought of Taylor as a pretty real monster yourself but actually admired the Apostle's uncompromising purity. What happened?"

"I got older and smarter."

A man came in who was obviously a detective, and Newman left the table to talk to him. When he returned, he finished his drink standing up.

"Looks like we've got another lead in the area. Probably nothing, but I chase them all. Thanks for the whiskey."

He shook their hands and left with the other cop.

The artist gazed after him. "Do you think he's got me this time?"

"I'm beginning to hope so."

Gaynor never knew for certain when a painting was done. He always tended to hold on too long. There was always that sick fear of letting go, that compulsion to add, to take away, to change, that dread of sending the poor thing forth, naked and vulnerable, into the cold places of judgment. And with this one, his big blue, there was even more reason for fear than usual.

Putting down his palette and brushes, he stepped back and looked at the figure he had created. For that was what the thing had finally evolved into, a life-size male nude painted almost entirely in icy tones of blue, the color itself harsh, soiled, and dirty. One could almost sense a whiff of rot coming off it as if from some malignancy not yet visible to the naked eye but there nevertheless. The figure was rendered broadly, impressionistically, yet nothing of its early promise had been lost. The mouth still howled its maniac speech, the demonic eyes still glared, the stump of a missing arm still flailed the heavens, and from the chest cavity, from that dark hole where a heart should have been, crawled things viscous and black.

Gaynor sat down at the far end of the studio. Enough, he thought, and turned away. But there was more. Indeed, the worst was yet to come. So he looked again, this time below the waist. Here, in the blue orchards of the loins, tiny worms chewed at what remained of the wrinkled fruit. Little was left, only a few pitted fragments, and these dangled between withered thighs. And if a howling madness came from the mouth, it screamed doubly loud among these chewed-up roots.

Behind it the background was dark, turgid, swollen with foul intent. If you believed in spirits and demons, in omens of evil, they would have dwelt in such a place as this. Beasts were hidden here. They prowled beneath a hurricane sky, crept through cities of shattered stone and burned-out rubble. You knew they were there but did not see them. All you saw were the ruins and suffering sky and a single vine, murderous and deadly, winding itself about the legs of the howling blue man.

He called his ex-wife at her office. "How about going to the stadium tonight and helping the Yanks win?"

The last time they had been to a ball game together was before the divorce and with the twins. They had been fans. They had also been a family, he thought, and wondered how kind he was being in asking her.

"Who are they playing?"

"The Red Sox."

"They'll be murdered," she said. "Boston's been hitting like crazy. Twenty-five runs, thirty-eight hits, and nine homers in their last three games." She paused. "Who's pitching?"

"Hank Emerson."

"I like Emerson."

"I'll call for you around seven. If it's okay, we can pick up some franks at the park."

"Why not?"

Emerson started off on fire, striking out seven in the first three innings and keeping Boston hitless.

Jane was beside herself. "My God, look what he's doing to those guys. Maybe he'll make it a no-hitter."

Gaynor laughed.

"It's not possible?"

"Our last no-hitter was in the fifty-six World Series. Do you know the odds against its happening tonight?"

"You've got to believe."

But only a small fraction of his attention was on the game. He was there for a different reason. He had not been to Yankee Stadium for a long time, and his mind needed refreshing on some of the details. Additionally, there were things he had never paid much attention to before that were suddenly of vital importance—the locations of entrances and exits, the height and spread of the upper deck, the relationship of seats to playing field, the distances between particular points. Tonight, the stands were only about three quarters full, so the nature of the expected crowd and its attendant problems on July Fourth would be very different. Not only would there be more than fifty thousand people, but there would also be a speaker's platform and extra seating in the center of the field. Gaynor tried to imagine how it would be, tried to picture it with the stadium packed to overflowing, crowds milling about and "Onward, Christian Soldiers" blasting from the loudspeakers. From which direction would Taylor be entering? How close to him would the guards let people get? Like most demagogues, the minister loved to move through swarming mobs, loved the touching and being touched, loved the closeness and electricity of the mass moment. But exactly how far Newman and his security people would let him go with all that on July Fourth was something else.

He noticed that the crowd seemed oddly quiet.

Jane tugged at his arm. "What's the matter with you? You're not even watching."

"I'm watching, I'm watching."

At the end of six innings, Emerson was still holding the Red Sox hitless, and the crowd had grown even more quiet and tense. Superstition said you didn't talk about what was going on or the pitcher would be jinxed. Everyone was trying to avoid any mention of it.

"You think I'm a fool, don't you?" said Jane quietly. "You think I don't know why you're here."

"I've never thought you were a fool."

She was leaning very close to him, her arm pressing against his. Its pressure was a boat, bearing them away. But where were they going?

"Why didn't you tell me the real reason?" she asked.

"I asked you along tonight, didn't I? I didn't have to. I could have come alone."

The answer seemed to satisfy her.

"I've been thinking about it," she told him. "I haven't said anything, but there's hardly been a moment I haven't had it on my mind."

Boston's half of the seventh ended with a ground out to short. There had still been no hit off Emerson. The crowd sighed. That was all.

"I want you to know that I understand," she said. "I understand everything—your reasons, your needs, the particular moment in time. Everything."

He glanced at her. She was smoking a cigarette and watching the field. There appeared to be nothing else on her mind but the game. But when she turned, there was a flash, like far lightning, as her gaze met his.

"I also want you to know," she said, this time speaking directly to him, "that it all applies equally to me. We share the same reasons and needs. Everything is the same for us. And that's why we're going to do this together."

The crowd cheered a Yankee double to right field, but Gaynor did not even bother to look.

"Don't talk foolishly. Do you know what you're saying?"

"I'm not talking foolishly. I know exactly what I'm saying." Her answer came in a gentle, singsong, almost childish voice, but her face had hardened. "I'm saying that if you're going to be here with a gun on the night of July Fourth, I'm going to be here with a gun, too."

Who was this woman? How could he not know her after all these years?

"I'm sorry. I only have one revolver."

"I'll get my own."

He stared off at the field but had no idea what was going on there.

"Richard, listen to me. I'm as serious about this as I've ever been about anything in my life. I'm going to help you."

"I don't need your help."

"Everyone in this world needs help." Her face glowed

with pious conviction. "I'm not going to let you shut me out."

"You have no choice."

"Yes I do."

Something in the way she said it made him turn.

"If you don't take me along, you don't go either."

"How can you stop me?"

"By calling your friend Lieutenant Newman and telling him you're the Apostle."

He sat there hearing sounds from the stands and from the field, yet not really hearing them. "You wouldn't do that."

"Try me."

Breaking through, it hit him like a kick in the groin. "You despise me that much?"

"No. I love you that much."

"Sure."

She took his hand in both of hers, gripping it as though to prevent him from leaving.

"I've lost both my children, Richard. My small world is two thirds gone. If you're going, too, I don't want to be left behind." Tears welled. "We all have our contracts. I broke mine when I left you. I know that now. Whatever may remain, I refuse to break it again."

Touched, he could only watch her weep.

"I have it figured out," she whispered. "If I'm part of it you won't be nearly as crazy, you won't be nearly as ready to throw both our lives away, as you might if it were yours alone."

"Jesus, you're as spaced out as I am."

"I just know you, Richard."

"You don't know anything. All you're going to do is end up dying with me."

She had stopped crying. Her eyes, as green as they had ever been, flashed that same far light.

"Maybe. But I don't really think you'll let that happen."

"What's wrong with you?" He looked helplessly at her. "Can't you see there's no way I'll be able to stop it?"

"You'll think of a way."

She said it with such confidence, such finality, that Gaynor saw no point in further argument.

Moments later Hank Emerson struck out the last Red Sox batter with a slider instead of his expected fastball, and he had achieved the first Yankee no-hitter in years. The crowd went wild, Emerson's teammates carried him off in triumph, and Jane hopped up and down, hugging Gaynor, beside herself with joy.

"We did it, we did it!" she shouted into the uproar. "I told you. You've got to believe."

He felt her delight, her wonder. How young she could be. From tears to euphoria in minutes.

"Now I *know* it will be all right," she told him.

"What will?"

"Us—it—July Fourth—everything."

He held her, not understanding.

"It will" she said. "I made a deal."

Who hasn't? he thought. "With who?"

"God, of course."

"Aah. What kind of terms?"

"His guaranteed protection on July Fourth if we got the nohitter."

"Great. And if we hadn't gotten it? What would *you* be paying?"

"I'd have thought of something." She grinned. "Though I'd have probably welshed, anyway."

He remembered now. She could do things like that. It was one of the things he had loved most about her.

17

Late in the day of June 18, Commissioner Westley appeared in the doorway of Newman's office. "Let's go to the club," he said. "We can take a hot tub and talk."

The detective cleared his desk and went along without argument. Although the thought occurred, he did not even question Westley's need to sit naked in steaming water in order to have a conversation. Newman was a stubborn man, set in his ways, but he felt he was adapting. The dinosaur had failed to adapt and where was the dinosaur today? He had even progressed to the point where he could ride uptown in the commissioner's stretched, dove-gray limousine and enter the sanctified halls of the Nineteenth Century Club without feeling like an impostor. No mean accomplishment.

Still, he was not wholly free of who and what he was and out of what he had sprung. So that once between the sweating, tile walls of the club's bathing rooms, it somehow became not too different from Rabinowitz's Russian Shvitz Baths down on lower First Avenue, where his father had taken him when he was seven years old and where he had first seen all those awesome folds of flesh and hanging parts that left him bug-eyed with wonder. Would he really look like that one day? Hard to believe. All those male giants, sitting and standing about on the hot tiles, sighing and groaning, unburdening by steam. It had been a treat, an affirmation, a sign of impending manhood. His father had trusted him enough to take him to this place without women. He had made him part of the great male conspiracy. Now Michael Westley was taking him, and what was the conspiracy this time?

They sat in a private alcove in a huge, round, wooden tub, sipping straight vodka. Steam drifted up in wisps, like patches of fog. Hidden jets sent streams of hot water pulsing against their backs. An attendant brought two trays of hors d'oeuvres, placed them on a shelf edging the tub, and disappeared without a word. A recorded string quartet, playing something that sounded to Newman vaguely like Bach, accompanied the strains of rushing water. Eyes closed, the detective nibbled caviar on a cracker.

"Whatever you're building up to with all this," he said, "it's working. I'm a softened, vulnerable man."

"Fine. Enjoy it." The police commissioner's voice was as gently insinuating as the music. His body, slender and almost hairless, could have been that of a young man. "What the hell. There's nothing in department Regulations that says a cop's life can't be halfway pleasant."

"Some halfway pleasant." Eyes still closed, Newman washed down the caviar with his vodka, relaxed enough at that moment to drift into sleep. "Okay. Who do I have to shoot?"

"Only the Apostle."

"Naturally." Newman sighed and opened his eyes. "You get nothing for nothing on this planet."

"How is the investigation going?"

"We're still going building by building. Unfortunately, it takes time. And I've broadened the search area."

"He might not be in that neighborhood at all, you know."

"I feel he is."

"And if he's not?"

Newman shifted his position in the tub, angling the jet into knots of pain in his lower back. "I can't work on that assumption."

"Maybe not, but I have to. We've got only sixteen days left, Jay. I don't want Taylor walking into Yankee Stadium on July Fourth with that homicidal maniac still on the loose."

"Our poor Apostle. No more Mr. Nice Guy. Now he's a homicidal maniac."

"I want you to know the FBI is coming in."

Newman stared at the commissioner through the rising steam, a mythic god of the waters stripped to the skin.

Sudden anger clouded his eyes. "What the hell for? Who needs a bunch of bureau hot shots nosing around? This is our case not theirs."

"I've been stalling them for more than two weeks. I can't anymore. You're going to have to let them into it." As Newman's voice had risen, Westley's became even softer than usual. "Why are you so upset? Why are you overreacting like this?"

Newman had no answer. The anger had been pure reflex.

"This is no reflection on you," said Westley. "It's just the law. Besides, we're suddenly faced with a potentially lethal deadline, and we both have too much invested in Taylor to risk losing him."

"The reverend isn't worried. He'd rather we didn't pick up the Apostle at all. He loves the publicity." Newman slowly relaxed in the swirling water. "Why is Taylor so important to you, Michael?"

"I've told you."

"Yes, but what haven't you told me?"

Naked and pink-skinned in repose, they sat looking at one another.

"You always were a hard-nosed sonofabitch," said Westley.

"I'm involved. Remember?"

"So you are." Nevertheless, it required several additional moments of consideration. "The truth is, this is the man who is going to move me into the White House within six to eight years. I've hinted at it before, so it should come as no great surprise. It should also help you understand my concern. Obviously, I have a lot at stake."

The lieutenant felt something stir inside him. It was not the vodka.

"And if you have any doubts that he can carry it off, let me remove them. The United States is the greatest working democracy in the world, but unlimited funds, political know-how, and the right pressure points can still influence elections. Even presidential ones. Joe Kennedy and his boys are the perfect case in point. From nowhere they all but created a dynasty. So you see it's quite possible."

"Congratulations," said Newman. "I'm impressed. I'm also curious. I know what my deal with Taylor is, but what's yours? What's the going rate on the presidency these days?"

"The same as you're paying for police commissioner. My soul."

They laughed together, the sound losing itself quickly beneath the swirling water and piped-in music, two old friends lounging inside a steaming room devoted to sensuous pleasures.

"I hope that's a joke," said the lieutenant.

"We laughed, didn't we?"

"I haven't sold out. Whatever I'm doing for Taylor, I honestly believe it to be for the best."

"Fine." The commissioner raised his glass in a toast. "To the best. Whatever that is."

Newman drank with him.

"But I'm not nearly as lucky as you," said Westley. "I'm willing to eat shit to be president, and that's pretty much what I expect to be doing for the next eight years. I also expect to be lying, kissing ass, laughing when I should be crying, and embracing people who would ordinarily make me want to puke. So I'm not deluding myself about the cost of what I want." He smiled with icy elegance. "You see, like our friend the Apostle, I too think of Taylor as a rather outsized, neoclassic focus of evil, if I may use so outdated and melodramatic an expression. But I also believe every evil can be put to some good use."

"Such as making you president?"

"*And* making you commissioner. Two equally worthwhile projects. Which I say without undue cynicism. Given the opportunity, I'm certain we'll both be outstanding at our respective jobs. But for God's sake, let's not fool ourselves about what we're willing to do to get them."

Newman drank more vodka, but it had no effect. Listening to Michael Westley suddenly seemed to have burned off all the alcohol.

"Tell me something. What if Taylor wasn't so important to your presidency? What if he was simply the arch demon you apparently think he is? How would you feel about the Apostle's threat then?"

"You should know me better than that, Jay. Assassination is hardly a viable solution to anything."

"Not even to the certifiably evil?"

"Evil by whose judgment?"

"Your own."

The commissioner's eyes were steady, a clear, moist blue

staring through the gray steam. "The instant I decide I'm free to fight evil with murder, I become evil myself. It's a no-win contest."

What about killing Hitler in '33? But Newman refrained from asking the rabbi's question aloud. Knowing what his friend's answer would be, he had no desire to hear it.

Special Agent Frank Peterson had been in Newman's office for more than an hour. A young, even-featured man with muscular jaws, he chain-smoked cigarettes at a furious pace and spoke with great earnestness and sincerity. He also had a law degree, from Northwestern University, and good enough manners not to appear too shocked upon learning that Newman's degree from Harvard had somehow failed to raise him any higher than a lieutenant of detectives.

For his own part, Newman did his best to cover his resentment at having the FBI intrude in his case at all. *His case.* His feeling of possession was total and irrefutable. The Apostle had been his from the beginning and still was. To which end, Newman had drawn his men into a small conspiracy of understanding before any of the agents had even appeared at Headquarters. "The Apostle is ours," he told them, and it took a conscious effort not to say *mine.* "Everything we've done so far in this case is ours, and we're not about to share it with a bunch of bureau desk jockeys in three-piece suits who can't even piss without getting their shoes wet. But since our orders are to cooperate, we'll have to go through the motions at least. We'll give them copies of our case files, but with any really significant material removed. We'll answer their questions, but not the answers that can do them any good. I feel we're only days away from a break in this thing, and I'm sure none of us wants these guys moving in just in time to get their pictures in the papers." He considered their three solemn and attentive faces, Mulcahy, Robbins, Loretti, suddenly his co-conspirators. "And no leaks. Not to anyone. Not to wives, girlfriends, buddies, or priests. If this ever does get out, it's our asses."

Now, two days later, with Peterson in his office and several of the agent's men already effectively handled as planned, Newman felt well enough in control to wax increasingly expansive as he went over the case. A couple of brother

Norman Garbo

lawyers, he thought, happily dedicated to the preservation of the common good.

Peterson lit a fresh cigarette from a dying one. There were seven butts in his ashtray. "I'll be honest with you, Lieutenant. When this assignment came into our district office, I pulled every possible string to get it, I wanted it that badly. To me it's a once-in-a-lifetime shot, a chance to do something few of us ever get."

"Why is that?"

"Hell, it's a textbook case. I've read everything ever written about it. Where else could you find so clear-cut a contest between right and wrong, light and darkness, order and anarchy."

Oh, Christ, thought Newman, he's one of those, a cliché dialectician.

"Yes, but which side is which?"

The bureau man looked at him. Then he laughed. "I'm a small-town boy, Lieutenant. Go easy on me."

He rose to study the wall map. It was not the same one that had been there before. The new map had different pin flags and different search areas marked off. Peterson took out a notebook and jotted down the streets and buildings that he and his men would be covering. It was going to be a futile search.

"What sort of weapon has he been using?" the agent asked.

"A thirty-eight police special. But all that sort of detail is in the forensic reports we gave you."

"I hate reading anything out of Forensics. I can never make head or tail out of their gibberish."

Newman didn't believe him.

"Do you know where he got the gun?"

"He hit a cop over the head and took it."

"What's the officer's name and precinct?"

"Reagan. He's in the Sixty-seventh. Up in the Bronx."

"No other weapon ever used?"

"A toy pistol. When he hit Reagan."

Peterson looked up. "Pretty cute. I don't remember seeing any of that in the newspapers."

"I kept it out. Reagan would have killed himself."

"You're a kind man, Lieutenant."

Newman watched him writing in his notebook. It made him

280

curiously uncomfortable, as if the mere recording of the information could somehow achieve subtle insights that would break the case.

"Eyewitnesses," said Peterson. "I'd like the names and addresses of anyone who has ever seen, heard, or spoken to him."

"That's also in the reports your people were given."

"There are things I want to ask as we go down the list."

Newman gave him what he wanted. None of it meant much, anyway. Or did the FBI have new, more sophisticated interrogation techniques that could strike hidden gold? *Now I'm really getting paranoid.* From time to time the agent interrupted with questions and wrote down Newman's answers with the same studied meticulousness with which he apparently did everything. He paused only to light fresh cigarettes. No real problem with this guy, Newman decided. He'll be dead of cancer in a week.

Peterson closed his notebook. "What about you, Lieutenant? Have you yourself ever spoken to the Apostle?"

Newman stared at him.

"Has he ever called you on the telephone? Disguised his voice? Anything like that?"

"Yes. He's called me."

"Aah." Despite his comparative youth, Peterson had dark, concentric circles under his eyes. They tended to give him the look of an anxious raccoon. "Would you tell me about it?"

Newman described the recurrent conversations, editing the more personal parts. What possible harm here?

"How did you know the Apostle might have been calling me?"

"My mother was a gypsy psychic, my father, the town drunk. Between them, they managed to give me certain occult powers."

"You're lucky. I could use some of that."

Peterson grinned. "The part about my parents is true. I also happen to have more faith in my instincts than in certain alleged facts. For example, you and everyone else around here have come across as nothing but pleasant and cooperative, yet I still know we're getting fucked."

"What's that supposed to mean?" Newman flared.

"Relax, Lieutenant. I don't take it personally, so don't you. I've gotten used to it. The locals always resent our coming in. Which is why I never expect much from these briefings.'' He paused to light his ninth cigarette. ''I'm sure you weren't the one to want us in on this. Who was it? The commissioner?''

''You know damned well it was.''

''Of course. July Fourth is getting closer and Westley is getting worried. How come you're not worried, Lieutenant?''

Newman did not answer.

''But getting back to my occult powers. Actually, I was once on a similar case in Chicago. It had nothing like the Apostle's scope and imagination, but it did involve disguised calls to the agent in charge. The calls all had the same friendly baiting you described, the same personalizing of the relationship, the same compulsive flirting with danger. So I figured what happened once could happen again.''

''Did you ever catch the guy?''

Peterson looked mildly surprised. ''I sure did.''

''Who was he?''

''A friend of the agent.''

Newman sat letting it wash over him.

''What do you say, Lieutenant? Have you checked out your friends lately?''

''I don't have any friends.''

''Too bad. You might have been able to find the Apostle somewhere among them.''

It had not been entirely a lie. Looking back, Newman had to admit that establishing lasting friendships had never been high among his talents or priorities. All these years of living, of being in the job, of working with hundreds of officers, he had remained pretty much a solitary creature. Taking latent inventory, adding up what might be close to a final score, he supposed he would have to call Michael Westley his only friend. Which struck him as rather sad.

Yet, in considering it, he would never have judged himself an unfriendly man. He had never consciously avoided getting close to people. But neither had he ever felt any real need for that kind of closeness. While he was married, whatever requirements he may have had in that area had always been well enough satisfied by Jenny. She had been his missing company of friends. She had been there to talk to and share with. Jenny never spoke of friendship as such, but it was her familiar. She lived in it as though it were her private room. No need to mention such things. Nothing to say about that except, *Hold my hand. I'm here.*

And not too long after she was gone, he had Mary. Or at least as much of her as he was willing to accept. It was a time when he was beginning to suffer loneliness in the face of advancing age and death. His senses were no longer as acute as they once were, and sometimes he had to grab a chair or a wall if he rose too quickly. The world disappeared at such moments, but Mary was there. Again, all by himself, he invented the idea of friendship with a woman.

Still, affected by this sudden concept of his aloneness, he shared it with Mary. She listened. She held him. Then she buried herself in what he was feeling. She looked over his years, his work, his lost wife. She looked over herself. She said, "Cheer up, darling. You've done better than most. With friends it's quality, not quantity. Besides, you've had love." She looked at him with her pale Irish eyes. "You have it still."

Newman was silent. He gazed off at the faded image of his history. It failed to reassure him.

"Listen to me," Mary told him. "Stop pouring ashes over your head. You've spent a quarter of a century in defense of eight million people. You've touched more lives than you'll ever know. You've even saved some."

"I know. I'm a big hero."

"Don't knock it. You're that, too. If you think not, call up Richard Gaynor sometime. Ask him how he feels about breathing. Ask him if he might be persuaded to call you his friend."

"Saving a man's life doesn't constitute friendship."

"Maybe not to you. But you can bet your teeth it does to him."

He dropped it there.

But some hours later, lying awake in the dark, he picked it up once more. It seemed a time for fate to be picked clean of old problems, or, failing this, to be defied. Maybe he owed Gaynor as much as Gaynor owed him. Hadn't both their lives been renewed that night in the burning grass? And they had certainly talked. Maybe not too often, but surely of things that mattered—of life, of love, of loss, of pain. Soul talk. All of which brought their own guarantees of value.

So we're friends, he thought.

"Jesus Christ."

It was said aloud, but so softly that Mary did not even stir beside him.

His three graces, Mulcahy, Robbins, and Loretti, were in his office well before seven the next morning. They were all putting in extra time since the FBI had come in. With the authentic case map pulled out of its special cabinet and taped over the fake one, they went through their morning ritual of submitting the previous day's reports and discussing any leads that seemed to hold promise. Today there were six possible suspects that fit this category and required further investigation. Three were on West 105th Street, two were on 106th, one on 107th. They were all men of the Apostle's reported physical stature, all were under forty years of age, and all were living alone. Additionally, one had been at home, ill, several weeks before. Robbins, who had the sick suspect, was especially hopeful.

Newman checked his detectives' schedules for that day. He occasionally helped out by covering a few buildings himself, and this morning he expected to give Loretti a hand. "Suppose I take the south side of a Hundred and Ninth Street," he told the detective. "I'll start at the corner of Riverside Drive and work east. Is that okay with you?"

"Please, Lieutenant. Be my guest."

Newman was careful to follow the same procedures he and his men had been using all along. He went straight to the building superintendent, said he was conducting a crime survey in the area, and requested a tenant list. Asking the usual questions, he chose twelve tenants for further inquiry, not telling the super who they were. Then he went through the building alone and rang their doorbells. Of the first eight on his list, four were at home, and he spent several minutes talking with each. The ninth bell he rang was Richard Gaynor's.

He stood there waiting, praying the artist was home. Delay at this point would have been intolerable. Then he heard footsteps approaching and felt something burning go out of his lungs.

Gaynor opened the door. He was wearing a sport shirt and

jeans and he was unshaven. His face stared back at Newman—successively surprised, curious, and finally just pleased.

He's glad to see me, thought the detective with a sudden flash of hope that he was wrong. This was a bereaved and withdrawn man, someone who was out of things, not an Apostle type at all. Besides, he was an artist, for God's sake, an abstracted dreamer. How could someone like that turn himself into an assassin?

"Well, Lieutenant. You're really up before breakfast."

Newman hesitated in the doorway. "I hope I'm not busting in on anything. Are you alone?"

"You've got to be the politest cop in New York. Come in. You're just in time for coffee."

The detective followed Gaynor into the kitchen. "Black," he said. "And you may as well lace it with something sensible."

Gaynor added some Irish whiskey to his own cup as well as Newman's, although the detective was certain he wouldn't ordinarily drink this early. What a nice man. He's trying to make me feel less of a solitary boozer.

"Still chasing the Apostle in the neighborhood?" Gaynor asked.

"I think I've found him."

Gaynor looked at him. If his face showed anything, it was pleasant expectation. "You *think* you've found him? What does that mean?"

"It means I haven't bothered preparing any hard evidence."

They considered one another across the kitchen table.

"I haven't the patience for cat and mouse, Richard. We're long past that, anyway. It's you I'm talking about."

Gaynor allowed himself the slowest and faintest of smiles. "You think *I'm* the Apostle?"

"Yes."

"But you just said you had no hard evidence."

"I don't need any."

"Then how can you arrest me?"

"I'm not here to arrest you," said Newman. "If I were, I'd have come with a search warrant and a couple of men. As it is, no one else even suspects you. And if you're willing to be sensible, if you're willing to listen to reason, maybe we can work it so no one ever will."

Gaynor carefully added more whiskey to his coffee. It was

his only sign of possible stress. "I don't quite follow. If you really believe I'm the Apostle, why are you being so good to me?"

"Because I know what you've been through and understand why you're doing this. Maybe I even feel a crazy kind of responsibility for you." The detective paused, his eyes solemn. "And because although I may not have thought much about it before, I've decided you may very well be one of the few friends I've ever had."

Gaynor looked off, suddenly unwilling to meet the lieutenant's gaze. "I appreciate that. I think of you as a friend, too. But I'm not the Apostle."

"Then I'm sure you won't mind stripping and letting me see if there's a fresh bullet wound somewhere on you."

"And if there isn't? Will that convince you you're wrong?"

"It might make me wonder."

"That's all?"

The detective was silent.

"Then I may as well save myself the trouble of getting undressed."

Newman took a deep breath. "It doesn't really matter. All I want is your word that you'll forget Clayton Taylor and this whole idea and quit as of now."

"You mean, if I were the Apostle."

"Say it any way you like."

"And what would you be offering in return?"

"I won't turn you in. You'll stay free."

"You couldn't arrest me without evidence, anyway."

"Don't be naive. I have plaster casts of the shoeprints and tire marks you left under the Verrazano Bridge. I'd just have to match them up. Besides, once I made you an official suspect, you wouldn't even be able to take a crap without our knowing it. So no matter what you do, the Apostle will still be washed up."

They drank their hot Irish coffee.

"The one thing I can't offer you," said the detective, "is protection from the FBI. They're on their own. But so far, at least, I've got them looking for you in all the wrong places."

"How did the FBI get involved?"

"You went to Georgia and shot Reese. That made it an interstate felony."

Gaynor seemed abstracted. "Just for curiosity's sake, why me?"

"Why *not* you? I must have been blind not to have seen it before. There you were, right under my nose with your tragic loss and accident trauma, with your survival guilt, with your need to justify living when all those others were dead. Looking back, I realize now that I may even have been partly responsible, that I may even have inspired the whole insane idea myself with my chronic bitching, my screaming about our lousy, revolving door system of justice."

Newman looked at Gaynor for confirmation. None was offered.

"Then, of course," he went on, needing to get everything neatly wrapped up and in order, still partly needing to convince himself, "there was your interest in the Apostle whenever we met, your approval of what he was doing, your constant curiosity about my investigation. But I admit that's all with hindsight. What really switched me on was when one of the FBI agents reported a similar case in which an anonymous caller turned out to be a friend of the investigator. It was only then that I thought of you and realized you actually lived in my prime search area."

The detective felt a curious weight of melancholy. Studying Gaynor's face, he saw it as solid, all of a piece, without seams. There were no open places. Had he gotten inside at all? They sat in silence. Then someone ran water in the kitchen overhead and the plumbing groaned between the walls.

"Just for the record," said Gaynor, "I deny everything."

"Deny what you want. Just give me your word that as of now the Apostle is no more."

"And if I refuse?"

Newman shrugged. "If you're going to act like a schmuck, then I'll treat you as one. I'll turn you in as a prime suspect and have you placed under twenty-four-hour surveillance."

"That's all?"

"No." Moving deliberately, the detective placed his cup on the table. Then he took out his revolver and pointed it at Gaynor's chest. "I'll also make you strip right now and show me what I'm sure is there. Once that's confirmed, I'll turn this place inside out until I find your mask, gloves, and gun."

"You have no search warrant."

287

Norman Garbo

"I'll get one later."

"That's against the law." Gaynor smiled. "A purist like you would never do that."

"The hell I wouldn't." Newman's face was dark. "You think you can piss on the law at will, then make it shine for you? You'll either give me your word or I'll walk out of here with enough hard evidence to put you on ice for forty years."

"I thought we were friends."

"Only if it works two ways. And your way better start right now."

"At least give me some time."

"Time for what? To get rid of the evidence?"

"You're pushing me. I don't like being pushed."

Something seemed to tear loose in Newman's head. He half rose, leaned across the table, and grabbed the front of Gaynor's shirt. Then, sticking his revolver in his belt to free both hands, he ripped the garment off the artist's shoulders. There it was. Pink and ridged, a fresh bullet scar marked the upper part of Gaynor's left arm. It somehow gave Newman little satisfaction.

"Now maybe we can stop fucking around."

Gaynor sat quietly watching him. He seemed wholly indifferent to what was happening. Newman picked up the whiskey, bypassed the coffee cup altogether, and drank straight from the bottle. Then he sat there, trying to keep his hands from trembling. Why was he so angry? Why was he so upset?

"Okay," he said. "Where's the mask and gun?"

"You're the detective. Find them."

Newman took out his handcuffs and walked to the back of Gaynor's chair. "Put your hands behind you."

"That's not necessary."

"Like hell it isn't."

Newman put the cuffs on him and began searching the apartment. It took him only a minute to find the Henri Bendel shopping bag in the closet. Inside were gloves, mask, gun, and nylon cord. He carried everything back to the kitchen.

"Some hiding place," he said flatly.

"I wasn't hiding anything."

That almost seemed true. Tiredly, Newman sat down. With his anger spent, the melancholy weight seemed to return. Gaynor's torn shirt exposed his body to the waist, and Newman saw the terrible, welted crash scars. They made him feel no

288

better. What did the poor sonofabitch want? How many times did he have to be saved?

"How about the handcuffs?" said Gaynor.

"Wear them awhile. They might help your thinking."

The detective picked up the mask and studied it. He drew it over one hand. He felt the cool rubber against his skin. He thought about what it had come to mean.

"How in God's name did you ever think of this?"

"It belonged to my kids. It seemed like a good enough idea at the time. It still does." Gaynor's voice was calm, but his face suddenly seemed involved in an elaborate effort. It affected his eyes and mouth and pulled at his chin. "Not that it really matters, but you were right before. You did inspire the whole concept, you and your thin blue line of knights errant. Like you, I just wanted to do what I could."

"I was talking about *within* the law, for Christ's sake!"

"The law doesn't always work."

"You're out of your goddamned head. You've killed two men and now you want to kill a third." Newman sensed dangerous human actions going on but felt helpless to stop them. "Aah, we've been all through that. I'm sick of talking. Now all I want is your God's honest word—on the souls of your poor, lost kids—that the Apostle is through. And if I don't get it, I'm marching you and your silly Bendel's shopping bag straight to the nearest precinct house."

"You're not giving me much choice."

"It's still more than you've ever given *me*."

Gaynor sighed. "All right. For whatever it's worth, you've got my word."

"I'll tell you this. It better be worth a lot. For both our sakes."

Newman unlocked the handcuffs and they sat finishing the whiskey straight, without the coffee. Slowly, the detective felt himself begin to unwind, felt himself moved by the sweet purity of the moment. Something good, something worthwhile, had surely been accomplished. His heart was so full that he was afraid to open his mouth to speak. Some part might escape.

18

Gaynor discovered his reactions coming in consecutive, gradually varying stages. Which was enlightening, he thought. He was still learning about himself. Yet it was, at best, a foolish course of study. By the time he knew anywhere near enough, none of it would really matter.

At first there was just shock. The danger of discovery had, of course, been constant from the start, yet somehow he had never expected it to happen. Not really. The ego was that strong, that ridiculous. And as time passed, it had grown even more so until he had finally felt untouchable, impervious. *Run, run, as fast as you can. You can't catch me, I'm the gingerbread man.* The old nursery rhyme danced tauntingly through his brain. In the end, of course, the poor gingerbread man was caught by a fox helping him escape across a river. Well, he had been caught, all right. He was just lucky the fox was Newman, not someone else.

So it was gratitude that swelled next. Bless Jay Newman, now and forever, and all who come after him. A lesser man, considering only the rewards to be reaped from bringing in the Apostle, would never have been swayed by friendship—and a totally one-sided friendship, at that. What had he ever done for Newman? But this thought somehow made him uncomfortable, as though heavy debts were piling up that he might never be able to repay. Carefully, he set it aside.

Then came an almost euphoric sense of relief. He had been

set free. Newman had granted him an eleventh-hour reprieve. He was no longer bound to carry out an act that would have led to nearly certain death or long-term imprisonment. And it wasn't that he had wavered in either courage or commitment. He had remained steadfast all the way. But having pledged his word to a friend, he had no choice but to quit. His responsibility to himself for any further action was finished, over. He was literally back from the dead, a latter-day Lazarus.

Still, the feeling of relief, of deliverance, was surprising. It puzzled him. When had he changed? At what point had it become so important to cling to a life that had lost all joy and meaning? What had happened to the indifference to possible harm that had been his greatest strength, his protective armor?

He began going over everything again. It was a reexamination that spun him around, tilted his horizons, rendered him dizzy and confused. He was a very peculiar animal. He invented attitudes and plots against his true feelings. If you're frightened, if you want to back out of this, he told himself fiercely, then go ahead and back out. But for God's sake, don't crap all over it with fake reasons.

He finished his recanting and looked at what he had. The euphoria was gone, but he felt better. He had caught himself in time. Lying to yourself carried a death of its own. From that, at least, he considered himself saved.

He had been calling Newman at home for three nights in a row with no success. On the fourth night, he heard the detective on the other end.

"Hi, Lieutenant. I've been trying to reach you for days." He was speaking to Newman for the first time on the phone without muffling his voice, but an instinctive caution still kept him from identifying himself by name. "Don't you ever sleep at home?"

"Not if I can help it." Newman seemed to hesitate. "Is this who I think it is?"

"Yes."

They were both silent, both waiting.

"What I'm calling for—" Gaynor stopped. He was finding this unaccountably difficult. "The thing is, the last time we met I'm afraid I was pretty much off balance, even overwhelmed. It was a hell of a shock for me."

"You seemed to handle it well enough."

"Not really."

Newman said nothing.

"I never did thank you."

"Thank me? I'm lucky you didn't go after my head with a piece of furniture."

"You could have been a hero."

"You've already made me a hero, remember? I figured once is enough."

"Anyway," said Gaynor, "I just wanted you to know that I appreciate it."

"Okay. So you appreciate it." The tone came over the wire flat, cold.

"What's the matter?"

"Talk is cheap."

"What do you expect?"

"If you don't know, we're in trouble."

Gaynor knew. But they were still in trouble.

He felt like a stage director, setting up a scene in which he also was going to be one of the performers. Jane and Kate were the other two members of the cast. They sat stiffly opposite one another in his living room, frigidly watching him fussing about, preparing drinks and a few snacks. Neither woman made a move to help. They intended this to be all his. The tension between them was almost palpable.

Still, Gaynor was finding that the moment was not without a certain appeal. Perhaps there were even subtle sexual overtones lurking somewhere in the blended fragrances of their perfumes. Surely two women, sharing the same man's body, must, perforce, share something of one another's.

So far, they had no idea why they had been brought together. He had told them only that something had come up that made it imperative for the three of them to meet. Both women had protested, although not too strongly. If nothing else, they were curious.

Amenities completed, Gaynor drew up a chair and let them have it straight out. "Newman knows about me. Everything. The whole Apostle bit. I'm afraid he has me cold."

Watching their faces for some response, he saw nothing. Had they somehow developed an immunity to bad news, the way some people develop an immunity to poison? Or had they been expecting it for so long that the event itself simply proved anticlimactic? Whichever, they just sat staring at him.

"How did it happen?" Jane finally asked.

More practical, Kate said, "What does it mean? Why aren't you in jail?"

He told them about the detective's visit and everything that resulted from it. They listened in silence, a solemn audience of two for his latest witch's tale.

"Thank God he considers you a friend." Jane sighed.

Kate was still staring at him. "Do you think he really expects you to keep your word and quit?"

"I doubt it. I think that was just a little game he had to play to justify his not arresting me. I'm sure he'll still be watching for me on July Fourth."

The windows were open to catch the evening breeze off the Hudson and the roar of a helicopter intruded. The vibration rattled the ice in their glasses.

"In case you're wondering," said Gaynor, "and just for the record, I still expect to go through with it."

"Doesn't giving your word to a friend mean anything at all to you?" asked Jane.

"Yes, but not when I had to give it with a gun at my head. That's what my soul-searching finally came up with, and that's what I believe. Anyway, since we all seem to be involved in this for one reason or another, I thought it might be a good idea to get together and talk."

Kate's eyes came alive. "Wait a minute. What do you mean, *all* involved?" She stabbed a finger at Jane. "Who brought *her* in?"

"I brought myself," said Jane.

Kate faced Gaynor. "If it's not asking too much, would you mind telling me what's happening?"

"Jane is with us."

"Since when?"

"Since she threatened to blow the whole thing if I didn't promise to take her with me on July Fourth."

"Take her with you *where?* Are you talking about right into the stadium?"

Jane answered for Gaynor. "If that's what we finally work out."

Kate rose, went to the window, and stared out at the

Hudson, a dark, silvery purple in the fading light. When she turned, her face was set for battle.

"I didn't like you when I threw you out of the hospital," she said, "and I like you even less now. You're pure ball-breaker. You walk out on a good man because he dares be less than perfect, and now that he has only this poor, crazy obsession left, you shove your way back in to take that over, too."

"Don't you dare judge me. I can at least give him a chance out there. I can at least keep him alive." Jane was fuming now. "What can you do? Fuck him?"

"Damn right. And a lot better than you ever could." Kate glared at Gaynor. "What is she talking about? What does she mean, she can keep you alive?"

The artist felt both amused and invisible. Nevertheless, he was penetrated by them. Or, rather, by their feelings about him. Yet this was precisely why he had brought them together. Better to have it out now than later.

"It's Jane's idea," he said. "I'll let her tell you about it."

"Do I have to?" asked his former wife.

"Please." Allowing them breathing room, time to cool down, he mixed fresh drinks. His women, he thought, studying first one, then the other. At this moment they were foreigners to one another, even enemies, yet both only wanted to keep him alive. Why was he so valuable to them? They gazed back at him, and in their angry, thickly lashed eyes he seemed young despite his years of turmoil.

"Actually," Jane began, "the whole thing has to do with Victor Lutovsky."

"You mean the gangster, the syndicate boss?" said Kate.

"Who else? Though the only way I've ever known him is as a legitimate real estate operator.

"Anyway, I've been doing his head-hunting for a long time now and we've become, well, good friends. In fact, at this point he even owes me a few favors. I've been able to get him some key people when other searchers either couldn't or wouldn't."

Kate looked puzzled but interested. "Meaning what?"

"Meaning I should be able to ask a favor in return."

"You're going to ask Lutovsky to bump off Clayton Taylor?"

Jame smiled for the first time. "No. But I thought it might

be smart to at least get some advice from someone long rumored to be the best in the business.''

"Lutovsky does public assassinations?" Kate was wavering between facetiousness and complete fascination.

"Not personally, of course. Not for years. And not in this country. He's too patriotic. But I've gotten the idea he's had people active in Central and South America. Also, he's Jewish. Which should make him a bit more approachable about something like this. In any case, talking to him strikes me as the most logical way to deal with this whole illogical project.''

"I think I love it." Kate looked at Jane with the beginnings of respect. "Can you really arrange a meeting?''

"No problem.''

"What about safeguards?''

"We can work something out.''

My women, thought Gaynor.

Jane handled everything with dispatch and with what was increasingly appearing to be characteristic efficiency. How little we know about one another, thought the artist. Who was the woman who had birthed his children, lived with him all those years? Suddenly, she was a stranger, a hard-nosed confidante of gangsters—was she also Lutovsky's lover?—an arranger of secret, delicately poised meetings. They lived in a spiritually and emotionally confused age. Or was it just he who was confused? He was beginning to think that even his own suddenly acquired strain of madness endowed him with an undeniable appeal. Much of the population hailed him as a hero while the two women in his life gazed at him with shining eyes and transposed his malaise into sexual excitement.

At a few minutes before nine o'clock on the evening of June 22, Jane drove a rented Mustang into the cobbled courtyard of Victor Lutovsky's town house on East Sixty-third Street and parked beneath a picturesque, turn-of-the-century gas lantern. Gaynor, seated beside her, slipped a white hood, fashioned from a pillowcase, over his head. The hood had eyeholes, an opening for his nostrils, and a smiling mouth, drawn in lipstick, that Jane had added as a whimsical touch. They got out of the car and Jane rang the doorbell.

A houseman big enough to be a pro linebacker let them into a marble-floored vestibule. He showed no surprise at Gaynor's hood.

"Good evening, Mrs. Gaynor."

"Hello, Arthur." Jane smiled at him. "How's the back?"

"A bit better, thanks." He looked Gaynor over with the cold, measuring eyes of a maître d'hôtel. "Would you raise your arms, please, sir?"

Gaynor did as he was told and the man went over his body lightly but thoroughly. Studying him, the artist saw the unmistakable bulge of a shoulder holster under his jacket. He then led them along a hall to a huge sitting room that seemed to be a combination library and art gallery.

"Mr. Lutovsky will be with you in a moment," he said and brought out a tray of brandies and liqueurs. "The usual, Mrs. Gaynor?"

"Please."

He poured her some anisette.

Well, thought Gaynor, and ordered a B and B for himself. The lady did get around. He looked at the paintings hanging about the room, each under its separate light, and picked out two Renoirs, a Matisse, and a Gauguin. There was also a series of small sketches that he knew had to be Goya's even before he saw the signature. Some gangster.

Lutovsky himself appeared a moment later. Gaynor recognized him at once from his photographs, a broad, deep-chested, physically impressive man with graying temples and an aging fighter's face.

Jane kissed his cheek lightly. "I do appreciate this, Victor."

"I haven't done anything yet." Lutovsky's eyes were on Gaynor's smiling pillow case. They were clear, dark, and coldly amused. "Hello, whoever you are."

"Hello, Mr. Lutovsky. Sorry to have to handle it this way."

"It's okay. I don't have to know who you are. All I care about is you're a friend of Janey's and you've got a problem." He poured himself some brandy. "Well? What's the problem?"

"I have to kill a man."

"Aah." Lutovsky sighed. "That's all?"

The artist said nothing. He found it utterly grotesque to be sitting here, talking casually about killing to this almost mythical mobster. Not that Lutovsky had ever been indicted for his alleged criminality. He was much too clever and careful for that. When someone had to pay, others went to jail in his place. Lutovsky himself obviously preferred collecting art and living the good life of a real estate baron.

The mobster looked at Jane. "You think I'm running some kind of school for hit men?"

"Let him finish, Victor."

"This is a little different than you might think," said Gaynor through his hood. "The shooting has to be done in a public place with tight security. If possible I'd like to be able to walk away from it."

"And if you can't walk away from it?"

"I'll do it anyway."

The dark eyes showed sudden interest. "Why must it be a performance? If you want to kill a man, there are a hundred ways to do it without making yourself a big star."

"It has to be done this way."

"That's final?"

"Yes."

Sipping his brandy, Lutovsky turned to Jane. "You're trying to convert me with a new Apostle, Janey? How long did you think it would take me to know?"

"About five minutes. You're right on schedule."

Lutovsky sat there, his size overwhelming the chair beneath him. His face, potentially communicative, seemed preoccupied with some irony of his own.

"You weren't worried about what I might do?"

"No," Jane said.

"You trust me that much?"

"I know you that well."

Gaynor was beginning to feel like a voyeur at a reunion of former lovers. Or were they current?

"You surprise me," Lutovsky told Gaynor's ex-wife. "But what's your part in all this? What have you got to do with this guy?"

"He's a close friend. I care about him and what he's trying to do." She hesitated. "I also expect to be involved myself."

Lutovsky took a moment to absorb it. Then he swung back toward Gaynor. "You're letting her do this?"

"I can't stop her. She's threatened to turn me in if I try."

"Forget all that, Victor," said Jane. "That's all settled. What we need from you is your knowledge of these things."

Lutovsky looked worried, an aging heavyweight with unexpected problems. "I don't want you dying on me, Janey."

"Then show us a way to do this and live."

"I'm no damn miracle worker."

Jane's expression was veiled, lost in shadow. "You did well enough in Santiago, Managua, La Paz."

"Hell, that was comic-opera land. You're talking about New York, about Yankee Stadium, for God's sake!"

"You once said there was nothing that couldn't be done if you did your homework, thought it through, and dealt only with the facts."

"Sometimes I talk like a schmuck."

Lutovsky stared broodingly at Gaynor's hood. "Do you know they're making book on you in Vegas? It's even money you'll go through with it and twenty to one you'll be wasted if you do. I'm impressed with the even money. They seem to be taking you seriously."

"I am serious. You should be, too, Mr. Lutovsky. Whatever else you are, you're also a Jew."

"You think you have to remind me?" Lutovsky's voice was pure ice. "You think I don't know I'm a Jew?"

Gaynor did not answer. He had evidently touched a nerve.

"I learned that dirty little lesson early. And if I ever forgot, there were always plenty of good, kind Christians around to help me remember."

Impatient with himself, with his own lapse, Lutovsky spoke to Jane. "I don't like the whole thing. But him, I can maybe understand a little. You, I can't understand at all."

"Yes you can."

"Aah, Janey, it's such a waste."

"No it isn't."

"My heart's not in it."

"It means everything, Victor."

Lutovsky sighed and stood up. "Well, we'll see."

They went back to Gaynor's apartment and to bed. Their bodies, heated by fires of their own, sought distraction, sought to fit together and hold. Yet some part of their separate hurts remained. It was mostly out of this that she said, "Is Kate really better in bed than I?"

"That's some question."

"It's all right. She doesn't bother me anymore. I've gotten over that. In a way, I'm grateful. She did help you through the worst of it. She's so sure, so strong. I wish I had some of her toughness."

"You're tough enough." He had meant it as reassurance, but it sounded more like indictment. How wrong some things came out. In many ways, they were still locked rooms to each other. "You sure did okay with Lutovsky tonight."

"That wasn't so hard. He happens to care about me."

They were lying in the dark. A soft blue light filtered onto the bed, the carpeting, the walls.

"I know," he said. "You're full of little surprises these days, aren't you?"

Their bodies touching, she stirred against him. "I think I wanted you to know about Victor and me."

"Why?"

"I guess I still have my ego needs. I didn't want you just feeling sorry for me. I wanted you to know I was appealing to other men."

"But Victor Lutovsky, for God's sake!"

Her laugh had a light, pleasantly girlish sound. "Aah, you're jealous. But he is an attractive man, isn't he?"

He liked the idea of her teasing him. It carried the illusion of normalcy. "I suppose so. Frankly, for a moment there, I was almost imagining him in bed with you. It was strange. I know you've had other men since you left me, but this was the first time I've actually been in the same room with one."

"How did you feel?"

He thought about it. "I don't know. How did you react to Kate and me?"

"When I was able to stop being furious with her, I think I found it rather exciting."

He was suddenly curious. "Is Lutovsky married?"

"He's a widower. His wife had just died when I met him. They'd been together for forty years. It was a bad time for him. He feels I helped."

"How about your own bad time? Did he help you?"

He could feel her body tighten. "Only you could help me with that. Who else could know what it was like?"

Lying in the blue, translucent dark, they were suddenly invaded by one another. Or by their common loss. The bedroom walls offered no protection.

"But I know one thing for sure," she said. "He's going to help me with you."

19

A few days earlier, Newman had found his own immediate response to unmasking the Apostle strangely frustrating. It had to be one of the more satisfying achievements of his life, yet there was no one with whom he could share it. Except Mary, of course. And this was almost like sharing it with himself. Still, something special, a glow, a warm, curiously adolescent pride existed even in that. He felt like a kid on an ego trip, bragging to his best girl. *Look. See what I've done. Now you can appreciate how clever I am.*

Yet Mary's first reaction had seemed to hold little that resembled appreciation. Listening, her eyes narrowed, her lips tightened, her breathing grew slower and deeper.

"Oh, my God."

He stopped in midsentence. "What's the matter?"

"If you don't know, I can't tell you."

"Try."

"Why can't you ever do anything the normal way? Why can't anything ever be simple and straight with you? Why can't you be happy unless you're hanging from a cliff by your fingernails?"

"Are those rhetorical questions or are you expecting answers?"

He spoke calmly, trying to hold back his anger. Or did she consider anger one of his pleasures, too? It was early morning and they were still in her bed. The light sifted in, gray and gloomy. He had arrived late in the night without waking her, and this was his first chance to talk about it.

"I'm sorry. Congratulations." She was making her own effort to stay calm. "It must be very satisfying for you. I know how hard you've worked, how obsessed you've been with this. But isn't it enough that you once saved the man's life? Must you also be his keeper?"

"I don't understand you. You're the one who described him as a friend. What do you expect me to do? Send him away for twenty to forty years?" He paused to light a cigarette. "Well, I can't do that. I feel for him. I understand his needs too well, everything he's gone through. In his place, suffering his losses, his pain, his need to justify, I can see myself striking out in much the same way."

"All I can see is you destroying yourself to protect him."

"Don't be so theatrical. I'm not destroying anyone, least of all myself. Everything will be taken care of. The Apostle will just disappear and never be heard from again. He'll be buried and forgotten as quickly as yesterday's news."

Mary switched on a lamp to cut the gloom. The light yellowed her face and shadowed her eyes. "Are you telling me you really expect him to keep his word?"

"Hardly. I'm not that much of a fool."

She stared at him, eyes suddenly wide. "Jesus, Joseph, and Mary! You're not planning to let him go through with it."

"You should know me better than that."

"Sometimes I don't know you at all."

A sour dryness scraped his throat. With some effort, he dragged himself out of bed and went for the bottle he had left on the kitchen table a few hours before. When he returned, Mary was sitting at a window, hugging her knees. She watched him as he drank, a pale-eyed woman fearful of further revelations. What would he tell her next?

"I admit there are problems," he said. "For one thing, there's no way I can have him placed under surveillance without making him a prime suspect. And of course neither can I spend my days watching him myself. But I think I've worked out a way to handle that."

"Marvelous." Her voice was flat.

He laughed. "Hey, come on. Cheer up. This is a great thing that's happened. I've got him. He's all mine. Can't you understand that?"

"All I can understand is that if anything goes wrong, one or both of these men could end up dead on July Fourth, and you could be finishing your career in prison."

He poured himself some whiskey and drank it down. New fires were rising from old ashes. His heart burned like a furnace. "No one is going to die and I'm not going to prison. I've thought it all through. You've got to have more faith in your old goat."

"I have it, darling. Except where the Apostle is concerned. You've been slightly off the wall about this man from the start." She took the remains of his cigarette from an ashtray and nervously puffed it. "All right. So what are you going to do about him?"

"It's simple. I'll just make sure he doesn't show up at Yankee Stadium on July Fourth."

"And exactly how are you going to manage that?"

He shrugged. "I haven't worked out the details, but it shouldn't be too hard. All I have to do is lock him away somewhere for a day or two. Maybe even tie him up in his own apartment. When the big night has come and gone and the Apostle has failed to show as advertised, I can turn him loose."

"So he can shoot Taylor the next day?"

"No. Not Gaynor. He's no murderer. I know who I'm dealing with now. With the Apostle discredited and the myth instantly dead, there'd be no point to it. The soaring moment of grace, the public martyrdom, would no longer be available. Besides, Gaynor would know I'd be watching him carefully."

"You can't really believe all that."

"Why else would I say it?"

"To justify what you're doing."

"To whom?"

"Yourself."

"There you go again with your textbook psychology."

Her smile was sad, rueful. "It happens to be basic, darling. You've reversed all normal reasoning, done everything backward. Instead of examining the facts, then acting on them, you first decided what you wanted to do—in this case, not have to lock up your friend, Gaynor—then you scraped together whatever ideas might make this utterly unreasonable action seem halfway reasonable."

"Why would I do that?"

"You tell me."

He had no reply for her. At least none that he was prepared to accept. And certainly none that he would have been willing to share.

The lieutenant fled from the synagogue into the rainswept darkness, his collar up, his head bent against the downpour. He had just finished addressing the West Side shul's wealthy and politically conservative congregation on the subject of Clayton Taylor, and he felt he had acquitted himself quite well. Although some of his most sensitive listeners' questions had been less than sympathetic, he had managed to handle them without great difficulty. He knew the pattern by now. The reactions to his comments had become fairly predictable. When there was antagonism, it was usually the antagonism of those wanting to be convinced they were wrong. He was, after all, offering them a very appealing package—two million a month, the promise of safer streets, a much-needed respect for real property, and a halt to creeping urban blight. All things worth believing in. And they were trying hard to believe. The lieutenant was simply giving them a little boost in their trying.

The flickering neon sign of a corner bar beckoned like a Siren from Columbus Avenue and he started toward it. His throat was parched from two hours of talking and he was chilled with what felt like the beginning of a fever. He hoped he wasn't coming down with something. He had neither time nor patience for illness.

"Lieutenant Newman!"

A slightly built man came out of an arched doorway. His dark hat sat crookedly atop a turban of white bandages. The lieutenant was unable to make out his face.

"It's Duv Glickstein," said the rabbi.

Newman stared at him, a small figure that seemed to be growing smaller. Was he melting down in the rain?

"I'd like to talk to you, Lieutenant. Could you spare a few minutes?"

Even the rabbi's voice seemed to have shrunk. Gone was the belligerence, gone, the sharpness, gone, the instant rush to attack. His clothing was soaked through. Rain speckled his glasses. How long had he been huddled in the doorway, waiting? He held out a knobby hand. A peace offering? The detective shook it.

"Come on," said Newman. "I'll buy you a drink. Or are you too holy for whiskey?"

"A rabbi is a teacher, not a holy man."

They walked silently through the rain to the bar and settled in a booth. The lieutenant had bourbon and soda, the rabbi, straight whiskey in a shot glass that reminded Newman of the way his grandfather used to drink a little schnapps at the table to stimulate his appetite. Glickstein's orthodoxy required his keeping his hat on indoors, which the waiter seemed to find coldly amusing. He said something to the bartender and Newman saw them laugh. The black, narrow-brimmed hat, sitting askew on its hill of bandages, looked funny, all right, but Newman doubted that this was why they were laughing. He filed the thought away for further consideration. The reaction was pretty much instinctive.

"I didn't notice you in the audience," he said. "I guess you were someplace in back. Less chance of contamination, right?"

Glickstein sipped his drink with delicacy and concentration. His eyes were closed. His body shuddered as the whiskey did its work.

"I must confess I wasn't there. I was outside the entire time you spoke. I don't think I could have borne listening to you again. I wanted to talk to you, not hear you."

"You really know how to make a man feel good."

"I'm afraid I'm not much of a diplomat. I make enemies easier than I make friends. I'm too judgmental, too frank, too abrasive. What's on my mind is on my tongue. I know I approached you incorrectly when we first met and I apologize. Now I'd like to try once more."

What a strange man, thought Newman. He insults me, apologizes for it, and now I'm sure he's about to insult me again. Still, the detective was finding it difficult to take offense. Actually, he was getting to like the myopic little rabbi. There had to be something about unequivocal belief, total certainty of purpose, that, agree with it or not, he found appealing.

I've been asking around," said Glickstein. "I've been doing a little quiet investigating of my own in your old neighborhood. I've learned a few things about you, about your family, about the sort of people you come from. Your parents and grandparents are remembered well, warmly. They were good people, good Jews. You are apparently a good Jew, too. They say you knew a few pages of Talmud.''

"That was a hundred years ago, on another planet.''

"I'm a great believer in background, Lieutenant. Acquired traits may not be passed on through the blood, but we can't help accepting them into our hearts. It's the same with anguish, with suffering. We may not personally have suffered the horrors of the Spanish Inquisition, of the Russian and Polish pogroms, of the Nazi Holocaust, but our knowledge and remembrance of such things mark and haunt us. As Jews, we're forced to carry the scars of the Jewish experience. We carry them till we die. That's why I feel I can talk to you. That's why I still hope I can make you understand.''

"Understand what?''

"I'm sure you know.''

Newman was silent. He was only half listening. The other half of him was watching the waiter, who seemed to be amusing himself by directing the attention of the bar's regulars to Glickstein and his hat.

"You're being used, Lieutenant. You think you're getting a fine deal from this man Taylor, but you're just being swindled. And every time you open your mouth, every time another bunch of our landsleit listens to you, they're being swindled, too. If you don't stop, we're all going to pay dearly for it. I beg you. Stop now. Stop while there's still time.''

"You mean well, but you're wrong, Rabbi. I know what I'm doing. I'm not a fool. And the people I'm talking to aren't fools, either. At least give them credit for that. They're certainly intelligent enough to hear what I have to say and make up their own minds.''

Glickstein's eyes fluttered rapidly, nervously, behind their lenses. They seemed to be going into spasm. "When it concerns their future, their welfare, they're a pack of cretins. What do they know? They're half dazed from reading their idiotic newspapers, watching their infantile TV programs, listening to their self-serving politicians. They can be led like children. They'll follow whoever promises the most, whoever tells them what they want to hear.''

"That's your opinion of the chosen people?''

"Chosen for what? Official victims? Are we so stupid and

self-destructive that we have to keep repeating our mistakes for two thousand years? Watching what you're up to, hearing what you're saying, I fear we are."

Newman was tired, wet, chilled, and getting bored with Glickstein's unchanging, single-note theme. He signaled the waiter for another round of drinks.

"Sometimes I see visions," Glickstein intoned vacantly, a barroom prophet newly descended from Mount Sinai. "I see visions of our people fifty years from now—our synagogues in ruins or turned into video parlors, our torahs buried deep in the forests, our old people praying in cellars because the practice of Judaism has been outlawed, our young converted to the Cross or dying in work camps. No future for us. No future anywhere."

The waiter put down their fresh drinks, and Newman wondered how much he had heard of the rabbi's poor, delusionary lament. A gross, thick man with pink, watery eyes, he was still smiling to himself, as at some ongoing private joke. Except that Newman knew what the joke was and failed to enjoy it.

"Something's funny?"

The waiter gazed thoughtfully at him for a moment. Not bothering to answer, he turned to leave.

Newman grabbed his wrist. "I asked you a question."

"Let go of me, you lousy Hebe."

The words were spoken very softly, yet the detective saw that the barman and others in the room had heard. The place had become quiet.

"I told you to let go of me."

The waiter's sensitivity not being the greatest, he still had no notion of what he was into. Trying to pull free, he was surprised to find himself locked in place.

"The gentleman you think is so funny," said Newman, "the one you've been having such a fine time laughing at with your buddies, happens to be a rabbi, a scholar, a respected and learned man who has more sense in his asshole than you've got in your whole, big, fat, stupid head."

Gradually twisting the waiter's arm as he spoke, Newman brought him down on one knee beside the table. "So I think it might be nice if you apologized to him, don't you?"

"Fuck him. And double for you."

The detective smiled. He saw Glickstein watching, fascinated, eyes anchored to the waiter's face. The bartender was also watching, but with a sawed-off bat partly visible in his hand. Newman added a bit more pressure and the waiter's eyes bulged. He grunted and mumbled something.

"I can't hear you," said Newman.

"I'm sorry. I . . . apologize." It broke out like a clot of half-dried blood.

Newman let him go. The barman, his expression flat, put away his pacifier. Those privy to what had been taking place resumed their drinking and conversations. They looked disappointed.

"A very interesting demonstration," said Glickstein. "But I'm not sure what it proves—other than that you're stronger and better trained in such things than that momzer."

"How about might makes right?"

"You're not that simple a man, Lieutenant."

"It also made me feel good. How about you?"

"I'd be lying if I said I didn't find it satisfying. But there must be more than that."

"What do you want me to say, Rabbi? That I think, feel, and react as a Jew?"

"Exactly." Glickstein nursed his straight whiskey. "Which, incidentally, I never really doubted. Despite what you're doing for Clayton Taylor. Which is also why I'm making this last attempt to talk some sense into you before it's too late."

"Forget it."

"You won't reconsider? You won't at least think about it?"

"I didn't go into this lightly. I've already done my thinking about it."

Glickstein looked into the detective's eyes, then shrugged, sorrowful and defeated. He stared off at nothing.

"I'm sorry. It was a forlorn hope, but I thought if I appealed to you reasonably I might be able to convince you. Aah, I suppose it was too much to expect."

Once more his eyes sought Newman's. "Listen to me, then. I feel it's only fair to warn you. I can no longer stand idly by and watch this happening. I'm going to fight Clayton Taylor and I'm going to fight you. From now on, everything the two of you do, every word you say, I'm going to challenge. Me. Personally. Duv Glickstein. I'm not sure where or how I'm going to do it, but I'm going to do it. So you'd better watch out for me. And tell your friend Taylor, too. Because I'm going to be dangerous to him. Every time he opens his mouth, I'm going to nail his lies to his lips. In the end, if it comes to it, I promise I'll nail him to his own cross.''

The rabbi started to get up, but Newman restrained him. ''Wait a minute. It looks like I'm going to have to tell you something. It's in confidence.'' He briefly outlined his involvement with Israeli Intelligence.

Glickstein listened without comment. When Newman was finished, he nodded. ''All right. That at least makes you a little less of a fool. But it still doesn't change the way I feel about Taylor. The cryptic needs of the Israeli Secret Service interest me far less than the well-being of our own American Jewry. Damage is being done here. Regardless of reasons, I refuse to just stand by and watch it happen.''

Glickstein rose, a small, dignified man with ruined eyes and a black fedora perched ridiculously on his bandaged skull. Newman watched him march out of the bar. He imagined he heard the sound of Joshua's trumpets.

Newman studied the media's growing attention to the impending July Fourth rally.

Making the most of the tension, the reverend's Atlanta headquarters now began each day with its regular early-bird special, a bulletin that usually contained a mix of religious and patriotic platitudes, along with the piously expressed hope that the Apostle would come to his senses in time and realize that he and the reverend were not enemies, but actually allies in the service of God.

Apart from Clayton Taylor's releases, the media itself were doing everything possible to generate even more concentration on the upcoming event. But it was the Apostle's sudden silence that seemed to be arousing the most public speculation. Richard Gaynor was following Newman's ultimatum to the letter. From the day he had pledged his word that the Apostle would go into forced retirement, it was as though the masked vigilante no longer existed. There were no messages from him, no declamations, no letters to editors, no replies to Taylor's steady stream of propaganda. Yet it was this very lack of response that caused the greatest stir. Had something happened to the Apostle? What did his uncharacteristic silence mean? Was it simply a new tactic, an ingenious public relations device to gain further attention? Or had the Apostle changed his mind, retreated from his threat, and decided just to disappear back into the anonymous darkness from which he had come?

Newman followed the varying reactions and suppositions with amused interest. Some commentators were certain that the Apostle had been frightened off when Taylor finally called his bluff. Others, with Harry Blake in the lead, vehemently denied any such possibility, pointing out that the Apostle had never made a single claim or promise that he had not fulfilled. But Blake himself did express concern that the Apostle may have been wounded or even killed in trying to apprehend some unknown criminal. Still others were convinced that all this furor over the Apostle's silence was being greatly overdone. Having issued his ultimatum, what was there left for him to say? When July Fourth arrived, he would simply do whatever his conscience and the circumstances demanded.

Of course, thought the lieutenant.

In the meantime, late-twentieth-century America being a society of sports fans and bettors, the nation's bookmakers took full advantage of the situation. With no surprise, Newman found them treating the event as though it were a world-class athletic contest. Steadily changing odds were quoted on whether the Apostle would or would not appear, whether he would succeed in killing Taylor if he did appear, and whether he would then be captured or killed himself.

But Newman had other things to occupy him. Still officially involved in not only the continuing Apostle investigation but in the planned security for the July Fourth rally, he found himself constantly squeezed between what he knew, what he was supposed to know, and what he could feasibly say and do in his relations with his men, with the FBI, with Michael Westley, and particularly with the media, who kept questioning him about his progress or lack of it.

And there was also Duv Glickstein. True to his warning, the rabbi had already launched a wire service attack on Newman and Clayton Taylor as an unnatural alliance dedicated to the betrayal of America's Jewry. The story ran in the *Daily News* under a dramatic picture of Glickstein's bandaged head and staring, halfblind eyes. "Orthodox rabbi attacks minister and police hero," read the caption. Sensational, thought Newman.

The lieutenant found the FBI man sitting in his office when he returned from lunch. Peterson was reading the *Times* and holding five cigarette butts in an ashtray on his lap. Newman shot a quick glance at the wall map. Had he remembered to replace the genuine with the fake before he left? With relief, he saw that he had.

Peterson folded his newspaper. "You don't have to worry about the map. I know it's a fake. I also know about your ordering your men not to cooperate with us on the case, along with the rest of your elaborate little deception."

The lieutenant sat down behind his desk. He felt utterly foolish and inadequate. There was some bourbon in a bottom drawer, and it was a real effort to keep from going for the bottle.

"Good for you," he said. "You get a gold star. So now what else do you want?"

Peterson lit a fresh cigarette from the remains of his dying one. "Reasons. I'm sure you've got a lot of nice, logical-sounding reasons for trying to mess up this case for me, but somehow I can't think of one. Other than a local cop's usual resentment of the FBI's busting in on him. And with you, I don't feel that's it."

To hell with the sonofabitch, thought Newman, and took his bottle out of the drawer, drank a solid belt without bothering with a glass, and carefully put it away. Peterson, he noted, did not even blink. Hell, he probably has a complete dossier on my drinking habits, anyway.

"Or maybe," the agent continued, "maybe you just don't want the Apostle caught at all right now and therefore are trying to protect him."

Newman felt a faint stir of interest. "For what reason?"

"Who knows? Maybe you're enjoying all the publicity and excitement. Or you might even be living vicariously through him, taking understandable pleasure in all the crime-busting fantasies he's acting out for all the frustrated, regulation-bound cops in the world. Can you deny secretly cheering some of the things he's accomplished?"

Peterson waited for a possible answer. When none was offered, he said, "And then, of course, you might not want to wash out the fantastic drama that's building toward a climax on July Fourth. Good Lord! Imagine the reaction if you caught the Apostle before he could play out his final scene. You'd be lynched. The public, the media, the betting syndicates, the hotel and restaurant industries, would all be going for your throat. Do you know how many hundreds of millions of dollars in lost revenue they would suffer if the Apostle was caught at this moment? It would be an economic disaster.''

''You've been seeing too many bad movies. They're beginning to soften your brain.''

The dark circles under Special Agent Peterson's eyes seemed to glow. A nocturnal predator on the prowl.

''Aah, but wait. I've saved the best for last. How about this? How about you already know the Apostle's identity and are afraid I might interfere with your superbly crafted plan to get the most out of this knowledge?''

Newman longed for the rest of his bottle. This guy was a beauty, all right. ''What superbly crafted plan?''

The FBI man took a moment to light another cigarette. He seemed to be enjoying himself. The only evidence of threat was in the furrow between his eyes. It cut too deep, Newman decided. It was not the mark of a man who took things anywhere near as casually as Peterson was pretending.

''To come out of this as dramatically as possible,'' said the agent. ''To delay the Apostle's capture and keep it for the perfect time and place—the night of July Fourth in Yankee Stadium.''

''You're wasting your time working for the Bureau. You could be making a fortune writing TV scripts.''

They sat studying one another.

''Just one question,'' said Newman. ''Exactly why are you telling me all this?''

Peterson stood up and stretched. He suddenly appeared bored with his own diversion. ''Professional pride. I hate being taken for a horse's ass.''

He said it with a faintly mocking smile. But whether it was for believing him or for not believing him, the detective couldn't quite decide.

Two hours later, at exactly four-ten that same afternoon, the phone rang on Newman's desk. It was Detective Loretti. His voice sounded strange, hoarse, oddly excited.

"I've got him," he said. "I swear to Christ I think I've really got him."

Something unpleasant took place inside Newman's lungs. "Who?"

"The Apostle, for Christ's sake! Who else?"

"Where are you calling from?"

"The guy's apartment."

"What's his name?"

"Langdon. Frank Langdon. Jesus, I'm excited. How do you want me to handle this?"

The lieutenant was able to begin breathing again. "Have you spoken to anyone else?"

"No."

"Give me the address."

"It's Five-eighty West One Hundred Ninth Street. Apartment Four-C."

"Don't move and don't make any more calls. I'll be there in half an hour."

Newman slowly put down the phone. He looked at his hand, found that his fingers were trembling, and once more dug the bottle from his drawer.

He reached the apartment in just twenty-seven minutes, siren going all the way. As far as he was supposed to know, it could be the real thing. It was important to behave accordingly.

Loretti let him in. His face was flushed and tiny beads of sweat dotted his upper lip. The suspect, Frank Langdon, sat on a straight, wooden chair in the living room, one wrist handcuffed to a radiator. A dark, angular-faced man of about forty, he seemed undisturbed by his predicament. The room was well cared for and tastefully furnished, with a grand piano standing in a deep bay window, oil paintings on the walls, and a large Oriental rug covering much of the floor. Whatever else he was, thought Newman, he was neither frightened nor poor. The detective found these facts consoling. Which, in itself, began to worry him.

"Please forgive my not getting up, Lieutenant," said Langdon. "You'll find the liquor in that corner cabinet. If you'd care to do the honors, I'd appreciate it."

Newman added to his estimate. An educated smartass. There was further consolation in that. Loretti, he saw, was finding it hard to contain his excitement.

"Okay, let's hear it. What have you got?"

"What he's got," cut in Langdon, "is this beautiful, if mad, illusion that I'm the Apostle. Which is probably the most flattering thing that's happened to me in years. I've always wanted to be a swashbuckling hero."

Loretti sniffed the air with a prizefighter's quick snort. His black eyes shot tiny darts of light, and he kept moving about the room in a nervous dance. "It's him, all right, Lieutenant. I've been on it for days now. I didn't say anything because I was afraid of looking like a dummy if I was wrong. I wanted to be sure." He picked up a small canvas carryall from the couch, unzipped it, and emptied its contents onto a coffee table. "Look at this."

The lieutenant looked. Spread out before him was a rubber Apostle mask, a pair of black leather gloves, a realistic plastic facsimile of .38-caliber revolver, and some three-foot lengths of nylon cord.

"I was just planning a little costume party," said Langdon. "It was supposed to be for July Fourth. I thought it might be a fun idea to dress up as the Apostle."

"Where did you find this stuff?" the lieutenant asked Loretti.

"In the trunk of his car. It's okay. I picked up a search warrant this morning. Like I said, I've been on it for days. I mean, the guy fit our specs from the start. Right age category, right height, right build, right street area, and he lives alone. The whole schmeer. He even bought some bandages and antiseptic at about the time we think the Apostle caught one."

Langdon laughed. "This is really very funny. I should be able to dine out on this little episode for at least six months."

Neither detective looked amused.

"What were the bandages for?" Newman asked him.

"I slipped in the bathroom. The edge of a glass shelf ripped my arm. It was a pretty nasty puncture."

"Did you see a doctor?"

"No."

"Why not?"

"There are no doctors anymore. Just bloodsuckers and moneychangers. If they don't earn half a million a year after taxes, the AMA considers them a disgrace to the profession and lifts their license to practice."

Loretti made a face. "I forgot to tell you, Lieutenant. He's also a stand-up comic."

Newman drifted over to the liquor cabinet and splashed some Jack Daniel's into three glasses. He gave one glass to his detective, kept his own, and approached Langdon with the third.

"I must say, Mr. Langdon, you don't seem very worried about all this."

"Why should I be worried? I'm not the Apostle." He accepted the drink with his free hand and nodded his thanks. "Although I've often wished I were. The man is absolutely magnificent. Lochinvar and Don Quixote rolled into one. Unfortunately, I lack his courage."

"You admit you admire him?"

"Of course. Don't you?"

Newman turned back to Loretti, who had absorbed most of his liquor in a single gulp. "What else have you got?"

"I checked with Forensics. You know the impressions they picked up under the Verrazano Bridge the night of that attempted rape? Well, Langdon has a pair of size eleven penny loafers that fit the shoe casts like a dream. He also drives a seventy-nine Vega, which is one of the models that carry the size and type of tire that left its marks in the mud."

"What sort of work do you do, Mr. Langdon?" asked Newman.

"I teach at Columbia."

"What subject?"

"Philosophy."

"You're obviously an intelligent man, Professor. Hasn't it occurred to you that you're in very serious trouble at this moment?"

"Not really. You see, I have inherent faith that one way or another the truth always comes out. And since I know I'm not the Apostle, I'm sure that you or someone of higher authority will soon know it as well."

The philosopher, thought Newman dryly. The ancient homily was right. There's no fool like an educated fool. Or is it an *old* fool? They were probably both right.

Loretti was growing increasingly impatient. "What do you say, Lieutenant?"

Newman ignored him. It was, at best, an insanely wrought situation. You didn't rush stuff like this. Not even when there was no doubt about what would finally have to be done. You still had to consider all sides judiciously, as if you were, in fact, a ranking police officer weighing the existing evidence and trying to decide whether or not an arrest was warranted.

"Have you any police record, Professor?" he asked. "Have you ever been convicted of a crime? A misdemeanor? A felony? Have you ever been in jail?"

Langdon sighed. "Now you've got me, Lieutenant. I'm afraid I was one of the original Wisconsin Eight. We blew up some draft installations in sixty-eight and sixty-nine. It was during all the Vietnam trouble. I spent eight months in prison." He smiled, showing even, healthy teeth. "But I've paid my debt and I've learned. Now I'm a solid citizen, a member in good standing of our free, democratic society. Now I accept the necessity of war. Now I know it to be an integral part of life and the continuing relationship between nations. Now I believe in war with all my heart."

"You're still taking this much too lightly."

"I'm sorry. I'm just not a weeper. Anyway what's the use of crying? Will it change Detective Loretti's mind about me? Will it make him any less joyously sure that he's finally caught the Apostle?"

"Do you have a family? A wife? Children?"

"No."

"Were you ever married?"

"Once. A long time ago. My wife happened to feel pretty much as you do about me, Lieutenant. She also thought I took things much too lightly. So she married an economist, a practitioner of the dismal science. Economists take nothing lightly. They're serious about everything. Except the important things."

"What's important to you, Professor?"

Langdon considered both Newman and the question. "Love," he said. "Loss. Good-byes. An awareness of time. And of course the rarest of all: being able to accept human frailty. Which is almost impossible." He thought for a moment. "I also believe that what the Apostle is doing is important. If only because he's willing to die for it."

Loretti said, "How much more of this crap do we have to listen to, Lieutenant?"

Newman stood there, staring at Frank Langdon. A not unpleasant man, he thought, handcuffed to a radiator as the

alleged perpetrator of crimes they both knew he had never
committed.

"I'm going to have to arrest you, Professor."

"I realize that."

"Please be advised that you have the right to remain silent.
Anything you say can and will be used against you in a court
of law . . . ." Newman quietly intoned the rest of the Miranda
warning.

At 7:16 P.M. on the evening of June 25, Franklin Langdon,
Ph.D., was booked into the Thirteenth Precinct Station as the
individual known as the Apostle.

~~~~~~~~~~~~~~~~~~~~~~~~~~~ **20** ~

The first reports of the Apostle's capture came as flash
bulletins on radio and television, the news judged significant
enough to interrupt the regular programming. The announcements were brief, stating only that a man tentatively identified
as Franklin Langdon of West 109th Street, Manhattan, had
been booked into the Thirteenth Precinct at 7:16 P.M., and that
the arresting officers were Lieutenant Jay Newman and Detective First Grade Albert Loretti. Further information was
promised as soon as it was received.

Gaynor was in his studio, still compulsively pecking at his
blue man, unable either to acknowledge his existence or let

him go, when the phone rang. It was Kate, her voice high with excitement.

"Did you hear the news?"

"There's a new war?"

"They've arrested someone as the Apostle," she said and told him what little she knew.

Gaynor listened and said nothing.

"What do you suppose our friendly neighborhood lieutenant is up to?"

"Who knows, with someone like Newman?"

"I'm on duty. One of the nurses just came in to tell me. I'll check with you later."

Gaynor sat by the phone, trying to make sense of it. He turned on a news station but learned no more than he already knew. On an impulse, he called the lieutenant's home. No one answered.

Half an hour later, the phone rang again. He knew it was Jane before he picked up the receiver.

"You're not going to believe this," she said.

"Yes I am. I've already heard."

"Victor just called to tell me."

"Victor?"

"Lutovsky. He wanted to know if it was you who had been arrested. When I told him they had the wrong man, he laughed. He said it figured."

"What else did he say?"

"He wondered how this would affect your plans for July Fourth. I told him it wouldn't."

"You're getting smarter by the day," said Gaynor.

"That's not smarter. It's just sicker. I'm starting to think like you."

He found himself grinning at the phone.

"Anyway, I arranged another meeting with him for two nights from now. He thought he should have something by then."

"My gangster's moll."

"Don't be so superior."

"What should I be?"

"Grateful."

"I'm that, too."

The wire was silent.

"What do you suppose Newman has in mind with this

Norman Garbo

crazy false arrest?'' she said. ''Do you suppose he's trying
something tricky?''

''We'll find out soon enough.''

''Why don't you call him?''

''I did. He's not home. If he's being cute, he wouldn't give
me a straight answer anyway.''

She took a long, deep breath that ended as a sigh. ''Is Kate
there?''

''No. She's on shift.''

''I'd rather not sleep alone tonight.''

''Lutovsky is busy?''

''Let's not be mean to our ex-wives.''

''Come on over,'' he said and went back to his blue man.
He seemed to be adapting, growing a bit more comfortable
with him. *His friend.*

It arrived in bits and pieces in a swiftly accelerating stream of
information, comment, and reaction. Albert Loretti became
an acknowledged hero. Newman, deferring to his detective,
gave him full credit for initiating and following through on
the investigation that resulted in the Apostle's capture.

''This was all Detective Loretti's,'' the Lieutenant told the
media at every opportunity. ''I just came along for the ride.''

The fact that the suspect was a philosophy professor at
Columbia University only added another dimension to an
already dramatic situation. Astonishment and disbelief were
voiced by many of Professor Langdon's students and col-
leagues. Others, recalling certain of his comments upon the
deteriorating controls and standards that were no longer holding together contemporary society, claimed they were not
really surprised by his arrest. The professor himself, revealed
as a rather charismatic man with an easy smile and crinkling
eyes, steadily denied being the Apostle. And he did not
appear especially concerned about the assortment of charges
under which he was being held. These ran all the way from
simple assault to illegal use of a deadly weapon, public
threats of bodily harm, and two separate counts of homicide.
A judge denied him any possibility of bail.

The Reverend Clayton Taylor, reached by the media while
on a speaking tour of the South, expressed his belief that in
this great land of ours, all men were to be considered innocent until proven guilty. He felt this should be applied no

differently to Professor Langdon than it was to any other suspect in any other criminal case. "I have never at any time wished this man who calls himself the Apostle the slightest harm," said Taylor. "And whether or not he truly turns out to be Professor Langdon, I still feel no antipathy toward him. I pray only that the Lord grant him the same grace and mercy that he, in his infinite compassion, grants to all members of his poor, faltering flock." Several wire services distributed a photograph of the reverend with his head bent in prayer. The shot was carried by several hundred client newspapers, who ran it along with Taylor's statement. The caption read: "The Reverend Clayton Taylor prays for the Apostle's soul."

God help us all, thought Gaynor.

Not to be outdone, Rabbi Glickstein continued holding to his pledge. He kept after Taylor. He blasted his hypocrisy. He called it a mortal sin for a supposed man of God to preach lies whose sole purpose was to inflame hatred. He alluded to the reverend as the reincarnation of Hitler himself, Satan's curse upon a planet apparently doomed to suffer such recurring afflictions. As for Lieutenant Newman, the rabbi thought a Jewish police officer's time would be better spent defending his brethren from enemies such as Clayton Taylor than by arresting those who had valiantly chosen to fight against him. "When," demanded Glickstein, "would the eternal hatred of the eternal people finally be laid to rest?"

The drizzle was like a damp shroud along the Potomac. Reverend Taylor drove beside the river until he saw Melissa Bradberry's Porsche parked on a dirt cutoff, partially screened by bushes and trees. The road itself dead-ended close to the water's edge. They had met here several times before, but only under emergency conditions. Taylor pulled up behind the Porsche and waited for Melissa to join him in the more comfortable Sedan de Ville he was driving

They kissed, but broke apart quickly. "What is it?" she said. "What's wrong, darling? Why couldn't we meet at the house?"

"Because you're under surveillance, and I didn't want you leading anyone there."

Her eyes, still cool, clouded over. "You're certain of this?"

"Yes."

"How do you know?"

"Because I pay a small army of security people to find out precisely such things."

Struggling to deal with it, her face suddenly looked pinched, less youthful and attractive.

"I believe you've been watched ever since Dexter was shot," he said. "Which isn't all that astonishing."

"Does that mean I was followed here, too?"

"I passed a car about a quarter of a mile back. It was parked off the road."

She stared helplessly at him. "But if you knew I was being followed, why—"

"I have to find out who it is. I don't know that yet. But I expect to shortly."

"My God! You used me as bait?"

He smiled. "You needn't worry. You're in no danger. It will all be taken care of within the next few minutes."

"I don't understand. What's going to happen?"

"Nothing monumental. My security people will simply do what they're being paid to do."

Melissa fumbled in her purse for a cigarette. When she lit it, her fingers were trembling. "I'm suddenly very frightened, Clayton."

Taylor glanced at his watch. He said nothing.

"And I've been so relieved for the past few days." She sighed. "With the Apostle madman safely in jail, I thought things might at least be quieting down for a while."

"I'm afraid quiet isn't exactly what my life is all about."

A look of hers tried to go through him but shattered, as if against stone. "What *is* your life all about, Clayton?"

Watching the rearview mirror, he did not seem to hear her. They sat in silence, cigarette smoke curling about them. Except for the smoke, the Cadillac's interior had a colorless and airless quality. A car with two men appeared in the mirror and the reverend got out.

"I'll only be a minute," he said, and he walked back to meet them.

They talked for several minutes while Melissa sat waiting nervously.

The two men drove away and Taylor returned.

"What is it?" she said. "Who was following me?"

"An Israeli Intelligence agent."

The center of her eyes seemed to widen. "But why? What interest could the State of Israel possibly have in my private life?"

"Don't be naive, Melissa. You're the wife of the secretary of state. Which means that under certain conditions you have no private life."

"What conditions?"

"A significant Mideast peace initiative was destroyed when Dexter was shot. The Israeli Secret Service evidently thinks you may have been the leak."

"I never said a word. Except to you, of course."

Taylor shrugged. "They don't know that."

"But some crazy Arab group did the shooting. It said so in all the papers."

"The Israelis probably know more than the papers."

It was warm in the car, but Melissa rubbed both her arms, as though chilled.

"I'm afraid we're not going to be able to see one another for a while," he said. "And you're not going to be able to phone me, either."

"Yes." her voice was flat. "What happened to the man who followed me here?"

"He's been taken care of."

"Is that a euphemism for 'killed'?"

Taylor did not answer.

"Is it?" she persisted.

"He was in a dangerous business."

"And what kind of business are *you* in?"

"Melissa—"

"What happens when they find his body? They'll know he was following me when he was killed."

"You needn't be concerned about that. His body won't be found."

"What about his car?"

"That won't be found either."

She nodded slowly. "You're really very capable at this sort of thing, aren't you?"

Drizzle dripped from the trees onto the car.

"Tell me, darling," she said softly, "what does this Apostle person know that I don't?"

She left without saying good-bye.

*   *   *

Harry Blake, writing in the *Post* and syndicated in another 247 newspapers across the country, devoted an entire column to the alleged Apostle's capture.

"Of course it finally had to be," he wrote.

> No single individual can stand for long against the massed power, the juggernaut, that we call society. Eventually, it must crush him. So our own Hamlet, our own poor star-crossed hero, is finished. "Now cracks a noble heart. Good night, sweet prince. And flights of angels sing thee to thy rest."
>
> But how wonderful that we at least had him for this brief time, this curious man who was so willing to give of himself. He had to know that things would not really be any better when he finished, yet he went forward with it anyway, hoping they might not be any worse. So we had this one valiant man to toss a plume and strike a noble pose and put the cause of justice into understandable language for us. But he apparently was the last. We seem to have run out of our inventory of his kind. Our Apostle was just a transient aberration. I doubt that we shall see any others. Indeed there was a heroically old-fashioned ring to him, like a bugle blowing for a nineteenth-century cavalry charge.
>
> There are no bugles anymore. Any horns we hear have a mocking and hollow sound to them. Yet we did, briefly, hear one.

Gaynor's second meeting with Victor Lutovsky took place at eleven-thirty on the night of June twenty-seventh. It again was held at the syndicate chief's East Side town house and under the same conditions as the first meeting. This time, however, there was a black suitcase and a roll of blueprints resting on a table in the library. Lutovsky had come straight from a charity dinner at the Waldorf and was wearing formal clothes. His tuxedo was impeccably tailored, and he carried it with the air of a man born to such things. He looks like at least a Supreme Court justice, thought Gaynor, and felt the aura of the man so distinctly it might have had physical substance.

Lutovsky's eyes appraised him. They noted his hood and build, flickered to his hands, then once more looked him over from his shoes up. "I'll be honest with you," he said. "When I first heard those reports, when I thought you'd been taken, I felt relieved. To me it just meant Jane wouldn't have to be risking her neck with you on July Fourth. Yet in a crazy kind of way I was also glad when I learned it wasn't you. So you can see I have mixed feelings about the whole deal. Because no matter what I do, it's still going to be a dangerous long shot. I can only cut down the odds a little."

He picked up the roll of blueprints and spread them out on a large coffee table. "What we've got here are the original building plans for Yankee Stadium, diagrams of the total renovation that was done some years ago, and a layout of the speaker's stand they'll be putting up on the infield grass for the night of July Fourth. They've all been gone over from top to bottom and a pretty workable idea has come out of it."

Gaynor drew up a chair. Marvelous. The man approached assassination with the detachment and precision of a general preparing for a major campaign. Well, why not? With all the emotion squeezed out, it was finally reduced to pure technique.

"But first," said Lutovsky, "exactly how good a shot are you?"

"Good enough, I guess."

"This is no guessing game. It's life and death. And not only your own. The way this is being set up, you're going to have to use a rifle from a distance of a hundred and sixteen feet. Which really should be no problem with a precision piece and scope sights. But you've still got to be able to shoot."

Jane said, "You don't have to worry. He can shoot." She looked at her former husband. "Remember when you took your boys to that shooting gallery? You knocked over twenty-two tin ducks in a row. They talked about it for months."

So she remembered that, thought Gaynor. "Tin ducks at fifteen feet are something else. Anyway, how am I going to get a hundred and sixteen feet from Taylor in Yankee Stadium, carrying a rifle?"

Lutovsky explained it to them. Using his charts to demonstrate, he pointed out a maze of old conduits that had once connected a series of electrical substations that had been blocked over when they were no longer needed. Unused for many years, some access points still remained through concealed trap doors. Two nights before, one of Lutovsky's people had made a trial run and feasibility study. It was possible to enter one of the trap doors, crawl through several hundred yards of conduit, and end up in a substation exactly 116 feet from the speaker's platform where Taylor would be standing. When the nearly invisible cover of a small ventilator grille was removed, there would be a clear field of fire.

Jane was exultant. "It sounds fantastic."

"There's a good chance it might work," said Lutovsky.

"But how does he get away? Won't they be able to figure out where the shots came from?"

"That's all been thought about."

Lutovsky opened the black suitcase. It was fitted with individual compartments, each of which contained a piece of ordnance. Gaynor saw the major components of a rifle, a set of telescopic sights, two boxes of cartridges, a cluster of tear gas canisters, and several breathing masks. It was a complete do-it-yourself assassination kit.

Lutovsky held a cartridge between his thumb and forefinger. "This is a specially made, thirty-caliber rifle cartridge. It's unique for two reasons. First, it's silent. There's only a soft, hissing sound when it's fired. Which means no one will be able to tell right away where the shot came from." He looked at Gaynor. "So there should be time to crawl out the way you came in and mix with the crowd."

"What if it doesn't work that way?" Jane said. "What if the cops do spot where the shot came from?"

"That's been thought about, too." Lutovsky gently laid down the cartridge and took the two canisters from the suitcase, a distinguished, elegantly garbed pitchman hawking his latest line. "Here's where you come in, Janey. These are tear gas canisters and a gas mask, which you'll pick up and put in your purse after you've gone through security and are inside the stadium. They'll be waiting for you behind a commode in the Ladies' Room. You'll get the exact details the night before. You'll be sitting twenty feet from the shooting blind. If anything goes wrong, if they seem to have your man spotted, just bend forward, quietly place the two canisters under your seat, and activate them. The area will be covered in seconds, socked in solid. No one within twenty yards will be able to see a thing. Then just slip on your mask and start working your way out of there. When the gas starts clearing, remove and drop your mask before anyone can see you in it."

He addressed Gaynor. "You'll have your own mask and tear gas in case you run into any trouble at the other end of your escape conduit. Have you both got that straight?"

They could only nod. In terms of the acceptable arithmetic of professionally conceived mayhem, it was awe-inspiring.

Lutovsky picked up the cartridge once more. "The second reason this ammunition is special is that it carries an explosive bullet. When it hits, it doesn't just penetrate. It explodes on contact. Which means if it strikes any part of the head, neck, or chest areas, it's not going to simply wound. It's going to kill. The rifle you'll be using is one of the best ever made for its purpose. It's a handcrafted, precision instrument that can deliver a bullet to within a hairsbreadth of where it is aimed. The aiming, of course, will be up to you. But with the explosive shell, you'll have plenty of margin for error."

He took the disassembled rifle from its several compartments and showed Gaynor how to put it together. Then he broke it down and had the artist assemble it himself. It was not difficult.

"A few nights before July Fourth," Lutovsky said, "I'll have a man take you into the stadium for a dry run. He'll show you exactly where the trap doors are, let you get the feel of the place, and leave your ordnance in the blind. You and I are going out for a little shooting practice tomorrow afternoon. I'll call Jane in the morning to make arrangements."

They went over the blueprints again, this time marking each conduit entrance and its relative exposure level. Three looked good. One was in a passageway leading to a locker room, another was through a first-level utility closet, and the third was under a ramp directly behind home plate. It was agreed that the final decision on which to use on July Fourth would not be made until after the trial run.

"Why are we so worried about security?" said Jane. "They think the Apostle has been caught."

"They have the wrong man. They'll know it by then."

Gaynor had stopped listening. He was concentrating on one of his mental paintings. This time it was of a giant mole burrowing through an endless maze of blind passages. He considered it one of his more perceptive self-portraits.

*　　*　　*

They were having a celebration of sorts in his apartment. It had not been planned as such. What, after all, was there to celebrate?

It was Kate who had initiated the mood. She had come straight from her four-to-midnight shift, eager to hear about the meeting with Lutovsky, and they had found her asleep on the couch. She had awakened blurry-eyed and anxious.

"Well? Tell me!"

Jane had done the telling, spinning a magical tale of hope and salvation in which all things were possible. Yankee Stadium floated in a soft golden haze. They had been gifted with wings. On the night of July Fourth, they would soar free.

"Wonderful," Kate had said, "but where do I fit in? Do you expect me to just sit at home, watching it all on TV?"

"What do you want?" Gaynor had asked.

"I want to be part of it. I want a canister and mask in my purse, too. I want to be there with Jane, ready to help."

They had agreed without argument. Why not? It could be a perfect rondelet for three voices.

The celebration had taken off from there. They had started with champagne and when they ran out followed it with straight whiskey. Now, well into the drinking, Gaynor felt a rare kind of heat rise out of him. Did you lift after death like a balloon? The two women must have felt much the same way because suddenly they were silent. Something hungry for pleasure was loose.

Again, and not unexpectedly, Kate was the one to make the first move. The friendliest, the slyest, of smiles came off her and Jane caught it in midair. She was ready to play. A new boldness was in her, along with a willingness to share. They had been sharing him separately for months. Now, joined in a common action, they were no longer adversaries. So why not share him together?

Kate giggled, the sound part girl, part woman, part alcohol, part fever. She winked at her new playmate. "Which section do you want?"

Together, they went at him, a couple of happy alley cats dividing the night's spoils. He held up his hands in mock terror. "Hey, come on. Give me a break."

But they were breathing erotic pictures into his brain and he soon lay back and let them romp, a prince of Baghdad enjoying his rank. They had their special talents, these two, pink lips and tongues aflutter, mouths and flesh all rosy and sweet. He touched them both, a hand for each, and felt his heart go quietly mad.

Yet, nearing the end, he was coming to that time when only one would do and the choice had to be his. Yes, but which? Whoever happens to be there to take me, he thought, even then not wanting to have to make any such decision. So he offered a moment for one and a moment for the other until finally, moving on sensation alone, he was quite beyond choosing.

"Oh, sweet Jesus," he whispered, although the Son of God was nowhere in his thoughts at that moment.

Somehow, neither woman, nothing, seemed there to receive him.

The afternoon of June 28 was mild, clear, and yellow with sunlight. Driving north on the Taconic Parkway, Gaynor saw a flock of crows rise from a field, circle gracefully, and settle in a stand of pine. He breathed deeply and took in the day.

Alone in a rented car, he was on his way to meet Victor Lutovsky for his private shooting lesson. Jane had passed on specific instructions. No one else, not even she, was to be present. Gaynor figured Lutovsky would either try to talk him out of the whole enterprise or else try to pressure him into doing something about Jane's part in it. This curious figure, he thought, putting all this time and effort into saving the life of someone he didn't even know. Again, he was impressed with Jane's obvious importance to the man. The current market value of one's former wife was impossible to judge.

Following his written instructions, he turned off the Taconic in the area of Mount Kisco and took a secondary road until he saw an abandoned barn on his right. A quarter of a mile later, he circled north and then east onto a narrow dirt track running off into a forest. The sun flickered in small, bright stains on the leaves of tall elms and maples, their trunks looking almost black against the pale green of the early foliage. Then the woods grew thicker and hardly any sun broke through at all. The trail twisted along until it widened and ended in a turnaround at the edge of a clearing. About a hundred yards away, a muddy Land Rover was parked just off the trail. Gaynor braked to a stop and put on his pillowcase hood. Then he parked a short distance behind the Land Rover. A white

327

notice nailed to a tree warned that this was private land and that hunters and trespassers would be prosecuted. At the bottom of the notice was printed VICTOR Z. LUTOVSKY. They left their cars and approached one another. Gaynor saw no sign of a bodyguard. Lutovsky wore faded jeans and a sport shirt that strained against his massive chest and shoulders. He was carrying the same black suitcase that had been in his library the night before. They shook hands.

"What does the Z stand for?" Gaynor asked.

"Zpinoza." Lutovsky laughed. "My mother meant it to be Spinoza, but she couldn't spell worth a damn."

He took Gaynor by the arm and began walking him across the clearing toward a rough, stone fence that marked the far end. "It must be hot as hell under that hood," he said. "If you want to take it off, it's okay. I know who you are. I've known since the first night we met."

The artist kept walking.

"Listen," said Lutovsky. "My mother drowned all her stupid sons early. I know Janey pretty well. She doesn't make attachments that fast or easy. So if she cared enough about you to put her own life on the line, I figured the only one you could be was her ex-husband." His eyes squinted into the glare. "You don't have to worry about me."

Without a word, Gaynor removed the hood and stuffed it into his pocket.

They climbed over the stone fence, and Lutovsky led the way into another patch of woods, this one of pine. The air, warmed by the sun, was sweet, giving off the full, clear promise of summer. In a narrow glade, a break among the trees offered a long line of sight that stretched for about a hundred yards.

Lutovsky stopped. "This should do it."

Using a steel measuring tape, he marked off exactly 116 feet and nailed a paper target to a tree. He opened his suitcase, removed the rifle components, and assembled them piece by piece. Then he loaded a cartridge into the breech and fitted a silencer around the end of the barrel. He did not want to risk using the silently firing but loudly explosive shells in their practice rounds. He would use one at the end, he told Gaynor, just to demonstrate the total effect.

Lutovsky handed the artist the loaded weapon. "Okay, let's see what you can do. You'll be firing from the prone position, using a rest to keep the piece steady." He brought over a small rock. "Use this to lean the barrel on."

Gaynor stretched out on the ground. The target looked to be about a mile away, and his eyes were suddenly so blurred he could barely make it out. Then he squinted down the scope sight and the black bull's eye leaped forward at him. He steadied the cross hairs and pulled the trigger. Nothing happened.

"You forgot the safety," Lutovsky said.

Gaynor released the button, aimed once more, and fired. The recoil slammed the rifle against his shoulder. The *whoosh* of the silencer was soft.

"How did it feel?" said Lutovsky.

"Not bad."

But when they approached the target, the hole was high and to the left."

"Two things," said Lutovsky. "You pulled the trigger instead of squeezing it. You also weren't holding your breath when you fired."

Gaynor went back and tried again. This shot caught the edge of the bull. The following four were right in it, a perfect cluster.

Lutovsky nodded. "You'll do." He unwrapped one of the special bullets from its plastic casing and gave it to Gaynor. "Now try this."

Gaynor loaded the cartridge, centered the cross hairs on the bull, and gently squeezed the trigger. The hit exploded with the sound of a large firecracker. A veil of blue smoke covered the target.

The two men approached the tree. Nothing was left of the target but a few scorched bits of paper. The bark of the tree had been ripped off, leaving a crater of blackened pulp. Tiny wisps of smoke curled from the center of the hole like vaporized blood rising from a wound.

"All you have to do is hit him," said Lutovsky. "The bullet will take care of the rest."

Gaynor swallowed dryly. The taste was not good.

Lutovsky missed nothing. "Take it easy. Dead is dead."

They sat on the stone wall while Lutovsky cleaned the rifle barrel with a ramrod and cotton patches, then oiled the metal parts. He seemed to enjoy the small ritual.

"I've been thinking," he said. "If you want, I can have

this taken care of for you. There's no reason for you to have to take this kind of risk. You're an artist. I respect that. You've been trained to create, not to kill. This isn't your line of work.''

"I've made it my line of work. I thought you understood all that."

"I don't think that way. You work on emotion and some pretty high-class theories. I'm more practical. All I care about are the facts. Once I know what I want, the facts are what tell me how to get it."

Lutovsky gazed off at a crow, sitting high on a dead tree. "Maybe I'm not much of a Jew, but I'm still a Jew. Sometimes this surprises me. Yet I guess I'll always be carrying a little Yiddish lox peddler somewhere in my belly juices. Remember how I got hot when you reminded me I was also a Jew?"

Gaynor nodded.

"It's one of my tics. I'm a big man now and dangerous to fool with, so people are polite to my face. But I know that behind my back they still call me a Jewish gangster. Okay. So I'm Jewish and maybe I'm still part gangster. Fine. But I've never heard people talk about Protestant or Catholic gangsters. They're just gangsters. Me? I'm always a *Jewish* gangster. A leper without a cure."

Lutovsky peered through the rifle barrel to make sure it was clean. Then he reversed the weapon and aimed it at a distant crow. "Bang!" he said and watched the bird fly off. "This Taylor doesn't really bother me much. His kind have been coming and going for five thousand years while we Jews remain. What bothers me more is that a goy, a Christian like you, should be the one taking a shot at him, not a Jew." He gazed broodingly at his rifle. "What you're doing is crazy. But maybe every once in a while it gets to be time for something really crazy to be done."

"You mean maybe it's time to forget the facts?"

Lutovsky shrugged. "I'm not sure what I mean. You're making me itch where I can't scratch. Rabbis are always screaming about how we owe something, about how all Jews have to work at keeping up our traditions or Judaism will disappear. Well, I don't buy that. I think if we've got to work at it, if Judaism ever stops having enough to offer on its own, then it's time for it to disappear. Then every once in a while something comes along that makes me start itching and I begin to wonder. I think maybe I do owe something, somewhere. Maybe there'll come a time when I'll have to straighten out my accounts and settle up. And I'm not talking about any Judgment Day. I mean something much closer. Which is probably why I'm here with you now. And that's apart from how I feel about Janey. But that's a whole different ball of wax, isn't it?''

He packed away his cleaned and oiled ordnance and they started back toward the cars.

"Here's what I'm going to do," said Lutovsky. "Since that's how you want it, you'll have it all your own way on July Fourth. But if anything goes wrong that night, if you somehow don't finish what you've started, I promise I'll have it finished for you at some later time. So either way, you can be sure it'll get done.''

Gaynor knew the offer was meant to be reassuring, but he failed to respond that way. It brought him no comfort. In an odd sort of way, it almost felt like an intrusion.

Thomas Mackley was alone, working with explosives, in the basement of the ACP's New York headquarters in Flatbush. He worked with grace and skill, as a good surgeon works, hearing the sounds of occasional traffic outside and the small, faint noises of the empty house itself. He had taken extensive demolition training in the Marines and had even, briefly, been an instructor, so he felt he knew what he was about. This was nothing for an amateur to fool with. He also had good hands and took a fair amount of pride in what they could do. Even if he didn't always approve of the purposes for which they were used, he still performed as best he could and tried to leave the moral judgments to those higher up, to those whose orders he usually was following.

Every line of work had its dirty secrets, but he had to admit that his had more than its share. Sometimes, as now, they were almost too much and he felt strangely oppressed, almost as if it was something beyond him, some ugly seepage from the nation's waste pipes. The more you held your breath, the more it stank. And at its worst, it seemed to be everywhere—at work, at home, at Sunday double-headers. Yet why? he wondered. Weren't most of us well fed and clothed, glutted with abundance? Wasn't America a lush, air-conditioned garden, where honest toil was nourishment, people lived in Hamburger Heavens, and the skies were not cloudy all day?

Maybe. But sometimes the thing he chose to call his work tore away the shiny wrappings and showed the worms beneath. Sometimes blood flowed like honey through ghetto walls. The hardheads got their livers chopped free of charge. Memorial candles burned day and night. Everyone had their own proving grounds. Those who peopled his turf were crazy types. They dared shake their fists at the land of opportunity, refused to bend to the mold. They wouldn't learn. So it was his job to teach them, and usually the hard way.

Mackley tightened a final connection and carefully went over the timing device for the third time. Forget something in this business and there were no second chances. His hands, steady until now, suddenly began to quiver like a dowsing rod, as if some nameless terror lay hidden and waiting. *Maybe I'm getting too old for this.*

Yet awhile later he was able to take some small comfort from part of one of the Reverend Clayton Taylor's radio spots.

"Take away all love and hatred," said the reverend, "all hope and fear, all anger, zeal, and affectionate desire, and the world would be motionless and dead. There would be no such thing as activity amongst mankind or any achievement whatsoever. And what is true in worldly things is also true in religion. Here, too, the emotions are the wellspring of all action. They are the life and soul of true religion. And since love is the chief of the emotions, the essence of all true belief in God lies in holy love."

But who do I really love? Mackley wondered; he felt his brief instant of comfort fade.

"**W**hats wrong with you?" the commissioner asked Newman. "I don't understand your entire attitude toward this arrest."

It was late afternoon and they were alone in Michael Westley's office. A heavily attended press conference had just broken up and the air was still blue with smoke. Newman was busy at the liquor cabinet. Turning, he handed a measure of straight bourbon to Westley and poured double the amount for himself.

"Why do you keep holding yourself in the background?" the commissioner persisted. "Why do you keep deferring to Loretti? The man may deserve a certain amount of credit for competent police work, but it was you who set up and headed the investigation, and it was your procedures he was following when Langdon fell into his lap. So why all this ridiculous humility?"

Newman gently eased himself into a chair. "It's no big deal. I just want to give the guy a break. Besides, it should make me a more popular police commissioner. People enjoy discovering humility in high places. It's so rare. Especially after your own patrician arrogance." He held his glass to the light, a miser savoring his treasure. "Relax, Michael. Just be happy the Apostle is ours, that Taylor will live, and that you'll one day be president of these United States."

Westley nibbled the end of a fresh cigar. He suddenly had

the look of a man with a great many problems, trying to decide which to worry about first.

"I can't help wishing Langdon wasn't who and what he is. I also wish we had a nice, neat confession from him."

"Why? You don't think he's our man?"

"Do you?"

"I arrested him, didn't I?"

"On the basis of the evidence Loretti came up with, you had no choice. But it's all so damned circumstantial. I'd feel a lot better if we had a real thirty-eight instead of that plastic toy."

"We're still looking for the gun."

The commissioner considered him through a cloud of expensive smoke. "I don't think you're any more certain about his arrest than I am. Maybe you're even less so. And I'm afraid that's the real reason you're trying to keep out of the limelight. You'd much rather let Loretti look like the ass if it turns out to be a false arrest."

Newman said nothing. The analysis was not unexpected. He was just surprised it had taken so long in coming.

"So unless you come up with the gun," said Westley, "or Frank Langdon suddenly decides to sign a confession, I want you to be quietly working on the assumption that the Apostle is still at large and as much of a threat as ever. And that goes double for our security plans on July Fourth."

Special Agent Peterson was about to indicate his own reaction to Langdon's arrest.

Seeking Newman out, he found him having a less than gourmet dinner of whiskey and hamburger at Paddy's Bar, just across from Police Headquarters. The FBI man slid, uninvited, into Newman's booth. His grin was more a baring of teeth than a smile.

"You're getting to be more and more interesting, Lieutenant. I'm not too sure what you're trying to pull on me this time, but whatever it is, I must admit I'm intrigued."

Newman went on eating.

"You've got no real case against Langdon," said the agent. "Why did you arrest him?"

"Why don't you bug off?"

"Don't be so unfriendly. We're supposed to be cooperating on this case. Or hasn't the commissioner told you?"

On an oversized television screen, a Met batter hit into a double play and a groan rose from those watching at the bar.

"You couldn't have arrested him just to be a hero," said Peterson, "because you're already a hero. And you're only going to look foolish when you have to let him go. So your motivation really puzzles me."

"You questioned the suspect and reviewed the evidence. What would you have done? Just let him wander around?"

"That's exactly what I'd have done. Then I'd have kept him under round-the-clock surveillance until he either led me to his gun or went out on his next hit. Which in all probability would have been on July Fourth in Yankee Stadium." Peterson gazed off at the TV as a Met error let two runs score. There was more pain at the bar. "At least that's what I'd have done if I really believed Langdon was the Apostle."

Newman put down his hamburger. He had lost all appetite. "I guess I'm just not as clever an investigator as you."

"Oh, but you are. That's what's so fascinating about your handling of the arrest. It makes me wonder why you did it that way."

"You forget. It was Detective Loretti's collar, not mine. He was the arresting officer."

Peterson leaned over the table, his arms enveloping it, his eyes bright and close. "I know that. Which must have made it very difficult for you."

"Meaning what?"

"Meaning you had to arrest Langdon on purely circumstantial evidence because the proper alternative, that of keeping him under surveillance, was evidently closed to you."

"Why would it be closed to me?"

"I must confess I'm not absolutely sure."

Newman picked up the remains of his hamburger. "But of course you've got another one of your theories."

"Would you like to hear it?"

"Why not? You're better entertainment than having to watch the Mets get mutilated."

The agent lit a cigarette. Newman wondered if he sucked his thumb at night. He obviously had strong oral needs.

"Here's my theory," said Peterson. "Let's say you found out some time ago that Frank Langdon actually is the Apostle, but you didn't want to arrest him until the right time. Which, of course, would be the night of July Fourth, in

Yankee Stadium, in front of a hundred million television viewers. Unfortunately, Loretti stumbles onto him, forcing you to arrest him now. But because the evidence is so thin, you feel sure he'll be released in time to take his assigned role in your big psychodrama, and you can once again play the supreme savior.''

"Do you actually believe that drivel?"

Peterson laughed. "No. Of course not. It's entirely too complicated. The truth is always much simpler." He rose. "I told you I'm not sure what you're up to. This is just by way of keeping in touch. I like you to know you're in my thoughts."

There were cheers and whistles from the bar as Daryll Strawberry hit a home run, but it was too late to save either the Mets or what remained of Newman's dinner.

Approaching his car to go to work, Newman saw a printed note under the windshield wiper. "I'm on the beach," it said.

He found Zvi Avidan, carrying his shoes and socks, walking along the water's edge behind some sandpipers. The Israeli squinted against the early sun.

"Congratulations. I hear you caught the Apostle."

"*Alleged* Apostle."

"There's a difference?"

"A big one." Newman fell into step on the hard, damp sand. "What's happening?"

"One of our agents disappeared."

"Maybe he defected."

Avidan was not amused. "Yitzkak was following the Bradberry woman. I don't expect to see him again. Not alive. Taylor's people are very good and very thorough. Even his car is gone." The tough face was brooding. "He was just married a month ago. I was best man."

"I'm sorry."

"Have you spoken to the reverend recently?"

"He called yesterday. He'll be in New York this evening. He wants to look at the alleged Apostle." Newman stared off at a line of fishing boats half a mile out. "I'm afraid I haven't been much use to you so far."

"You'll get your turn. Everyone does."

The detective had no idea what he meant.

"Taylor is Taylor," said Avidan, "but women like that make me sick. They want everything all ways and everyone else ends up paying. Because the self-indulgent bitch had to have her cunt tickled by a preacher, her husband is lying in a hospital, three men are dead, and a good chance for peace is destroyed.''

"I'll be honest with you. Phony as he is, I still find it hard to accept Taylor as the consummate demon you paint him.''

"Of course. You've been raised on purity, goodness, and Walt Disney. You're a native-born American.''

"I'm also a cop.''

"Yes, but your criminals are either just crooks or murderers. They're rarely demons.''

"I don't believe in black arts practiced by devils.''

"Come live in our beloved Holy Land for a few years," said Avidan, "and you will.''

Even alone in the car, driving to work, there was no escape; one of the inevitable sermons came over the radio.

"Those who ignore God are stupid and senseless and have hearts of stone or they would know better. For he will surely break those who will not bow, having wrath and power enough to crush a poor human as easily as one would crush a lowly bug or spider. Listen to me, you who now hear of hell and the wrath of the great God yet sit in your seats so easy and quiet and go away so careless. Very soon you will tremble and cry out and gnash your teeth and finally be convinced that there is no salvation unless you repent and fly to Christ . . .''

Newman opened his glove compartment and flew to his bottle.

Two uniformed guards escorted Frank Langdon into a small, square interrogation room whose walls and ceiling were painted a pale, bilious green (a psychiatrist had once had a theory about the color's effect upon a suspect's composure and had sold it to the commissioner). It was late evening, and Newman felt pretty much the color of the room. He handed his service revolver to one of the guards and the officers left, locking the door behind them.

"Professor Langdon,'' said the detective, "this is the Reverend Clayton Taylor.''

The two men stood considering one another. They were both tall and angular and about the same age. But where

337

Norman Garbo

Langdon slouched casually, a rather soft man at ease with himself and his surroundings, Taylor stood as straight and unyielding as a bayonet. Performing his function as host, Newman seated them at opposite ends of a scarred table and tossed out cigarettes and matches.

"The reverend asked to meet you," he told Langdon. "If you object, you have the right to be taken back to your cell."

"No. It's all right." Langdon lit one of the cigarettes from the table and gazed benignly at Taylor. "I've been revolted by you for a long time, Reverend. It's a pleasure to be able to tell you so to your face."

Taylor nodded as though in polite acceptance of a compliment. "Yet you still insist you're not the Apostle?"

"Regretfully, I can't claim that distinction."

"Then why aren't you making more of an effort to clear yourself? From what I've been told, you're doing everything possible to remain in custody. You won't call a lawyer of your own, you refuse to speak to a court-appointed one, and you're making no attempt to bring in anybody who might provide evidence of your guiltlessness. That's hardly the behavior of an innocent man, Professor."

"You've got it backward. That's exactly the behavior of an innocent man, of someone who knows that no effort is really required to prove his innocence, that finally it's going to be proven for him."

"Even if true, that could take a long time."

"No longer than the five days that still remain before the real Apostle finishes you."

Taylor stared thoughtfully across the table.

"And I really don't mind staying locked up until then. Even longer, if necessary. Actually, I'd welcome the opportunity. When I do finally get out, I'll be happy to wear my time behind bars as a badge of honor."

The philosophy professor was no longer casual or at ease. Nor was he slouching. He sat very straight in his chair.

"A frightening thing has been happening in a lot of places lately, Reverend. It's something called Hitler chic. The marketplace has suddenly become deluged with Hitler diaries, Hitler TV shows, Hitler paraphernalia. Hitler and the whole Nazi pestilence have become hot items, big business. Publishers keep grinding out books about the Nazi experience because that's what sells. Fortunes are being made with this sick filth.

There's even a disgusting sexual tingle in the very horror of it. *Hitlermania.!* It's all over the media and army surplus stores. Nazi helmets, guns, daggers, boots, Gestapo uniforms, insignia, battle flags. Memorabilia of the glorious Third Reich—the very things that are now banned in Germany. The market for this human excrement covers all of Europe and South America, but do you know where the demand is greatest?"

It was obviously a rhetorical question, yet Langdon looked hard at his audience of two. He stared first at Taylor, then at Newman, and finally settled on the cleric. "The biggest market in the world happens to be the heartland of America, our own Midwest and South, the places where your voice soars loudest, Reverend. You're building your own bull market in this pornography of violence, and every item keeps going up in price."

"You're not being reasonable, Professor." Taylor's voice was soft, his tone mild, but a pulse had begun to flutter in his temple. "You can hardly blame me for some of the less attractive facets of human nature."

"Oh, but I do blame you, sir. Because that is exactly where you make your strongest appeal—to the dark underside of our poor species, to the same side that causes us to slow down and stare at bloody accidents on the highway. One of the most dreadful parts of our nature is that millions, in the secrecy of their hearts, actually admire and applaud Hitler for what he did to the Jews. It helps them lift their own heads out of the filth and feel superior. Hitler is a dark mirror held up to the human race. Take a good look, it tells us. This was a man just like us, an Austrian child who grew up and did these things. He didn't simply drop from outer space. And you, a man of superior education and background, who for poor, sweet Jesus' sake alone should know better, are on your way to doing much the same thing."

Professor Langdon paused, a disciplined debater scrupulously awaiting rebuttal. None came.

"But what bothers me more than anything," he said directly to Clayton Taylor's face, "is that both you and all this Hitlermania are just cheapening our Holocaust martyrs, our poor millions of victims. It demeans their suffering. It mocks their deaths." He sighed. "I'll tell you. I thank God I'm not the Apostle. Do you know why? Because this way I know he's still out there someplace, waiting to put an end to you.''

Langdon stiffly got out of his chair, went to the door, and knocked. When one of the guards came and opened it, he said, ''Please take me back to my cell.''

A steady rain was falling as Newman drove Taylor back to the Waldorf. The high-speed wipers stuttered and clicked, slightly out of sync. Broadway was wide, black ice, reflecting the lights. Taylor's retinue was in a chauffeured limousine directly ahead, but the reverend had wanted to talk to Newman alone and had chosen this arrangement in which to do it.

''Impressive, wasn't he?'' Taylor said.

Newman's hands were sweating on the wheel. One at a time, he wiped them on his thighs. ''Hell, he's a professional lecturer. It's what he does. He's probably made the same speech to his classes a dozen times.''

''That's unimportant. He was impassioned and effective.'' The cleric smiled wryly. ''One of my greatest strengths is never underestimating the opposition. At one point I was watching your face. You weren't happy, Jay.''

The detective left it alone. He wished that Taylor would, also. There was too much in what Langdon had said that he wasn't quite prepared to deal with.

''But with it all,'' said Taylor, ''he still isn't the Apostle.''

Newman glanced quickly at the man beside him. In profile silhouette, the clergyman's face might have been stamped on a Roman coin.

''Are you serious?''

''Completely.''

''How do you know? The evidence against him may be circumstantial, but it was still strong enough to have warranted his arrest.''

''I've met with the Apostle. I told you. Remember?''

''But he wore a mask and disguised his voice.''

''That was our second meeting. I never mentioned our first.''

Taylor briefly described the incident at his Atlanta headquarters and his later association of the interview tapes with the Apostle's voice on the telephone. ''Langdon is definitely not the same man I talked to in Atlanta. I had my doubts when I

340

saw the news photos after his arrest, but I thought it best to see and speak with him in person.''

Newman braked for a red light behind the limousine. Two men peered anxiously back at him through the car's rear window. ''You're full of little surprises, aren't you?''

''There was no reason to tell you before.''

''Then you're ready to make a statement to that effect? You want us to release Frank Langdon with our apologies?''

''Yes. Of course. You can't keep an innocent man in jail.''

The detective drove carefully through the traffic and rain. Poor Loretti. His fame was about to be short-lived.

''I've been meaning to ask you,'' drawled Taylor. ''Who is that rabbi, this Duv Glickstein, who has been beating on me so hard lately?''

''He runs a little broken-down Orthodox shul on the Lower East Side. He's harmless.''

''No zealot is harmless. And this one seems to be attracting an unusual amount of attention. Maybe you could talk to him and explain things, show him the light.''

Newman tried to imagine anyone showing Duv Glickstein the light. ''I've already talked to him. I'm afraid he's declared a holy war on us both, a Yiddish jihad.''

''You told him everything we're trying to do for his people?''

''I told him. And you're still the devil, while I play Judas.''

''Then you see no hope in quieting him down?''

''None whatsoever.''

''Too bad.'' It was said softly and with genuine regret. ''Things like that can be upsetting.''

''I wouldn't worry that much about him, Reverend.''

The limousine stopped in front of the Waldorf-Astoria and Newman pulled up behind it. Taylor's bodyguards, a secretary and a media woman, got out and stood on the sidewalk, in the rain, waiting for him. A gold-braided doorman approached with an open umbrella. Hotel guests in evening clothes stood talking just inside the lobby.

The reverend said, ''Why don't you come up for a drink? We don't really talk often enough.''

Newman weighed Taylor and brandy against Mary and bed. It was no contest. Still, the imagined sensation of the Napoleon warming his chest caused him to hesitate. It was just enough to let him notice a man crossing Park Avenue. He wore a dark raincoat and he was coming against the light, a small man with a heavy limp, picking his way through the speeding traffic as casually as he might have crossed his own living room.

He was less than fifteen feet away when the raincoat opened down the middle and Newman caught the glint of blue steel. "Aah." He sighed, and in a single motion slammed Taylor's head down against the dashboard and went down himself just as the first burst exploded the driver's window and the windshield. Then he was diving low through the open door and firing before he hit the rain-slick gutter. His shoulder took the impact and he rolled, squeezing off shots without counting until his revolver clicked empty. He heard shouting and the squeal of breaks and saw the man lying, face down, just a few feet away. The machine pistol was still in his hands.

Newman crawled forward and rolled him over. He was an elderly, gray-haired man, a stranger to the detective. One shot had caught him in the forehead, sucking the bone backward. It didn't much matter about the other shots or the rest of the carnage. The single shot was enough. The man was dead.

The lieutenant turned to look for Taylor and saw his bodyguards hurrying him across the sidewalk and into the hotel. He was apparently unhurt.

Moments later, three patrol cars were on the scene, revolving lights flashing. An ambulance soon followed, and the man was placed on a stretcher and lifted inside. Newman went in after the body, looking for identification. Inside a worn leather wallet was a driver's license and a Medicare card issued in the name of Jacob Fein. There was also a small, gold Star of David hanging from a neck chain. The detective knelt there, feeling something thick and heavy in his throat. For the moment, he was alone with the man. He put the wallet in his pocket. Bending, he unhooked the chain and took that, also. Then, without knowing why, but sensing that the very light of his life would begin to fade if he did not do it, he lifted one of the dead man's arms and pulled back the sleeve. There were the blue numbers, marked as indelibly as he had somehow known they would have to be. And how was he going to put that particular memento in his pocket?

He left a sergeant in charge of the shooting scene and went into the Waldorf and up to Clayton Taylor's suite.

GAYNOR'S PASSION

The reverend embraced him, gripping him tightly with both arms. "You saved my life, Jay. I'll never forget that."

The lieutenant felt the leanness of Taylor's body and breathed his cologne. "I'll take that drink now."

Taylor got rid of his people and they sat alone with the Napoleon. Newman drank much too fast but felt the brandy going down like love.

"Who is he?" asked Taylor.

"He's no one anymore. But his name was Jacob Fein. Did you know him?"

"No."

Thirty-one stories up, they heard the wail of police sirens.

"I'm sorry," said the clergyman. "I know how it must be for you."

"What's that?"

"Having to shoot one of your own, a Jew."

Newman replenished his drink. He felt as though he were dragging sobriety after him like a load of rocks and ached to be rid of it.

"Not just any Jew," he said. "He turned out to be one of our survivors. He carried the blue tattoo."

"Oh, Lord." Taylor closed his eyes. He seemed in pain.

He's either the best actor I've ever seen, Newman thought, or there are dimensions to this man I haven't even begun to touch.

"A terrible, terrible tragedy," The reverend's voice was barely a murmur. "During my worst times, I've had nightmares of something like this happening. Except that I was always the one to do the dying."

Newman groped through his pockets for a match and fingered the dead man's Star of David. Oppression stirred.

"Did it ever occur to you that I may have been the one he was trying to kill?"

"No. I'm afraid I can't allow you that much credit."

"We were talking about Rabbi Glickstein before. People like that could condemn me, as a Jew, even more than they would a Christian like you."

"I don't believe any rabbi would ever favor killing as a solution to anything."

"Maybe not. But that doesn't mean some anguished, half-demented old man like Fein, hearing Glickstein's attacks, wouldn't pick up a gun."

343

Clayton Taylor sat looking at him, and the two men drank in silence. There were reports to be filed and a dozen details that required Newman's attention, but he put off leaving. There was a turn of mood in the room that he did not dare break by getting to his feet.

"I once had an older brother I loved very much," said Taylor out of nowhere. "He always talked about being a minister when he grew up, but my father had other plans for him. One day he wasn't there anymore. He got up and left for school, but he never reached it and no one ever saw him again. My parents thought he had been kidnapped and waited for a ransom note. It never came. The police theorized that some pervert had killed him and left his body in an unmarked grave. I never believed that. I was sure he had simply followed God's voice and become a minister somewhere. So I became a minister, too. I felt that in this way God might be able to talk to us both, and in his own good time, bring us together."

The reverend smiled and savored his brandy, struggling to spin a few threads of communication between them. "It hasn't happened, of course. Still, I never go into a city or enter a street without some small part of me looking for my brother. When I noticed this figure crossing through the traffic toward us tonight, I indulged in the mad little fantasy that it might at last be Charles. I fantasized even as his coat opened and I saw the machine gun. I would have undoubtedly still been sitting there as he fired if you hadn't shoved me down. And do you know what I thought when I saw the gun? I thought, Why does my brother want to kill me? All I ever did was love him."

Mary awoke, saw the light on in the kitchen, and found him asleep with his head on the table beside Jacob Fein's Star of David and an empty bottle of Jack Daniel's. It was 4:10 A.M. Sensing her presence, he opened his eyes.

"I killed a Jew," he said. "A survivor."

She let him talk. Then she took him to bed.

She always takes me to bed, he thought. What would I do without her to take me to bed? The Star, somehow, was still in his hand.

"Let's get married," he said in the darkness, speaking to

the approximate area where he figured her head to be. "Why don't we stop this fooling around and finally just do it?"

She kissed him. "Ah, darling, you're really gone tonight, aren't you?"

"Some of us . . . we're a bit slow. It's not always easy to know what to do."

She murmured something, making a soft, human sound in the silent air. It was her reassurance. He was unable to understand the words, but it didn't matter. He needed only her voice.

"What's happened to me?" he asked. "When did I suddenly get so fucking Jewish?"

"It's not sudden. You were born that way. Remember?"

"I haven't prayed in a synagogue in forty years."

"That has nothing to do with it."

He fingered the Star of David. "I feel as though I blew away my grandfather tonight."

"That man wasn't your grandfather. Your grandfather wouldn't come at you with a blazing machine gun."

Through the bedroom window, the moon was a cold stone in the sky. The curtains were silver. Newman's heart rumbled with bourbon and panic.

"I just hope to God I'm not doing the wrong thing," he whispered.

She held him.

Asleep, he dreamed of Clayton Taylor's brother. Charles looked enough like the reverend to be his twin. He was smiling and holding out his hand. But when Newman reached for him, there was a flash of light and the spastic, rapid-fire lurching of a machine gun.

He awoke in a cold sweat. Some nameless grief rose in him. His throat was parched and his eyes burned. He lay very still but did not sleep again until the sky turned light.

22

Kate was due to work the eight-to-four ICU shift so they were awakened by the six o'clock news on the clock-radio. The lead item was the attempt on the life of the Reverend Clayton Taylor and Lieutenant Newman's killing of the would-be assassin.

"Jesus Christ!" said Gaynor.

Kate was still half asleep. "Did he say—"

"Let's listen."

But these were just the headline bulletins. The second piece of news involved the withdrawal of all charges against Professor Langdon in the Apostle case.

Gaynor reached for a cigarette, although he rarely smoked before breakfast.

"Give me one of those," said Kate.

They lay there, listening for details. But apparently there was very little available. Returning to the lead bulletin, the newscaster reported the time, place, and primary features of the shooting. He emphasized that Clayton Taylor had escaped injury and lauded Lieutenant Newman's further heroism in gunning down the would-be killer, a man tentatively identified as Jacob Fein, age seventy-three, of 148 Rivington Street on the Lower East Side of Manhattan. A human interest sidelight was pointed up by the indelible blue numbers on Fein's arm, which, for the past forty-odd years, had served as a tragic souvenir of the Nazi death camps. No specific motive had been established for the attempted assassination, although speculation did indicate the possibility of Fein's being aroused by Taylor's often virulent attacks on American Jewry.

As for the dropping of charges against Frank Langdon, the announcer offered no information other than that the philosophy professor had been cleared by newly acquired evidence, which the authorities were not free to make public at this time.

"I feel a little sick," said Kate.

Gaynor was not sure what he felt. He turned off the radio and, responding to a sudden, powerful need, picked up the phone and dialed Newman's home number. He counted six rings and was about to hang up when the detective answered. His voice was hoarse, thick, drugged with a mixture of sleep and alcohol.

"I guess I woke you," said Gaynor.

There was a rasping cough, in spasm, from the other end. Silence followed. Newman needed a moment to identify the voice.

"What the hell time is it?"

"Six-fifteen."

"Terrific. I've slept exactly forty-seven minutes." The coughing started again and Gaynor listened to the phlegm rattle.

"I just heard the news."

"That's what you woke me up to tell me?"

"It seems you're a hero again."

There was no response.

"Why didn't you just let the poor old man shoot the sonofabitch?"

There was an explosion in Gaynor's ear as Newman slammed down the receiver. The artist slowly hung up.

"Well, what did you expect?" said Kate.

"I don't know."

They lay on the bed, smoking.

"I can't help wondering," said Kate. "What if Jacob Fein had succeeded? What if Taylor was the one lying dead this morning? How would you feel?"

"Cheated." The windows were open, and he could hear the early traffic moving six stories below. "What about you?"

"I haven't your needs, darling. I'm afraid I'd just be grateful."

He began an imaginary painting of the late Jacob Fein. With no idea of what the old man had looked like, he turned him into a composite, the quintessential Holocaust survivor forty years later—face gaunt and lined, eyes dark, deeply set, haunted, body bent and meager. What amount of food could ever replenish such ravaged flesh? (Not true. He had seen plenty of fat, even obese, survivors. Pictorially, however, they would never do.) For composition, he had Fein lying face up in front of that soaring art deco monument to all the wrong things, the Waldorf-Astoria Hotel. It had been raining when it happened, so he painted the old man's blood shimmering in the wet gutter, mixing with the drizzle and running in small rivulets along the curb. Then, because he felt particularly bitter at that moment, he painted Lieutenant Newman standing over the body with a smoking gun in his hand.

Gaynor signed the painting, placed a rough, wooden frame around it, and added it to his collection.

The artist called his dealer later that morning. It was the first time he had called Sanders or made any kind of overture since he was out of the hospital. But it was getting very close to July Fourth, there were good-byes to be said (just in case), and there were things to show him.

"Can you come over this afternoon?" he asked.

There was a pause. "Are you telling me you've been working?"

"After a fashion."

"What the hell does that mean?"

"You'll have to see."

"I'll be there at two o'clock."

The dealer arrived at one thirty-five, his excitement naked in a face that found it impossible to hide a thing. "I couldn't wait," he said, heading straight for the studio.

The blue man was on an easel with a sheet draped over him. The others, the half-dozen smaller paintings, stood exposed against the walls. Sanders studied these first, taking his time, moving slowly and without comment from one to the other. Gaynor looked along with him. With another pair of eyes present, it was like seeing them for the first time. His freshly minted ghosts. No. They were no longer phantoms. They suddenly had life. The unlovely, gross-featured men and women were actually there. Gaynor could feel them, all of them. Not just flesh, bones, sinews, hair. The rest, too. It blazed out of their eyes and hooked into Gaynor's chest. They hated him, hated anyone young, strong, whole, hated the little that God had granted them and the still less that lay ahead. These people would not go gently to their final night. They would fight all the way, scratching, kicking, and biting, hanging on with the last few wobbling teeth in their bleeding gums. And every brushstroke screamed it. There was no other sound in the room. Gaynor soaked it in, lost himself in it. Standing there, he could feel his body relax. A sweetness gathered in the deep part of his throat. Today, this afternoon, he was an artist. Maybe not yesterday or the day before, or the day before that. And maybe not even tomorrow. But now, this afternoon, yes.

Sanders finished looking and turned. "I don't know what to say, Richard. They're like nothing you've ever painted."

Gaynor stood silently. Disapproval or praise? The dealer was a kind man as well as his friend. Also, he knew about artists, knew the terror, the terrible vulnerability, of these moments. Attack the work and you strike the man. They were one. Thirty years in the business had made it no easier for the gallery owner. He had gotten so he could see artists' faces without looking. Slowly melting wax. The cheeks sagged, dripped over the chin. The eyes died. Their lights went out.

"They frighten me," Sanders said at last, "but they're undoubtedly more powerful, carry more passion, than anything you've ever done." He sighed. "What's that you've got covered on the easel?"

"If these frighten you, you'd better skip this one entirely."

The art dealer walked over and pulled off the sheet. For several moments his face showed no reaction, no emotion, nothing. But it was only becauses his skin kept it that way. The nerves beneath moved in separate broken bits. One bit wept, another was angry, a third was horrified, a fourth trembled minutely. Then the sweating began. It started at his hairline, ran down his forehead and cheeks, and stained his shirt. He wiped it with a handkerchief but it did no good. He had turned to water.

Gaynor poured some straight whiskey and handed it to him. "I'm sorry, Marvin."

"You should be, you sonofabitch." Sanders took the whiskey in two gulps. ''Where the hell do you get off turning out something like that? Do you want to know how it makes me feel? Like killing myself.''

The artist smiled.

''I'm not trying to be funny. I think if I believed everything you've said here, I couldn't see much point in getting up in the morning. And if I thought you believed it yourself, I wouldn't feel much better.''

''Don't you think I believe it?''

Something strangled in Sanders, some wistful desire to change what was beyond alteration. ''I pray to God you don't. There's no hope here, Richard. Not for any of us.''

Gaynor was silent.

''I know of your terrible loss. I know what you've suffered. I'm sure there are parts of you that will never recover. But all that still doesn't justify creating such an abomination.''

''It's only a painting, Marvin.''

''We both know better, don't we? It's your statement. And the only thing I'd like do with the thing is burn it.''

Gaynor was touched by the intensity of his friend's reaction. In a field not famous for its loyalty, the gallery owner had always hung in there with him, had never swerved an inch, had never pressured him to run with the fads of the moment, had never berated his stubbornness, had never offered him anything but encouragement when God knew there was precious little of that coming from anyone else. Too bad I can't offer him a better return on his investment, he thought.

They stood looking at one another.

''All right,'' said Sanders more quietly. ''I've got the feeling you didn't bring me up here just to look at this. What do you want to tell me? At this point, I can't imagine its being anything I'll want to hear.''

''I may be going away. I didn't want to leave without seeing you.''

''When are you going?''

''Sometime within the next week.''

''For how long?''

''I'm not sure.''

''Where can I reach you?''

''If I can, I'll reach *you*.''

Sanders stared at him. ''What are you trying to say?''

''I've already said it.''

The gallery owner, looking miserable, turned back to the blue man. "Worst of all," he said, "is that if you live to be a hundred and work twelve hours a day for the rest of your life, you'll probably never paint anything as good."

Gaynor picked up a late afternoon edition of the *Post*, in which a eulogy of sorts was carried on the second page. It had been written by Rabbi Duv Glickstein and said:

I don't know where Jacob Fein ever found a submachine gun or learned to shoot it. He was not a man given to violence. Until last night, he spent a lifetime simply being its victim. Indeed, in all the years he came to my synagogue, I never saw anything more threatening in his hands than the Old Testament. Or are there threats implicit even in the word of God?

Still, it was Jacob who last night lay dead in the rain, of police bullets, a just-fired machine gun beside his body. And how far he had come, searching for this end. Out of the cobbled streets of Cracow, across Poland and Germany in a cattle car, through the unspeakable horrors of Buchenwald, across thousands of miles of ocean, to his violent moments in a New York gutter. How far, how far. God tells us to love our enemy as our brother, but this is not always easy to remember. In the end, Jacob forgot. And in his forgetting, he picked up a gun.

Yet let us not be too self-righteous in our condemnation of this man. For was it not our own indifference to the spread of lies and hatred, our own weakness of spirit, our own deafness to Jacob's silent warnings, that allowed someone as insidious as Clayton Taylor to reach his present power and preeminence? Jacob prayed, he wept, he waved his poor, indelible numbers in front of our eyes to remind us of what had once happened and could well happen again, and we said, "We see nothing. That was almost half a century ago in another place. That has nothing to do with us."

Then, in his despair, feeling it was the only way left for him to shout a warning that might be heard, Jacob picked up, aimed, and fired his machine gun. And then, finally, we said, "Now we hear him. Now we know he is a dangerous man, an assassin. Now let us kill him."

Norman Garbo

So we killed him, Jacob Fein, Number 8463728 of Buchenwald, near Weimar, Germany, a small man with a poor liver and digestion, impossible veins, and a leg once deliberately broken in four places and never allowed to mend properly.

May he rest in peace.

Gaynor read the article three times. He suddenly had great hopes for this Rabbi Glickstein. But it was not until several hours later that he realized Glickstein was the mugging victim whose assailants he had tied up near the South Street Seaport Museum, then called upon Lieutenant Newman to handle personally. He saw no particular significance in this, yet somehow found it satisfying.

The phone rang just as he was about to leave for his trial run at Yankee Stadium. It was Victor Lutovsky. "There's been a change of plan. I'll be taking you through myself. Not the man you were supposed to meet."

Gaynor was surprised. "Are you serious?"

"Why not? You think I'm too old?"

"No. Too important."

Lutovsky laughed. "Listen. I used to do everything myself. That's how I got so important. Besides, this way you won't have to go through all that nonsense with your mask." At 1:00 A.M., Gaynor parked his car five blocks from Yankee Stadium and walked due north along a road on which all the shops were closed for the night. A corner drugstore and a pool parlor had lights on in the distance, but only a few people were visible on the street, and even they soon disappeared.

Gaynor heard footsteps behind him and saw Lutovsky about twenty yards back. He had no idea where he had come from. They kept walking, maintaining the twenty-yard interval. As they approached the great mass of the stadium itself, Lutovsky's pace picked up until they were side by side. Neither man spoke. Lutovsky was wearing a dark shirt, jeans, and running shoes. Seeing Gaynor glance at his feet, he smiled. "I jog five miles before breakfast every morning. My pressure is like a kid's. Want to run?"

"Hell, no. I wouldn't last fifty yards."

The Yankees were on an extended road trip, so the streets

around the stadium were comparatively free of the litter that Gaynor usually associated with the area. The silence, too, seemed strange. It was the brooding stillness of ancient ruins. He thought of the way it would be four nights later and for the first time felt it in his stomach.

Lutovsky was evidently experiencing much of the same sensation. "I was once in the Roman Colosseum at night. I swear you could almost hear the crowd, the iron clanging on iron. And it was all two thousand years ago. Imagine."

He's enjoying this, thought Gaynor. It's a kind of picnic for him, fun and games under the Bronx moon. No wonder he wanted to come along. It was a lot more exciting than charity dinners.

Lutovsky stopped in the shadow of a building. A security patrol was due in a few moments, and they waited until they saw the car slowly drive by. Then they crossed a broad, open area, and Lutovsky opened a locked gate with one of several keys he had on a ring. They were in. Gaynor felt his life simplifying, its separate parts coming together in a single piece. Whatever remained to be done was right here.

Inside the stadium itself there were two guards on foot patrol, but Lutovsky had both their routes and call box sequences timed to the minute. They spotted first one, then the other, a pair of bored, nocturnal sentinels earning their lonely keep. When they were finally out of sight, the two intruders followed one of the entrance ramps to the grandstand and came out in the area between home plate and first base. The moon was almost directly overhead. It silvered the grass and basepaths of the playing field. The construction of the speaker's stand had already started, the raw wood looking pale, almost white, on the infield. Gaynor half expected to see a gallows rising above it, but there was only part of a railing.

Lutovsky took out a diagram. Following it, they found the three trap doors they had decided were most feasible. Lutovsky's advance man had worked graphite into the locks and they all opened easily by key. The conduits themselves were narrow but quite passable. Using small, high-intensity flashlights, they crawled through on their hands and knees. Electrical cables ran on both sides of the conduit of poured concrete. The air was stale, damp, and cool. A tomb, thought Gaynor. In the lead, he suddenly heard movement in front of him. He raised his beam in time to see two dark, furry shapes scurrying away. Rats.

Lutovsky grunted. "They don't care much for us, either."

The conduit ended in an electrical substation, a six-by-four-foot concrete box with a tangle of dusty wires and equipment and a square, steel plate set into the forward wall. Lutovsky loosened four thumbscrews and removed the plate, revealing a ventilator grille beneath. The openings in the grille were large enough to accommodate a rifle barrel. Gaynor looked out and saw the skeleton of the speaker's platform directly in front. As Lutovsky had promised, it was no more than 116 feet away.

They stood together in the concrete tomb. Gaynor stared through the grille. A cloud passed over the moon and the silver glow disappeared.

"How do you feel?" Lutovsky asked.

"A little cold, as though parts of me were packed in ice."

"Good. Hold on to it. For your purpose, it's better than heat."

There was something about the place that held them.

Lutovsky said, "I'll have your ordnance brought in the night before. You'll come in on July Fourth with everyone else. But a bit on the early side so you can get set."

"Which trap door will I use?"

"Which looked best to you?"

"The one in the utility closet."

"Let's take a final look to be sure."

They crawled back, the rats once more scurrying off in the darkness ahead. On second examination, the utility closet did indeed appear best. It was easily accessible yet secluded. Nevertheless, Lutovsky gave him the diagrams of the other conduit entrances in case of emergency. He seemed pleased with the trial run.

"I'm glad I came with you," he said. "Most things are better done yourself."

"Exactly."

Jane was asleep in front of the television set when he got home. She awoke as he entered the room. She had not told him she would be there, yet he had half expected to find her. Kate had been with him the night before. The two women seemed to have reached a tacit understanding that they would alternate. It was all right with him.

Jane stretched herself awake. "I tried to wait up. How did it go?"

"Okay," he said and told her about it.

In bed later, the same silver light as in the stadium touched them, the room, with its glow. She turned to him. It was a mild, even a warm night, but her flesh carried the chill of winter.

"Hold me," she said. "Please. Just hold me."

Her voice was flat, a soft monotone. He held her and felt he was holding air. He thought she wanted to be made love to, but when he touched her she moved his hand away. Her eyelids fluttered as if he had touched her there. Moonlight glinted in a point of moisture in one eye.

"I think I'm frightened," she whispered.

Gaynor held her more tightly and her flesh felt leaden on her bones. She had every right to be frightened.

"You'll be all right," he said. "You know, you don't really have to be there at all. The way it's set up now, there's no need."

"Not for myself, dummy. I'm frightened for you."

"I'll be all right, too. Your friend Lutovsky has done a beautiful job for us."

"It's crazy," she said in her new monotone. "I didn't really care at all before. Not about either of us. I mean, I felt what difference did anything make? How much more could we lose?"

Lying beside her, he had one of his recurring visions of flaming horror. In it, there were no reasons anymore—no reason for love, for work, for getting up in the morning, no reason for hope or prayer. He lived in a tight box whose sides kept him from toppling over and falling.

"Yet now . . ." Jane stopped. "It's crazy. Why should it be easier, not caring?"

23

Newman was in his car, heading for the Brooklyn-Battery Tunnel and home when the bombing report crackled out of his police radio. For a moment, the address meant nothing. Then it hit him like the echo of a scream. Swearing softly, he made a screeching turn at the next corner and drove back uptown.

He saw the smoke as soon as he reached First Avenue, a black dome that grew like a mushroom and blotted out the sun. When he got to the street where the synagogue was, his path was blocked by two police cars with whirling lights. He pulled over, identified himself, and ran the rest of the way. The air was thick with smoke, and in it, along with the bitterness of paint and chemicals, Newman felt he could sniff out the essential smells of piety—the old prayer books, the tallithim, the sacred scroll in the ark of the covenant. Fire hoses were everywhere, hissing from their joints. People leaned from tenement windows, waiting. They would not be disappointed.

Two firemen came rushing out of a hole in what had been the front of the synagogue, carrying a body. Newman stood beside an ambulance, knowing who it was going to be even before he saw Glickstein's blackened face. The rabbi's eyes were closed and he was covered with blood. He looked finished, gone. But from the speed with which the firemen were moving, Newman figured he was just unconscious. No one ever rushed with the dead—certainly not city employees. They loaded Glickstein into the ambulance and drove off, siren wailing.

Newman approached one of the firemen, a black beetle in a shining wet slicker. "How bad is he?"

The man shrugged. "He's alive. Which is more than the kids are."

"What kids?"

"The three who were with him when the bomb blew. Hebrew school kids."

Newman watched as they brought them out, three small packages in green body bags. A cluster of screaming women tried to rush forward but were held back by the police. The women seemed isolated. The other spectators—the neighbors, the friends—had backed away in respect for the immensity of their grief.

Newman went over to a sergeant he knew from the local precinct. "What have you got on it, Charley?"

"Plastic bomb. Three dead kids and a blown-up little rabbi, and the mother-fuckers want credit for it." The sergeant, a tall black man with soft, worried eyes, shook his head in disgust. "I mean, they called in two minutes before it went off."

"Who are *they?*"

"Bunch of paramilitary, underground crazies. You know. Hate all kikes, niggers, and spics. Call themselves the American Crusade Party." The sergeant walked off in search of witnesses.

Newman stared at the green body bags lying in the gutter, awaiting a coroner's wagon. He had never seen the three young Hebrew scholars but felt he knew them, felt he also knew their books, their *sefers*, with their worn pages and tiny Hebrew lettering spiced with truths from some learned Reb in pre-Christian Jerusalem, passed on to the Rebs of the Diaspora, and finally relayed to this just-blown-apart Reb in New York City, U.S.A., truths five thousand years in transit and somehow preserved amid pogrom, famine, and the systematic cruelty of so-called Christians.

The lieutenant stood there as the shattered synagogue was hosed down. He was listening to the wailing women—mothers, grandmothers, sisters—all still needing to be restrained from rushing to those terrible green bags. An old sickness sank through him like soot. He wished he could put it down as just bad luck or God's will, but he had never been much of a believer in either. Maybe they were both up there someplace, but blame stopped for him in the human world. And for this, once he got past the American Crusade Party, the highest he somehow was able to get was the top of his own head.

He was waiting in the corridor when they rolled Duv Glickstein past him, toward the recovery room. The rabbi had been in surgery for five hours and was still unconscious, his head swathed in bandages, his body shapeless under a green sheet. He was very pale, and without his glasses he looked oddly naked and vulnerable.

How small he is. I had no idea he was so small, Newman thought.

He found the surgeon in charge of the emergency team. "How is he, doctor?"

"You family?"

"No." Newman hesitated. "A friend."

"Call tomorrow." The surgeon started to leave.

Newman stepped in front of him and showed his badge. "I happen to be interested."

"Why didn't you say you were a cop?"

Newman was silent. The man clearly didn't like cops. Well, he wasn't crazy about doctors.

The surgeon had a deeply tanned face and eyes that seemed to have been trained to transmit bad news. "We took off what was left of his right leg. Just above the knee. I think we saved the other, but we'll have to wait and see. He also suffered severe internal injuries, multiple lacerations, and a fractured skull."

Newman stood there. He felt that certain parts of him were melting, floating off. Breathing deeply, he sucked in air flavored with pain, sickness, drugs.

The surgeon was looking at him closely, with new interest. "Aren't you Newman?"

He nodded.

"I'm afraid I've got some tough news for you, Lieutenant. He's going to live." The surgeon walked away.

There was a pay phone in the corridor near the elevators.

Newman called the precinct house. A Sergeant Jennings was at the desk.

"Sergeant, this is Lieutenant Newman. Who was on duty when that call on the synagogue bombing came in?"

"I was, Lieutenant."

"Do you have the transcript handy?"

"Yes, sir."

"Would you read it to me?"

There was the sound of rustling papers. "It came in at sixteen-o-six hours, Lieutenant. I'd just taken the desk. A guy said, 'A bomb's going off in Beth Israel Synagogue in exactly ten minutes. This is a warning from the American Crusade Party. Let Glickstein the antichrist stick to his kikes and stop meddling with Christians.' "

"That's it?"

"Yeah. I called Beth Israel as soon as I got the number. The phone was ringing when I heard the explosion. It was no more than two minutes after the guy phoned."

Newman thanked the sergeant and hung up. Then he found a bar right across the street from Bellevue, downed two quick doubles, and once more started home. It was more than seven hours since his first try.

He stopped at the hospital on the way to his office the next day. Glickstein was in an intensive care unit, with a great many tubes carrying fluids in and out of him and the red and white lights of electronic monitors flashing. The rabbi's face, framed by bandages, was not nearly as ashen as the last time Newman had seen him. His eyes were closed. But as Newman stood there, the lids fluttered and slowly lifted. There was no sign of recognition. Without his glasses, Glickstein was functionally blind.

"It's Newman," said the detective.

The rabbi sighed and closed his eyes. Things were taking place inside him.

"I'm sorry." Newman put a cigarette in his mouth, then remembered where he was. He chewed it, unlit.

Glickstein's lips worked. "My . . . my students . . ."

The detective said nothing.

Glickstein lay there. He again opened his eyes, but they were sightless bubbles. Silently, he wept. The tears ran down his cheeks and darkened his pillow. He was melting. There seemed to be no end to his tears. Then they stopped. "This man, this . . ." He licked parched lips. "Aah . . . he's not human."

"No," said Newman. His face ached strangely. "You're wrong. It wasn't Taylor. He had nothing to do with it."

"Who . . . who else?" Even the whisper was almost gone. "*You* . . . ?"

The detective looked down at the place, under the sheet, where Duv Glickstein's right leg should have been. When he looked up, the rabbi seemed to have drifted off.

He felt as though he was walking a high wire in a windstorm. He swayed first one way, then another. What was he looking for? A soft place to fall? He saw none anywhere. In the meantime, he seemed to be after something else.

He sought it first from Michael Westley. He charged into the commissioner's office unannounced, chased out two startled clerks, and slammed the door after them. Then he went for the bourbon. But when he finally spoke, it was with a delicately balanced softness.

"Okay. We've got three blown-up little kids in the morgue, a one-legged rabbi in intensive care, and a pile of rubble that had been a synagogue for a hundred years. What are we doing about it?"

Westley studied the detective from behind his desk. "I'll tell you what we're *not* doing," he said in his gentlest murmur. "We're not running around like wildmen, breaking into offices, and indulging ourselves in barely suppressed cases of galloping hysteria. This is a terrible, utterly senseless tragedy, and everything possible is—"

"Come on, Michael. You're not holding one of your fucking press conferences. Just tell me what we've got so far. What the hell is this American Crusade Party?"

"Extreme right-wing hate group. Obviously violent. Lost their charter a while back, were outlawed and went underground. But we're not even sure they did it."

"What about the warning call?"

"A voice on a phone can say anything. We've got no witnesses, no evidence, nothing. The only thing the call tells us is that whoever set up the bomb doesn't know too much about timing devices. I don't think anyone was meant to be hurt. That's what the ten-minute warning was all about."

"Tell that to Glickstein and the kids' mothers. I'm sure it'll make them feel a lot better."

Westley watched Newman working at his bourbon. "Since you're so anxious to place blame for this, why don't you try placing some on the rabbi himself. If he had kept his nose in his torah where it belonged instead of sticking it in politics, none of this would have happened."

"That's a hell of a thing to say."

"But unfortunately true. I don't mean to be unfeeling, Jay. The tragedy of this event is very real. But those children would have been alive today if Glickstein hadn't called so much attention to himself with his attacks on you and Taylor."

Newman swayed on his wire. He felt he was losing his fine edge of control. Before he lost it entirely, he gulped the remains of his drink and left.

If he had tended to forget about the Apostle during the past thirty-six hours, Peterson was waiting in his office to remind him. Ignoring the FBI man, Newman sat down at his desk, picked up a handful of reports, and shuffled through them without interest.

"I knew you'd release Langdon before July Fourth," said the agent, "and I was right on target. But I never thought Taylor would be the one to clear him. Did you expect that?"

"How could I? I haven't your clairvoyance."

Peterson smiled. "As a matter of fact I've had another vision—my best yet. How about you yourself being the Apostle? Imagine that for an idea. A cop heading an investigation to track down himself. Who would suspect him?"

"Obviously, you."

The agent lit another of his endless chain of cigarettes. "I've been going over things from the beginning. Face it, Lieutenant. You've always been a maverick. Everyone knows you'd have been dumped long ago if it wasn't for your friendship with the commissioner. You're a clever, tough, functioning alcoholic who has always flouted regulations and made no secret of his impatience with our entire criminal justice system. You're also a hopeless romantic to whom the whole idea of a vigilante psychology would have enormous appeal."

Newman slowly put down his unread reports. What an

intriguing mind this man had. But hadn't Mary once said much the same thing?

"So I started building from there," Peterson went on. "Knowing cops' off-duty habits, it was easy enough for you to ambush Officer Reagan in that Bronx parking lot and get his thirty-eight. Then you did a little work on your friend Westley, and had yourself put in charge of the whole investigation. A stroke of genius. You now knew everything that was going on. Your only bit of carelessness was in letting yourself be tailed by your own men when you set up that rapist near Sheepshead Bay. But you even turned that to good advantage by abandoning your stolen car near Riverside Drive and then cleverly wasting weeks of investigation by having your people check through the whole area."

The detective nodded his approval. "Very good. But what about the blood in the abandoned car and on the sidewalk? Are you assuming I was really wounded?"

"Not necessarily. You might have deliberately planted the blood to add spice and reality." Peterson sucked at his cigarette as though his intelligence itself was rooted in the tobacco. "But, of course, all of this is nothing more than mildly amusing conjecture. I think what really turned me on to the entire notion was that along with everything else, you were also Jewish. Because, finally, I'd have to believe the whole thing hinges on the minority theme."

"What minority theme?"

"The idea that the Apostle would have to be a Jew, a black, or a Hispanic, someone willing to risk his life, even martyr himself, defending his people. I'm surprised this didn't occur to me before. It only hit me when Jacob Fein tried to blow you and Taylor away the other night."

The dead survivor's grave opened up between them. "But I was the one who shot Fein."

"It was your life or his. Besides, you had no way of knowing who he was until it was too late." He gazed thoughtfully at the detective. "The one thing that doesn't quite fit is your continuing endorsement of Taylor. Oh, I know all about his assurances to you and his two million a month for the UJA. It's just that I can't quite believe that would be enough to allow you to support a man you've pledged to kill on July Fourth."

Newman was silent. All he was doing now was listening.

"Unless, of course," Peterson continued, "it's just a device to help you get close to him to facilitate your assassination plans. Anyway, I hope that's it. Because I must confess I've fallen madly in love with the whole idea of your being the Apostle."

The lieutenant's concern was still building, accelerating by the hour until it began to seem almost metaphysical. Was there automatic morality just in devotion to those of your own religion? Could there be some crazy idea of duty and mutual love in what was nothing more than a random act of biology? Why was he carrying this load on his back like an old Yiddish peddler? Was he becoming his own grandfather?

It made no sense, thought Newman. Yet by late evening it had become bad enough to drive him toward the thirty-first floor of the Waldorf, where Clayton Taylor was in residence, preparing for July Fourth.

The clergyman looked at his face and brought out the brandy. "Is there anything new on the bombing?"

His drawl was as heavy as ever, yet Newman found that he hardly noticed it anymore. Maybe they were getting to sound alike. My brother, he thought.

"They'll never find anything new. They'll just bury the three kids along with Glickstein's leg and that'll be the end of it." He gulped some brandy. "I saw what's left of the rabbi this morning. He thinks the blame lies mostly with us."

"That's unfair."

"Maybe. Yet all those attacks of yours on non-Christians . . . my public support of you. It's a wonder more bombs haven't gone off."

The reverend's face was troubled. "We can't be held responsible for every psychopath with a TV set. We're people in public life, Jay. All any of us can do is follow our own heart and conscience. Neither of us intended a tragedy like this to happen. May God forgive those who did." He sat staring at nothing. "I've never asked. We've never had that kind of relationship. But I'm sure you must have your own very strong, very definite feelings about God . . . what he is, what he expects of you."

"Not so strong," said Newman, "not so definite. Often, I have no feelings about him whatsoever. I've been a cop too long. You get a dark, twisted view of things. Sometimes I'm even sure that if he exists at all, he's got to be a committee. I think no single God could have screwed things up this badly. When I was a kid, my grandfather used to tell me it was my duty as a good Jew to love God. And since I loved my grandfather, I tried. But is it really a duty to love a God who produces things like the Holocaust and Hiroshima? It's like the duty of a good German to love Hitler."

"I understand. I had much the same problem in the seminary. My professors talked about the love of God, never about the world's horrors. They saw no problem in that. What they talked about was man's free will, man's responsibility for his own actions. That was their excuse for everything bad that happened. If there was evil in the world, it was blamed on man or the devil."

The minister paused, as though for breath. But he was studying Newman. "So I had to work out my own way of handling that. I decided that since God created us in his image, our evil also had to be his evil. How could we love him if he were not like us? We are inescapably linked to one another. As we change, God changes. When we do something bad, it adds to his dark side. When we do something noble, it helps his good side. It's a constantly altering process. He and we never stay the same. Sometimes it's quite awful, and the God I believe in endures as much agony as we."

"It seems much simpler not to believe in him at all."

"Maybe," Taylor admitted. "But then you're alone. There's only yourself. And I can't think of anything more terrible. What do you do for that?"

"Mostly, I suppose, I drink."

"Does it help?"

"For a while."

"And then?"

"There's always another drink."

Taylor took him seriously. "Then God, for you, is in a bottle?"

"At least I know where he is when I need him. And he never fails me. Which is more than I can say for yours."

They sat drinking in their separate silences.

"I've prayed for the souls of those poor children," Taylor said softly. "I've prayed for Rabbi Glickstein's recovery. Still, you feel so helpless in the face of such tragedy. I confess I'm not always as certain as I may sound. There are too many questions to which I have no answers. Sometimes I wonder about the value of everything I'm trying to do—all this hoopla, all this striving. Weighed against the deaths of those three children, it's not even a contest. If I felt I was in any way responsible, it would be hard for me to face another day.''

Amen, thought Newman. Whatever that meant.

It was close to midnight when he got home and drove into his parking space. He turned off the motor and lights and sat there for a moment, wondering if Mary would be in his bed. If not his God, then surely his opiate. He started to get out of the car, and it was suddenly as though Jacob Fein was coming at him all over again, this time across the darkened parking area. Except that Fein was dead and the approaching figure was much bigger, a tall man who moved with a fluid grace. He wore a short-sleeved shirt and both his hands were visible. Newman drew his revolver and waited.

"Take it easy, Lieutenant. It's only me."

He recognized Richard Gaynor's voice.

"I know," said the artist. "This has to be a pretty dumb way to approach a cop who's recently been shot at."

Newman replaced his revolver.

"I'm sorry about my call the other morning. It was stupid and insensitive of me. I should have known how you were feeling."

"Do you always do your apologizing after midnight in parking lots?"

"Only when I'm running out of time. I have to talk to you."

They got into the car together. Newman knew why Gaynor was there. He could actually feel the pressure of his motives. Or had he somehow conjured him up for his own needs?

"During the past forty-eight hours," Gaynor said without preliminary, "your friend Taylor has been directly responsible for four killings and a crippling. And as far as I can see, this is only the beginning of—"

"Hold it!" Newman cut in. "I know what you're trying to do, but let's just stick to the facts. Taylor had no part in those disasters. I was the one who shot Jacob Fein, and it was a bunch of lunatic Nazis who did the bombing."

"Taylor's Jew-baiting was still what clicked something off in the poor survivor's brain. It was also what made Glickstein start attacking Taylor so strongly he had to be silenced."

"By those American Crusade nuts, not by Taylor."

Gaynor shrugged. "Same thing."

"The hell they are."

"These are the types that support him, that take seriously every lie he spews. And it's going to get worse because that kind of thing feeds on itself."

Newman wanted to get out of the car right then, but something held him. It was a warm, still night, and the surf could be heard rolling into the beach three hundred yards away. A late flight came over, its landing lights on, heading for Kennedy.

Gaynor said quietly, "I want to go for him. I want out of my pledge."

"No."

"You must know what this man is."

"I know him better than you. He's not simple. He's not what you think."

"Aren't four dead enough for you? How many are you waiting for?"

Why is he bothering with this performance? Newman wondered. As if his pledge would stop him. The detective had begun to feel that he and Clayton Taylor were running in the same dark blood. The apartment house where he lived, the cars in the parking lot, seemed to stand about them like angry witnesses.

"I refuse to sanction murder. Call it what you want."

"What I call it is blind ambition. Is being police commissioner really so important that you can't see anything else?"

Newman opened the car door and started out.

Gaynor grabbed his arm. "I'm sorry. I really think more of you than that. I'm just frustrated. There's less than forty-eight hours left and the dead are piling up like cordwood. I was hoping all this might change your mind about things. I was hoping you'd give me back my IOU. But I guess not. Okay. Then I have one last favor to ask."

This time the detective made it out of the car. "Enough is enough. No more credit."

"Please." Gaynor followed him and again took his arm.

"It's not just for me. It's for you, too. You might not be able to live with yourself afterward if you don't at least listen."

Newman kept walking.

"Go to Atlanta."

The detective stopped. "For what?"

"To talk to an old lady who probably knows more about Clayton Taylor than anyone alive."

"You mean that preacher's widow you saw?"

"Yes. Mrs. Forsythe."

"What could she possbily tell me that would change anything."

"I have no idea. But you can be sure it would be the truth."

Newman walked away.

"Please," Gaynor called after him. "As a last favor."

"No more favors. I've run out."

Newman's grandfather came in the night. It was not a dream because he felt Mary sleeping beside him and saw the curtains at the window with the moonlight breaking through. Still, his old zayde, Israel Newman, was right there in the room, telling his pogrom stories, reciting his terrible tone poems of mutilation and death at the hands of the goyim. None of the tales were new. He had heard them many times before. But they seemed to hold a new freshness tonight, as though he had just discovered that pain in this world must continually be remembered anew, that if it were ever (God forbid) forgotten, it would be bound to return in many times its original strength. The earth had for five thousand years been enriched by the bodies and pieces of bodies of Jews. It seemed that for the goyim there existed this historical nostalgia for the infliction of suffering and death. For pagans, Christians, Moslems— whatever—it appeared that life could only be reasserted as true by murdering Jews. The feeling had proven universal.

"Understand, boychik," his grandfather had told him when he was thirteen and considered a man, someone old enough to be presented with the hard truth. "All of us, everyone ever born, must at some time wait for death. It is no great tragedy. It is only natural. But for a Jew, what he often waits for turns out to be murder."

Most of a lifetime later, lying in bed beside a sleeping Christian woman whom he loved, Newman could almost feel his grandfather's hand softly touching his head. "You don't have to be afraid, boychik," said the old man. "Just be careful."

Early the next morning the lieutenant called Headquarters from La Guardia to let them know he would not be in his office all day. Half an hour later, he was on the 9:00 A.M. Delta flight to Atlanta.

〰〰〰〰〰〰〰〰〰〰〰〰〰〰 **24** 〰〰〰

The White Christ stood on the crest of its hill, arms outstretched. Lines of pilgrims genuflected and took pictures to paste in their albums and show to their friends. Recorded hymns floated on the warm, clear air. The three soaring towers of the American Fundamental Church's tabernacle and headquarters glistened against an azure sky. Television and radio antennas rose in steel silhouettes.

Newman saw it all as he drove by in his rented Chevrolet. He was impressed, even a trifle awed. You didn't see such grandeur every day. Still, there was something about the very size and majesty of the complex that made him uncomfortable. It kept him from stopping for a closer look. Maybe after I see the old lady, he thought.

He reached the crumbling, one-story cottage in the early afternoon, with the half-dead pines throwing their shadows across the lawn and an old iron table and chairs still rusting

beside the entrance path. A 1967 Plymouth was in the driveway. Brown stains reached from the gutters to the ground. A
broken railing leaned from the front steps. Newman parked
behind the Plymouth and walked to a peeling white door.
What am I doing here? He knocked and stood for a long time
before Mrs. Forsythe opened the door.

Leaning on a cane, she peered at him from under her white
bangs. "Are you here to sell me something? If you are, I'm
afraid we're both going to be disappointed."

"I'm a police officer, Mrs. Forsythe. My name is Newman,
Lieutenant Newman." He showed her his badge and identification. "I'm from New York."

"You've come all this way to arrest me?"

"No, ma'am." He liked her immediately. She had humor.
Lately, the elderly seemed to be about the only ones who did
have it. The young were too arrogant, too self-absorbed, too
busy picking their sores. "I'd just like to talk to you."

"Talk is pretty much what I do, Lieutenant. Come in."

She sat him down on a couch with broken springs after
chasing off the cats. Without asking, she brought him a glass
of sherry. The drink was apparently one of her few remaining
ceremonies. The cluttered room and faded furniture indicated
there was little else. An elderly basset struggled over to
Newman and he scratched her back.

Mrs. Forsythe settled into a wicker chair by a window.
"What is it you want to talk about, Lieutenant?"

"Clayton Taylor."

"I had an unpleasant feeling you were going to say that.
Someone else from New York came to see me for the same
reason awhile back. He left a dead man as a memento."

"I know. He was the one who asked me to talk to you."

The old woman looked doubtful. Frowning, her skin went
taut, turned almost translucent.

"He calls me from time to time," the detective explained.
"It's a little game he likes to play. He said you knew more of
the truth about Clayton Taylor than anyone else around."

"Why should that interest you?"

"Because it's my job to keep the reverend alive on July
Fourth."

"Aah . . ." Perception shone. "And learning the truth
about him might perhaps make you a bit less conscientious in
your work?"

369

Norman Garbo

"That's what your friend seems to think."

"And what do *you* think, sir?"

"I've been a police officer for almost thirty years, Mrs. Forsythe. I believe in the law, not murder. Not for any reason."

"Then why have you traveled all the way down here to talk to me?"

"I'm not sure." Rubbing the hound's back, Newman suddenly wished he had a dog. They offered so much in return for so little. "Maybe I've been a cop too long. Finally, you can't resist knowing whatever there is to know."

The old woman was staring at his face. Again, perception shone. "Of course. I should have realized it. You're Jewish."

Newman said nothing.

"My late husband, Hanson Forsythe, always preached love for the Jewish people. When he was attacked for it by our local anti-Semites, he would laugh and say, 'They hate me like a Jew. Thank God. Because this, more than anything else, tells me I'm a true Christian.'"

"I think I would have liked your husband."

"Hanson believed that if Christians were true Christians there would be no anti-Semitism, no prejudice, no hate of any kind."

The basset dozed under Newman's touch. The cats watched indifferently.

"Ah, I'm rambling," said Mrs. Forsythe. "A hazard of old age. You came to hear about Clayton Taylor, not my husband. A clever, devious, evil man. But I fear there's not much I can tell you about him that you haven't already heard. Besides, they would only be more words . . . and from an obviously prejudiced source. I do despise the man, you know, unchristian though such feelings may be. Still . . ." She thought for a moment. "Can you stay through the evening?"

"If there's a reason."

"There may be." Using her cane for leverage, she lifted herself to her feet. "Just allow me a moment to telephone," she said and went into the kitchen.

When she returned, she seemed pleased. "It will be arranged. I think you'll find it enlightening. It might even be worth your trip."

He looked at her.

"You'll have to trust me," she said. "In the meantime, I can offer you another sherry and a modest dinner."

"You're very kind."

"A guest from New York is a rare treat." Her eyes turned almost coquettish. "Aah, but I'm not kosher."

"Neither am I," said Newman.

They rode in silence for the first ten minutes. The man driving had described himself as a mathematician and as such, he had made a point of telling Newman earlier, was given more to equations than to conversation. A gaunt, dour man without apparent humor, he had also made it clear that he was taking part in this enterprise with extreme reluctance, having agreed to it only because of Mrs. Forsythe's insistence. Besides, it could be dangerous. Great care would have to be taken. These people had proven themselves capable of anything. The detective, more curious than concerned, had solemnly promised to follow all instructions to the letter.

It was early evening, and a light breeze made a summertime murmur through the pines. Straight ahead, an orange sun sank peacefully behind a line of hills. The road, running in a dark, winding stream among the trees, was empty, and the occasional farmhouses in the distance seemed to have been deserted for a long time.

The man switched on his headlights as the shadows deepened. "A few points before we get there. I don't know a thing about you, not even your name, and that's how I want to keep it. I can't tell what I don't know. The same applies to you. The men you'll be hearing tonight are all men of prominence in their respective fields. As I am in mine."

He paused and almost allowed himself a smile. "Incidentally, I'm not really a mathematician, but I do have a penchant for equations. So that part, at least, is true. There will be six men at the meeting this evening, including myself. Five of us make up our southeastern regional council, or junta, if you will, and we meet regularly four evenings a month. The sixth man will be here tonight because he's slated to head one of our new units in another city. We're expanding so rapidly that recruiting new leaders is becoming a major problem."

He braked and turned into a rutted dirt trail. It was night here. He drove more slowly.

Norman Garbo

"I'm the official traitor," he said. "I've been in the junta from the beginning, but only to monitor what's going on. Our growth has been enormous, frightening, if you feel as I do about it. We currently have a hundred and eighty-seven units operating in forty-three cities, and we're adding an average of three a month."

Newman had questions to ask but smothered them.

"I can only assume you're someone exceptional," the man drawled. "This is the first time Mrs. Forsythe has ever asked something like this of me. Which is why I didn't turn her down. It was she who gave me the idea as well as the courage to do what I'm doing. It hasn't been easy. Some things I've had to agree to were enough to turn my stomach. I just pray to God it's all finally worth it."

The trail grew narrower, then dead-ended in a clearing. At the far end was a dark, shingled bungalow. It had a peaked roof, a wide porch, and two stone chimneys. A waning three-quarter moon offered enough light to see by as they left the car. There was the sound of rushing water, and Newman saw the glint of a stream through the trees. A squirrel bounded by and disappeared. "This is my place," said the man. "We've been meeting here for almost two years now. I built it for hunting and fishing, which happens to be about the best in the state of Georgia. So it all seems innocent enough. Our records are kept in a concealed safe. There's no electricity or telephone."

He unlocked the front door, led Newman inside, and put a match to a pair of Coleman lanterns. There was a fireplace at each end of a long room, with deer heads mounted over them. The furniture was rustic, even rough. A gun rack held half a dozen rifles and shotguns, and a cluster of fishing rods stood in a corner. Three doorways led to other rooms. Half of the ceiling, showing exposed beams and rafters, rose to the peaked roof. The other part was lower and flat and put together with unfinished pine planking to form an attic of sorts. It was above this second section of ceiling that Newman was suposed to conceal himself. A bat in a belfry.

The gaunt man glanced at his watch. "They'll be starting to arrive in about twenty minutes. Better get up there now in case someone shows early."

He brought in a stepladder and opened an almost invisible sliding panel. The detective climbed through.

372

"Get as comfortable as you can, and for both our sakes please stay quiet," said the man. It was his fourth such warning. "There's a mattress up there you can use. Do you see it?"

"Yes." Newman sat down. The mattress reeked of mildew.

The panel was closed. It cut out all light except the hairline cracks that showed between the planks.

"I'm speaking in a normal voice. How do you read me?"

"Okay," said Newman.

"We'll be directly under you, so there should be no problem hearing. Good luck."

Like Pavlov's dog responding to his dinner bell, Newman's hand went for his cigarettes and had to reject them. With a sigh, he stretched out on his back, the dark rafters close above him. A branch scraped across the roof in a breeze, and there were other small sounds he was unable to identify. So here he was, lying on a mildewed mattress in a dark attic in the Georgia woods. Waiting to hear what?

He must have dozed, because he was suddenly sitting up in a sweat, hearing voices, and trying to figure out where he was. Then it all came flooding back and he tried to pick up scattered words and make some sense of them.

He apparently had missed nothing because the last of the expected group just seemed to be arriving. There were greetings exchanged, followed by the easy small talk of men long and closely associated. Newman pressed an eye to one of the cracks in the planking. He was able to make out movement but little else. Ice clinked into glasses, and there were the sounds of drinks being poured. He swallowed and tasted whiskey.

Someone called the group to order and they settled down to business. There was lengthy talk of budgets and fund-raising and the attracting of recruits to maintain their accelerating growth pattern. Newman smothered a yawn. The whole thing sounded like the local Rotary meeting. Then he heard the words "American Crusade Party," and everything abruptly changed.

Eager for details, he saw he was going to have to wait. The new unit leader was being given a combination pep talk and orientation lecture. The council member spoke in a strong, sure voice that carried the ring of authority.

"You're good, Vincent," the voice was saying now. "One of our best. If you weren't, we wouldn't be putting you in charge of a key unit. But you do display an occasional tendency to softness and sentiment that could prove dangerous if left unchecked. We must regard ourselves as the shock troops, the front-line fighters in this cause. It's the only way we can prevail. A soldier's view of things is the only real truth that exists for us. Everything else is just so much talk, just so much Sunday school sermons for children. We may very well be a Christian organization, but we must never be misled into thinking we'll get what we want by following Christ's gentle precepts."

The man paused, apparently to let his words sink in. He's made this speech a hundred times before, thought Newman. It's probably his standard orientation lecture to the troops, honed and polished to a minor art form.

"We're not going to fail at what we're doing," the voice went on, "because we simply won't allow it. But if we do fail, it will only be because we are not hard enough. Often, to achieve our ends, violence is called for. If we waver, if we're filled with remorse because innocent lives may occasionally suffer, we're lost. We must learn the lessons taught by Christian immortals like Ignatius of Loyola. We must learn to be cruel in order to abolish cruelty, to sacrifice lambs so that someday no more lambs will be slaughtered, to use the whip and the scourge so that people will learn not to let themselves be abused without reason. Most especially, we must learn to accept the hatred of the very ones we are trying to help because we know it is the only true way to help them."

Newman's face dripped sweat into the mattress. Was he really hearing this? In the reeking dark of the attic he might have been anywhere, but he somehow felt himself back in thirteenth-century Spain, listening to a tribunal of the Holy Office during the Inquisition. It was the same line of reasoning.

"The sad truth is," the voice was saying, "there are those among us who even now are stricken with remorse over the deaths of those three children in New York. And perhaps you are one of them. Well, let me tell you, Vincent. For us, remorse, conscience, and self-doubt are the worst of all vices. There's no room in our politics for the sweet, anguishing comfort of penitence. I and every other member of this council would be willing to blow a hundred children to bits tomorrow because we know it is being done to advance our purpose. And we would weep over none of them. Unless, of course, the weeping itself might in some way be used to our benefit.''

Listening, the lieutenant's initial anger faded. He felt himself grow calm because he knew this was going to be much worse than he could ever have imagined and he wanted his wits about him.

''If you are ever tempted to weaken, to grow soft,'' said the voice, ''always remember that we have history on our side. And history has no scruples, never hesitates, never makes mistakes. You and I may make mistakes. Never history. History moves steadily toward her goals regardless of the corpses she deposits beside her path. As we must. Anyone who doesn't believe this one hundred percent doesn't belong in the American Crusade Party. Remember that, Vincent. Let it be your guide.''

The indoctrination finished, congratulations and good wishes were offered the new unit leader. Toasts were drunk to his future with the organization. After a while, Newman heard good-byes being said and Vincent left. Now the five members of the council were alone.

''All right, let's get down to it,'' said the same authoritative voice. ''The bombing was a disaster. It was so badly bungled I don't even want to talk about it. And we're to blame. It was our responsibility to see that it was carried out correctly and we failed.''

''I don't see why we should have to—''

''Stop it!'' The leader's voice cut off whoever had started to speak. ''I want no whining excuses. The ultimate responsibility for everything within the fifteen states of the eastern region of this country lies with this council. If the bombing went wrong, it was because we picked the wrong people to do it.''

''What now?''

It was the voice of the man who had brought Newman to the cabin.

''We wait and see what happens with the rabbi. If he behaves, we'll leave him alone. If not, we'll have him finished right.''

''Is that what Clayton wants?''

"I spoke to him this morning. That's precisely what he wants."

Newman shook his head as though trying to clear it. His carefully sought calm had exploded and all the keepers of his house were trembling. There was damage inside him. He felt lonely, helpless, betrayed. He was certain that the best of his life had passed and that every last moment of it had been without profit.

He was able to catch the last flight out of Atlanta. With delays and missed connections, it took him back to La Guardia at a bit past three A.M. He had left his car at the airport, and instead of going home he drove straight to Manhattan via the Triborough Bridge. Even at this hour, lights glittered like those of a magic city. At three forty-eight he reached the East Side apartment building where the police commissioner lived. It was July 3.

A uniformed security attendant stopped him in the lobby. "Commissioner Westley," he said and flashed his badge. "I'm Lieutenant Newman."

The man looked worried. "At almost four in the morning?"

"Emergency."

"He'll shoot me if I ring him at this hour."

"I'll shoot you if you don't."

The man looked at Newman's face and picked up the house phone.

Westley was waiting at his open door as the detective stepped out of the elevator. He wore a rich navy robe over silk pajamas, his hair was combed and glistening, and he seemed to have just shaved.

In the middle of the damn night, thought Newman.

Westley's eyes swept over him. "I was sure you had to be bleeding."

"I am."

"It's that bad?"

The detective nodded.

Westley took him into the library and closed the door. He poured two whiskeys, then waited until Newman had drained most of his glass. "All right," he whispered. "What is it?"

"I just got back from Atlanta. Do you know who those American Crusade creeps take their orders from? Do you know who was really responsible for that synagogue bombing?"

The commissioner sat looking at him. Elegantly robed, poised, drink in hand, he might have been posing for a *Town and Country* ad.

"None other than our own sweet messenger of God, Clayton Taylor."

A muscle twitched in Westley's jaw. "You're quite sure of that?"

"Yes."

"How do you know?"

Newman told him, letting it drain out like pus.

"Unfortunate," Westley whispered. "But I'm afraid there's not much we can do about it. Your having overheard a group of anonymous voices in a backwoods cabin hardly constitutes a case. And I doubt that your equally anonymous informer would be willing to expose himself publicly by turning state's evidence to back you up."

"What the hell has that got to do with anything? The man is a murderer. He's directly responsible for killing three children. And if Rabbi Glickstein doesn't keep his mouth shut, as I'm sure he won't, he's going to be killed, too. And you're saying we're supposed to just sit around with shit-eating grins on our faces?"

"I'm not saying anything. I'm simply pointing out the facts."

"Well, I think your facts stink."

"They're not *my* facts, Jay."

Newman felt his drink begin to flutter in his hand. Why did everything always turn out to be so much dirtier than he expected?

"What do you want to do?" Westley asked.

"Something!"

"Yes. But what?"

Newman had no answer.

"I'll tell you what we'll do," said Westley in his softest of whispers. "For the time being, we'll do exactly what we've been doing all along. We'll make full and proper use of this man until both our goals have been achieved. We'll be sensible. Confronting him now would be pointless, even counterproductive. Not only would we be warning him in advance, arming him with information we could effectively use against him sometime in the future, but we'd be turning him into an instant enemy rather than the powerful supporter we both need. And that, you have to admit, would be pretty damn stupid.''

Newman admitted nothing. But neither did he argue. What did he have to argue with? Unfortunately, his friend was right. All his evidence was in his ears. And about the only thing that it might turn out to be good for was protecting Glickstein when he needed it.

Leaving awhile later, he felt something sharp in his pocket. He took it out and found himself staring at Jacob Fein's Star of David. Lovely. He was collecting all sorts of useless Jewish souvenirs. A long-forgotten snatch of Hebrew returned. *Ma tovu ohaleha Yaakov.* How goodly are thy tents, O Israel.

So?

There was no dawn. The morning light could not free itself of mist. He had not slept in twenty-four hours, yet he felt no need to close his eyes. He could feel Mary watching him over his third cup of coffee. She watched very carefully. She's afraid I might drown in it, he thought. Two hours and finally he was all talked out. Or so he believed. He believed wrong.

"I can't do it, Mary."

She didn't ask what it was that he couldn't do. She knew. She had known long before he himself knew.

His eyes were wistful. "Promise you won't laugh if I tell you something?"

"I promise."

"I made a secret vow. I vowed I'd stop drinking the day I was sworn in as police commissioner."

She shrugged. "I don't think I'd have been able to stand you sober, anyway."

"I might have been an entirely new man."

"I don't want a new man, love. I wouldn't know what to do with him."

He put his hand tentatively on her shoulder. She was still in her nightgown and he felt the warmth of her flesh. He also felt a curious need to comfort her. He had no idea why. Nor did he even know how to go about it.

"Just one question," she said. "Are you sure you're being practical?"

"Jesus, when have I ever been that?"

"But you told me there's no legal evidence against him."

"There isn't."

"Then what can you do?"

"Nothing. But maybe, if things work out right, that won't matter."

This time she had no idea what he was talking about. "I don't understand."

He poured himself a fourth cup of coffee. He needed a moment. He was not quite ready to tell her. Certain accommodations had to be made. Certain parts of him still needed to be convinced. He had told the old lady he had been a police officer for almost thirty years and that he believed in the law, not murder; this was all true. It was not easy to dump this kind of thing. You didn't just toss it away like a worn coat. You could be left naked in the cold. You could stand alone in the dark with drips and shadows. There was even an antique terror. Your flesh could turn blue.

But there was also a little world of pain in his heart that shrieked like an eagle. He could see Cossack sabers dripping Jewish blood, and he had, after all, been born a Jew. That was first. Being a cop had come much later. He could no longer bow his head and quietly wait for the next sword to fall. He was no longer consoled by reason.

All of which came with his fourth cup of coffee. Finally, he considered himself ready to give it voice. "I can't let him just walk away from those three kids. And the way things are set up, that could be only the beginning."

Even now he was unable to say it easily. Some part of the thirty years still clung. Mary waited.

"I've decided. If I can't get him legally, if I can't stop him within the law, I'll let Richard Gaynor stop him outside it."

She sat staring at him.

"All I have to do is not tie him up as planned and let him go ahead with his big number tomorrow night."

"You don't mean it." But looking at his face, she knew he did. "This isn't you, darling."

"Maybe yesterday it wasn't. But today it's me."

"I don't like it."

"Neither do I. But there's no other way I can think of to stop him. Can you?"

Silently, she sought other methods, other guarantees of value. She found none. Nature offered life, but also took it away.

379

His voice softened. "You know me, Mary. Do you really think I could just walk away from this, just go on as before?"

"Gaynor did give you his word not to go ahead with it. Maybe he won't."

"We both know better."

"Then you're willing to let him die, too?"

"If a man wants to die, how can he be stopped?"

"That's not the way you were talking a week ago."

"It's not a week ago anymore."

"Maybe they'll be able to stop him in time," she said without hope.

"There's always that possibility, isn't there?"

"What will you do if that happens?"

"Surrender my soul and become police commissioner."

She sought to penetrate his smile. But its limits remained, unredeemed.

~~~~~~~~~~ **25** ~~~~~~~~~~

July fourth came in hot. There was not even a hint of a breeze, and a morning fog hung low over the Palisades across the river from Gaynor's apartment. To prevent any last-minute emotionalism and its possible complications, the artist had thought it best to sleep alone the night before. The two women had agreed. Kate, having arranged to be off shift for thirty-six hours, had gone home with Jane. Gaynor had slept little but was clear-eyed and alert. He felt stripped down, ascetic, prepared for whatever lay ahead. Incredible. A single night without a woman and he was an instant monk.

He had his usual breakfast of juice, toast, and coffee and went over the morning newspapers. The hoopla was still going on, with a sold-out house expected at the stadium that night and the gates scheduled to open as early as six P.M. to avoid a possible entrance crush. Although several editorialists continued to express doubt that the Apostle would appear, Harry Blake, in the *Post*, insisted that his continued silence was only a ploy to heighten tension and keep security off balance. In regard to the latter, there were separate statements from Lieutenant Newman and Special Agent Peterson that all possible safeguards were being taken but that the risk factor in dealing with fanatics always remained high. There was also an article by a Dr. Hennessy, professor of psychiatry at Harvard, who had written extensively on the psychology of extremism. Gaynor read with interest that the professor believed that avowed terrorists such as the Apostle resort to violence, paradoxically, in order to affirm their own vitality. He claimed that threats and acts of violence, even if they ultimately turn out to be suicidal, can be judged life-enhancing because the terrorist sees himself as sacrificing his own life in order to affirm the life of a principle or a belief he considers more important than himself.

So that's what I'm doing.

The telephone rang. He hoped, somehow, that it would be Jay Newman. But he heard Lutovsky's voice.

"Good morning. Still nicely packed in ice?"

The man listened and remembered, thought Gaynor. Not many did. "I'm okay."

"Everything is in place and waiting."

"Good."

"You'll find a handgun there, too—an eight-shot automatic. It's loaded and ready to fire. Just release the safety. Have you ever fired an automatic?"

"No."

"I'm sure there'll be no need for it, but I had it left anyway. A little extra insurance. If you do have to use it, hold it loosely. It tends to kick up a little."

"What about the women?"

"They're all set. Their material was left behind a commode in the Ladies' Room as planned, and all your reserved-seat admission tickets were dropped off at Jane's. You've got two exceptional ladies. You're a lucky man."

Gaynor was silent.

"That was stupid. I'm sorry." Lutovsky paused. "Anyway, I hear they're opening the gates at six, so it might be a good idea to be there at about six-thirty. That way you'll be able to beat the main part of the crowd and have time to get yourself in order. From what I've read, Taylor has turned this into a real fundamentalist religious festival, with marching bands, gospel singers, and Christ only knows what else. And he's made it a big fundraiser, besides, making them pay through the nose to hear God's voice and his. And damned if he hasn't given himself top billing."

"Why not?"

The wire hummed softly.

Lutovsky cleared his throat. "Well, good luck. I'm sure it'll go great. But if for some reason it doesn't, remember what I told you the other day. It will be taken care of."

"Thanks for everything."

"My pleasure, son."

Gaynor hung up. He sat considering the phone. It took him fully ten minutes to decide. Then, carefully assuring himself he expected nothing, he dialed Jay Newman's home number and heard him answer.

"It's me," he said.

"Naturally."

"I was hoping you might call with some good news."

"This is the planet Earth. There is no good news."

Gaynor found his hand sweating on the phone. "I was hoping you might have gone to Atlanta."

There was no response.

"It was just a hope."

The detective was silent.

"I had no right to ask something like that," said Gaynor. "You've done enough for me. I just couldn't help going for one last long shot."

"Well . . . ." Newman's voice sounded strange, like someone else's. "We all do what we have to."

"No hard feelings?"

"Hey, come on. We're friends, aren't we?"

The artist felt his first twinge of guilt. "I'd like to feel we are."

"We are," said Newman in his strange new voice.

"I've never really done anything to prove it."

"I'm sure you will if it's ever needed."

Gaynor felt no such certainty. In fact, there was something odd about the whole conversation. Newman didn't sound like himself. He was being much too polite, much too careful.

It was only after he hung up that Gaynor was able to figure out what bothered him. Not once in the entire conversation had the detective so much as mentioned either Gaynor's pledge or what today's date was.

The six private jets flew into Washington's National Airport within minutes of each other. They had come, respectively, from Los Angeles, Houston, Atlanta, Boston, and two from New York; by nine A.M. their passengers were gathered in the study of Clayton Taylor's house in McLean, Virginia.

The emergency meeting had been called just twelve hours earlier for two reasons. Having grown increasingly concerned about their chairman's safety that evening, the council members hoped to persuade him to feign illness and cancel his appearance. Failing this, they thought it at least might be provident to choose a successor . . . should one be needed.

The reverend, annoyed by the last-minute distraction, let them argue and complain but paid little attention. He had heard it all before. At one point he did find himself mildly amused. Did they really consider him mortal?

When the essentially pro forma discussion appeared to have ended, he gave them what he felt they had really come for, a few strokes for their self-esteem and reassurance for their fears. He managed both with his usual skill, projecting his appreciation for their concern and his absolute certainty that he would be as safe in Yankee Stadium that evening as he would in his own tabernacle. He also made known his personal recommendation of Bob Harding as his successor as chairman, a choice that was quickly voted upon and accepted.

Since they were all together, it was decided to turn the session into a working meeting. Plans were made to double the existing fund for operations to two hundred million dollars, with further assessments to be levied on the basis of need. The bulk of these new funds would be held in numbered Swiss accounts, with working capital kept in a dummy division of Reginald Stafford's New England Financial Corporation.

Domestically, on the basis of the ACP's recent nationally

Norman Garbo

coordinated test, full-scale action would be launched within six weeks. It would take the form of an accelerating nation-wide campaign of incitement, terror, and violence that would hurl black against white, Jew against gentile, and Hispanic against Anglo. Only one overall objective would be recog-nized: the creation of a cry of rage in the country so loud, so anguished, so filled with fear and pain, that its backlash would scourge the hides of liberals for years to come.

The council agreed, in carefully spelled-out terms, that in politics as in war the message was the same: divide and conquer. Tactically, anything that held the slightest hint of humanism had to be judged a handicap. It was that concept that made politics the most intriguing of all enterprises be-cause it most closely fit the basic nature of man, which was predatory and egotistic. "The scrupulous," declared Harding, "can be found on the losing side of everything. Morality is what the rulers impose on the ruled to make sure they both remain exactly that."

"Divide and conquer, gentlemen." It had come to be Franklin Burns's favorite expression. He had already used it three times. "And if for a while a state of anarchy may seem to prevail in our cities, and if our besieged government officials are forced to take ugly, repressive measures to re-store order, so much the better. That in itself will mean we're halfway home."

There were also major involvements to be handled on the international scene, with particular focus on the Mideast and the unending Arab-Israeli confrontation. Much of the action here would continue to be funneled through Franklin Burns's Abeco Enterprises, which maintained a steady run of building contracts in Arab countries and financed more than a dozen Palestinian terrorist units in Libya, Syria, and Jordan. It also backed other teams based in Algeria, Turkey, Greece, and southern Italy. Planned for the immediate future were the purchase and shipment of increasingly sophisticated weaponry for Arab groups on the West Bank and the supplying of qualified experts as training instructors. Included in such ordnance would be explosives using mercury trembler fuses and remote-control bombs triggered by radio devices similar to those used in model aircraft. As currently set up, a drilling team out of the International Division of Turner Land and Oil would be facilitating these arrangements while operating from one of the company's newer concessions near the Persian Gulf.

On the lengthy propaganda front, stretching all the way from the United Nations in New York to London, Paris, Rome, Cairo, and Beirut, twenty million dollars was earmarked for the continuance of the Arabs' single most effective ploy and greatest hope in their battle against the Jews in their midst. Namely, that by the simple expedient of creating and keeping alive an Arab-Palestinian identity (though, of course, at the sacrifice of the well-being and the very lives of the Palestinian refugees themselves), they might yet accomplish politically, and through terrorism and guerrilla warfare, what they had so far failed to achieve in military combat—the destruction of Israel. For all of which an appreciative Islam continued to demonstrate its gratitude with increasingly lucrative concessions and grants.

The session turned out to be an unexpectedly fruitful one.

Still, because he was after all a man of God, Clayton Taylor thought it only proper that he make a final statement before adjourning the meeting.

"We must think always in the framework of our political goals, gentleman. It makes what we're doing and what we'll continue to do that much easier. It takes time to build a new national consciousness. Right now we're starting with a totally revolutionary point of focus. What people fail to realize is that all political invention has to grow out of disunity, violence, and cruelty. Later, perhaps, we'll be able to afford the luxury of benevolence."

The reverend brought out a bottle of Napoleon and passed it around the table. "Politics is a cold, fickle bitch, gentlemen, but I do believe she loves us today."

Rising, they touched glasses and drank.

Jane and Kate arrived shortly after eleven with the elements of Gaynor's disguise. They seemed relaxed enough at first, but their nervousness quickly showed in their posturing, giggling, and almost nonstop chattering as they fooled with the artist's hairpiece and beard. His two schoolgirls preparing for their first varsity show. Yet, watching them, he found himself moved. *You've got two exceptional ladies,* Lutovsky had said. *You're a lucky man.* And in this, at least, he was.

Then the chatter and giggling faded and their expressions

took on a look of thoughtful, cool reserve, which they clung to with great care. The drill also helped. It was a good distraction from the threat of too much thought. So they went over Lutovsky's meticulously worked-out procedures again and again. The mobster had reserved seats for the two women that would place them no more than twenty feet from the grille through which Gaynor would be firing. If everything went well and the blind remained undetected, Jane and Kate would simply leave with the crowd. But if the grille was spotted, the women would release their tear gas canisters and blot out the whole immediate area. They would then put on their masks and work their way partly clear of the gas. The masks would be discarded before they reached a point where the air was clear enough for them to be seen. It was this latter possibility that bothered Jane.

"I don't like that," she said. "If we wear the masks a few seconds too long and they're noticed, we're in trouble. I think we'd be better off not using them at all."

"But then you'll be as blind as everyone else in the area," said Gaynor. "You'll never be able to get out of there."

"So we'll stay with the crowd. In all that confusion, the police will just be trying to prevent a panic, anyway. They're certainly not going to be rounding up three or four hundred possible suspects."

They discussed it for a while. The final decision was to take the masks along, but not to use them unless they were locked in and threatened.

Kate asked, "What do we do about Newman afterward? Even if things go perfectly tonight, he's still going to be waiting when you get home."

"Don't worry about him," said Gaynor. "He may love me a bit less, but he can't really turn me in without making himself an accessory before the fact. All his evidence means nothing unless he's willing to sit in jail beside me."

They had Gaynor's disguise to take up a bit more time. They covered his dark hair with an iron-gray wig, stuck on a mustache and beard to match, and whitened his sideburns with a liquid tint. Then Kate used some theatrical makeup to darken the shadows under his eyes and deepen whatever facial lines he had.

"My God, you look ancient," said Jane.

He looked at himself in a mirror and saw an old man

staring back at him with rheumy eyes. The effect was startling. Where had his life gone?

As though compelled to preserve the last of his days, he began an imaginary portrait of what he had finally become. He painted himself stooped, bent over, and walking painfully with a cane. He made his hand on the cane knobby with arthritis and covered it with brown liver spots. He turned his mouth bitter, as though just the sight of anyone younger and in better shape was a personal affront to what the years had done to him. If he died tonight, at least he would never be like this. There were worse things than dying.

But he didn't really believe it. Fool, he thought. You haven't even an idea of what you might be missing. Ah, but I do. Yet how would it help me to think about that now?

About fifteen miles away, on the south shore of the Rockaway peninsula, Mary Logan sat in Newman's bedroom, watching him dress. Hands folded primly in her lap, back straight, she sat on the edge of her chair like the obedient Catholic schoolgirl she had once been. Newman, having showered and shaved, stood in his underwear, brooding over his ties.

"The red and blue stripe," said Mary. "It looks smashing with your light gray suit."

He stood staring at the recommended tie immobilized, a man suddenly rendered incapable of decision. Mary rose, took a blue oxford shirt from a bureau drawer, and helped him into it. Then she gave him the striped tie.

"I couldn't get myself to tell him," the detective said dully. "Do you think it would have been such a terrible thing if I told him?"

"Maybe not to someone else, but to you it would have been a terrible thing." She slipped the tie out of his hands and put it around his neck. "I still say there's a chance he might actually keep his word."

"No. He'll be there." Newman's eyes were dark, without discernible light. "That's why he called. It was his way of saying good-bye."

Standing in front of him, she silently tied his tie.

"He's going to die tonight," said the detective. "There'll be a thousand guns waiting in that stadium. I don't see how it can be avoided."

"Yes you do. You can get to him right now and tie him up."

387

"No I can't."

"You mean you won't."

"Whatever."

Mary lost patience. "Then shut up and stop beating your breast. It's not doing anyone any good."

He strapped on his shoulder holster, removed the .38, and checked it. Then he slid the revolver back under his arm.

"Are you going to shoot him yourself after he does it?"

Newman looked at her.

"You'll be the only one there who knows what he looks like. It should be easy enough to spot him and stay close. Then, after he does his number on Taylor, you can shoot him and be a hero all over again. Once for saving him and once for killing him."

"I don't think that's very funny."

"I didn't mean it to be."

The detective put on his jacket. It was cut full on the left side, so there was no visible bulge from the revolver. "I expect he'll be wearing a disguise of some sort. He knows I'll be watching for him."

"You'll still pick him out."

Tiredly, he faced her. "Please don't be angry with me."

"I'm not angry. I'm disappointed."

"I'm Jewish. I follow a vengeful God."

"Suddenly?"

"Maybe not so suddenly. It's just taken a while to break through."

Her expression was flat. "You mean killing Clayton Taylor is going to help make you a better Jew?"

"I'm not doing any killing."

"Yes you are."

They stood looking at one another. When it became too much for her, she worked at straightening his tie.

"I love you," he said. The words felt awkward and strange on his tongue and he realized how few times he had ever said them to her.

"I know you love me."

"I'm sorry I'm such a disappointment to you."

"I just said that to hurt you." Her voice faded. "You could never disappoint me. You're the best I've ever known. Even when you do wrong, you do it with such pain it breaks my heart."

He touched her face and found she was crying. "Hey . . ."

"Isn't that dumb?" She wiped her cheek. "It's just that no matter what happens tonight, I know it's going to be terrible."

What could he tell her? Instead of speaking, he explored her face. Her eyes shone moistly and the tip of her lovely Irish nose glowed pink. His instinct was to reach out, pet her, do something gentle, loving, as you would to a kitten. But all he did was hold her.

Still, he had to turn at the door. "Are you going to be watching on TV?"

"I'm sure I'll have to. Whatever happens, it would be worse not knowing."

It made him feel no better.

A final security conference was held in the police commissioner's office at noon, although all plans had actually been set for more than a week. These included 1094 uniformed police, plainclothes officers, detectives, and FBI agents assigned precise positions in and around Yankee Stadium and another 120 on roving patrol.

Including Newman, there were nine New York City police officers at the meeting along with Peterson and two of his agents. The three FBI men sat together and slightly apart from everyone else, as if to establish their independent status. The commissioner was addressing the group from in front of the fireplace, directly under the portrait of former Commissioner Theodore Roosevelt. Westley looked tired and strained to Newman, with dark circles under his golden eyes. He's affected, too, thought the detective. Finally.

"I spoke to Reverend Taylor less than an hour ago," Westley was saying, "and he still refuses to take this whole thing seriously. Which is not how I feel about it. I take the threat to his life very seriously. And that's exactly how I expect it to be treated. I want every man in this room and every man assigned to this security detail to perform as though the reverend's life depended solely upon his personal alertness and behavior. Which, in a very real sense, it does. Because we have no idea how this fanatic is going to strike and no way to anticipate it."

The commissioner paused, looking as though he were in pain.

"It is virtually impossible," he went on softly, "to prevent a public assassination by a fanatic who is himself willing to

Norman Garbo

die. Our only hope is that when it finally comes down to it,
this man, this devil's Apostle, will prove sane enough to want
to preserve himself. Because if he tries to kill and get away,
he has a fair chance of failing. That's our one hope. And it
does exist, since everything the man has done up to this point
has been controlled and rational. So that's how we've set up
our security measures—against rational attack. Taylor will be
picked up at his hotel and driven to the stadium in a bulletproof limousine. All hotel and stadium employees will be
checked for weapons, and there'll be metal detectors at the
entrance gates. All members of our own security force will be
issued special lapel badges no earlier than five-thirty this
evening in case the Apostle tries to disguise himself as a
police officer.''

Westley stopped to light a cigar. The room was quiet.
From somewhere in the streets below came the faint sound of
firecrackers, although such Fourth of July celebration had
been banned in New York for years. Newman, half turning,
saw Peterson looking at him. The agent smiled, but his eyes
were faintly mocking, and Newman wondered what was going
on in that curious mind of his. Whatever it was, it suddenly
made the lieutenant uncomfortable, as though the man had
been given a talent for predetermination that was sure to
complicate further what already promised to be the single
most complicated night of his, Newman's, life.

"I've tried to get the reverend to wear a bulletproof vest
under his jacket," said Westley, "and to speak from behind a
panel of bulletproof plastic, but of course he refused. He's
afraid any such safety measures might be construed as a lack
of faith in God's protective hand. Unfortunately, gentlemen,
we can't allow ourselves the luxury of depending upon any
such divine intervention. We'll be going more by the Police
Security Manual. Which doesn't necessarily rule out prayer if
any of you are so inclined. I'll happily accept whatever
additional help you can muster for us, celestial or otherwise.''

There was more laughter than the modest attempt at humor
warranted, and Westley waited for it to die.

"The route being taken by our limousine from the Waldorf
to the stadium is not known at this moment," said the commissioner, "and will not be determined until immediately
before departure time. This should forestall any possibility of
remote-control explosives being set up along the way. Al-

390

though I frankly don't believe the Apostle would be interested in that sort of thing to begin with. It's too impersonal, too ungallant, and too lacking in possible media coverage. I tend to expect a bullet, from fairly close range, with as many witnesses and TV cameras as possible on hand. Which means I expect the attempt to be made within the stadium itself—either as Taylor is approaching the speaker's platform, while he is on it, or as he is leaving it. These will be the most dangerous periods for him, when we can offer little real protection.

"Still, whatever we can do will be done. The reverend will walk from his limousine, through the stadium, to the speaker's platform between two rows of our tallest officers and he will leave the same way. A similar row of police will be lined up in front of the platform while he is speaking. Every man will be constantly scanning the crowd for anything or anyone that looks the least bit suspicious, and there will be two sharpshooters concealed high in the area usually reserved for the press. The sharpshooters are our very best and will be using precision rifles fitted with telescopic sights. But they'll be severely handicapped by the crowd presence and therefore will fire only if they have a clear, unobstructed shot at the perpetrator. Which, of course, isn't too likely to happen."

The commissioner drew thoughtfully on his cigar. There was nothing new in what he was saying. The overall plan had been formulated days before and everyone knew his assigned role. Westley's speech merely was a last-minute pep talk to emphasize the gravity of the situation and inspire the highest possible level of performance. He stood there now, a slender, almost theatrically handsome man whose stated ambition was to become president of the United States. Too bad he's not going to make it, thought Newman.

"I'll be frank with you," whispered the commissioner. "When I last spoke to the reverend an hour ago, I asked him to cancel out. I asked him to call the whole thing off. No. I didn't just ask. I begged. And I haven't begged for much in my life. I felt that a human life, regardless of whose it may be, was worth begging for." He smiled ruefully. "But as you've probably learned, you never get what you want by begging for it. Still, I begged. And in this case I'd even be willing to beg again. Which should give you some idea of exactly how frustrated I feel."

Norman Garbo

Westley sighed. "Good luck. Do the best you can. God
bless you all."

Newman was conscious of the heavy, unnatural silence of
twelve men sitting without movement, without a sigh, a
whisper, or a cough. Slowly, they started to get up and leave.
Newman hung back. He wondered if there was perhaps something he should say to his friend at this moment, some word
that might make what lay ahead a bit easier for them both.
Then he thought, What do you say to a man whose hopes for
the presidency you were probably about to dash for all time?
He left with the others.

Driving alone toward the stadium, the lieutenant tuned out the
police calls on his radio, adjusted it to a commercial station,
and moments later was rewarded with another of the reverend's recorded sermons. Had it been predestined?

"Because man is essentially evil," said Clayton Taylor,
"God has determined that a certain number of us, completely
helpless in and of ourselves to achieve virtue, shall by the
irresistible force of his grace become truly good. In this way
God resolves for us the terrible dilemma created by his doctrines of depravity and virtue, doctrines that appear to offer us
no hope. Man, given over to selflove, is evil. Virtue, Christ
tells us, exists wholly in benevolence. The grace that God
offers is all that can bridge the gap . . ."

Not for you. Never for you, you murdering bastard.

26

It was almost as hot at 6:30 P.M. as it had been at noon. Walking toward Yankee Stadium with a crowd that jammed the sidewalks and spilled over into the gutter, Gaynor felt his shirt cling moistly to his back. The shirt was white, had long sleeves, and had been carefully selected by Jane as the kind of shirt a gentleman of advanced years might wear on such an evening. Additionally, the long sleeves covered Gaynor's arms, whose flesh and musculature in no way matched his gray hair and beard and lined face. Slightly stooped over, shuffling his feet as he walked, Gaynor felt like a neophyte actor auditioning for his first part. He also felt rather ridiculous since Newman was nowhere in sight and no one else had any reason to pay the slightest attention to him.

Police cars crawled through the gutter with the crowd. Uniformed patrolmen were spaced along the curb, studying everyone who passed. Gaynor saw them stop several people carrying large packages and attaché cases and make them open each piece. Motorcycle cops traveled slowly back and forth between the stadium entrance plazas and the subway exits from which the crowds were pouring. Gaynor himself had arrived by taxi. Jane and Kate were scheduled to follow the same way in about half an hour.

Moving along with the crowd, he gazed up at the mammoth stadium directly ahead. Flags and colored pennants hung limply in the still air. A flock of pigeons swarmed, then came to rest along the parapets. Peddlers hawked souvenir pennants and lapel buttons bearing the Apostle's bearded face. From somewhere inside the stadium, a marching band could be heard banging away at a brassy rendition of "New York, New York."

America, America, thought Gaynor.

Wooden barriers funneled the crowd toward the entrance gates, where attendants were going over ticket holders with metal detectors and where additional police were watching for any packages that might have been missed earlier. Gaynor himself was watching for Newman. He found he was terribly thirsty, as though he had not had a drink in days and the last of his body fluids had leaked out. And it was not simply the heat. He felt as tight as a guitar string. *I guess I'm more nervous than I thought.* Pressed by the crowd, he took several deep breaths and began to feel better. An officer with a metal detector examined him and waved him on. It was then that he saw Newman.

The lieutenant stood with two uniformed cops, scanning the crowd as it entered. He was several gates down from Gaynor, but his glance seemed to sweep the entire area. The artist shuffled forward a foot at a time. As he was handing an attendant his ticket, Newman's eyes, moving in smooth passes like a gun turret, briefly touched his and continued on. Gaynor pushed ahead. There was no one else he had to worry about at this point.

Then he was walking once more with the crowd, hurrying slightly now and forgetting all about his old man's shuffle. The band was louder here, the big bass drums going *boom . . . boom . . . boom* and forcing him into step. They were playing "The Battle Hymn of the Republic," surely the most moving, most inspiring marching song ever written. "Mine eyes have seen the glory of the coming of the Lord . . ." Who wouldn't march anywhere, do anything, to words like that?

He turned right and entered the refreshment area, where the smell of hot dogs and popcorn was thickening the air and people were already lining up to eat. God help them if they couldn't keep their mouths full for half an hour. There were uniformed police here, too, most of them strolling in pairs. Gaynor was also able to pick out a few plainclothesmen from the way they stood with their feet planted.

When he came to a Men's Room, he stepped off to one side to light a cigarette. Directly behind him was the narrow passageway that led to the utility closet he had to reach. A souvenir stand partly hid him from view. When he felt certain he was unobserved, he backed into the passageway, reached the utility closet, and let himself in with the key Lutovsky had provided. Hearing nothing behind him, he turned on a small, powerful flashlight, opened the trap door in a corner of the closet, and entered the conduit. He closed the trap door over his head and sat down. He was breathing heavily. Under his wig and beard, his face dripped sweat. It was cool in the conduit, and the wet shirt, sticking to his back, made him shiver. He was in.

Newman thought, My God, look what he's done to himself, and found it hard not to stare. The old man disguise was actually pretty good, but not if someone was watching for it. There was enough gray hair there to stuff a pillow. The only real surprise was that Gaynor had arrived so early. Newman had expected him much later in the evening so that he would have less time to wait for Taylor's arrival and therefore face less chance of discovery.

Leaving his two officers to their gate-watching, the lieutenant followed the tall, gray-haired man who had entered a moment before. He stayed well back in the crowd, barely keeping a tip of gray in view over the intervening heads. His caution, he soon realized, was unnecessary. Evidently considering himself safely past the entrance and free of detection, Gaynor did not once glance back. Still, because it was simply good tradecraft, Newman maintained his proper interval. He strolled casually, nodding to some of his men at their assigned posts as he passed. For all intents and purposes, he was just making a routine check.

He watched Gaynor turn off into the refreshment area. He saw him slow, then stop by the Men's Room to light a cigarette. Newman stopped also. Better be careful, he thought, or you'll light up your silly beard. The detective searched his pockets for a cigarette of his own and found an empty pack. The move took only a few seconds, but when he looked up for Gaynor, the gray head and beard had vanished.

He watched the Men's Room for almost ten minutes. When Gaynor failed to reappear, he went in to check. The suddenly aged artist was not there. Nor were there any windows or other possible exits. Leaving the room, he checked both sides and discovered a narrow pasageway on the left. He followed it to the end and came to a utility closet. He tried the door. It was locked. He stood staring at it for a moment. Then he took out a ring of wire thin skeleton keys and had the door open in less than a minute. Using a pen flash, he searched the walls and floor of the small utility room until he found the outline of a trap door. Gently, quietly, he eased it open. When he flashed his light into the opening, he saw the conduit stretching off and disappearing toward what had to be the front of the stadium.

"Beautiful," he breathed. He felt so great a surge of relief, something approaching so pure a state of elation, that he almost went light-headed with it. For this surely was not the undertaking of a crazy kamikaze. This was no suicidal attack of a death-oriented fanatic. Somehow, Gaynor had worked out a plan. Newman had no idea what it was, but, it did seem to promise at least the prospect of a controlled shot, from good cover, and perhaps even the possibility of survival.

Tempted to see where the conduit led, he rejected the idea as pointless and dangerous. Why tempt fate? There was no telling what protective measures Gaynor may have set up behind him. So he replaced the trap door and left the utility closet.

Once outside, though, he had to know more. Following the direction the conduit had taken, he found that it led to the forward grandstand area directly in front of the speaker's platform. Of course. Where else?

He walked very slowly and casually now because he had spotted Peterson about fifty yards up in the stands and the agent was watching him. All about the stadium, in every aisle and at every level, uniformed police and plainclothesmen were patrolling their assigned areas as the crowd continued to flow in. To put on a small performance for Peterson, the lieutenant stopped a man carrying an oversized thermos, showed him his badge, and asked to inspect the bottle. When the man complained that it had already been inspected three times, Newman said, "Great. Now let's go for four." The thermos held two quarts of iced tea.

He went down to the front row of box seats, where three workmen in hard hats were installing a pair of floodlights directly below. Feeling Peterson's eyes still on him, Newman leaned down. "What are you men doing here?"

"Christ! Not again!"

"Let's see your IDs."

He made a five-minute show of checking through their equipment and identification.

"Why wasn't all this done earlier?" he asked. "Why now?".

"Because now is when those TV faggots decided their goddamn cameras needed more lights hitting the speaker's stand. I mean, we've been fucking around with this shit for a week, but *now* is when they decided."

The lieutenant walked away. A fresh marching band had appeared, strutting across the infield to a blaring rendition of "Onward, Christian Soldiers." Newman seemed to be watching the band, but he was actually noting the position of the lectern and microphones on the speaker's platform. Then he tried to figure out where the conduit would be most likely to surface in relation to where Clayton Taylor would be standing. It could be anywhere within a radius of several hundred feet. And although he crisscrossed the aisles and steps of the entire area, he saw nothing. Which was exactly what he should have expected to see, he thought. If he could have found it that easily, others would have, also. He had to assume that if Gaynor had given the project this much thought, he would have had to come up with something more effectively concealed.

The idea pleased him. He had obviously underestimated the artist. Turning, his glance happened to fall on Jane and Kate, who were sitting together in what appeared to be the exact center of his target area. Pretending not to have noticed them, he kept walking. A whole new range of possibilities began to form.

High up in the glassed enclosure reserved for the media, Harry Blake was doing the commentary for the Continental Television Network. Several cameras covered the action on the field and in the grandstand; others were set up outside the stadium in anticipation of Taylor's arrival. Occasionally, one of the cameras focused on Blake himself as he spoke. His face glistened with perspiration despite the air conditioning, his cheeks were flushed, and his hands and body moved with the quick, almost spastic, lurching of someone approaching the extreme limits of control.

Seated beside him was the Apostle dummy, wearing the earphones of a co-anchorman. Earlier, to help fill the long stretches of empty waiting time, Blake had carried on one of his fictional dialogues with the mannequin. But as the crowd poured into the stadium, the reporter's mood changed, and he seemed totally caught up in the tension and drama of the event building before him.

"Ladies and gentlemen, we don't get the chance to say this very often," he told his audience of millions with the quiet intimacy of a friend confiding something important, "but there's a feeling here in this stadium that what we're about to witness may end up in the history books.

"We say this regardless of what you may think of the two participants involved. Because, approve or disapprove, there's a new kind of happening taking place tonight. You might even say we're sitting in a unique sort of cathedral of the absurd. And if this is so, we may be about to see a passion play with such powerful forces at work that the political, moral, and religious traditions of this country—traditions that have seen preachers becoming politicians and assassins changing the course of history—might never again be quite the same."

Gaynor crawled along the conduit, following the white beam of his flashlight. The passageway appeared much longer this time, and he began to wonder whether he might have unknowingly turned off on one of several connecting branches. A rat moved in front of him. Was it one of his old friends or a stranger from another district? Then his light picked out the substation directly ahead and he was home.

Again, he found himself breathless. Either he was in terrible shape or was more tense than he cared to admit. He placed his flashlight on a ledge and started to loosen the thumbscrews that held the ventilator grille's steel cover in place. Then he stopped. Stupid. With the cover off, someone might just happen to spot the grille and begin asking questions. Also, he would have to keep his flash on while getting things in order, and the light was sure to be seen. The cover would be better left on till the last possible moment.

He opened the suitcase that had been left for him and found everything in place. He took out the rifle parts and assembled them without any problem. Then, very delicately, he slid one

398

of the explosive cartridges into the open breech, pushed the bolt forward, gave it a half turn downward, and put on the safety. His weapon ready, he carefully stood it in a corner.

He next went over the gas mask and tear gas canisters, although he did not really expect to need them. He tried on and adjusted the mask, which was very small and compact and, according to Lutovsky, had been especially designed for CIA use along with the canisters. All three items fit neatly into a green canvas webbing that could be belted about the waist and worn, without detection, under a loose shirt. Finally, he took out the automatic that Lutovsky had mentioned on the phone that morning. Extending his arm, he squinted along the barrel and caught the flashlight's gleam in the V of the rear sight.

He glanced at his watch; it was not quite seven-thirty. Clayton Taylor was scheduled to mount the platform at nine o'clock. He had an hour and a half to wait.

He turned off his flashlight, sat down in a corner, and tried not to think. The grille cover was not airtight and he could hear a band playing and many voices singing "Nearer, My God, to Thee." He wanted a cigarette very badly but was worried about where the smoke might drift. Just relax, he told himself, and stay properly packed in ice. But it was not easy, and after a while the darkness became too much and he turned the flashlight back on. Being able to see somehow made it easier. Stop whining, he thought. You're not here to make anything easier.

To help pass the time, he began one of his mental paintings. He made it a sunrise because it was his favorite time of day, with the early mists floating free and the slow lightening of the sky that came before the actual appearance of the sun. He placed a stand of pine against some clouds, painting the trunks solid and brown, the branches a cool, lacy green. He breathed deeply, imagining the sweet smell of the pine needles and feeling their softness beneath him as he lay on the ground. And he thought, I'm never going to breathe and feel anything like that again because I'm going to die here tonight.

He thought it, not in panic or fear, but in his properly controlled and icy way. Which meant he was ready to stop playing let's pretend and to face things as they were. All this planning and cleverness had made it easier for everyone, but now it was time to accept the facts. There was no way he was going to be able to shoot this man and walk away from it. Which was all right with him. He had accepted this part, had made his own special peace with it a long time ago. As long as Clayton Taylor didn't walk away from it either.

He looked at his watch and saw that it was just a minute or so past eight o'clock. What the hell, he thought. Cutting the light, he loosened the four thumbscrews on the steel grille cover, took the plate off, and peered out.

He saw nothing unusual. There were the two bands playing in the middle of the infield and a huge chorus of white-robed men and women lined up in front of them singing "Rock of Ages." At the far end of the field, the stadium was dark with people, and the flags and pennants above them still hung without movement in the dead air. Looking toward the speaker's platform, he saw three men on ladders working on some floodlights. The lights were mounted on brackets attached to steel poles and were evidently being focused to hit the precise center of the platform, where the lectern and microphones were. At least Gaynor assumed they were there. Because, from his carefully worked-out position behind the grille, his view of that particular area was sufficiently blocked by the new construction to prevent his seeing any part of them.

At 8:05, the lieutenant was still trying to work out the details of Gaynor's operation. He had to know for himself. It was more than just curiosity. He felt an overpowering emotional commitment to its success. It was blossoming inside him. Jehovah's secret plan of vengeance. No. It was Gaynor's. The same thing. Weren't we all part of God's long arm on earth? Or was he just turning into a religious nut, a mystic, a Jewish Holy Roller? Which had to be the craziest thing yet. Still, he might be able to help in some way.

At one point he had almost considered approaching the two women. He had wanted to go over, take them to one side, and say, "Listen. It's okay. I'm your guy's friend. I know he's here and I approve of what he's doing. But I have to know more. Tell me how, when, and where, and maybe I can do him some good." But of course he had done nothing of the sort. Not with Peterson still watching him. Besides, the women would never have trusted him enough to tell him anything. Nor could he blame them. Thirty-six hours ago he would not have trusted himself.

Nevertheless, it was Jane and Kate who helped establish the logical parameters of his search. The location of their seats was no accident. They were not here as spectators but to offer some kind of help. So Gaynor had to be concealed fairly close to where they were sitting. Newman imagined a fifty-foot circle with the two women at its hub. He patrolled the aisles, ramps, and steps with apparent casualness, but his eyes missed little. Yet nowhere did he see anything like an opening through which a hidden sniper might aim a bullet at the speaker's platform.

Bands are playing, thought Newman, choirs are chanting their hymns, and more than a thousand armed security people are watching for a man who at this very moment is buried in concrete, pointing a rifle at what is certain to be his carefully prescribed killing zone.

He tried a different approach. Leaving the grandstand, he walked out onto the infield grass. He climbed the steps to the speaker's platform. The rostrum's front and sides were hung with bunting, and a row of chairs was lined up across the rear. The chairs were still empty of their expected dignitaries, who were not scheduled to occupy them until 8:55. The police commissioner and the mayor would be arriving with Taylor himself, at nine o'clock.

Pretending to check out the platform, Newman approached the lectern, where a communications specialist was adjusting the microphones. He asked for and was shown the man's identification. Then he stood there for a moment, staring off toward the grandstands, seeing pretty much what Clayton Taylor would be seeing when he stood at this same spot in just about forty-five minutes. He saw several squads of exceptionally tall policemen standing at ease on the grass as they waited to take their positions in front of the platform. He saw the three workmen still belaboring their new floodlights and, behind them, the kaleidoscope of bright summer clothing that now filled the stadium. He was even able to pick out his friend Peterson, who at this point was watching him from behind the first line of box seats.

Zeroing in on the section of stadium directly in front of the lectern, he looked for Jane and Kate in order to orient his search. For a moment he was unable to find them. Then he saw that they were partly obscured by the newly installed lights. He looked all about them within his imaginary fifty-foot circle. Nothing. There was no visible opening for a rifle. Puzzled, he left the platform.

He was halfway to the grandstand when he saw it. Walking back at a slightly different angle, he saw the small, barely perceptible grille. It was in a concrete abutment supporting a line of forward seats; the detective wondered why he hadn't seen it from the lectern.

He turned, walked back, and again climbed the platform. He was still unable to see the grille, but this time he understood why. The new lights were in the way, blocking his line of sight. Just as they would also block Gaynor's carefully set-up line of fire. His entire scheme was dead, scrubbed, finished.

Hollowed out and desperately in need of a drink, Newman slowly returned to the stadium.

Man makes plans and God laughs, Gaynor thought.

Still, he was no worse off than before he had met Victor Lutovsky. He was, in fact, better off. At least he was in the stadium, he had a loaded automatic, a gas mask, and a pair of tear gas canisters, and he had a diagram of possible escape routes if he ever got that far. It had never really been part of his original idea to get out of this, anyway. That was Jane's contribution. Strange, though, how he had almost known it would come to this. Maybe he was getting psychic. It was said that those near to dying often develop such powers.

But it was still a shock and his mouth tasted of bile. Or was it just fear? There was nothing wrong with being afraid, he told himself. Everyone ended up afraid. It was only bad if you thought about it too much. What he had to do now was stay with what he believed and just take it from there. That was all he could do. It was 8:19. At this point, his only real chance would be to get him on the way in, while he was glad-handing the crowd. Otherwise he would never be able to move in close enough. But I still mustn't be stupid. I still must think this through and do it right.

He put the cover back on the grille. Then he turned the flash to his diagram to determine the most logical place for Taylor to make his entrance. If he knew the man at all, it would have to be through the main gate and the center ramp. Entering in triumph, the holy shepherd would want his flock pressing close about him. His security people might try to talk him out of so exposed an approach, but no true demagogue would be able to resist it. Should the high priest be asked to steal into his tabernacle like a poor thief in the night?

He studied the diagram for possible escape routes. If he was lucky enough not to be blasted away the moment he opened fire, he just might have a chance. Not only would there be panic in the immediate area, but if he could release his tear gas canisters, he might be able to create enough cover to let him reach one of the trap doors.

According to his diagram, there were three such possibilities within a reasonable distance of the entrance ramp. The two closest were actually under the ramp itself and about a hundred feet apart. The third was the one in the utility room. If he could get to one of them without being noticed, if he could stay holed up there for a while . . . Sure, he thought. If, if, if.

But at least it was a hope, something to work toward. Which was infinitely better than just going out there to die.

Then he remembered Jane and Kate. He had to let them know, but how? Not by sitting in this hole, he thought, and he took off his shirt. Then he tied the canvas webbing about his bare waist and slid the two canisters and gas mask into their respective pockets. When he put his shirt back on, it buttoned over everything with room to spare. He let the ends hang loosely over his belt, into which he now stuck the automatic. Nothing bulged and he was able to move his arms freely. He was as ready as he would ever be.

At 8:32 he left his bunker and crawled back through the conduit.

He's not going to let those lights stop him, Newman was thinking. Not now, not after all he's been through to reach this point. He's going to have to come out of there and do it the hard way, but he's still going to do it.

It was 8:40.

But what a bloody shame, and after all that lovely planning. You had to have a little luck in this world. Mazel was what his mother used to call it. But mazel was something Richard Gaynor seemed to have run out of a long time ago.

Roving the aisles, Newman was watching Jane and Kate. If he had been able to spot the problem, they must have seen it, too. And since they obviously had been scheduled to be part of the original operation, they would also be involved in any contingency plans. Assuming there were contingency plans. In any case, he was sure that by watching Gaynor's women, he would soon be seeing Gaynor. Which made him feel better. Also, Peterson seemed to have disappeared. The agent was no longer tracking him like an omniscient eye—in itself, cause for celebration.

At 8:46 the stadium was full, although people were still milling about the aisles and ramps, hoping for a glimpse of their messiah's arrival. On the speaker's stand, surrounded by great banks of flowers, the line of chairs now held most of the expected dignitaries. Bands and choruses continued their celestial strains while the unctuous voice of a master of ceremonies soared above them through the loudspeakers, expounding the significance of the occasion and whipping up additional fervor. The American way of life and the greater glory of God were mentioned often, with the implication clear that the two concepts were irrevocably entwined. There was also a protracted comparison between conditions in America today and the collapse of the Roman Empire, when hedonism, sexual debauchery, and godlessness were everywhere and the disciples of Christ were being martyred by the antecedents of the same unbelievers who were the antichrists of the twentieth century.

God! thought Newman, open your ears in the greatest city on earth, and this is the kind of shit you hear.

The ugly, historically inaccurate peroration reached its climax in thundering boasts about the inner strength of the American people and the American Fundamental Church and warnings to those who threatened its leaders. Newman looked at those about him, well-dressed, orderly men and women, whose faces, attentive to every word, were suddenly proud, defiant, exalted. It was as if they could see before their eyes a shining symbol, perhaps even the Second Coming, and themselves—each of their poor, mean souls—redeemed. All right. But why on the bodies of innocent children? Could it be that God was not impressed or moved by their deaths? If so, he, Newman, was.

The gray beard and hairpiece he had been watching for suddenly caught his eye. Ah, he was out. Newman had not seen him emerge, but at this moment Gaynor was pushing through the aisle directly in front of where Jane and Kate were sitting. He slowed as he passed and looked their way. Then he walked on.

A moment later, the detective saw the women leave their sets and follow him. When they had gone about fifty feet, Newman also followed, keeping a long interval and staying well hidden in the shifting crowd. He checked the time; it was 8:52. If Taylor arrived on schedule, he would be making his entrance in eight minutes. The lieutenant tried to think like Gaynor. Since he could only be carrying a handgun with an effective range of no more than fifteen feet, he would have to get in close. Which meant he was heading for Taylor's entrance route. The next idea occurred, and it hit him with all the warmth of a solid shot of whiskey on a mean winter night. He doesn't have to die, he thought. He can do it and I can still keep him alive. I saved him once, I can save him again.

Newman felt as though he had blundered through a barrier and was floating free. He would just have to watch him and stay close. When Gaynor finally fired, when he had done what he had come to do, he, Newman, would be on him before either the FBI or his own cops could blow him away. And with a good, skillful psychiatric defense, how could so obvious a mental case not be declared legally insane? They shot presidents these days and got away with no more than a vacation on a funny farm. The artist would be free in five years.

Gaynor, too, was feeling better. Fortunately, Jane and Kate had needed no red flag waved in front of them. The instant he caught their eyes in passing, he had seen that they understood. Newman had turned out to be a happy bonus. For which Gaynor was grateful. Some part of him had never really expected to deceive the detective with his amateur's disguise. Another part of him had not even wanted to, a faint hope having persisted that when it finally came down to it, Newman had to feel as he did. If not, the detective surely would have found something more binding than the charade of a forced vow to ensure his not being here tonight. Still, catching sight of Newman standing quietly off in the crowd, watching Jane and Kate—and knowing, too, that the lieutenant had seen through his disguise and was offering tacit approval by doing nothing about it—had brought a special exhilaration of its own.

He worked through the crowd and headed for the main ramp. Police were spaced at regular intervals, trying to keep the aisles clear, but it was futile. There was too much electricity in the air, too much heat and excitement. Turning left toward the central entrance gates, he saw Jane and Kate a short distance back, Newman about twenty feet behind them. My convoy, he thought.

The massed choirs were singing another hymn, and thousands of voices in the stands were picking it up and joining in. Was that really what God wanted to hear? Was he so shallow that clichés of praise were enough to touch him? Gaynor hoped not. If he was destined to stand before him within the next ten minutes, he hoped he might be judged by other criteria. Such as? he asked himself. But he had no answers. His willingness to die was certainly no answer. God had never yet shown himself to be touched by death. Not by any single one and not even by millions.

He saw two lines of uniformed police standing at the base of the ramp where Taylor and his entourage would be making their entrance. An impatient crowd pressed close. Gaynor eased his way through, elbows held close to protect his ordnance. Taller than most of those around him, he was able to see and maneuver without trouble. Sweating profusely under all his false hair, he looked for his convoy. Jane and Kate were there, struggling to stay close, and Newman was right behind them. The detective seemed to have abandoned the last of his pretense. He was no longer even bothering to disguise his presence or interest. Above the crush, their eyes met and held briefly. For Gaynor, there was no longer any doubt. They felt the same.

The artist worked toward his chosen position. Remembering his diagram, he was trying to station himself as close as possible to the trap door under the main entrance ramp. He was thinking survival. Which both pleased and disturbed him. Was there a special morality in simply wanting to stay alive? A biological duty? The hell with that. All he wanted to do was shoot the bastard. It was about then that Newman saw Peterson. The FBI man must have been following him for some time because he was just off to the right, slightly behind him and not more than seven or eight yards away. Newman also saw two of Peterson's agents. All three men were shoving their way through the crowd, but they were not even looking at him. They were headed straight for Gaynor, whose hairpiece and beard, askew with sweat, were suddenly so obviously false they seemed to scream it.

Newman swallowed a mouthful of panic. He felt like a child ready to weep. I've led them to him, he thought dully. They've been watching me all along for this very reason and I've taken them straight to him. Once they were this close, his silly disguise did the rest. Without a plan, without the faintest idea of what he was going to do, he started after the three agents.

There were shouts and cheers at that moment, and he saw Taylor stepping out of his limousine. The mayor and Michael Westley were close behind him. Somewhere, a band was playing music from Handel's *Messiah*. With his first glimpse of Clayton Taylor's face, primitive feathers of malice began stirring in Newman's brain. They had been there, growing, ever since Atlanta. He had some savage notion that demons were adrift in this human devil, this great horned goat, this congenital liar, this purveyor of hate and murderer of children, who rose on his hind legs and walked through adoring throngs like a savior. But dread also came in and he thought, What good am I, of what real value can I ever be to myself or anyone else, if I do nothing to stop this pestilence from infecting us? Yet a fear broke loose in him, too, like the funk that comes on a man who is forced into a fight he does not want or feel ready for.

Stop it! he told himself furiously. Stop pissing in your pants and do something. Yes, but what? Anything, he thought, anything that will keep that smartass agent and his apes from interfering with what that poor guy, buried under all that fake hair, is about to do.

But he was finding it hard to make forward progress. The crowd, pressing toward their approaching leader, packed itself tighter. Peterson and his men were having much the same problem. Still, they were closing in.

Oblivious to what was taking place behind him, Gaynor watched the reverend and his retinue approaching through the two lines of cops. Caesar entering Rome in triumph. It was classic. The only thing missing, thought Gaynor, were the flower petals being strewn at his feet. Bands and choirs echoed from the center of the stadium, adoring followers shouted his name, and there were even those who struggled to reach past his embattled police guard just to touch some part of him.

The reverend responded graciously. He smiled, he waved, he shouted greetings. He paused to shake hands and exchange words with those able to get close enough to make contact. When several of his security people nervously tried to hurry him along, he shook them off. It was his only show of impatience.

Gaynor was in the third row of disciples behind the police line. Taylor was still about fifty yards away, advancing slowly, squeezing the most out of every second for the television cameras. When he passed directly in front of where Gaynor was standing, there would be no more than ten feet between them. It would be hard to miss at that range.

Gaynor no longer bothered to glance behind him. He knew exactly where Jane, Kate, and Newman were. He wondered when and why the detective had changed his thinking and come around. Regardless, Gaynor felt only gratitude for the result. The feeling came up in him the way the words of a half-forgotten song might remind an old man, alone and near dying, that he had once known love.

Still, looking at this man, this Clayton Taylor, approaching, was not too different from leaning over the edge of a high balcony and feeling your stomach sucked out of you. Gaynor could almost sense the fall.

Someone in the reverend's party spoke into his ear and pointed to his watch. Taylor started to move more quickly. Gaynor reached for his gun.

They're going to get him, thought Newman. I'll never make it in time. It hit him with all the shock and sickness of a kick in the groin, and he could feel a full twenty-four hours of whiskey turning rancid. At that moment he would have been willing to pray, had he believed in such things. But whatever good was due him had to be born of valor, not religion. Terrific. *Then show some guts, you whiskey-livered schmuck, and do something.*

Lurching forward, he drew his revolver. It was an absolutely idiotic move, yet it somehow felt right. He saw Peterson turn and look at him. There was raw satisfaction in the agent's stare, perhaps even triumph, and it stung like salt. Yet what was he supposed to do, shoot the man for being smarter than he, for only doing his job? There would still be the other agents to stop, anyway, and it was impossible to wipe out the whole FBI. Besides, the only one he wanted wiped out, obliterated, surgically removed from the earth's crust like a new form of cancer, was that devil's son marching along like a grand marshal of an All Saints' Day parade.

Just the thought took the air from his lungs. Yet he pressed ahead, shoving aside those in his way, while the revolver in his hand trembled like a divining rod as if straight in front of it, yes, in this very direction, it was pointing towards some as yet unveiled absolute of evil. Do it, just go ahead and do it, he thought, and he sensed a vital point of balance going wild in his brain. Which made it easier, because there wasn't even logic or fear to hold him back now. There was a lot of noise, a lot of shouting, but he barely heard. He knew he had lost some part of himself. Yet he knew, too, that he was better off with it gone, that all it had ever been was the willingness to accept failure and compromise and be ready to die without complaint whenever it was so ordained. Die he might, but, sonofabitch, not with failure and compromise, and most surely not at anyone's choosing but his own.

The revolver, seeming alive, tugging at his fingers, carried him forward. When he felt close enough and had a clear line of fire, he lifted the gun and aimed with both hands. Calmly, he squeezed off a cluster of three quick shots. *That's for the three kids, you murdering shit, one for each.* He was going for the chest rather than the head because he did not want to risk a single miss. Then he got off his second group of three. The first shot was for Duv Glickstein, the second for his grandfather, Israel Newman, who understood such things and would have approved, and the last was for himself because he had come late to such understanding and needed it badly.

All six shots were squarely in the killing zone.

Gaynor was reaching for his own weapon when the first shots went off. There was so much other noise that he thought they were firecrackers until he saw the red flowering on Clayton Taylor's shirtfront. Then he spotted Newman. The detective was just getting off his second cluster, his revolver raised above the heads and shoulders of those in front and the three shots exploding so close together they sounded like one.

Gaynor stared dumbly. *Why?*

It was the only question he had time for. With the last explosion still echoing, Jane and Kate released their canisters, and a cloud of tear gas enveloped the area.

There was instant pandemonium. People shouted, cried out, and groped blindly. They fell to their knees and tried to crawl, but it was no use. Their eyes streamed. They were unable to see. Off in the stadium, the music and singing went on.

God bless my ladies, thought Gaynor. Reacting quickly, he slipped on his breathing mask and headed straight for where he had last seen Newman. It was no more than ten feet away, but he had to climb over people to get there. He was bursting with love. Imagine that man.

He found him groping blindly with everyone else. Three uniformed cops were kneeling nearby, unable to see him. His empty revolver was still in his hand. The artist pressed close, lifted his gas mask slightly, and spoke into his ear.

"It's Gaynor. I've got a mask. Let me lead you."

The detective nodded. He stood very tall and straight, his head tilted upward. A blind man, listening. Tightly closed eyes streamed tears. Gaynor took the revolver from his hand and put it in his shoulder holster. Then he led him like a child among and past the late messiah's weeping, coughing disciples.

The gray mist had spread and the canisters were still pumping. Gaynor glanced around for Jane and Kate. They were nowhere in sight and he assumed they had lost themselves in the crowd. Even with the mask it was not easy to see. But it was only a short distance to the trap door under the ramp, and Gaynor lifted the cover and helped the detective down. No one was near. Mass coughing and wailing rose from the gas-shrouded area. Incongruously, the bands and choruses almost drowned out these sounds. Gaynor lowered the trap door over his head and the sounds faded.

They crawled along the conduit and branched right until they reached the substation where Gaynor had waited earlier. He sat the detective in a corner and wiped his eyes with a handkerchief.

"Well . . ." Gaynor began, but it all clotted in his throat.

Newman sat exactly as he had been placed, a blind man weeping gas. Through the grille cover, the music could still be heard. Then it began to die out in small pieces as the news filtered through the stadium. Finally, there was only the sound of a bass drum beating, *boom . . . boom . . . boom.* The drummer, lost in his own vibrations, was apparently the last to receive the word. When this, too, ended, all that remained was the hum of thousands of voices.

Wearly, Gaynor pulled off his hairpiece and beard and tried again. "I don't understand. What in Christ's name made you do it?"

Newman just blinked. He was blind and mute.

"He was supposed to be mine," said Gaynor.

"You'd never have made it. Three agents were on your back. Another few seconds and they'd have had you."

"That's not possible."

"It's the truth."

"But how?"

His voice dull and toneless, Newman told him.

"But that still doesn't explain why you did it," said Gaynor.

The detective looked vaguely surprised. He hadn't the energy or heart to explain. "Someone had to."

Gaynor turned off his flashlight to conserve the battery, and they sat together in the darkness. Outside, the murmur of voices gradually died as the stadium began to empty. It took a long time, as though everyone was reluctant to leave. The performance they had paid to see had been played offstage, out of sight. They felt cheated. Still, an important man had died there that night, and they were alive. It was impossible also not to feel superior.

When the last of the voices was finally gone, Gaynor said, "Go easy on yourself. It's all over."

"Maybe for you. For me, it's just begun."

"You said it yourself. Someone had to do it."

It took the detective a long time. "That was how I felt when I was firing."

"It's still true."

"No." The word was barely audible. "I believe what I've always believed. I did the worst. I murdered a man. And I'm not making any excuses because murder is inexcusable."

Gaynor heard faint shouts off in the distance as the police still tried to clear the shooting area. "Yet you were ready to let me do it."

"There are no excuses for that, either. But your finger on the trigger still wouldn't have been mine."

411

Gaynor was silent.

"Aah . . ." The sound came as a sigh. "The thing is, I never thought I'd have to live with it. There were a dozen guns on me. I thought I'd die. You miserable bastard," whispered Newman. "You really fixed me good, didn't you?"

And he means it, thought the artist.

Just before dawn, there was a tapping on the outside ventilator cover. A man's voice said softly, "Are you there?" It was Lutovsky.

Gaynor put his mouth to the grille. "We're here."

"The last of them is gone. You can come out."

Gaynor switched on the flashlight and began collecting his ordnance.

Newman touched his arm. "Who the hell is that?"

"Victor Lutovsky. He was the one who set everything up."

The detective stared at him, his face shadowy and drawn in the narrow beam of light. "*The* Victor Lutovsky?"

Gaynor nodded.

"Jesus, I should have known. A megalomaniac artist and a fucking yid gangster."

27

Newman might have been swimming underwater. Alone in the back of the car, he felt pretty much the same sensations he remembered feeling as a boy, with the lovely silence and the weightlessness and all the sharp edges pleasantly rounded off.

For a while he had been aware of Gaynor and Lutovsky quietly talking in front, but he had managed to reduce their voices to a faint murmur and now even that was gone. Still, there they were, all three of them together—a mythical syndicate boss, an artist with a Lancelot fixation, and a lieutenant of detectives turned assassin. Three dolls in a Jaguar.

They had left the Bronx and were driving north, taking a circuitous route of back roads. Lutovsky had come prepared with a documented list of police checkpoints on the major bridges, tunnels, and parkways, and these had to be avoided. The detective had gathered that they were headed for someplace around Mount Kisko, where Lutovsky evidently had a country house. It all seemed part of an insanely elaborate conspiracy to preserve him, as if the act of shooting Clayton Taylor had suddenly made him enormously valuable. Indeed, Lutovsky seemed to be treating him with the quiet deference and respect generally reserved for either a highly esteemed holy man or someone dying of cancer. Newman himself felt much less estimable and holy than terminal. All this trouble, and in the end they would get him anyway. He despised wasted effort. It would have been simpler for everyone if he had been finished right there on the spot.

Then, for the first time, as if he had unconsciously been protecting himself from so painful a perception, he thought of Mary. Ah, God. She had seen it all on television. Diving deep, he took himself back underwater.

"Lieutenant?"

It was the third time Lutovsky had addressed him. This time, looking up, he saw the racketeer's eyes in the rearview mirror. They were not bad eyes, as such things went. They were dark and Jewish and might even have seemed caring if he had not known better.

"Yes?"

"There's something you should know. It was all over the news before." Lutovsky hesitated, a man searching for the best way to make the implausible seem less so. "They think you're the Apostle."

Newman kept his eyes on the rearview mirror, but Lutovsky was watching the road now, a ribbon of light with dark trees crowding in on both sides.

"What are you talking about? Who thinks I'm the Apostle?"

"Everyone. I guess it was just taken for granted. The

Apostle was the one who threatened to shoot Taylor in Yankee Stadium, you're the one who shot him, so naturally you have to be the Apostle.''

"That's crazy."

"Only to the three of us and a few others. To everyone else, it's an accepted fact.''

The detective stared at the back of Gaynor's head. "Not to the cops. They may be a little slow, but they're not morons.''

"Maybe to them, too," said Lutovsky. Some of the commentators are predicting confirming evidence within twelve hours.''

"What evidence?'' said Newman, and quietly slid back underwater.

Lutovsky's country place was modest for a millionaire syndicate boss—no more, really, than an oversized cabin of half-round logs. It had a two-story living room and a few bedrooms leading off a balcony. The three men were alone, Lutovsky having gotten rid of his bodyguards along with everyone else. Around them were five thousand wooded acres to ensure privacy.

It was daylight when they arrived, with the sky a pale orange and the rising sun throwing purple shadows on a stretch of lawn in front of the house. A fast-moving stream was in back and mountains showed above the tops of the trees. Birds called. A pair of cottontails bounded across a clearing. It was idyllic, but Newman felt no better. He felt nothing at all. He was a dead man, peering through a crack in his coffin.

Lutovsky made some eggs and coffee, but Newman just sat drinking Irish whiskey while the other two men ate. A tranquilizing numbness was beginning to take over. Pretty soon he might even try to surface.

"Why are you doing all this?" he asked Lutovsky. "What am I to you? Once, years ago, I even collared you on an illegal gambling rap. Do you remember that?''

"You were just doing your job." Lutovsky smiled. "Besides, I was never indicted.''

"He's like you," said Gaynor. "A born-again Jew. He's also got lovely humanitarian instincts.''

Newman studied the color of his whiskey. The connoisseur. "He's a crook and a killer, probably the biggest running loose today.''

"You overestimate me."

"I've seen your file. If anything, I'm on the low side."
Newman made a small mock bow. "I'm sorry. It's not polite
to drink a man's whiskey and insult him. It's just that I'm a
little upset. I've never shot an unarmed man before."

"Stop beating your breast," said Lutovsky. "All you did
was what needed doing."

Newman retreated once more into silence. I'm losing my
mind. Now I'm talking high-level moral issues with a career
rackets boss.

"I'll tell you something, Lieutenant. A few days ago I let
our friend Gaynor know that if he wasn't able to handle this
deal, I'd have it taken care of for him. So cheer up. That momzer would have ended up dead whether you shot him or not."

They kept the radio going throughout the morning. At
noon, a police bulletin confirmed what previously had been
only rumor. In an official statement attributed to Commissioner Westley, it was announced that new evidence indicated
that Lieutenant Newman, who last night had shot and killed
the Reverend Clayton Taylor, did, in fact, appear to be the
long-sought suspect known as the Apostle.

Why would Michael be party to that kind of lie? Newman
wondered.

Further details were added as the day wore on. The most
conclusive evidence was the discovery of a Henri Bendel
shopping bag in the closet of Lieutenant Newman's apartment. The bag contained not only the Apostle's mask and
gloves, but the same .38-caliber service revolver that had
been stolen from a police officer in a Bronx parking lot.
Ballistics now showed it to be the same weapon used in the
shooting of the Apostle's earlier two victims in New York
and Atlanta.

Newman brooded over a fresh glass of Lutovsky's good
Irish. A new kind of lie seemed to be building. It was
composed entirely of truths.

The lie expanded.

With the infallible wisdom of hindsight, a small parade of
witnesses marched forth to add their own personal truths to
the growing falsehood. Michael Westley came first, recalling
Newman's eagerness to be placed in charge of the Apostle
investigation and his angry response when the FBI was called
in. In looking back, declared the commissioner, it now was

Norman Garbo

easy enough to understand Lieutenant Newman's concern. More truths were offered by Special Agent Peterson, who carefully detailed the lieutenant's conspiracy to confuse and render ineffective the FBI's investigation of the case.

Although no further documentation of Newman's guilt was needed at this time, it nevertheless was presented by Detectives Mulcahy, Robbins, and Loretti, all members of Lieutenant Newman's squad and all unanimous in corroborating Peterson's testimony. Newman had indeed given them specific orders to do everything possible to thwart the FBI's probe into the case. Finally, the lieutenant's height and build matched perfectly the descriptions offered by the few witnesses who had actually seen the masked perpetrator in the past months.

Gaynor had been watching the detective. "So how do you feel about our hallowed system of justice now?"

"It's in even deeper trouble than I thought."

"It doesn't bother you?"

"What?"

"Being taken for the Apostle?"

Newman's dark eyes looked back. "We once talked about this. I said if you compromise, you're a fake, and that the only one I knew who never compromised was the Apostle. Do you remember that?"

"Yes."

"I also said that this might be bad for everything else, but it had to be good for his soul. Do you remember that, too?"

Gaynor nodded, and they sat in the high-ceilinged room, not quite looking at one another. The radio was still going. Lutovsky stood at a window, not moving, gazing out at the distant hills.

"Well, the point of all this remembering," said Newman, "the point of my prattling on like this while you sit there with that smug grin, is that you asked whether it bothered me to be taken for the Apostle." He managed a kind of smile. "What I'm trying to say is that the answer is no. It doesn't bother me."

The detective called Mary, although he was sure her phone would be tapped by now.

"Hello?" she said.

"I'm okay. Don't worry."

"Oh, lordy . . ."

416

"I love you."

"Yes. I know."

"Just be patient."

"Haven't I always?"

He hung up before there was any chance of the call's being traced.

Gaynor was faced with no such concern. As poor as his old man's disguise may have been, it had still been good enough to hide his identity. He called Jane's apartment, assuming that Kate would have stayed over. He heard their voices as the two extensions were picked up almost simultaneously.

"You were beautiful. You saved the day. Both of you."

He heard what sounded like a double sigh.

Kate asked first. "Are you all right? Where are you?"

"I'm fine. So is our friend. We're both up at Lutovsky's place."

"What made him do it?" asked Jane.

He told them.

"It's wild," said Kate. "Have you been listening to the news?"

"Every word."

"What about the lieutenant?"

"Lutovsky will work something out. He can do anything," said Gaynor.

"Come home!" chorused his women.

It was not until close to evening that Newman thought of Zvi Avidan. He called the Israeli Embassy in Washington, was connected with Colonel Netter, and told him he had an important message for Major Avidan.

"Can you tell me what it is?" asked Netter.

"No."

"Where can he call you?"

"He can't. I'll have to call him."

"What is your name, please?"

"Newman."

There was a brief silence. "*Lieutenant* Newman?"

"Yes."

"Aah," said the colonel, and gave him a New York number.

Avidan answered on the first ring.

"This is Newman."

417

It took the intelligence agent several beats. *"Mazel tov!"*

"I've finally got something for you," said Newman and told him what he had learned in Georgia.

The wire hummed softly. "Why didn't you let us take care of it?"

Newman had no answer, at least none that made any sense. What could he say? That he had never even thought of the Israelis until ten minutes ago? That whatever sort of madness had taken place in his brain since his visit to Georgia had somehow eaten away all rational consideration and behavior? Or was the truth of it that he had simply done what he wanted to do and that nothing, not even the deepest psychological and metaphysical probing, would ever come up with anything better than that?

"What's the matter?" he said. "You feel cheated?"

"There was nothing personal in this for us."

"Well, there sure as hell was for me." Maybe *that* was it. "Anyway, I've got a few others for you."

He gave Avidan the names that Mrs. Forsythe's man had passed on to him.

"Adoshem!" The major sounded impressed. "Those are big ones. You're sure?"

"I've no reason not to be."

Neither man spoke.

"We appreciate this, Lieutenant."

Newman said nothing.

"I don't know what your plans are, but we can take very good care of you in Israel."

"I'm still an American. Remember?"

"It's not going to be easy for you here."

"It never was."

28

On July 11, five apparently unrelated incidents took place within hours of one another in widely separated parts of the United States.

In the salt marshes near Galveston, Texas, William Turner rowed out to the same duck blind he had been using for seventeen years, and put out his decoys. He was alone, which was how he preferred to hunt these days—without dogs, boatmen, or shooting companions and nothing to break the quiet other than the ripple of water and the soft whisper of wings when the flights came over.

It was not yet daylight, but the sky was turning pink in the west. Turner was wearing hip boots and an old olive-drab camouflage jacket as protection against the early morning chill. He had brought two guns, and he placed them against the wall of the blind, with his shell bag hanging on a hook between. He moved his shooting stool to where it would allow him the widest possible swing from left to right. Then he opened a box of shells and filled his pockets.

In front of him the water was still. Beyond that, as the sky lightened, he could see more marsh, and in the distance, the open sea. He felt a breeze on his face and knew it would grow stronger as the sun came up. Which meant that some birds would come flying in from the sea when the wind disturbed them. He loved shooting birds about as much as he loved anything and was looking forward to one of his better mornings.

Rarely one for philosophical introspection, he had been in a foul, brooding mood all week. Clayton Taylor's death had affected him more strongly than he liked to admit. It was such a stupid waste. Not that he had ever cared much for the man. The reverend was much too pious and superior to ever really get close to. But something like that shook you, made you wonder about things.

Then he saw the rowboat.

Lying low in the water and with a single man at the oars, it eased out from behind a spit of marshgrass. Turner was furious at the intrusion, but what could he do? Not even he owned the wetlands. Still, his solitude was broken and his anticipated morning ruined. And probably by some stinking nigger who couldn't shoot worth a damn, anyway. He watched, scowling, as the boat drew closer.

But the lone boatman turned out to be white, not black, and no one that Turner had ever seen before: a wide-shouldered man with dark eyes, who brought his boat right up against the blind and shipped his oars.

"Mr. Turner?" The man's speech was not from around here.

"That's right. Who the hell are you?"

"I have a message for you, sir."

The man held out his hand and Turner looked at it. He saw nothing else.

His body was found late that afternoon by another hunter. He had been shot at close range by one of his own guns. The Galveston Coroner's Office listed it officially as death by accidental gunshot.

The girl sighed into James Billings's ear as he entered her, and offered him a kiss that was full of the smell of honeysuckle. Indeed, it was very like a first kiss except that it was just a trifle too practiced. Whatever true passion might have once been in it had long before been replaced by technique. Still, she was young, unbelievably lovely, and her body was about as perfect as mere flesh could be. But perhaps most stimulating of all to Billings was that she was someone other than his wife.

There had never been any promises between them. The girl knew she was just one of many for the media mogul. But she was more than content with an arrangement that had already taken her immeasurably further as a news personality than her talents alone would have allowed. Even now, in a Philadelphia hotel to which she had flown from Chicago and he from New York, the act of love was not the sole reason the Galatea chairman was there. He had simply summoned her to provide a pleasant interlude between corporate meetings. And she, of course, had dropped everything to come.

Having exorcised his small demon, he lay quietly beside her. The room was high in the hotel and outside, the wind was up. Billings could hear it too well; it had the sound of a hungry gale at sea. Somewhere a siren was screaming, and he could all but sniff out the sour rot of blood in the streets. It spoiled the moment because he knew there were mysteries to which he would never find solutions. And he had a sudden hatred of all mystery, an instant when he despised all that he was and just wanted his life reduced to clear, simple events with logical answers. Had he believed in God, he would have prepared a long list of questions for him to answer. Yet Clayton had been a believer. What good had all his divine answers done *him?* So he had to settle for his usual sexual feast in a hotel, with its inevitable bitter aftertaste.

They were in one of the larger suites. Music was drifting from the stereo system, so neither of them heard the door open in the adjoining sitting room. Their first indication of anything was the sight of a tall man in a ski mask, pointing a silencer-lengthened revolver at them.

"Don't be afraid," he said. "I just want money and jewelry."

Naked, they lay staring at him.

"You'll never get away with this," said Billings.

"Over on your stomachs," ordered the man.

They did as they were told. Pathetically, the girl tried to cover her nakedness with a sheet. Moving as though to help, the man tapped her neck with the hard edge of his hand. It was a light blow, but it left her unconscious. Billings, his face in the pillow, was not even aware it had happened. Nor did he see the man lift his revolver, take deliberate aim, and squeeze the trigger. Even then, there was only a soft *whoosh*.

Later, there was a certain amount of awkwardness because of the circumstances of Billings's death. He was, after all, a nationally known figure as well as a married man. As the weeping girl tried to piece things together for the police, she could only assume that Billings had somehow tried to attack the gunman while she was unconscious and had been shot in the attempt. Since everything of value had been stripped from the room, there seemed little doubt that robbery had been the primary motive.

It was a wet, ugly night with the rain hitting the coast highway in sheets and the Pacific pounding hard at the cliffs below. The weather had been bad all the way from Los Angeles, but Franklin Burns was driving his Ferrari, and this in itself was about as close to a peak experience as he was capable of achieving these days. Apart from the automobile's sheer physical beauty, just listening to the almost lyrical hum of its engine and feeling the power of its response was a consummate joy.

Especially made for him, the sports car had cost more than two hundred thousand dollars—the most expensive, nonprofessional racing machine in the world. That itself meant little to a man who had, after all, turned barren deserts into modern cities. What did matter was that this exquisite piece of handcrafted machinery was capable of giving him more pure pleasure than anything alive and human.

Swinging right, he left U.S. 1 for the spiraling road that led up to the Condor's Nest, the huge stone and redwood aerie he had cantilevered two thousand feet over the Pacific. The road climbed at a steep thirty-degree grade, but the Ferrari took it in high gear without any effort. High-speed wipers swept the windshield clear of rain, and wide beams cut a path of light through the darkness. On the right were scattered rocks and trees and a swollen stream racing downhill. Off to the left, the foam-flecked dark of the ocean pounded the cliffs.

Burns's hands on the wheel and the violence of the night heightened his sense of control. Just as the sudden death of someone you knew heightened your own sense of life. Which was exactly how he had responded to Clayton Taylor's assassination. There was no real feeling of loss, only relief that it was the reverend who was lying dead and not himself. Fortunately, with Bob Harding already selected as the new chairman, the transfer of leadership had been managed with a minimum of bickering and confusion.

Rounding a blind curve, the Ferrari's headlights suddenly picked out a highway maintenance truck blocking the road immediately ahead. Slightly beyond the truck were two striped barriers hung with flashing lights. As Burns braked to a stop, a highway worker in glowing orange rain gear left the truck and came toward him.

Burns lowered a window and squinted against the pelting rain. "What's the trouble?"

"A tree's down ahead." The man bent to look at his face. "You're Mr. Burns, aren't you?"

"Yes." Impatience showed in his voice. "Listen, I've got to get home. When will you have the damn thing cleared?"

The worker, a big man with a craggy face, seemed to consider the question. Then, almost casually, he thrust a hand through the open window and pinned Burns's head against the back of the car seat. His other hand slammed against Burns's larynx. As the builder slumped forward, a cold chop broke his neck.

The Ferrari was found smashed against the rocks at the base of the cliff early the next morning. It had evidently skidded on the curve and jumped a wooden guard rail. A large rock, clearly loosened by the rain and discovered on the road, was the apparent cause of the accident.

Reginald Stafford swam easily, letting his body roll with each stroke, feeling strong, loose, and tireless in Nantucket Sound's early morning calm. There was an occasional gentle swell, and he could feel himself lifted in a long slow glide. But mostly the water held him steady. Gazing out toward the horizon, he sensed the long, sleeping bulk of Hyannis Port behind him. The beach was far off and fading and he was quite alone.

He knew there really was no sense to it. Cramp out here and it was all but certain you were through . . . fish food. Well, fish had to eat, too. But he was neither amused nor ready to turn back. As if gripped by an implacable current, he kept swimming. It was one of his major conceits. Decades before, he had just missed an Olympic bronze, and he still took pride in his ability in the water. Yet swimming alone and this far out every morning had to be more than that. He swam in a silence that had no air left and that somehow made him feel wonderfully free of waste and guilt. Sometimes he even felt that if there were mermaids around somewhere and that if they could speak, he would have no trouble understanding them.

423

But he had also spent enough years on the couch to recognize an obvious compulsion to self-destruct. Why else this need to place himself at risk? He wasn't too different from the reverend, in that respect. Good God! For the man to have walked deliberately into a self-imposed death trap. Still, it was easy enough to be smart with hindsight, and who was he to throw stones at the dead?

So he swam. Pushing himself harder and farther, he had the sensation that something of him was passing through a corridor. Then a hot breath came over his face. When the breath turned suddenly cold, he swung around and started back toward the distant shore.

"Mr. Stafford!"

At first he thought it was just an echo in his brain. Hearing it again, he lifted his head and saw a launch coming up alongside him. It's motor had been cut and it was drifting close. He treaded water, seeing the rising sun pink and low over the windless surface. A bald, middle-aged man leaned over the side of the boat, one hand extended as though to help him aboard. His first thought was of a possible emergency at the office; his second, that his father, riddled with cancer for two years, had finally died. In either case, he was more curious than concerned.

Then, without apparent reason, the reaching hand was suddenly on his head. It grasped his hair and pressed him downward. Helpless, he felt himself go under. He fought to get free, but the hand was incredibly strong and he was unable to break its grip. A new and unidentified fear broke loose in him and all he wanted was to escape, to be some sort of rational, producing man again, nailed tight to ordinary details, blind to the pull of the dark.

It was too late. Somewhere near the end, a dim sense of dread opened wide inside him, as if he knew that this was where he had been headed all along and that there was nothing he possibly could have done to change it.

It was several days before Stafford's body washed ashore. Its discovery caused little surprise among Hyannis Port's summer residents, well acquainted with the banker's unorthodox swimming habits. Their only wonder was that he had not drowned sooner.

High on the thirty-second-floor penthouse of Atlanta's newest residential tower, Robert Harding was spending a relaxing evening tending his plant collection and listening to Brahms. With his wife at her mother's for the week, he felt pleasantly free of her chronic nagging and the social pressures she consistently created for him. Sometimes he wondered why he had married at all. He and his wife were childless, and after the first few years, there wasn't a thought or idea of any significance that he could remember Genevieve contributing to the possible enrichment of his life. Of late she was actually becoming abusive, the other night having gone so far as to accuse him of being incapable of demonstrating even the slightest evidence of human compassion. My wife, he thought.

The statement hadn't really bothered him. In the world in which he functioned, compassion could be a dangerous weakness. It was the classical form of betrayal, in which the temptations of God were usually more lethal to a proper course of action than those of the devil. As long as money, position, and power were the going things, God was a risky indulgence. Clayton Taylor had put his faith in God when he entered that stadium, and now he was dead. If you heard Christ's voice when key decisions were to be made, the safest thing was to cover your ears.

Well, they would all miss Clayton, but in the end his vanity and faith had made him behave foolishly. Now that he himself was heading the council, that part would be very different. Only their goals would remain the same, unalterable constants.

He paused in his pruning to gaze out over the lights of Atlanta. It was a fine, clear night, and off to the southwest the faint glow of the reverend's floodlit White Christ was visible on its distant hill. His memorial.

Harding heard a slight sound behind him and turned to see a man coming through the terrace doors. He was carrying a metal toolbox and wearing the white uniform of a building handyman.

"Sorry, sir. When you didn't answer the doorbell, I thought no one was home and used my pass key."

Harding had never seen him before, a short, fair-haired man with a slender build. "What is it? What are you doing here?"

"You have a leaky shower, sir. I was sent to fix it."

"There's no leak in my shower. You people seem to give your best service when there's nothing wrong."

The man smiled. He had straight, white teeth in a sensitive face. He should be carrying a violin, not a toolbox, thought the new council chairman. The man was very close now, and Harding saw pinpoints of light in his golden eyes. Then there was only the dark.

As the Atlanta police later put it together, it was simply one of those unpredictable accidents that all too often happen in the home. The tall potted shrub that Harding had evidently been trimming had landed beside him in the gutter, along with the pruning shears. A small stepladder was found against the penthouse parapet where the shrub had stood. Harding had obviously lost his balance on the ladder, made a desperate grab at the shrub to steady himself, and pulled the plant over with him. It was noted without comment that when the police entered the apartment, a Brahms requiem was playing on the stereo.

On July 12, Major Zvi Avidan arrived at Kennedy Airport more than three hours early for El Al's 7P.M. flight for Tel Aviv. It was not at all unusual for him. He was and always had been a confirmed worrier about time and everything else beyond his immediate control. It was a trait that was often difficult to live with, but it had not only kept him from ever missing a plane, it had also kept him alive.

In the next two and a half hours, the five men he had been worrying about flew in from their different parts of the country. When they were all finally gathered in a secured lounge, a bottle of perhaps a bit overly sweet Mount Carmel red was opened and poured.

"L'chaim," said Avidan. Which meant "to life."

"L'chaim," said the five agents.

No irony was intended. It was about as solemn, even sacred, a toast as a Jew could offer.

EPILOGUE

It has been said by those who should know that the Federal Bureau of Investigation is best noted for three qualities: its limitless resources, its long memory, and its unwillingness to forgive.

For the approximately twelve weeks following July Fourth, Special Agent Peterson saw to it that Mary Logan was kept under twenty-four-hour visual and electronic surveillance. Day and night, she went nowhere and spoke to no one without being observed; her home and office calls were monitored, and she received no mail that previously had not been opened and read. Peterson was a devout believer in the constancy of emotional attachments. Particularly for a man with the tried and proven loyalties of Jay Newman. It was simply a matter of having the necessary time and patience. He was certain that Newman would run short of both long before he himself did.

Then on the morning of October 2, Mary Logan left her apartment and went to work just as she did every day except Saturday and Sunday. She remained in her office until 1:05 P.M., when she went out to lunch. She dined alone at a small Italian restaurant, where she had eaten several times before, and started back to her office at 2:10. On the way, she stopped at a branch of the Manufacturers Hanover Trust Company to take care of some banking. She left the bank at 2:36 and hailed a taxi, which drove west on Forty-ninth Street, turned north on the Avenue of the Americas, and somehow was lost to the agent following her before it reached Central Park. When a computer check was made on the license number, the taxi turned out to have been stolen.

Mary Logan never returned to her apartment. Nor did she appear again in the office in which she had worked for the past fourteen years. All of her clothing and other possessions remained behind, but she had closed out her checking and money market accounts and withdrawn their entire proceeds ($47,522) in cash. Special Agent Peterson sent out Wanted bulletins on her to every police department and FBI office in the country. Later, he also sent them abroad. It was all without result. Mary Logan had vanished. As far as Peterson was concerned, neither she nor Jay Newman would ever be seen again.

Some months later, however, a man and a woman calling themselves Arthur and Francine Foster moved into a cheerful white cottage not far from San Francisco Bay. Their minds and bodies were clearly those of Jay Newman and Mary Logan, but their faces were not. When they looked at one another or gazed in the mirror, each of them saw a stranger. The only features they could recognize were their eyes, which had remained the same. The rest belonged exclusively to Arthur and Francine Foster, who had sprung full-blown into the world, complete with backgrounds and documentation that included driver's licenses, credit cards, and Social Security numbers. In addition, there was a Master of Social Work degree for Francine and a Doctor of Law for Arthur, both miraculously authenticated by their universities of origin. All of which was presented through the courtesy of a grateful Victor Lutovsky, a born-again Jew with the power to work miracles.

So they lived together in the golden light of the bay, gazed into one another's unchanged eyes, and were pleased by what they saw. People, unfortunately, were still being burned, shot, and blown up. Newman guessed they always would be. But at least they were not exclusively Jews, blacks, and Hispanics. There was some small satisfaction in that. Besides, what more could he do? He had already made his personal contribution—which he still felt compelled to label murder—and had found it was not for him. What absorbed him now was studying the law again, loving Mary, and enjoying the substance of their days.

They looked younger now. They were also more beautiful.

"Why not?" said Lutovsky's friend the surgeon. "A little bonus. No extra charge. Young and beautiful might not be everything, but old and unbeautiful are a lot less." Even the doctors had become stand-up Yiddish comics. Still, it was not too bad to scrape off a few years. Lines and bags were nothing to be ashamed of, but neither were they any great honor. Actually, Newman enjoyed looking at Mary's new face and she seemed to delight in his. But the feeling they shared was still the same. As were the ghosts, which were not always easy to escape. Sometimes they talked about them. When they did, it was usually Newman who initiated it. They bothered him more. They were, after all, essentially his.

"I wonder if they're still looking for me," he said.

She knew enough just to listen and not answer.

"I think Michael Westley would be just as happy to let it die," he told her, "but not Peterson. He'll spend the rest of his life looking. It's a personal thing with him. Apart from everything else, I made him look like a fool. God, how he must despise me."

"Let him. *I* love you."

He looked into her blue, unaltered eyes. It did seem so.

"And for whatever it's worth, so does Rabbi Glickstein."

That, also, was true.

On July 5, the rabbi had issued a statement to the media from his hosptial bed. "Last night," he declared, "Lieutenant Jay Newman, a Jew, struck a strong personal blow for his people. Today he is being hunted as a murderer. Which, in a strictly legal sense, he undoubtedly is. Yet within the broader, truer context of history, would he not be better judged as having merely made proper retribution? Haven't Jews died graciously long enough? For two thousand years we've turned the other cheek, and lost not only both cheeks but our heads as well. In this latest and most enlightened of centuries alone, we have more than six million bodies silently testifying to this. If they could speak, surely they would say, 'No more. Enough is enough.' To survive among predators, it is finally necessary to become part predator yourself. This is sad but true. Wherever Jay Newman may be, I do not condemn him. I understand what he has done and why he has done it. He has grown me a new leg. I feel more whole now than before that bomb exploded. I bless him and I pray for him."

His new champion. There were few such in evidence. At

429

times, it seemed, none at all. Against all good judgment, he had watched Clayton Taylor's funeral on TV and found it less than consoling. He apparently had shot a saint. Dozens of dignitaries were there to pay their last respects and a senator delivered the eulogy. He extolled Taylor as a dedicated man of God, an outstanding patriot, and a true prophet of his time. Not a word about the American Crusade Party, Duv Glickstein's missing leg, or the three murdered children. Newman wondered if he had just imagined all that.

What he did not imagine was hearing himself described as a renegade police officer who had not only betrayed his sacred oath to uphold the law but who had viciously taken the life of a man who considered him a friend and supporter. If God was in his heaven, the senator declared, he would surely make payment. Sitting before the senator's large-screen, full-color image, Newman had waited for God to strike. He would have been happy to make payment right then and there. When nothing happened, when he remained untouched by divine vengeance, he could only assume that God had left his heaven for someplace else. Which came as no great surprise.

Then there was Michael Westley, an especially difficult ghost to exorcise because he had been a friend.

"You don't just walk away from thirty years," he told Mary. "And without a word of explanation."

"Forget him."

"I've tried, but it still bothers me."

"Then explain."

Newman looked at her.

"He can't see your face over three thousand miles of wire," she said. "Call him."

Newman thought about it for a month. Finally he called him at home, on his private number, at three o'clock in the morning, New York time. He wanted him straight out of sleep, before he could button up his defenses. His wife slept in another room, so Newman knew he was alone when he picked up the phone on the third ring and whispered a shaky "Yes?"

"Hello, Michael."

It took several long beats to work through. "Jay?" The whisper cut out like a faulty engine. "I was wondering when you would get around to calling."

"I felt I owed you some word."

"Naturally, you would feel that way. You're just that kind of congenitally self-righteous boozer. But what I can't figure out is how, being what you are, you're able to live with murder."

"It's not always easy." Newman paused to fortify himself from a pint bottle he had brought into the booth. In case Westley later tried to trace the call, he had flown all the way to Chicago to make it. It was that important to him. "But when it starts getting to me, I just think about the American Crusade Party and those three kids."

"I should have known you couldn't hold still for it."

"How could *you*, Michael?"

"I wanted to be president."

"And I wanted to be commissioner. But my God!"

"I was never as virtuous as you."

"What kind of virtue," said Newman flatly, "turns a man into a murderer?"

"Obsessive. The most dangerous kind. I was a fool. I should have let them kick you off the force a long time ago."

After more than thirty years, they seemed to have nothing to say to one another.

"Are you all right?" said Westley.

"Reasonably. Considering."

"I assume your lady is with you."

"Yes."

"You did a lovely job of getting her away. They tell me Peterson chewed up a whole carton of cigarettes." Westley chuckled softly. "He's still looking, you know. So don't get careless."

"I won't."

They tried to look into one another's hearts across seven hundred miles. In a way, they did.

"Just one thing," said Westley. "Where it counted, you were usually smarter than I, but I don't want you to think me a complete fool. I know you were never the Apostle. I never believed that nonsense for a minute."

Newman stared at the phone. "Then why—"

"Do you think I'm going to be silly enough to tell the FBI they don't know what they're doing? Besides, I thought you'd appreciate the irony."

"You're really a very nice man."

"I don't mean to be."

"Yes you do."

Again they were silent.

"I appreciate your calling," whispered Westley. "Keep in touch. I might still be president someday."

"I hope so, Michael. You'd make a damn good one. You're unprincipled enough to be the very best."

Richard Gaynor's exhibition was scheduled to open on the Saturday evening immediately before Easter Sunday. It was to be launched with a major reception at the Sanders Gallery in its new, larger quarters on East Fifty-seventh Street. The evening was being projected as a lavish, black-tie affair, with many notables invited along with a carefully selected list of critics and collectors. The prospect of viewing Gaynor's first collection of new work since his miraculous and celebrated escape from death had made the invitations the most eagerly sought of the current art season. And being nothing if not the quintessential showman, Marvin Sanders was intending to go all out in his arrangements.

"I've waited a long time for this," he told Gaynor. "And we both know there were moments when I never expected to see it at all. Now I'm really going to milk it."

Benignly, Gaynor let him enjoy himself. Why not? He had been loyal, a friend and supporter when such items were in painfully short supply. Gaynor made only one stipulation. No one was to know of the exhibition's theme or see a single canvas until the night of the opening. Sanders was pleased to agree. So much the better. As far as he was concerned, it would only add to the interest and suspense.

The art dealer went all the way, even to the hiring of two Brinks guards to escort the crated canvases from Gaynor's studio to the gallery. Then he and the artist unpacked and hung the paintings and arranged the lighting themselves. When they were satisfied with the overall effect, they locked the doors to the exhibition room. No one would be allowed in until ten o'clock that night.

It was an extraordinary approach for an art show. At most such openings, the guests would drift in over a two-or three-hour period, pick up their obligatory champagne, and wander about, looking lightly at the paintings and deeply at one another. Not this time. When people arrived that evening, they were served hors d'oeuvres and champagne in a large anteroom, where they were entertained by a celebrated string quartet as Sanders greeted and moved among them. Gaynor himself was nowhere in sight. He was behind the locked doors, alone with his paintings.

There were fourteen canvases in all. Which, for Gaynor, was a considerable amount for the time involved. He generally was not a fast painter. Yet this time, having once decided what he was going to do, everything seemed to have come together and flowed. There were no dry periods, no days of uncertainty, no overworked passages, no angry smears, no brushing or scraping out. It was as if it had all been collecting inside him, waiting for release. He had heard about artists working through such cycles of spontaneous gestation, but this was the first time it had ever happened to him. Usually he labored, pushed, poked, suffered, and changed direction a dozen times before he finally achieved what he wanted. Sometimes, not even then. But this had been only the purest kind of joy.

He also was grateful to Sanders for his understanding. Art dealers were known to be opposed, on principle, to any sort of controversial theme, and what he had wanted to do was about as controversial as you could get.

"To be honest," said Sanders, "I don't know why you feel the need for this. But if that's what you want to paint, I say go ahead and paint it."

"A lot of people are going to be angry. They'll hate it."

"So they'll be angry. So they'll hate it. You can't please everybody. If you did, you'd be a lousy artist."

"You might not sell a single painting."

"If it has your name on it, I'll sell it. And remember, Goya's controversy helped start the Spanish Revolution, and Daumier's polemics got social justice for the French."

How could you not love a guy like that?

Jane and Kate had been wild about the idea but worried about the possible danger.

Gaynor had been amused. "After what we've been through, you're worried about a few paintings?"

But everybody bore their own marks of danger and sacrifice. This was theirs. Besides, there were different standards now. When the problems were no longer so clearly life-threatening, you tended to adjust downward. They had the right to be prosaically nervous again, even petty and jealous.

433

Yet, with it all, there turned out to be astonishingly little of that. They remained two women who claimed to want the same man, yet some sort of accommodation seemed to have been made. Or did they prefer it that way? Maybe they simply had shared too much too successfully to want to risk breaking up the triumvirate. Gaynor himself was not complaining. Forced to choose between them, he had no idea what he would do. Or perhaps Victor Lutovsky, still curiously patient with Jane yet surely unwilling to wait forever, would one day try to offer a final solution even to this. Jewish gangsters had their needs, too.

So he sat alone with his paintings, the murmur of music and voices drifting softly through the locked doors. This was normally a difficult time for him. These last few moments of waiting were usually the worst of all, with that stripped-down feeling that left you naked before strangers. You were most vulnerable then. They could attack you reasonably or unreasonably and there was no way to fight back. And never mind those fools who told you not to take it personally. How else could you take it? That was *you* nailed up there on those walls.

But not tonight. This time it was different. He really didn't care what they thought tonight. These were his own tics, his own batch of poems. With these, there was no way they could touch him. At 9:55 he took his last look. He was certain it was the closest he would ever come to true satiety.

His back to the doors, Gaynor offered himself the same sweeping view that the more than two hundred guests would share as they entered. There were no chandeliers. The only light came from a circle of pinpoint spots in the ceiling and focused on each of the fourteen canvases.

Directly opposite the entrance, in what was obviously the focal position of the show, was a large, almost life-size rendering of a fourteenth-century knight in glistening armor. He was astride a great white horse, rearing against a background of clouds. The canvas was painted in the classic style of the old masters, with strong umber and gray shadows and a golden wash glazing everything with a beatific light. The knight carried a lance in one gauntlet and, incongruously, a whiskey bottle in the other. The visor of his helmet was lifted and the tough, proudly Semitic face beneath it was unmistakably that of Jay Newman.

The other thirteen canvases were not as large but were painted in the identical Renaissance manner, showing strong lights and darks throughout and warm, luminous colors. Their mood was soft, almost mystical, and the unifying theme was a graphic representation of the brief, flaming career of that same contemporary knight who had called himself the Apostle. Each painting depicted another trial, another ordeal, in his pursuit of grace through justice. They did not, of course, come close to resembling the true Stations of the Cross, but those with even a faintly religious bent might have sensed a hint of such an analogy. For a quiver of heavenly hosts seemed to shine from each, along with the distant glow of jeweled cities. Indeed, nothing under God's own sky appeared capable of offering anything but pleasure. Which, in some undefined way, seemed entirely the Apostle's doing.

There were his fourteen canvases. He felt no great certainty about their artistic merit. Perhaps they even leaned closer to illustration than to fine art. But that was not important. What mattered most was what they had to say and that he had been able to say it at all. Part of his brain was still in mourning. He had seven far better, far more creative, canvases (including his Blue Man) covered up in his studio to attest to that fact. But the rest of him was back among the living.

Of course every piece he had done, those here and those in the studio, were only paintings, only scraps of stretched canvas covered by dry bits of paint. They had no real substance and were not even close to being flesh. Still, in a way, you could feel what they said. They might even create feelings in others, affect their beliefs, move them to action. Also, they would last, would stay behind when you moved on.

Don't get so pompous, he warned himself. Now you're talking immortality, and in this country, that lasts no longer than next month's headlines. This is America.

But he had learned some things about America, too, had seen a few blemishes scarring its otherwise perfect veneer. He had discovered history, had found there was hate, ugliness, and injustice even in this shining new Eden. He had so far failed to make the other discovery—that to survive you cultivated a distance from such facts and events. He could not yet understand that kind of funkiness. Or if he sometimes could, he was not yet ready to surrender to it.

He turned and opened the doors.

* * *

He kept himself in the background for much of the evening, watching the reactions. There were no real surprises. There were those who were shocked, those who were amused, those who were impressed, those who responded mostly to the neoclassical technique, and those who were outraged at the whole concept of glorifying a known assassin. Of the latter group, some few went so far as to walk out in protest. The overall response was positive. Which was due, Gaynor felt, not only to his recent celebrity, but to the traditional insistence of art lovers on placing creative considerations above the political, ethical, or even moral aberrations of the artists in question. Dostoyevsky, after all, had confessed to raping a ten-year-old girl.

"Mr. Gaynor?" It came in a soft whisper of a voice. "I'm Michael Westley," said the police commissioner, and held out his hand.

Gaynor shook it. "I recognized you, Mr. Commissioner."

"Congratulations. It's a fascinating show, a tour de force."

"Thank you. I thought you might find it interesting."

They stood looking at one another. It was late, and they were alone in a corner of the gallery anteroom.

"I don't know whether you're aware of it, but Jay Newman and I were the closest of friends for more than thirty years."

"You use the past tense. Does that mean you're no longer his friend?"

Westley smiled. "Not publicly, Mr. Gaynor . . . hardly in public. But since you and I share a more significant confidence, I don't mind telling you that Jay will always be my friend."

"I admire loyalty, but what confidence do we share?"

"The knowledge that Jay Newman wasn't really the Apostle."

Gaynor said nothing. He was suddenly very glad that Jane and Kate had avoided being there tonight. He became conscious of two thick-chested men standing near the main exit, looking uncomfortable in their tuxedos. They had to be detectives.

"Jay called me awhile back," said Westley. "I told him then that I knew he wasn't the Apostle. But it wasn't until tonight that I finally put it all together."

He offered Gaynor a cigar, which the artist refused. Westley took a moment to light his own.

"You must have had a very compelling need to paint these pictures. Which I can understand. You're an artist, and an artist must affirm, must nail down, must make public his strongest, most deeply rooted convictions." The commissioner's smile was faintly wistful. "Still, these paintings did make you vulnerable. Until now, I had completely forgotten about you, about Jay having been the one to save your life, about the kind of involvement there must have been between the two of you because of that. Seeing this show brought it all back. And once that association was made, the rest wasn't very difficult to figure out."

Gaynor glanced at the two detectives near the door. One of them caught his eye, then quickly looked away. "I don't know what you're talking about."

"Naturally, I didn't really expect an instant confession. I wouldn't have accepted it, in any case. I'd very much prefer leaving things as they are. I'm sure Jay does, too. It tickles his personal sense of justice to be thought of as the Apostle. And whatever your own ego needs are in that area, they should be taken care of adequately enough by your art."

A smile came off Westley. It shimmered about him like a red warning light in a fog. "Just one small favor, Mr. Gaynor. Don't get any ideas that might embarrass us all. Our criminal justice system is far from perfect, but it's still pretty much the best around. So please, leave it alone. Just go on making whatever statements you feel compelled to make about it with a brush rather than a gun. We'll all be better off."

Gaynor watched him walk away, a slender, handsome man with a far more youthful stride than he had any reasonable right to possess. An elegantly appointed woman joined him at the door and they left together. The two thick-chested men followed close behind.

All of which meant what? Gaynor wondered. That the Apostle was finally buried forever? Perhaps. Yet who could look into the future? Who could know about such things? With everything that had happened, with all he had seen and done, he still couldn't really understand evil. He supposed he could only meet it when he had to, recognize it, and continue to live and do his work despite it. Many could do that. A rare few refused to make the necessary concessions.

About the Author

Norman Garbo is the author of CONFRONTATION
(with Howard Goodkind), which won the Harper
Find Award. His other novels are THE MOVE-
MENT, THE ARTIST, CABAL, TURNER'S
WIFE, and SPY. In addition to being a novelist,
he has also been a syndicated columnist and
a painter whose work has been shown at the
Metropolitan Museum of Art, the Chicago Art
Institute, and the Philadelphia Museum.